Dear Reader,

Thank you for picking up Lynne Gentry's fabulous first novel and the beginning of the Carthage Chronicles!

A mysterious disappearance, archaeology, time travel, medical suspense, political intrigue, plagues, gladiators, star-crossed romance—what more could you ask for? When I first picked up *Healer of Carthage* to read, I was immediately drawn in and could not stop! I'm sure you know the feeling, and if you don't, then you are about to.

I am convinced that you will love Lisbeth and Cyprian and their breathtaking adventure as much as I do, and so for a limited time we're offering *Healer of Carthage* at a special introductory price of $9.99 as an invitation to readers everywhere to leap through the portal with Lisbeth into ancient Roman Carthage and see for themselves!

We can't wait for you to join the ride and become one of Lynne's first fans! Thank you for supporting new authors.

Best,

Becky

Becky Nesbitt
VP, Editor-in-Chief

Praise for *Healer of Carthage*

"*Healer of Carthage* held me captive from the first page to the last. Lynne Gentry's authentic voice and rich detail in this breathtaking time-travel adventure delight with every twist. Gladiator games, plagues, romance, and high-stakes political intrigue carried me from the filthy streets of ancient Tunisia to its lavish palaces with a cast of characters I won't soon forget. Highly recommended!"

—Carla Stewart, award-winning author of
Chasing Lilacs and *Sweet Dreams*

"Until recently, I didn't think there could be a time-travel book that was also Christian. This book blew that idea right out of my head. Lynne Gentry has written a wonderful time-travel story that has elements of medical suspense as well, one of my favorite genres. Her characters leapt off the page, grabbed my heart, and pulled me through the portal. I lived every minute with them. The only problem is that I will have to wait awhile before the next installment comes. Write faster, Lynne!"

—Lena Nelson Dooley, award-winning author of
*Love Finds You in Golden New Mexico, Maggie's
Journey, Mary's Blessing,* and *Catherine's Pursuit*

"With her debut novel, Ms. Gentry has proven to be a masterful storyteller. *Healer of Carthage* is full of depth and emotion, twists and turns that carry the reader away to ancient Rome. From the first page to the last, the reader is instantly taken into a world of emotion, secrets, and political intrigue. Ultimately, this is a story about healing past wounds and discovering love . . . in its many varied forms. I highly recommend accepting this author's invitation to fall into another world. A wonderful trip awaits."

—Kellie Coates Gilbert, author of *Mother of Pearl*

"What a wonderful premise! *Healer of Carthage* follows Lisbeth, a modern-day doctor, as she's transported through time to ancient Carthage. I found it fascinating to watch Lisbeth apply her knowledge of medicine to a group of very early Christians. This novel is rich in detail and drama. A unique and terrific debut by talented author Lynne Gentry!"

—Becky Wade, author of *Undeniably Yours*

"Lynne Gentry's debut novel pulls you in from page one and never lets you come up for air as you follow Lisbeth Hastings into the turbulent world of third-century Carthage in a gripping tale of mercy, passion, sacrifice, and deceit."

—Lisa Harris, author of *Dangerous Passage*

"From a modern-day emergency room to third-century back alleys, *Healer of Carthage* pulls readers into a riveting story that will keep pulses racing and hearts twisting. Beautiful writing. Compelling story. Enough twists and turns to keep you on your toes every step of the way. Kudos to author Lynne Gentry for this remarkable, haunting storyline. Highly recommended!"

—Janice Thompson, author of *Queen of the Waves*

"Extraordinary writing. Exceptional story. I've just discovered my new favorite author in Lynne Gentry. With an incredible, compelling new voice she weaves the past and present together in a fascinating tale that I couldn't put down. I can't wait to read more from her, and while I'm waiting, I think I'll read *Healer of Carthage* again!"

—Elizabeth Goddard, Carol Award–winning author of *Treacherous Skies, Riptide,* and *Wilderness Peril*

HEALER
of
CARTHAGE

A NOVEL

Lynne Gentry

HOWARD BOOKS
A Division of Simon & Schuster, Inc.
New York   Nashville   London   Toronto   Sydney   New Delhi

Howard Books
A Division of Simon & Schuster, Inc.
1230 Avenue of the Americas
New York, NY 10020

The map of Carthage on page ix and the swimmer image on page 25 were created for *Healer of Carthage* by Jackie Castle and are used with permission.

First Howard Books trade paperback edition March 2014

HOWARD and colophon are trademarks of Simon & Schuster, Inc.

For information about special discounts for bulk purchases, please contact Simon & Schuster Special Sales at 1-866-506-1949 or business@simonandschuster.com.

The Simon & Schuster Speakers Bureau can bring authors to your live event. For more information or to book an event contact the Simon & Schuster Speakers Bureau at 1-866-248-3049 or visit our website at www.simonspeakers.com.

Interior design by Davina Mock-Maniscalco

Manufactured in the United States of America

10 9 8 7 6 5 4 3 2

Library of Congress Cataloging-in-Publication Data

Gentry, Lynne.
  Healer of Carthage : a novel / Lynne Gentry.
    pages cm
  ISBN 978-1-4767-4633-3
  1. Residents (Medicine)—Fiction. 2. Texas—Fiction. I. Title.
  PS3607.E57H43 2014
  813'.6—dc23
                                        2013021353
  ISBN 978-1-4767-4633-3
  ISBN 978-1-4767-4635-7 (ebook)

For Megan, a healer of bodies
and
Eric, a healer of souls

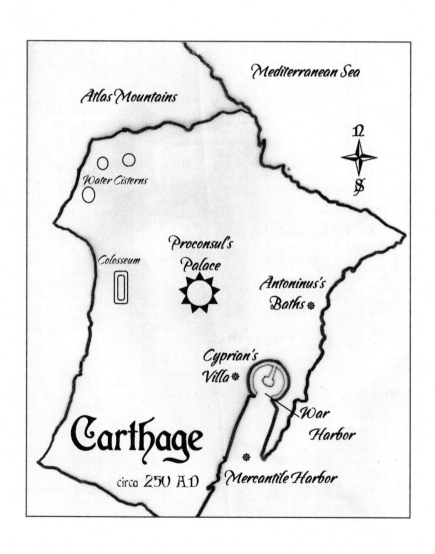

HEALER

of

CARTHAGE

1

TIME IS A COMMODITY first-year residents can't afford to waste, Dr. Hastings." Nelda, the chunky ER charge nurse, held out two charts. "Which one do you want? The diabetic with a necrotic foot ulcer? Or the questionable TB hacking his lungs out?"

What Lisbeth wanted was a bite of the tuna sandwich she'd just purchased from a vending machine, ten minutes off her feet, and a chance to read the letter burning a hole in the pocket of her white coat. But if she had any hope of catching a break in the next fifteen hours, tonight was not the time to spout off to the snarling brick house who had the power to make a thirty-hour call seem like sixty.

Frigid temperatures, combined with the loneliness of the holidays, had driven the uninsured of every age, sex, nationality, and state of mental duress into the county hospital. Regurgitated Jack Daniels, exhaust fumes, and too many nights on the streets fouled the emergency room air. Vagrants slumped in the upholstered chairs or lay sprawled across every inch of shiny floor tiles. Bearded men and frazzled women scrapped for an inch of real estate and clamored for the attention of a doctor.

The desperate begged for someone like her.

Lisbeth's eyes flitted from the stale sandwich she clutched to the occupied gurneys lining both sides of the hall. A grizzled man wearing a filthy, oversize army jacket and combat boots without laces sat up, flashed a toothless grin, then coughed blood into a tissue.

So much for her appetite. Lisbeth slid her sandwich on top of the letter in her pocket.

"I haven't got all night, Dr. Hastings." Nelda waved a chart under Lisbeth's nose. "Choose!"

Choices. Decisions she'd made that she could never undo. When she chose to go into medicine, Papa said he could see how she might enjoy saving the living after spending her childhood watching him resurrect the dead. He'd been supportive of her choice, even tried to share all he remembered of her mother's medical career: First-year medical residents lived in a constant state of sleep deprivation. Days off were rare. And scariest of all . . . what kept her awake at night even when she wasn't on call, the possibility that she'd screw up and kill someone.

"Which one?" Nelda barked in the voice that had earned her the nickname of Nurse Ratched.

Something about the desperation oozing from the old man's yellowed eyes pumped a new round of adrenaline into Lisbeth's sagging system. She snatched the chart in Nelda's left hand. "TB it is."

Thirty minutes later Lisbeth exited the old man's exam room fully aware that her lecture on the importance of taking the medication tablets regularly had fallen upon deaf ears. To rule out TB, she called medical service to admit him, then dropped the signed chart on the stack at the nurses' station. Thankfully, there was no sign of Nelda. With any luck, she could disappear long enough to choke down her sandwich before Nurse Ratched cornered her again.

Strong arms circled Lisbeth from behind, and she jumped with a start. "Hey, beautiful." A male voice whispered in her ear, "I need an examination."

"Knock it off, Craig." Lisbeth wiggled free before Nelda appeared and caught her making out with her fiancé, a handsome first-year surgery resident on an ER rotation. "Nurse Ratched has spies everywhere."

"You speak Arabic, right?" Craig Sutton's dark eyes were too darn dreamy for a surgeon. Every time he came around she melted like one of his many drooling fans.

"Yeah." Her aptitude for languages had been a leg up when she interviewed for this residency, but whenever the attendings needed a translator stat, she felt it a curse. "So?"

"A triple gunshot just came in." He cranked up the charm. "You know I want in on this surgery, love. But Nelda dumped an Arabic lady and her baby on me. Projectile vomiting." Nose wrinkled, Craig thrust a triage chart into Lisbeth's hands. "Women are better at this kid stuff than men."

"What?"

He held up his hands to block the possibility of her slapping him, which she was seriously considering. "You know what I mean: more nurturing."

"A baby?" Pediatrics wasn't her specialty. In fact, she didn't do kids. She liked the idea of them, even wanted a couple someday, but she'd been too busy climbing sand dunes and charting stars with Papa to develop her nurturing skills. What would her future husband think if she confessed babies made her squeamish?

Craig kissed her hard on the lips. "You're an angel. No wonder I love you." He spun on his heels and plowed through the congested hall. "Got her vitals, but no history," he shouted over his shoulder.

"You owe me." Lisbeth's protest got lost in his hasty retreat. "A baby? What was I thinking?" She gave a quick tug to her sagging ponytail and stepped inside exam room 1.

An anxious woman dressed in a black silk *abaya*, a dark veil covering all but her face, perched on the edge of a straight-backed chair. She rocked a crying infant wrapped neck to toe in a blanket. Inky ringlets capped the child's scrunched features and stuck to its olive skin.

Shouting to be heard over the piercing wails, Lisbeth introduced herself in Arabic.

The mother's almond eyes brightened. She obviously understood the Carthaginian dialect Lisbeth had chosen. "My Abra cannot keep anything down. Help, please."

"How old is—" In midyawn, Lisbeth realized the action must have seemed rude, because the mother's confidence level dropped dramatically. Lisbeth covered her mouth, applying extra pressure to her cheeks in the hopes of jump-starting blood flow to the few remaining brain cells she had left. "How old is your"—she glanced at the chart—"daughter, right?"

The woman nodded. "Eight months."

Lisbeth skimmed the vitals recorded on the chart. Numbers and letters blurred together. She blinked in an effort to fight back the fog of exhaustion. Low-grade fever at 100.4 degrees F. Slightly tachycardic for an eight-month-old. Decent blood pressure and good O2 sats on room air.

"How long has she been vomiting?"

"Two days." Worry weighted the mother's voice.

Lisbeth set the chart on one end of the exam table. "May I take a look?"

Abra's mother nodded consent, then carefully placed the screaming infant on the crinkly white paper. Keeping a firm grip on her child, she looked to Lisbeth, expecting a magical end to the little one's suffering. Four years of med school had not prepared Lisbeth for the unspoken pressure patients and families heaped upon doctors to perform miracles.

Lisbeth fished a pair of glasses out of her pocket, hoping the sturdy brown frames made her appear a little more experienced. "I'm not going to hurt her."

The mother reluctantly released her hold. Lisbeth used this break in the woman's defenses to better position herself to complete the exam. She palmed the child's damp head and gently slid an otoscope tip inside each ear. Abra's tympanic membranes appeared intact, non-bulging, no sign of infection. Clear rhinorrhea drained from each nostril. Dry mucus membranes in the mouth indicated dehydration.

Lisbeth returned the scope to a wall charger and ran her fingers along both sides of the infant's chubby little neck. No lymphadenopathy.

"I need to listen to her heart. Let's remove these strips of cloth."

The woman shook her head. "Swaddling is her only comfort."

"But she could be ob—"

"No." The woman stayed Lisbeth's hands. "She must remain bound." The mother's breaths quickened, and her eyes darted to the door as if she expected trouble to burst in should Lisbeth not comply with her wishes. "It is our way."

Lisbeth realized she'd set off some kind of fear. Of what, she didn't know.

Maybe this mother didn't trust twenty-eight-year-old doctors. But then, who did? Lisbeth wasn't sure she trusted herself. Maybe this woman didn't trust that Lisbeth was part white, part Mediterranean. She couldn't blame her. Since 9/11, the world had gone crazy with suspicion.

"Okay, calm down. I can work around it."

Lisbeth maneuvered the engraved bell of her stethoscope under the crisscrossed folds of fabric. Abra's heart raced, but Lisbeth heard no detectable murmurs. Lisbeth rolled the child to her side and pried down the swaddling across her back. Abra screamed louder. Lisbeth did her best to listen for wheezing. Magnified screams but no crackly sounds of pneumonia during the fleeting pauses for inspiration.

"Let's turn her on her back."

The child bucked and wailed. Her tiny features screwed into angry wrinkles.

"This kid is wrapped to the hilt. I can't tell what I'm dealing with," Lisbeth spit out in English. She paged her attending. *Need you to see baby. Rm #1.*

"I don't understand." The mother waited for an Arabic explanation.

"Never mind." Lisbeth gently pressed the baby's belly.

The baby's tummy felt slightly distended. Hard to distinguish between what was child and what was layered fabric. Lisbeth listened for bowel sounds, but Abra's piercing screams made it impossible to hear anything except the sizzle of her own rising temper.

Lisbeth checked her pager. No response. Where was her attending? Nelda wouldn't let her dillydally in here all night, too afraid to make a decision. Lisbeth draped the stethoscope around her neck. "Looks like she has viral gastroenteritis."

The woman's face puzzled.

"A stomach bug," Lisbeth explained. "She appears a little dehydrated from all the vomiting. She just needs fluids. We'll get an IV started, and she'll be good as new in no time. Any questions?"

The woman shook her head and scooped Abra into her arms. "Thank you, doctor."

Doctor? Assembly line worker suited her job description much better.

Lisbeth stepped into the hall. She scribbled an order, signed her name, and added the chart to Nelda's stack. "Kid's dehydrated."

Nelda's brows gathered to form a hairy caterpillar on her

forehead. "Dr. Sutton was supposed to be with that baby. Where is he?"

"Gunshot surgery." Lisbeth played like she didn't see Nelda's displeasure. "Paged my attending, but he never came. If you see Dr. Redding, make sure he signs off on my diagnosis." She turned and beelined it toward the elevator. "Need a restroom break. Be back in a few."

"Whoa, little missy!" Nelda shouted. "What about the foot ulcer?"

Her threatening tone stopped Lisbeth in her tracks. As a first-year resident, she was years away from being able to control her schedule. "Right." With an exhausted sigh, she spun and snatched the diabetic's chart, ignoring Nelda's smug smile. "Got it." Lisbeth bit back the urge to shout, "Happy now?"

Once she had the rank ulcer irrigated, she tried to break away again, but Dr. Redding, her attending, finally appeared on the floor. If she didn't take advantage of his presence, she'd have to track him down later to sign charts. She mentioned the baby, and he said he'd take a look before he left on a family ski trip. It would be years before she got the holidays off.

Just when Lisbeth thought the coast was clear, Nelda caught her again and insisted she check some labs on the computer . . . pronto . . . which Lisbeth managed to do while simultaneously standing on her irate tongue and aching feet.

Three hours later, she stumbled to the deserted doctor's lounge in desperate need of coffee and a bathroom break. CNN played on the muted TV mounted to the wall.

Lisbeth emptied the last of the coffee dregs into a Styrofoam cup. Serious shots of caffeine made her jumpy, but what choice did she have? She'd promised Craig he wouldn't have to spend Christmas Day watching her sleep.

The thick brew smelled like burnt camel dung and tasted

scorched, but Lisbeth was too hungry to care. Her last sustenance, a stale donut, had been gobbled down sixteen hours ago at the daily noon lecture. Were it not for her roommate Queenie's secret stash of Pringles, residency would be a forced weight loss plan.

Lisbeth swiped Queenie's chips from her locker and dropped into the nearest chair. She removed her smashed sandwich and Papa's letter from her pocket. Surely it wasn't a Christmas card. Mama was the one who had made a big deal about Christmas. After her mother's strange disappearance, she and Papa had made a fairly happy life for themselves, but they never again made a big deal about the holidays.

Drawing the envelope to her nose, Lisbeth closed her eyes and inhaled deeply. The orange and lemony traces of her father's Erinmore pipe tobacco lingered along the seal. Suddenly she was five years old and wondering if she'd caused the fight between her parents that dark and chilly night.

She pressed the guilt from her mind and studied the postmark on the envelope. *Carthage.* There was only one reason Papa would base from there. A chill ran up her spine. How long had Papa been in the desert? Sometimes he carried coffee-stained missives around in his shirt pocket for weeks waiting on Nigel's supply plane to skirt the plateaus and land on the barren expanse of sand that always surrounded his archaeological excavation camp. How ironic that the lifestyle of a man devoted to accurately dating rare artifacts made it impossible to assign a valid shelf life to his news.

Lisbeth tore a clean slit along the envelope's edge. She pulled out a single sheet of yellow paper. Bits of sand and dust left from the *ghibli,* a dry southern wind that rearranges the Sahara dunes every spring and fall, fell into her lap. Precious images whizzed through her mind: Papa sitting on an overturned bucket under the shade of a tattered tarp. His faded dungarees filthy from days of sifting through mountains of earth. A tablet perched upon his long, sinewy legs. The lined pages aflutter as he struggled to write a message to her.

She smoothed the wrinkled page, running a trembling hand across his scribbled words.

Have found your mother at the Cave of the Swimmers. Come quickly.

Lisbeth's breath caught. Her mother had died when she was five. At least that's how Papa had explained Mama's sudden disappearance. His crew had searched the area desperately, but when they never recovered a body, Papa had been forced to conclude that Mama had lost her way in the dark. Lisbeth had accepted his explanation—loved him too much not to—but deep down she'd always wondered what really happened after the argument she'd heard outside their tent. She'd probably never know, and neither would Papa.

The bigger question now was why her father had returned to the Cave of the Swimmers. When he came to the States for her med school graduation, he'd said his next project was a sarcophagus excavation in Cairo. Why risk the political dangers of returning to an obscure cave tucked away in the farthest region of the desert hinterlands? More important, why risk upsetting her? Hadn't they agreed they would never go back?

"Touch my Pringles and die, Hastings." Queenie stood in the doorway, hands on hips, her licorice eyes trained on the chip cylinder. "Swiping snacks is so ghetto."

Lisbeth tossed her the can, hoping her best friend wouldn't pick up on the fact that she was near tears. "So call security."

"I'm too tired." Queenie plopped down in an empty chair. "Besides, who has time for all the red tape? We don't even have time to pee."

"Nelda's against bathroom breaks." Lisbeth's pager buzzed.

"Aren't you going to answer that?"

"I just need five minutes off my feet." Lisbeth reached into her pocket and clicked the device to vibrate. "Nurse Ratched has been hammer-paging me all night. I'm sure she has ten new homeless guys who can't live without me."

"It's your funeral." Queenie rattled the chip can, then dumped the last few remaining crumbs into Lisbeth's palm. "Make your last meal count."

Pager vibrations coincided with an alarming voice on the intercom.

Code Blue. ER. Code Blue.

Lisbeth leapt from her seat, crammed the letter into her pocket, and bolted out the door.

2

FAILURE TO PRACTICE SOUND medicine" echoed in Lisbeth's head as she exited the customs queue in the Tunisian airport. Her residency coordinator had said she should consider her probation a lucky break, an opportunity for all concerned to apply the rehabilitative properties of time. He claimed two weeks off would help her regroup and refocus . . . the lie doctors have to tell themselves to beat back the shame of screwing up.

One lapse in judgment had killed a baby. In her mind, the mistake would never be history. If she'd failed once, she could fail again. The past was a wicked taskmaster that shaped the future with no regard to time.

Lisbeth pushed from her mind the peers that had avoided her, as if monumental mistakes were contagious. She hoisted the strap of her bag over her shoulder and strode into the oppressive humidity of the Mediterranean coast.

Across the street, sooty exhaust huffed from the tailpipe of a dilapidated bus pulling away from a hand-lettered cardboard sign. BUS STOP.

"Wait!" Arms waving, she raced across the street, dodging men on bicycles and speeding cars. "I can't miss my connection!"

Breathless, she pounded the slow-moving vehicle's door. The driver reluctantly flipped the lever, the door creaked open, and she hopped aboard. Heat-ripened bodies sucked every ounce of oxygen from the sticky air. Lisbeth dumped a few dinars in a tin can nailed to the dash. Behind the bus driver, she spotted a woman holding a basket of salted sea mullet. Next to her a small boy wrestled a scrawny chicken. No wonder the vehicle reeked of the same earthy scents that fouled the county hospital's waiting room on Christmas Eve. The native woman made no effort to share her seat, so Lisbeth discreetly offered a coin.

The young mother snatched the money without a word and drew the boy with ebony eyes tight against her slight frame. Lisbeth perched on the wooden bench. Careful to stay clear of the chicken, she swung her bag into her lap.

The bus swerved through narrow streets lined with whitewashed houses trimmed in the cobalt blue of the sea. After they passed the amphitheater ruins, Lisbeth fished Papa's letter from her bag.

Cave of the Swimmers. Had Papa lost his mind going back there? According to recent news reports, this part of the world had become a keg of dynamite with a short fuse. She was only a child when the Egyptian government shut down exploration of the mysterious chamber the first time, but she remembered enough to know she had to get her father out of there. Lucky for both of them, she just happened to be free . . . maybe permanently.

Lisbeth stuffed the envelope next to the stethoscope in the pocket of her cargo pants. It was stupid carrying such a cherished possession around. She wasn't fit to use medical equipment anymore, and having it with her wouldn't bring Mama back. But she couldn't bring herself to leave the last piece of her mother behind. Lisbeth buttoned the pocket flap and gave the bus driver a quick tap. "This is my stop." She slung the strap over her shoulder and stepped from the bus.

When the dust cleared, she stood alone on the end of a short, single-lane runway. In the opposite direction, a potbellied man kicked the tires of a prehistoric bush plane. A minute to gather her courage would have been nice, but her pilot was on time . . . a rarity for this part of the world. Lisbeth took a deep breath, plastered a smile on, then trudged toward the Cessna.

"I thought I hired a pilot, not an old buzzard," she shouted over the whir of the propeller.

The sun-weathered man eyed her oversize bag as he wiped his ham-size paws on a bandanna. "You said nary a word about stayin'." Although Nigel's hair had thinned considerably, he still had those keen blues eyes and a hint of Irish brogue that refused to succumb to the native languages he'd taught her around the campfire. "I ain't lettin' a wee lass linger at your da's haunted cave."

"Good to see you again, too." Lisbeth's extended hand went unshaken. "I'm not exactly a kid anymore."

He shifted the tobacco bulge in his cheek. "I don't care if you've become the bloody queen of England; the desert's no place for you now."

"You've carted me all over the Sahara."

"And the last time I hauled your bony backside out, it was so you could make a life for yourself amongst the living. Become one of those fancy doctors like your ma. Marry some nice boy, and settle in one spot for more than a diggin' season."

"Plans change." Her hand slid to the stethoscope in her pocket. "Besides, this isn't your call, Nigel."

"No." He spit a brown stream, barely missing Lisbeth's boot. "But it's me plane."

"Not really. My father's grant money pays your bills." Lisbeth pushed past him, his sturdy frame a comfort she'd missed. She opened the cockpit door, stowed her duffel behind the seat, and climbed in. "Don't stand there gawking like an offended lepre-chaun. We've got a thousand miles to cover before dark."

Nigel shook his head. "Too much political unrest in Egypt." He swiped his brow with his sleeve. "I'm going to have to sneak this crate down Libya's spine, then fly smack dab over blisterin' sand to get to your old man."

"When has working for the great Professor Hastings ever been easy?" Lisbeth belted in.

"Even with the added patrols, that godforsaken sandbox he's diggin' in again ain't no place for a camel, let alone a pretty lass."

Lisbeth retrieved the letter and showed Nigel the single sheet of notebook paper. "What does 'found your mother' mean?"

Nigel glanced at the shaky script. "That I best be haulin' your arse to that cave, I reckon."

"Don't you think twenty-three years is a long time to hope for the impossible?"

Nigel patted her hand. "When hope's all a person's got, they can act a little daft."

"Daft?" She slipped the letter back into the envelope, fear thumping in her chest. Had years in the sun fried the brain of the man who'd taught her how to use a soft-bristle toothbrush to free a fragile artifact from its tomb, or how to layer tobacco leaves in the meerschaum bowl of a calabash pipe, or how to search the stars to find the one that would always lead her home? "You don't really think Papa's losing it, do you, Nigel?"

"You wouldn't spend your life looking for your lost love?" Nigel folded into his seat. "Bet the man that put that rock on your left hand would be a bit disappointed if you said no."

Craig had been conveniently tied up in surgery during her morbidity and mortality conference. His testimony might have smoothed things over, but he hadn't wanted to risk tarnishing his reputation defending her mistake . . . or her.

"Are you going to help me get Papa out of there or not?"

Nigel's sigh vibrated his mustache. He slammed the door and revved the engine. The plane bounced toward a cluster of fishermen's dwellings blocking the end of the airstrip. At the last possible second, Nigel pulled hard on the stick. The plane's nose lifted. They skimmed over several flat roofs.

Lisbeth used her sleeve to wipe grime from the window. "Can we buzz the Roman ruins?" She glanced at Nigel. "For old times' sake?"

A crooked grin lifted his mustache. They banked toward the shimmering emerald waters.

"I forgot how beautiful it is here." Lisbeth pressed her nose to the glass.

Passing centuries had taken a bite out of Carthage's circular historical treasure. A few crumbling stone walls, a smattering of stubby pillars, and a steady stream of cruise ship tourists were all that remained of the ancient harbor that once ported Rome's powerful navy. Like Papa, she despised the visitors who tramped through archaeological ruins with their new sneakers, cheap guidebooks, and total disregard for the forgotten. Maybe she should have become an archaeologist like Papa instead of trying to fulfill his wish that she be more like Mama. Mummies didn't circle the drain and die without warning.

Lisbeth let her hand slip inside her pants pocket. She fingered the steel bell of the stethoscope engraved with the initial *M*. Mama was the real doctor. If Papa was slipping mentally, Mama should be here making the decisions. That's what families do. They take care of each other, support each other, and make decisions together. They don't disappear and never come back.

"Seen enough?" Nigel shouted over the roar of the engine.

She could never get enough of this exotic land she'd once called home, but she gave a reluctant nod. Nigel cranked the stick. The plane abruptly circled back toward the scrappy mountain range that sliced this huge continent into two very different worlds.

They cleared a series of barren peaks and a thin ribbon of grassland. Miles of sand stretched in every direction. Unlike the lesser deserts that dotted the globe, the Sahara had varying degrees of hell, each one more damnable than the last. Of course, her father *would* choose to make camp in the most condemned sector.

Blinding sunlight warmed the tiny cockpit. Lisbeth fought claustrophobia by allowing the rising heat and steady engine hum to quickly sedate her. She slept, deep and hard, for the first time since Abra's death.

Several hours later, Nigel elbowed her awake. "Cave's up ahead."

Lisbeth shifted and dug at her eyes. In the distance, the immense flat-topped shelf of Gilf Kebir rose from the desert floor. The plane skimmed a series of highland cliffs, then dropped over the edge into the Aqaba Pass, a dry river valley lined with huge white dunes.

Twenty-three years ago her family had approached the cave from the ground, yet even from this totally new perspective, she immediately recognized the strange rock formation. The upside-down ice cream cone had haunted her dreams since she was five.

In the shade of the giant conical granite, Lisbeth spotted tents. Fear, nerves, and excitement tangled in her throat.

"Shall I buzz 'em?" Nigel teased.

She shrugged. "Aisa will poison your supper."

"That dodgy fry cook's been tryin' to kill me for years. Might as well give him a reason."

"It's your funeral." Lisbeth's stomach tightened over the memory of Queenie saying those exact same words right before Abra's Code Blue.

Nigel whizzed low over the makeshift settlement, tipping the wings at the series of white tarps stretched over PVC poles. A wiry little man, his head wrapped like a sheik, hopped around, shaking his fist at the sky.

Lisbeth released a nervous laugh. "It'll be camel chips for you tonight, Nigel." A flash of metal on the bluff quickly sobered her. "What's with the armed guard?"

"The good professor's sittin' on a volcano about to blow. Government's threatening to shut him down."

"After they just let him in?"

"Bandits."

"Oh." Maybe she shouldn't have ignored the international travel warnings. She slid Craig's engagement ring over her knuckle and slipped it into her pocket for safekeeping. "The skeleton of a twenty-first-century woman can't be worth *that* much on the antiquities market."

"It's the water they want."

"Well, who doesn't in the desert?" Lisbeth remembered Papa's insistence that a labyrinth of underground caverns, full of fresh water from rains that occurred over ten thousand years ago, existed thousands of feet beneath the Sahara's sand. "Papa couldn't possibly have tapped those subterranean aquifers."

He rubbed the back of his neck. "Hard tellin' with the professor."

"How many guards?"

Nigel looked over his shoulder, his eyes meeting hers. "Not enough," he said. "Not nearly enough, lass."

The plane touched down with a jolt. Sand pelted the fuselage. Nigel held a steady course toward the cave. Two wheels sliced through the crusty riverbed, leaving a deep incision that rivaled the work of an accomplished surgeon.

Lisbeth's mouth went dry.

Time had changed the size of the cave. Or had time changed her? The entire geological structure seemed smaller than she remembered, not nearly the mammoth demon of her memory. Yet, something about returning to the place she'd hated for years felt like coming home.

They taxied to a stop less than thirty yards short of her reckoning with Papa.

She fiddled with the latch on her seat belt. Someone yanked open the passenger door. Heat engulfed the cabin.

"Lisbeth." Her father's cook smiled up at her, his mouth a dental student's dream of rotting or missing teeth. He held out two stringy arms.

"Aisa!" Lisbeth bailed from the plane.

"I told the professor that when the moon was right, you'd come." Aisa's Arabic had an Egyptian spice, mild with a surprising afterburn. His scraggly beard, a bit grayer than she remembered, had not been trimmed since she left for med school. Duct tape held together dark-framed glasses that sported thick lenses etched by the desert winds. The vision correction magnified his black eyes to twice their normal size.

Lisbeth gave the camp a quick survey. Except for a muscled man toting a cooking drum to the shade of a tarp, the place appeared deserted. "Where is he?"

"Hardly eats. Digs in the cave all hours of the day and night."

"I'll fetch Papa, Aisa."

While Aisa and Nigel continued their ongoing battle over the missing supplies, sand in the soup, and who had the bigger grievance against whom, she set out for the cave.

"Papa," she called.

"Beetle Bug!" Papa's radio-perfect bass boomed from the cave entrance. "You came." His unbuttoned, faded chambray shirt flapped behind his lean body as his long legs ate up the distance with the agility of a man half his age. "My beautiful girl." He scooped her into his arms and twirled around.

Lisbeth held on tight, burying her nose in the smell of pipe tobacco and dust. "I missed you, Papa."

"Your mother will be so glad you've come."

"Mother?"

He set her on the ground, clasped her shoulders, and leaned back. They exchanged their first up-close looks at each other. He'd aged ten years in the six months since her med school graduation. Why had his physical health declined so rapidly? She didn't know what she'd do if his mental capacity had followed suit.

"*Doctor* Hastings." The prideful way her father said "doctor," as if his dreams had materialized and she had miraculously become just like her mother.

It seemed he was not so mentally gone that he'd lost his expectations. The truth of her failure would gut him like a double-edged sword. How could she disappoint the man who'd taught her everything he knew and sacrificed so much to send her to learn more? She couldn't tell him, not until she knew for sure how much he could handle.

Trying to forget that her father was carrying on as if a dead woman were busy in the camp kitchen, Lisbeth said, "Let me look at *you*, Papa."

Hazel eyes clear, focused, free of cataracts, and completely without a trace of the insanity she'd anticipated. Papa appeared more than lucid. In fact, this brilliant son of an Arkansas chicken farmer seemed sharper than ever. But she knew not to get ahead of herself. Accurately diagnosing dementia or Alzheimer's required more than an initial evaluation. She needed a complete medical history, a mental status evaluation, a clinical examination, and a battery of lab tests. Even if Papa managed to jump through all of those hoops, she wouldn't have a definitive diagnosis. Time was the truest test.

Lisbeth pulled free of her father's grasp. "When can I see

Mama?" She couldn't help quizzing him to see if he'd abandon this impossible notion.

Papa's eyes shot toward the cave, then darted back to her. "There's time. Let's get you settled, Beetle Bug."

Her father's tent had been arranged to his usual meticulous specifications. A Coleman lantern sat upon a wooden trunk wedged between two cots. An extra pair of work boots waited at the foot of Papa's perfectly made bed, socks pulled over the openings to keep out sand and snakes. Neat stacks of reference books on the Roman Empire took up every other spare inch of space. The warped card table sagged under his selection of brushes, trowels, stakes, and string. She noted that a stack of small brown paper bags designed to hold recovered artifacts appeared untouched. So far, Papa had collected nothing.

"Papa, exactly what have you found?"

"A way for you to forgive me." Had her resentment been so obvious? It must have, because instead of giving her a straight answer like the papa she knew would have, he quickly changed the subject. "We have forever to catch up." He kissed her forehead. "Rest."

The retreat of Papa's boots upon the sand stirred to life eerie similarities to the night her mother had walked away from this very place and never come back. Papa's outlandish claims reminded Lisbeth that there was more than one way her father could leave her alone.

What would she do if she lost Papa, too? If she could no longer access the brilliant heart and soul of a man who had made her feel cherished, despite the empty spot created on that night so many years ago?

Lawrence Hastings was the only family she had left, and she would fight to keep him.

3

THE AROMA OF LAMB kabobs roasting on a spit prodded Lisbeth from a fitful nap. She poured water into a tin basin, splashed her face, and finger-combed her hair into a thick ponytail.

Feeling inadequate to tackle her father's possible declining mental health, Lisbeth left the tent and joined Aisa at the Land Rover.

"Where's Papa?"

Aisa alternated between slinging balls of bread dough onto the truck hood and flattening the rounds into tortillas with a jack handle. "Where he's been since he claimed he saw your mother. At that blasted cave."

"Have you seen her?"

Aisa handed her a pronged grilling fork. "Fry the pitas. Take your mind off your worries."

Her question had clearly made Aisa uncomfortable. Had he seen her mother's spirit drifting among the dunes? Was he worried she'd freak out if he said something? She remembered Aisa's insistence that the cave was haunted on her family's first expedition. Considering how upset the little fry cook had been after Mama's disappearance, she couldn't believe Papa had talked him into returning. Papa was lucky to have such a friend, someone who'd stand up for him no matter what.

Just as the sun began to drop behind the plateau, ten armed

guards hustled Papa from the cave and back into camp. Guns slung over their shoulders, they eyed her carefully as they shoveled mounds of charbroiled lamb onto the fried cakes. Most of them appeared to be Libyan nationals. If a border war erupted, a few dinars would not keep them loyal to Papa. No wonder Nigel did not consider Papa adequately protected.

"Join us at the fire." Papa took the fork from Lisbeth's hand. "I'm anxious to hear about this doctor who wants my daughter's hand in marriage." He cupped her chin. "Another doctor in the family. Your mama will be so proud."

Lisbeth cringed at the confusion bottled in his words. Caring for her father seemed a bigger job than she was prepared to handle. She wiped her hands on her pants. "Let me get my sweatshirt, and I'll tell you about him."

"You'll need a light." Aisa rummaged through one of the Land Rovers for a flashlight.

What had come over her? When had she become such a coward? She was five when Mama disappeared. She remembered Papa searching the cave and the surrounding desert night and day, refusing to bathe or eat. The whole camp had feared him temporarily insane, but Lisbeth had not run from her responsibilities. She'd combed his hair, held his hand, packed his pipe, and removed his boots when he finally collapsed upon his cot. If only she could stuff her fear and summon a bit of that childish naïveté.

Lisbeth thanked Aisa for the flashlight and set off for Papa's tent.

She lifted the flap and strode to her bag. She considered changing out of the cargo pants she'd worn all day, but Papa's open journal caught her attention. Normally she wouldn't pry into his private life, but this was a medical emergency. She lifted the spiral book from his bed and began reading the shaky script. The entry was dated the day before.

*My wife insists that I wait on Lisbeth. But our daughter has
her own life now. What if she doesn't come? Won't come?*

Lisbeth closed the book. What on earth was going on? Had
Papa stumbled upon Mama's skeletal remains? Had the finality
sent him into shock? She read the entry again. Had his grief and
loneliness from Lisbeth's recent absence driven him over the edge?
It had been Papa and Beetle Bug against the world for so long. It
saddened her to think about how hard it must be for him to suddenly be going it alone.

Investigating what Papa's digging had uncovered in the cave
could be put off no longer. Papa had to let Mama go. Lisbeth
wriggled into her UT sweatshirt and stepped back out into the
darkness.

In the short amount of time it had taken to read her father's
brief diary entry, a chilly wind had crept over the dunes and swept
her footprints from the sand. Everyone had deserted the campfire,
even Papa. Where was he? Had he returned to his digging? Lisbeth
tugged at the sleeves of her sweatshirt.

A full moon made Aisa's flashlight unnecessary. She flicked the
off switch and took a moment to get her bearings. Engulfed in the
immensity of the desert, the infinity of the stars, and the peace of
so many miles of nothingness, she wondered if Papa could forget
what had happened to Mama. Would he soon forget her? Forget
himself? If he had Alzheimer's, the cruel disease could not be buried in the mountainous dunes or stowed away inside a cave, never
to be found again. Dementia would carve away his memories bit
by bit. She would have to deal with her father's fragmented mind
just as she would one day have to deal with her own failure. Both
sounded terribly lonely.

"Lisbeth."

She wheeled in the direction of the thin, reedy voice. "Papa?"

The sketchy outline of a person backlit by moonlight hovered over the sand. "Papa, is that you?" She blinked, forcing her eyes to adjust to the shifting shadows cast by the moon's silvery haze. What if bandits had sneaked into camp?

A woman with long, black hair drifted into view. The lower half of the woman's face was shrouded by a gauzy veil. If this woman belonged in the camp, why had Papa kept her hidden? She'd not been completely truthful with him. Perhaps he could no longer be truthful with her?

"Who are you?" Lisbeth demanded.

"You know me, Beetle Bug." Despite the internal warnings to run, Lisbeth remained rooted to the spot, desperate to place the voice. "I've been waiting for you." Long, lacy fingers beckoned Lisbeth closer. "Come."

Instinctively, Lisbeth reached out. "Mama?" She caught hold of nothing.

The breeze suddenly changed direction, kicking up a skiff of sand. Lisbeth clawed frantically at the burn in her eyes. When her vision cleared, the smoky wisp had disappeared.

"Where'd you go, Mama?"

Peals of intertwined male and female laughter rippled from the cave. Lisbeth didn't hesitate. She sprinted toward the strange harmonies, bursting into the cave. "Mama!"

Desperation echoed in the musty darkness. Lisbeth fought to stave off panic. She remembered the flashlight in her hand and clumsily clicked on the light. A pale yellow glow illuminated her boots.

Lisbeth raised the beam to her left and slowly panned right, searching for something tangible, something that would explain the impossible.

Granite walls arched into a shallow cathedral ceiling twenty feet above her head. Scores of tiny, handpainted figures decorated the cave walls. Ancient swimmers. Frozen in acrobatic joy. Frozen in time. Silent. Their voices lost some ten thousand years earlier.

"Get a grip, Lisbeth." Her voice reverberated back to her, complete with the terror tightening her vocal cords. "It's just the wind." Those exact words bounced around the tomb-like quiet.

Breathing through her nose to keep from hyperventilating, Lisbeth dragged the beam around the impressive art gallery that had snared her father's curiosity years ago. She took a cautious step toward the magical world captured on the walls. Some nameless Neolithic artist had painted scores of tiny blood-red swimmers. Ten centimeters from the tips of their outstretched arms to the toes of their graceful legs, it looked as if their rounded bodies were being propelled through nonexistent water.

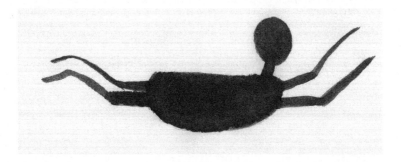

She knew these pocket-size revelers. She'd intruded into their carefree lives before.

These happy water nymphs were the tormented recollections of her childhood.

The fruity trace of pipe tobacco jogged her senses. "Papa?" Lisbeth lowered the beam and searched the sandy floor in case he'd passed out or fallen asleep.

Against the far wall, she spotted a row of tools arranged in Papa's precise habit. She eased over to investigate. A whisk broom. Nesting screen. Shovel. Flashlight. Digital camera. And one of Papa's old record books.

But no Papa.

Lisbeth picked up the ledger and blew away the dust. Except for the brief peek at his diary moments ago, she'd never poked around in her father's private papers. Curiosity overrode her sense of guilt. Hands shaky, she opened the leather cover and focused her light on the first yellowed page.

February 25, 1988.

Twenty-three years ago. Hungry for clues, she raised her light. The first thing she noticed was the clear, firm hand. So different from Papa's current journal. She began to read:

> *Set out for the lost, perhaps mythical, oasis of Zerzura ten days ago. Navigating hostile landscape proved quite the chore. The toll on my wife was great. More than once she mentioned her longing for the sea. No complaints from my Beetle Bug.*

Mythical oasis? Lisbeth carefully turned the brittle page.

February 27, 1988.

> *Found Almásy's Cave of the Swimmers. Convinced my girls to join me for a cursory inspection of the cave's cool interior. All of us captivated by the paintings. I surmise the cave was carved by an ancient underground spring. Where did the water come from? Where did it go? Must investigate.*

Lisbeth flipped the page, intent to find the common denominator that could possibly string the lost pieces of her life together.

Two weeks later:

> *My wife threatens to take our precious Lisbeth back to*
> *Carthage and resume her practice. The secret to the water*
> *source is here. I begged her to give me a few more days . . .*

"Lisbeth."

She whirled. The beam of light hit Papa squarely in the eyes. "You ruined our lives to find a mythical river?" She shook the book at him. "So what if rivers once existed in the Sahara? Who cares?"

"I do." He took the ledger. "A hidden water source is the only possible explanation for what could have happened to your mother." He waved his arm toward the plethora of swimmer graffiti. "The secret these people knew." Papa rubbed the book's weathered leather. "The secret I intend to find."

She regretted handing over the journal. Having an expert compare Papa's old entries to his more recent writings would have been a very useful diagnostic tool.

"You've seen her, haven't you?" The conviction in Papa's voice dared her to lie to him.

"Papa, I—"

"She summoned you here, just as she summoned me. I follow her night after night, as I did years ago, but . . ." His shoulders slumped, and he let his words trail off. He stared at the book, confusion on his face. "I can't find her."

"She left us, Papa. I heard you arguing that night. How could you have risked our family for a myth?"

"I'm sorry."

Lisbeth strode toward the cave opening. She hadn't meant to hurt him, but darn it, part of this was his fault.

The arc of her flashlight beam caught a grouping of three

rather sylphlike swimmers. Sandwiched between two yellow figures was a small, blood-red figure with tiny outstretched arms. A
child begging them to take its tiny hand.

Lisbeth moved in, drawn by a force she couldn't explain, for a
closer examination. "Tell me about this family, Papa."

His eyes met hers. "I call them the Hastings."

"The Hastings?" Despite the sting, the ironic humor pleased
her. If he could understand sarcasm, maybe he could comprehend how demented all of this sounded? "I've never been that
chubby."

He smiled. "You've always been as beautiful as your mother."

Was she? Lisbeth couldn't remember exactly what her mother
looked like. Longing drew her even closer to this tiny swimmer
family. She placed her hand over the pleading child.

Stone burned beneath her flesh. Lisbeth's mind ordered her to
step back, but her hand refused to let go. A rumble shook the
earth. Suddenly the cave floor shifted.

"Run!" Lisbeth dropped the flashlight.

The earth gave way, draining out from under her feet like sand
falling through an hourglass. Slowly at first, then the hole grew
wider and wider at a greater speed. She lunged for the decaying
cave floor, clawing at the crumbling soil. Water roared far beneath
her. Her feet pedaled for solid ground, kicking hard against icy fingers tugging at her ankles.

"Papa!" Strangled cries ripped her throat. "Help!"

"Beetle Bug!" Papa ran toward her and dropped to his belly,
his hand extended over the growing hole. "Grab hold!"

A large chunk of earth broke loose. Lisbeth lost her grip. She
dropped with the debris.

"No!" Papa's panic echoed in the growing gap, twisted with
her screams, then slowly died away.

Somersaulting end over end, she crashed into the sharp edges of a dark shaft, rocks pummeling her from above as she fell.

An eternity later, she plunged headfirst into cold, wet silence.

4

L ISBETH AWOKE DESPERATE FOR breath, gasping and sputtering as if she'd been submerged in water for a week. Her attempt to sit up sent jolts of pain through her branded palm. How
long had she been out? She remembered falling through the cave
floor, but how did she end up face-planted against cold stones that
reeked of urine? Had bandits raided their camp? Knocked her unconscious?

Red sandals adorned with an ivory crescent on the strap
stepped into her line of sight. "This one, Felicissimus? Or the one
on the wall?"

From the nasal tenor of the voice she could tell the speaker
was male, but the pounding in her temporal lobes garbled his dialect. What did it matter if he was Libyan, Egyptian, or Tunisian?
She wasn't alone. Help had come.

Lisbeth tried to lift her head.

A foot from behind came down hard upon her cheek. "And
where do you think you're going, whore?" The man towering over
her spoke the same language she'd just heard. Her mind sorted
through her repertoire of languages and landed on a form of Latin,
words similar to the ones Aisa used to curse Nigel.

Lisbeth writhed beneath the pressure. Every bone in her body
hurt. Bile burned the back of her throat. The foul taste of regurgi-

tated lamb tortillas mingled with the metallic tang of blood in her mouth.

She freed an arm, made a fist, and hammered the foot grinding into her cheek.

Greater force from the shoe sole threatened to snap her jaw. "Bind this tiger." Someone grabbed Lisbeth's free wrist and held it while they yanked her other arm out from under her aching body. Before she could react, her hands were bound together. None of this made any sense.

"You're gonna regret hurting me," she ground out.

"I believe you've found a spirited one, Felicissimus." Male. Condescending. Definitely speaking a more refined form of Aisa's Latin. Maybe he would help, but then again, she couldn't tell what was real or what was a head-trauma imagining.

"Make them let me go," she pleaded between pressed lips.

"Inflict any more damage, and I won't pay you a copper, old boy." The cultured voice demanded respect. The foot was promptly removed.

Someone suddenly jerked Lisbeth to her feet and crushed her hands while cutting the bindings from her wrists. Freedom. Except for being held in place. That's when she noticed the tall guy next to her. He had a shaved head and wore only a towel wrapped around his waist. She wondered what Craig would think of some half-naked guy manhandling her. Her fiancé was not nearly as sculpted as this brute, but he was wiry and fast. Craig could at least get in a couple of good punches if he were here. Wherever *here* was. Probably some godforsaken hole across the Egyptian border.

"Craig?" Lisbeth swayed, her balance as questionable as those dizzy homeless drunks who frequented the ER. "Papa?"

People she did not recognize spun in her blurry vision. A naked boy she guessed to be no older than ten. Two glassy-eyed women stripped to the waist. And three people dressed like toga-clad statues in Italian fountains.

"Where's Papa?" Lisbeth dug her nails into the arm of the tall guy with an iron grip. "What have you done with my father?"

A barrel-shaped man wearing a white, king-size sheet trimmed with a crimson braid lifted her chin. "Wherever did you find this little Thracian, Felicissimus?" Bulging black eyes and a dough-ball face indicated the possibility that this guy had a thyroid problem. Jewels dripped from his thick neck. Fishy halitosis, symptomatic of chronic kidney failure, soured his breath. Definitely a cut above the TV rebels that tossed homemade grenades on the streets of Libya. "One of the best properties you've brought me in years." He spun a wicked glance in the direction of a matronly woman draped in emerald silk and wearing a thin veil across the bottom half of her face.

"Think," Lisbeth muttered to herself. "What happened? Am I dreaming?" She concentrated on regaining her focus. She surveyed the dank cell again. Her breath caught. How had she missed the chains that attached the wrists of the little boy and the half-naked women to the wall? "Wait until my father finds out you've taken me captive!"

Felicissimus, a slimeball with a dribble trail down the front of his dingy yellow dress, continued his conversation with the fishy dough-ball guy. Neither one of them seemed to understand English. Either that or neither was the least bit concerned about the accusations she yelled at the top of her lungs.

"I knew you'd like her, Aspasius. But if I can guarantee the *quality* of the treasure, does it really matter where I acquired it? Such a rare beauty was meant to grace the proconsul's palace, would you not agree?"

The richly dressed guy in the sheet limped forward and grabbed Lisbeth's chin. His fingers squeezed off her string of curses. While his globe-shaped eyes raked her body, he yanked her face from side to side. "Good teeth. Passable complexion." His smile, more a pleased smirk, sent a jolt of alarm through Lisbeth's tense body. "She is not to be exhibited in the common slave market."

"Slave?" Lisbeth jerked her chin free and kicked him in the shins. "I'm not for sale, you sorry son of a—"

"Owww." Aspasius grabbed his injury. "You little vixen."

"Shall I have Metellus use the whip on her, proconsul?" Felicissimus nodded to the guy in the towel. In a flash, Metellus's thick arm coiled around Lisbeth's neck. "Or I have the iron hot if you want her ear pierced to break her spirit a bit."

Lisbeth wrenched against the pressure closing off her air supply.

Aspasius held up his hand, his pointy-tooth grimace transforming his face into an angry weasel. "No additional marks. I want nothing to mar her beauty." He leaned in close, his breath a nauseating combination of sardines and some sort of gastrological problem that made Lisbeth gag. "If you can give me some kind of assurance that she can learn the language of the empire well enough to at least follow commands, we have a deal."

With any luck, the visual daggers she hurled in the dough ball's direction would prick his pompous head and let the air out of those oversize jowls. Summoning her linguistic command, Lisbeth spat out, "I not only speak your foul tongue; I read it and write it."

The room went silent.

"Beautiful and smart." Aspasius stroked her hair with the back of his hand. He dragged his large signet ring across her face. "Intoxicating."

The matronly brunette stepped forward. "Do we really need another slave?" Although the woman spoke to the proconsul, her kohl-rimmed eyes drilled holes into Lisbeth.

Aspasius turned and backhanded the woman, nearly knocking her out of her pearl-crusted sandals. "If you will not serve me, I'll buy one who will."

"Hey!" Lisbeth lunged. "What do you think you're doing?" A strong arm reeled her in. "Leave her alone, you barbarian."

The rigid woman righted herself without so much as a rub to the welt his ring had left upon her cheek. "May she bring down curses upon your house."

"As did you." Aspasius spit at her, then turned and clamped a hand on Lisbeth's face. "Know this, my Thracian beauty. Displease me, and you too will be replaced." He turned to Metellus. "Strip her, and take her to the sunlight. I have a right to know exactly what I am getting beneath these filthy rags."

"And miss the thrill of surprise when you drag her to your bed?" The new voice entering the mix smoldered with disgust.

Aspasius glanced over his shoulder. "Cyprian!"

Lisbeth strained against her bindings.

"How little regard you have for your toys." The owner of the commanding voice filled the doorway. Even in this poor light, she could tell that the latest arrival to her crazy dream was tall, blond, and exceptionally well built. Maybe he was also kind, or at the very least willing to help her get free of these bindings, because she was too banged up to walk far, let alone escape their pursuit. Daring to hope, she shouted for help using her best Latin.

Aspasius protectively stepped between her and the intruder at the door. "Old friend, what brings you to my private showing?"

Lisbeth rose on her tiptoes.

"Reports that my least-favorite client is once again dabbling in illegal slave trading." This possible knight in shining armor looked past Aspasius and locked cool blue eyes on her. "Have you acquired this property from looters, Felicissimus?"

"Oh no, my *patronus*." Felicissimus rushed forward. "Since you so eloquently secured my acquittal, I've put my unscrupulous trading days far behind me." The greedy little slave trader scurried back to Lisbeth and raised the shredded cuff of her pants. "See, Cyprian, she has the whitened foot of one purchased abroad. All quite legal, I can assure you."

Lisbeth glanced at her feet. The hiking boots were gone, and her entire left foot was covered in some sort of white chalky substance. What kind of crazy dream was she having? She remembered touching a painting in the cave, but after that, things got fuzzy. If she was lucky, she'd fallen and hit her head, and this was simply a concussed hallucination.

Since when was a head injury better than dealing with desert bandits? Feeling unhinged by either possibility, Lisbeth thrashed and kicked. The arm of the bare-chested man continued to crush her windpipe.

"If you came by this property legally, why would you not do as the law allows and give me first rights, Felicissimus?" Cyprian ducked to avoid the doorframe and strode into the room, an intimidating presence decked in swirls of cream silk that conformed to his muscular chest. "Surely you've not misplaced your patron loyalties?"

"No. Never." The nasty little man tugged at the neck of his tunic. "It's just that our esteemed proconsul put in his order quite some time ago. I simply fill the requests as the merchandise becomes available." Sweat glistened on the old man's brow. "Happy to do the same for you, Cyprian? What with the emperor's campaign season coming to a close, all sorts of new conquests are sure to go on the block. Give me but a week, my good man. I'll find you a tasty delight. You prefer your maidens dark or fair?"

Fire ringed Cyprian's piercing blue eyes. "I prefer my pro bono clients to remain free of disreputable entanglements."

"Where's the fun in that?" The trader's brows quirked. "Or the profit for either of us?"

Cyprian reached for the knife tucked in his belt. "Felicissimus."

With a resigned sigh, the slave broker waved his hand. "Release her, Metellus." He shoved Lisbeth, and she stumbled toward Cyprian. "Here, examine the slut for yourself."

"Now see here, Felicissimus!" Aspasius's cheeks flamed. "We had a deal."

"Feel free to counter, consul." The slave broker grinned. "A decent bidding war would go a long way toward feeding the many mouths that populate my household, especially since the unfortunate arrival of my mother-in-law."

"I'm not a slave." Lisbeth searched Cyprian's eyes. "Help me. Please."

Not even a flicker of compassion warmed the icy blue pools that seemed to look past her. "How much, Felicissimus?"

"I don't belong here." Lisbeth bolted for the door on wobbly legs.

Cyprian reached out and snagged her arm. He pulled her tight against his rock-hard body. His hot breath burned her ear. "Say nothing more, fool." He ignored her hammering fists and the blows her heels landed on his shins. "How much, Felicissimus?"

"Two thousand sesterces."

"Three," Aspasius sputtered.

"Five," Cyprian countered coolly.

"Five?" Aspasius bellowed. "Have you lost your mind, man? I paid four for an entertaining Germanic dwarf, and I can rent him out for parties." He wrinkled his nose. "Look at her. A mule would be easier bedded."

"You have a point, but I love a challenge." Cyprian squeezed Lisbeth's arm. "Six thousand sesterces. And I take immediate delivery."

"Sold!" Felicissimus thrust his greedy hand at Cyprian. "Your marker will do until I can send Metellus to collect the full sum."

"You little cheat." Aspasius seized the neck of the trader's soiled tunic, his nostrils flaring. "I'll see you thrown to the lions." He released him with a shove, grabbed the woman in green silk, and stormed to Cyprian. "Don't think this is over, old friend."

"Don't think us friends," Cyprian replied with a commanding air.

Muttering Latin curses, the proconsul dragged the woman dressed in silk from the cell, his gait beating an uneven rhythm on the cobblestones.

The matron craned her slender neck and shouted over her shoulder, "Run while you can!" Her perfect English stung Lisbeth's ears.

5

I CANNOT GUARANTEE HER ABILITIES, patronus." Felicis-simus's eyes darted in the direction of Metellus, then back to Cyprian. "She had no papers." He dropped the silver marker into the small bag on his belt. "Her name and nationality are . . . sketchy."

Cyprian acknowledged the warning with a slight nod. "This one does not need an identifying scroll about her neck." He clamped a firm hand around the thin wrist of his newly acquired property. "Foreign-born flashes in her eyes."

"She'll run the first chance she gets." Felicissimus patted his belly. "But that could be just as well, since I cannot guarantee she's free of the usual diseases brought in from the barbaric regions."

"Diseases?" the woman he'd just purchased shrieked. "I'll be lucky if I didn't catch something fatal in this little rat's nest."

"She screeches like one of those foul parrots Aspasius keeps caged in his palace." Cyprian tightened his grip. "I'll take her as is."

"Take me?" She tugged hard trying to get free.

Felicissimus raised his hands in deference and spoke to Metellus. "Let the record show Cyprian declined a moment of private inspection and that I upheld my patron obligations." He leaned in close to Cyprian and whispered, "At great risk of irritating the most powerful man in the province, I might add."

"She'll not be returned." Cyprian scooped up his prize, tossed her over his shoulder, then cast a glower at Felicissimus. "In a way, Carthage would be better off if Aspasius followed through with his threats and shut you down."

Felicissimus smiled and patted his money belt with a wink.

"Hey, buddy!" The female pounded Cyprian's back, cursing him by the sound of it. "I'm not going anywhere with you."

"*Where* exactly did you say you found this one, Felicissimus?" He added pressure to his hold on her strangely clothed legs. "I do not recognize the native tongue as wicked as her fists."

The squatty little slave dealer shrugged. "Who needs words when it's so obviously love at first sight between you two?"

"If the opportunity to release you from my patronage ever presents itself, little man, I will not hesitate." Cyprian hauled the kicking woman from the slave cell and into the street.

"Enough." He set her abruptly upon her feet, keeping a firm hold on her wrist. Despite the cuts and bruises, he found this dark-haired beauty with eyes the color of a stormy sea even more fascinating in the late afternoon sun. He had done the right thing to risk another run-in with Aspasius.

She lifted her chin as if she intended to spit in his face. "Look, I don't know who you think you are, but—"

He removed his cloak. "Cover yourself."

She glanced down, then her head snapped up. "What happened to my sweatshirt?" She snatched the cloak and wrapped it around her shredded garments. "This is crazy. I've got to get home."

Her Latin was elementary, but an educated fire leapt from beneath the heavy fringe of black lashes, a heat capable of igniting fear in a lesser man. "You can run, but Aspasius has men everywhere. You'll be recaptured. The proconsul of Carthage will see you stoned before he returns you to me." He offered his hand. "What will it be?"

She stiffened. "I'm going home." Pulling tight the cloak he'd given her, she gathered the dragging hem and exposed the bare foot that marked her as a slave. "My father will be sick with worry." She stormed three paces toward the market, then stopped. "What is this place?" She made a slow circle that brought her face-to-face with him once again. "Where is the bus station . . . which way is . . . I'm not quite sure . . . ?" She touched the cut on her forehead, confusion clouding her eyes. "Where am I? Who are you?"

"If you are so determined to go"—Cyprian waved her on—"then go." He spun on his heels.

"Wait!"

He turned to see his cloak swaying in the middle of the street. "I don't know how to go home." Her eyes rolled back in her head.

He caught her right before she dropped onto the cobblestones. In one swift movement, Cyprian draped her limp body over his saddle, then swung up behind her. The sooner he had her safely out of sight, the sooner Aspasius would forget that he had been bested yet again.

6

SIX POWERFULLY BUILT LITTER bearers came to an abrupt halt, jolting Magdalena from her cushion.

Aspasius threw back the transport's fringed curtains. "Someone will pay."

Magdalena's left eye had swollen completely shut on the ride home. "I believe *someone* already has." She did her best to glare at him with her right eye.

Aspasius clasped her face and yanked her so close that his salty sardine breath mingled with hers. "Next time, you might not be so lucky."

He shoved her away and leapt from the cushions. He stormed toward the fortified doors of his palace with the uneven stride of a small man in built-up shoes. Royal cobblers did their best to compensate for the damage caused by the poorly set bone of a childhood injury. Magdalena remembered that Aspasius's first act as the newly appointed proconsul of Carthage had been to hunt down the physician to whom his mother had paid their last copper and to cast him adrift upon the sea. Aspasius consulted a bevy of seers and healers, yet no matter what magic potion he smeared across his shriveled flesh, his body continued to list to one side. The paucity of Aspasius's physical prowess was never more apparent than when he stood toe-to-toe with the levelheaded Cyprian. An inadequacy Aspasius hated almost as much as Magdalena despised him.

She slid her trembling fingers along the folds of her cloak. The souvenir she'd managed to snatch from the pocket of the feisty slave chained to the block was still safely tucked away. Why had she taken such a foolish risk? No matter. It was too late for regrets. What was done was done. She didn't dare examine her booty here. Cyprian's little show of defiance had already aroused Aspasius's temper beyond what she considered safe.

Magdalena gathered her skirts and dragged her bruised body from the litter. She must act, and act quickly, to close the distance between them before Aspasius had her permanently removed.

Hurrying along the cobblestone walk of the vine-covered porticoes, she returned to the palace that had become her prison.

The atrium, a large, airy room lit by an opening in the roof, was furnished with several golden cages containing an impressive collection of exotic birds. Nightingales, Ringneck parrots, and swans for the massive fountain. How she longed to return them all to their native woods.

Aspasius opened a cage door and reached for his favorite bird. Magdalena felt her own heart flutter, aching to be free. Three slaves he'd collected since his appointment to the Senate flitted around him.

Kardide, a hook-nosed Turkish wench shipped to Carthage on a Roman freighter, removed the master's heavy toga.

Iltani, a slender Christian woman, silently lifted the scandalous golden wreath Aspasius wore in public to cover his receding hairline. Fiery disapproval of her master's determination to set himself up as a god leapt from her eyes. Iltani's mouth would never utter the curses the proconsul deserved, since her failed attempt to return to lower Mesopotamia had cost her three fourths of her tongue. When the proconsul's bounty hunters caught her near the city gates, they had performed the bloody procedure then and there. No analgesics. No antiseptics. No mercy. A vivid and unforgettable message to the masses.

Saddest of all was Tabari. The small, dark-skinned waif crouched before the knots of the proconsul's red sandals. The child had lost the pinkie on her right hand fighting off Roman soldiers as they plundered the indigenous tribes bordering the African desert. For two years, Magdalena did her best to keep Tabari from the clutches of Aspasius. In the end, he snuffed the light of innocence from the girl's large black eyes in the same cruel manner he'd stolen her virtue. Failing to save this child from such irreparable harm felt like failing to save a child of her own . . . one of the many regrets stoking the revenge that burned in her belly.

A scowl drew the brows of Aspasius into a bushy awning that framed his seething eyes. "Hurry, fools." He set the bird upon his shoulder, offering it a scrap of something he withdrew from his pocket.

Today, the master of the house was not content to accept his servants' sham of welcome or the adoration of a bird. Today, he wanted respect. To be treated as if he deserved the appointment he'd weaseled from the emperor despite the Senate's refusal to confer on him his desires. To exact a little revenge of his own. If she did not act with speed, she would not be the only one sporting a black eye. All of Carthage would pay.

Magdalena drew a fortifying breath and stepped inside the room adorned with wall paintings of bare-chested cupids playing hide-and-seek.

All servants' eyes darted to her. They immediately took in her disheveled appearance. Except for Kardide, the others dared not stop their tasks or show concern that their friend had once again suffered at the hands of their master.

"The same will be your fate," Aspasius snarled at Kardide. Throwing control around in his own house seemed to fade the bruise on his ego. A surge of power pumped an evil snarl to his lips. "I'll scatter every one of you like the worthless chattel you are if you continue to dawdle."

Except for the concern flitting from eye to eye and the anxious cock of the bird's green head, no one moved, especially not Kardide.

Magdalena had long since passed the point of desiring pity. All she needed to complete her mission was a few more months of her fellow servants' continued silence. Aspasius's term as proconsul would be up sooner than he expected if her anonymous letters detailing the unrest brewing in the empire's southern quadrant had reached the emperor. She'd bribed a personal postal carrier she'd met in the market to avoid trusting her secret to Aspasius's faster government couriers.

Had the scrappy messenger made it to Rome? She prayed so. Despite the threat of another beating if Aspasius discovered her secret, hope of her master's removal and ultimate disgrace gave her reason to live. Until she had definitive word, she must let nothing tip Aspasius to her plan, not even her fear.

She tucked a strand of hair behind her ear and gave a discreet nod. Kardide resumed her work. Tension in Magdalena's neck and shoulders eased a bit, but she kept her guard drawn.

These servants were more than a seamless team. They were the family she'd pieced together in this hostile place. Without them, the years would have been unbearable. And she knew they felt the same love for her.

If Aspasius suspected *she* had become the true master of this house, the problems of this morning's run-in with Cyprian had distracted him to the point of letting such an impropriety slide. This temporary reprieve did not mean she'd escaped the arena, a fate she would have welcomed years ago were it not for her secret. No one who dared defy Aspasius escaped the arena's caged cats. Aspasius counted on the hungry roar of wild beasts to keep his subjects in line. And so far, they had.

Magdalena's stomach clenched at the tortures the proconsul of Carthage would use to shred her little family if he ever discovered the truth hidden beneath his palace floors.

"Away with you." Aspasius rubbed his temples.

The servants disappeared into the various alcoves and side rooms yet most assuredly remained well within hearing distance, loyal and willing to come to her aid if needed.

Magdalena slipped off her sandals. "Let me fetch your headache powders, master." She started down the great hall, grateful she'd conjured another excuse to delay closing the space between them.

"Bring that new scribe to my chambers, slut!" Aspasius shouted after her. "And plenty of parchment and ink. I intend to petition Rome."

Magdalena froze. Did the proconsul know what she'd done? Had someone betrayed her? Or was Aspasius simply allowing Cyprian's ballsy show of defiance to feed his fear of losing his position and power? Something was propelling her captor's unsettling campaign to remove her from his bed. She'd prayed to be free of him. Imagined herself sprinting toward the arms of her husband from the very first night she'd suffered under this man's sweaty body. Her mind spun through the different evacuation scenarios she'd constructed, emergency plans in case this very thing happened.

Magdalena captured her racing thoughts. Now was not the time to reveal her hand or to react without solid facts. She would skip the lavender petals in his wine and double the mugwort. Aspasius wouldn't miss her until morning. With her tormentor knocked unconscious, she could go to the home of Cyprian. After today, the secret she kept beneath the palace was not the only thing at stake.

She turned to face him with the practiced grace that had kept her alive beyond what even she dreamed possible. "As you wish, my love."

7

"O PEN THE GATE." DEEP, rich commands beckoned Lisbeth from hazy dreams of terrifying water slide rides and horrible men.

Somewhere in her foggy subconscious, metal hinges creaked and dogs barked. An uncomfortable combination of intense pressure on her midsection and the sensation of forward motion sent bile spewing from her mouth.

Something rough and wet lapped her face. She opened her eyes and worked to focus. Black canine eyes, set in a big square head, stared back at her. The hulking beast sniffed her tingling hands; then his large, pink tongue swept her face again. Mosaic tiles swirled in the sound of blood rushing to her head and the distinct stink of horseflesh and vomit. Had she passed out again? She had absolutely no bearings or a better explanation for why her head felt lower than her feet.

"Fetch Ruth." Feet scurried away as two large hands clamped around Lisbeth's waist and gently lifted her to the ground. "Can you stand?"

Fighting dizziness, Lisbeth swiped at her mouth. Her eyes traveled slowly upward. Before her, a huge black horse snorted and pawed at two big dogs scrambling beneath his feet. No wonder the person holding her steady smelled of musk and leather. She must have died and gone to a zoo.

"Feeling steadier?" Whose arms held her upright?

Lisbeth moved her eyes slowly for a sideways peek. The strong arm flanking her belonged to the same man she'd seen in her dreams, the one who had started a crazy bidding contest for her, the guy who'd given her his coat and dared her to make a break. That she found him even the tiniest bit charming while at the same time loathing his very existence meant she must still be dreaming.

She tried to speak, to articulate something intelligible. Clanking sounds of a gate closing behind her slammed the words against the roof of her parched mouth. If the bandits had taken her to some secret compound, how would Papa ever find her?

The handsome hunk wrapped his arm tighter around her waist. "Come. Let's get you some help." He practically carried her toward a palatial mansion surrounded by arched porticoes and lush greenery.

Suddenly, a door burst open. "Cyprian!" A woman flew out. "Another stray?" Topaz eyes, two sparkling jewels set in a perfect heart-shaped face, triaged Lisbeth in seconds. "She's beaten half to death." The woman raced to hold the door open.

Cyprian scooped Lisbeth into his arms and strode over the threshold. "Felicissimus had to allow her to be roughed up a bit, Ruth." He bypassed intricately carved benches and strode down a long hall, the dogs loping behind.

"It's only a matter of time before Aspasius discovers your arrangement with the slave trader."

"Rescuing those the proconsul keeps in bondage is worth the risk. Besides, the information I glean is invaluable." He halted for a second. "Aspasius plans to replace the healer."

Ruth gasped. "What will become of her?"

"I'm not sure." He turned to the woman with the milky white skin of a Celtic. "Don't worry. We'll do what we can."

Lisbeth squirmed. "Look, I don't know who you people are or what you're talking about, but I'm not—"

"From the looks of this stray cat, she tried to claw someone's eyes out." Ruth trailed their progress along the ornate passage.

"She has fight." Cyprian stopped, his attention fastened on the blur of voices floating from a room farther down the long hall. "The bishop has returned?"

"He has. The news from Numidia is not good." Ruth grabbed his arm. "How much did this one cost you?"

"Is there a price too great?" Cyprian commanded the dogs to stay. They dropped with an obedient whine. He ducked into a nearby room lit by a single oil lamp. "Clean her up. Tend her wounds before you bring her before the bishop." He gently placed Lisbeth on the bed. "It's too risky to fetch the healer."

"Wait!" Lisbeth jumped off the bed. Despite the dizziness, she ran after him. "I'm not staying."

Two dogs immediately flanked Cyprian, low rumbles vibrating from their droopy muzzles. "You are." He banged the door shut in her face and clicked the latch.

"I'm not." Lisbeth kicked at the brass-studded oak. Pain shot through her toe. "And your dogs don't scare me."

"Best to save your strength for what is to come."

Lisbeth wheeled and held up her hands. "Back off, lady. I don't belong here." Her eyes darted around the room, quickly taking in an ornate wooden bed, a matching nightstand, and a young girl hiding in the shadows. "Wherever *here* is. There's been some huge mistake." She rubbed her throbbing foot against the back of her other leg. "I was just talking to Papa when—" Lisbeth stopped, suddenly aware that the exquisite woman calmly studying her had only spoken Latin. She probably wasn't catching a word of what she was saying. Lisbeth drew a slow and measured breath, hoping that extra oxygen would blow away any language cobwebs and settle her stomach.

"Collecting yourself is wise," Ruth said. "Cyprian's generosity toward you has cost more than a few coins." She snapped her fingers, and a mousy-haired girl not more than twelve and dressed in a brown woolen tunic slipped from her hiding place. Keeping her chin tucked close to her flat chest, she waited for instructions. "Naomi, we'll need a hot bath prepared, some food, and fetch a bottle of raisin wine. Oh, and bring my herb box." The girl scurried out a side door.

"What is this place? It reminds me of a page out of history." Lisbeth's rudimentary Latin glanced off the frescoed wall mural of muscular men clothed in golden wings. "Some kind of palace stuck in a time warp or something."

The Barbie-shaped blonde who looked to be only a few years older than Lisbeth smiled. "So you do speak a bit of our language? Good. Then you'll understand when I tell you that this is your new home." Ruth indicated Lisbeth should sit upon the luxurious bed linens. "What you make of it is up to you."

Lisbeth knew if she went anywhere near that bed she wouldn't wake up for a week, and she had no intention of remaining in this nightmare any longer than necessary. "Lady, this is *not* my home."

"Let's get you out of those rags before you meet the bishop."

"Bandits have bishops?"

"Bandits?" Ruth laughed. "Caecilianus is most certainly no bandit." She clasped Lisbeth's shaking shoulders, a jolt of unexpected kindness communicated in her firm touch. "Your questions will be answered . . . in God's time."

"Time's one thing I don't have, lady. I've got less than two weeks to convince my father to leave that godforsaken cave and get him home."

The girl in the tunic returned, her hands full of towels, bath supplies, and a clean garment similar to the shapeless sack she wore. She dumped them on the bed and fled.

Lisbeth locked eyes with her blond warden. "Now what?"

"You are in a precarious position." Ruth smoothed a fold that ran the length of her cornflower blue silk gown. "Run and risk capture. Stay and acquire freedom. If you're as smart as you look, you'll do the latter." A smile tugged at the corner of her ruby lips. "Tell me your name."

"You first." Lisbeth hugged her torso. "I mean, I know Cyprian called you Ruth, but are you, like, . . . uh . . . *Mrs.* Cyprian?"

The woman's porcelain brow furrowed. "Mrs.?"

Lisbeth searched her mind for the correct phrasing, wishing she'd paid closer attention to the times Aisa blasted Nigel with the ancient language. "You know, how do you say . . . are you married to Cyprian?"

"Oh my, no." A becoming blush of pink flushed Ruth's cheeks. "Cyprian is the finest legal advocate in Carthage. He is from the family of Thascius, and he is also my husband's latest convert." She curtsied, then presented herself formally. "I am Ruth of Antioch, wife of the *bishop* you believe to be a bandit. And you?" From the perfect arch of Ruth's brows, remaining anonymous wasn't an option.

For reasons Lisbeth couldn't explain, divulging her name felt like she was committing to some sort of long-term relationship, and frankly, she didn't see the point. This prissy woman seemed nice enough, but they were not friends. The minute Lisbeth got the chance, she was going home . . . precarious position or not. Exactly how she was going back to the cave, she didn't know. But, in the meantime, answering Ruth's kindness with silence seemed rude. Besides, she had to admit, Cyprian's conversation about someone called the healer had stirred her curiosity. Until she could come up with a workable plan, she had to play along.

"Lisbeth . . . of Dallas." The moniker sounded nearly as strange as the first time she had entered a delivery room and introduced herself as *Doctor* Hastings to the perspiring woman huffing in the stirrups. She added a tiny smile to beef up the credibility lacking in her voice like she had that exhausting night in the ER not all that long ago.

"Dallas?" Ruth rolled the word awkwardly around in her mouth. "A province to the north, perhaps?"

If she had been smuggled to the coast, it wouldn't be wise to stir animosities against foreigners. "More west."

"No matter." Ruth's eyes roamed Lisbeth's tattered clothes. "I can see that you are far from home and have been through quite an ordeal. I'm sure you'll tell me all about it when you're ready." She smiled and offered what looked to be a luxurious robe. "In the meantime, I'm sure there's a nice figure beneath that cloak and whatever it is you're wearing on your legs. To the bath with you, Lisbeth of Dallas."

From the expectation lighting Ruth's face, she was offering more than the chance to clean up. She was offering friendship, a relationship where two people trust each other enough to share their fears. The idea of having a girlfriend was a luxury to a girl who grew up in male-dominated excavation camps. Queenie still chafed at the distance Lisbeth kept between them, and they'd been roommates since their freshman year of college. Being a loner had served her well, especially on the solitary trudge through the incredible hours of study required for a medical degree, but how was she to proceed in the face of such an offer?

Lisbeth didn't count herself all that successful at forming friendships. Becoming friends was a long, involved process, a process that wasted valuable time. Time Lisbeth could not let tick away if she was to get her father out of here and salvage what was left of her career.

Papa.

What had become of Papa? Had he been sucked into this nightmare, too? What if he'd managed to cling to the cave wall? What would happen to him if she didn't return? The thought of her father wandering the cave in some fruitless search broke her heart. Would losing his only daughter push him into complete insanity? She had to get back to her father. The sooner the better. Papa deserved to know the truth, to know that she'd failed miserably in trying to be just like her mother. She had to tell him that she was sorry for the things she'd said. That she didn't really blame him for what happened to Mama.

"Looks like I don't have a choice." Lisbeth undid the clasp on Cyprian's cape, flung it on the bed, and wriggled out of the cargo pants. "Let's do this."

Ruth slipped the silky garment over Lisbeth's straggly pony-tail, then scooped up her dirty clothes. "Follow me."

"Hey, wait. What are you going to do with my pants?"

"Dispose of them."

"No!" Lisbeth snatched the filthy garment. Fumbling with the buttoned pocket flap, she muttered, "My phone will be ruined." Sure enough. Inside the pocket she found the soggy remains of Papa's letter, a shattered cell phone, her engagement ring, and . . . "Wait!" She tore through the other pockets. "Where's my stetho-scope? I know I stashed it here." Maybe the instrument had fallen out while she was unconscious. More likely it had been stolen by that sticky-fingered sex trafficker. She clasped Ruth's arm. "Look, I think that guy who tried to sell me took something very important to me. I've got to go back."

"Too dangerous."

Making a break for it would do no good. She didn't know

where she'd been or even where to look. She'd never find that awful dungeon on her own. Like it or not, without the help of these strangers, she was lost.

"If we could just retrace our steps—" Her plea fell upon deaf ears. Ruth wasn't interested in allowing a scrappy slave to alter her plans. Lisbeth slipped the ring on her finger, but she felt no closer to home. "Tomorrow I'm going back for my stethoscope."

"None of us are guaranteed tomorrow." Ruth took the letter and the phone from Lisbeth and laid them on the bed. "Come with me." She led her from the room and down the luxurious hall.

Cool marble underfoot didn't soothe Lisbeth's burning desire to rip into the paunchy slave trader or the muscled man who'd dragged her here. She'd make these black market traffickers regret the day they'd messed with the camp at the Cave of the Swimmers.

They entered a bathroom bigger than Lisbeth's entire Dallas apartment. Intricate floor-to-ceiling murals covered three walls. A stone throne that resembled the primitive commodes she'd seen around the world and a sunken bathtub the size of her apartment complex's communal whirlpool took up the rest of the room. From the base of the far wall, a long concrete trough carried water that splashed upon the tiled mosaic of Neptune. The bearded god of the sea rode a carriage pulled by four sea horses. His maniacal grin and pointed trident dared her to enter the swirling water or make a move toward the silver chalice and a plate of bread, fruit, and cheese waiting on the stone steps.

There must be money in kidnapping. Lisbeth started to peel out of the robe. "Uh, I've got this. You can go now, Ruth."

"I cannot."

The determined set of Ruth's chin cut short any argument. Lisbeth considered her alternatives. Fight, and squander what precious little energy she had left? Or give in, and possibly win Ruth over to helping her escape in the near future? Resigned to humor her warden for now, Lisbeth shrugged out of the robe. She stuck a foot into the steamy water. Trying not to think about Ruth or Neptune's watchful eye, she slid in among the floating flower petals.

Ruth insisted she take the wine goblet. Lisbeth's first sip of the sweet nectar burned the back of her throat. By the third gulp her aches and pains began to dissolve. Hunger pangs prompted Lisbeth to reach for the bread and cheese. When was the last time she ate? She licked her finger and mopped up the crumbs, talking with her mouth full, "A girl could get used to this."

A cascade of water sluiced over her head.

Bolting upright, Lisbeth wiped her eyes. "Hey, what are you doing?"

Ruth quietly reloaded the pitcher and drowned Lisbeth again. "Searching for signs of the beauty Cyprian must have seen beneath this filth."

Sputtering, Lisbeth slammed the wineglass on the ledge. "I can wash my own hair, lady!"

Acting like she hadn't heard a word, Ruth opened a cobalt blue glass bottle and poured a generous stream of golden liquid into her palm. Hands lathered, she waited on Lisbeth's return to a reclining position. "Whether or not this is pleasant is up to you."

Offering reluctant cooperation, Lisbeth slid deeper into the water and rested her neck on the tiled edge. She couldn't remember the last time she'd slowed down long enough for a salon shampoo and haircut, let alone spa-like pampering.

Ruth's fingertips burrowed through the knots in Lisbeth's thick hair and found her scalp. Eyes closed, Lisbeth allowed the aromatic smells, coupled with the circular motions of Ruth's nimble fingers, to carry her back twenty-three years, to a time when her mother used what precious little water they'd hauled into the desert to wash her hair over a basin outside their tent.

How could she miss something she barely remembered? Something lost so long ago?

Ruth filled a ceramic jug and rinsed the suds. "I'd like to know how Felicissimus acquired you."

"Me, too." Tension eased under Ruth's very capable hands. "Unfortunately, I was unconscious, so I don't remember." Lisbeth gave a dreamy shrug. "All I know is, one minute my life was headed one direction, the next I'm lost in some ancient nightmare." Lisbeth shot upright, nearly pulling Ruth into the tub with her. "*Ancient?* Wait a minute." Water trickled down her face. She stuck a hand under the waterfall filling the tub. Cool. But the tub water was comfortably warm. "This is a *Roman* bath?" Her brittle voice hung in the steamy air. Lisbeth plunged both hands beneath the sudsy water and felt the warm tiles. "The water pours in cold, but then it's heated by underground steam piped through the floor, right?"

Ruth's face contorted in confusion, the front of her gown wet from Lisbeth's splashing about. "You need to settle down."

"I'm not settling anywhere until somebody tells me what in the world is going on." Lisbeth scrambled out of the pool and grabbed a towel. "I helped my father excavate a place like this in England. Even though we found the underground furnaces where slaves stoked the wood fires, we wondered if this plumbing actually worked, but . . . wait a minute. Am I . . . is this . . . some other time?"

"I'm not sure of the time." Ruth shook her head. "The sundial is in the courtyard. But the light is fading. If we don't hurry, we'll be late."

Why hadn't the possibility she'd traveled in time dawned on her before? She knew why. Because the idea was ludicrous! Falling down a hole in the Cave of the Swimmers could have broken her neck, but the crazy accident could not have dumped her into another time.

Time travel was just an unsubstantiated theory. Michael Crichton beach reads for the gullible. Santa Claus fantasies on par with the possibility of a supreme god. Science couldn't support these flimsy theories, and neither could she. In all her years exploring ruins, not once had Papa found a place like this . . . an inhabitable domicile that was actually inhabited.

In an attempt to keep her heart from beating out of its cavity, Lisbeth wrapped the towel tight across her chest. "Ruth, is this . . . where am I?"

"Let me check your scalp again. Maybe I missed a serious bump that requires a physician's attention."

Stuffing the urge to scream that she *was* a doctor, Lisbeth dodged Ruth's reach. "Where? Please tell me."

"Carthage."

"As in *Roman* Carthage?" Lisbeth sorted through mental snapshots of the crumbling stone pillars she and Nigel had buzzed what seemed only a few hours ago. She knew every inch of Carthage. Her eyes darted around the fully operational bathroom. Nothing this elaborate or complete remained of the strategic port ancient Romans had fought three wars to own. "How can that be?"

"Someone brought you here."

She must have been out for days if someone had transported her all the way from her father's cave. "Who?"

"I'm guessing it was one of Rome's many conquering legions. Pagan barbarians who won't rest until they own the entire world. One of those surly brutes probably sold you to Felicissimus."

"I thought I was kidnapped from a cave in southern Egypt . . ."

"Possibly. War always plagues the border provinces."

Lisbeth paced, her mind racing to pinpoint the century. "Who's in power?"

Ruth scowled and lifted a comb from the dressing table. "Emperor Decius, of course."

"Mid-third century?" Some parents drill their children on multiplication facts. Lisbeth's father had quizzed her on Roman history.

Ruth came at her with the comb. "I don't care what Cyprian says; as soon as possible we must let the healer have a look at your head."

"And Saint *Cyprian* is bishop?" Lisbeth's vocal pitch had ratcheted up several ugly notches.

"Saint?" Ruth shook her head. "Cyprian would never elevate himself to the level of our Lord. I told you my husband is the bishop, remember?"

"This can't be." Lisbeth buzzed around the bathroom, intent on gathering her things when suddenly she realized she had nothing to gather. Panic clogged her airway. "I've got to get home."

"Where is this Dallas of which you spoke?"

"It's"—Lisbeth wasn't sure how to explain that she'd somehow slid almost eighteen hundred years down a time continuum—"very far from here." With nothing more to say and no strength in her legs, she plopped down on the nearest bench.

"Maybe you'll feel like going later."

Tears scalded Lisbeth's cheeks. "How?"

"I don't know." Ruth let Lisbeth have a good cry, which only served to make Lisbeth more upset.

She never cried. Not even during the long torturous days of searching for her mother. Papa had cried enough for the both of them. She was the strong one. This rare breakdown must be chalked up to sheer exhaustion. Physical limitations had derailed her once again, and that made her even madder.

Between Lisbeth's sobs, Ruth chattered on about how she would find her place in this house as she gently tended Lisbeth's scrapes, plaited her hair, and layered her naked body with yards of flowing pink fabric.

Lisbeth worked to regain control of her emotions. Angry tears would not help her stitch illogical fragments into some sort of logical explanation. Strangely dressed people. Slave auctions. A male model dressed like he was ready for a frat house toga party. The faint smell of the sea that had swirled in the back of her mind from the moment she'd awakened in the cell. The fact that she'd passed over that clue far too easily hit her hard. How many other important pieces of information had she foolishly failed to register? Assigning each part a place in this crazy equation was the only way the truth would emerge.

No matter how she calculated or recalculated, the odds that she'd fallen down an *Alice in Wonderland* hole and ended up in the third century came up zero.

None of this made any sense.

A tug at her shoulder brought Lisbeth back to the present, which, to her muddled thinking, was really the past.

"This gown color is good with your dark hair." Ruth smoothed the wrinkles. The touch of this foreign woman's hand pressed reality into Lisbeth's situation. This was not some crazy dream.

Lisbeth shuddered. Even though she knew Ruth meant to distract her, to comfort her with the tangible, sorting out this time-travel thing had given Lisbeth a tremendous headache and left her in no mood for chitchat. If the impossible had really happened, she was both miles and years away from Papa. She couldn't bear the thought of her father facing his uncertain future without her. How was she going to get back to him? Could she even go back? What would become of Craig? Or her job at the hospital, tenuous as it was?

Ruth gathered the soft fabric at Lisbeth's left shoulder and pinned the folds in place with a golden brooch topped with an amethyst cameo. She cinched Lisbeth's waist with a belt of shiny coins. In short order, heavy jeweled earrings pulled at Lisbeth's earlobes, and two hammered metal bracelets dangled from each wrist.

"Much better." With a pleased smile, Ruth spun her around to face a wall of highly polished bronze. "What do you think?"

Lisbeth considered her distorted reflection. Her gaze flitted between the cotton candy confection in the mirror and the beaming stranger peering over her shoulder. How could she tell anyone what really tumbled in her mind? No one would believe her.

"You could be mistaken for nobility," Ruth said. "Cyprian will be pleased."

Whether or not some guy strutting around in a toga found her attractive was the least of Lisbeth's worries. What did bother her was that this woman, who couldn't be more than five years older than her, lived in this moment. A naive bishop's wife who didn't have a clue how dire the future was about to become. Ruth probably couldn't comprehend the terrors even if Lisbeth spelled out everything she could remember from Papa's history lessons. Third-century Roman writings recorded a bloody, volatile mess in the African provinces. Everything this innocent woman believed to be true about her world was going to change rapidly and drastically.

And not for the better.

Lisbeth clasped Ruth's hand. "If you want to live, you'll leave this godforsaken time with me, and you'll do it now."

8

MAGDALENA PRESSED HER EAR against the master's chamber door. She listened for the sound of silver bouncing
across the marble. Once she heard the clank of the chalice, she
counted under her breath. At the number ten, a muffled thud
seeped through the cedar. Slowly, she lifted the latch and forced
open the carved slab.

Golden lamplight flickered on a small table in the far corner.
The smooth-faced, wide-eyed scribe perched like one of Aspasius's
parrots on the dictation stool, a wax tablet in his lap and a stylus
pointed toward the bed. "I don't know what happened," he muttered.

Magdalena waded through the litter of discarded tunics, robes,
and half-written scrolls scattered over thick carpets imported from
Egypt. She hated how the disorder of Aspasius's personal life repeated itself in his erratic and spendthrift governing. Doing what
she could to bring his reign to an end would benefit more than just
herself. History itself would thank her one day.

Aspasius lay sprawled facedown upon sheets, sheets she'd
wanted to shred every time he dragged her bruised body across
them. Naked, except for his loincloth and red shoes, he resembled
the beached whale she and her husband had spotted during their
honeymoon on the eastern coastline of Africa.

She chose the safest path to the bed. She had always thought Aspasius a dirty old man, perverted in a way that made her blood run cold. But in the last few months, unexplained chills had caused the proconsul to take on another habit of old men. Every morning Aspasius ordered Tabari to wrap his feet in strips of woolen cloth to keep his feet warm and his shoes from rubbing blisters. As she neared his upturned soles, she could tell that his efforts were failing. Yellow pus oozed from the bindings that stank of festering ulcers.

Careful not to touch the infection, Magdalena nudged the thick sole of his built-up shoe. Aspasius didn't move. She placed her knee upon the down tick and reached for his neck. Working her fingers beneath the fleshy folds, she searched for the sweet spot, the place where she kept tabs on his beating heart after a slug of his headache powders. Exact dosing was something she'd yet to master. She only wanted him unconscious for a few hours.

Aspasius mumbled something unintelligible. She sighed with relief. He sputtered, turned his flushed face toward her, and eyed her with a glassy stare. Magdalena froze. Despite a drug-induced glaze, he seemed to take her in. Would he remember this night?

She smiled and patted his cheek. "There, there, my love."

His eyelids fluttered, then sank against the weight of the drug.

Magdalena stood. "You may go, Pytros." She watched the smooth-faced scribe gather his wax tablets, his eyes darting between her and their master. The eager scribe's name meant babbler, a singing canary who would not keep what he'd seen to himself if she wasn't extremely careful with her words. She summoned a concerned scowl to her face. "Our master is overwrought. He suffered a great loss today. We must let him rest, not mention his humiliation beyond these doors. Do you understand, Pytros?"

The scribe's halfhearted agreement did not grant Magdalena

the assurance she preferred, but more pressing matters deserved her worry at the moment. Securing Aspasius's slumber took more time than she'd planned. Changing her tunic would delay her further, a risk that would put her waiting escorts in greater danger. She would have to wear her silks.

Magdalena snuffed the lamp and followed Pytros from the room. She quietly pulled the door closed. "Remember, not a word."

She waited until the scribe was well on his way to his quarters, then turned in the opposite direction. The click of her heels made too much noise on the polished marble. Arousing the birds would not be good. She stopped and removed her sandals. Straps hooked on her finger, she continued down the corridor that led to Aspasius's office. A light rap on the thick wooden door elicited a muffled response. She released the latch and slipped inside. Slivers of moonlight filtered through the shutter slats.

"We're here, my lady," a gruff voice whispered in the darkness.

Once Magdalena's eyes adjusted to the dim light, she spotted Kardide, Iltani, and Tabari huddled in the far corner. The undeserved respect they heaped upon her had helped restore her purpose, but excess adoration also brought with it greater responsibility.

Magdalena hurried across the carpets and fell into their embrace. "We have but a few hours."

"You mustn't go to the assembly tonight." Kardide, as vigilant as her name, gripped Magdalena's shoulders. "Aspasius has added extra patrols. I heard him give the order to kill anyone out past curfew."

"I'll be careful." Magdalena tried to keep the fear from her voice. "Did you bring my cloak?"

"Have you not heard a word I said?" Kardide asked with a hiss. "You can't go."

"My dear Kardide, do you trust me?" Far below the palace balcony, the roar of the ocean crashed against the harbor breakers.

"Yes," Kardide finally admitted. "But—"

"Then you must pray." Magdalena felt a little hand slip into hers and squeeze. "And you too, my sweet Tabari."

"At least take Iltani with you," Kardide begged. "She could be of assistance should you encounter trouble."

"No. It's too risky."

"Then why are you going?" Kardide asked. "Ruth will care for the sick if you can't make it tonight."

"Something happened today . . . and I must find out more about it. I have to."

Iltani held out a coarse woolen tunic, her concern communicated in the mute tears that spilled onto her cheeks.

Magdalena slid her arms into the sleeves and lifted the hood over her head. If, for some reason, she was spotted, she preferred to be mistaken for a tenement peasant. An arrow through the heart would bring an instantaneous death, which would be God's blessing. She could not bear the agonizing worry that would accompany a slow demise in the arena.

Iltani pulled off her wooden shoes.

Magdalena traded her jewel-crusted sandals for plebeian slave footwear. She hugged each woman tightly. "Stay alert, my friends."

Kardide moved aside, grumbling her disapproval. Magdalena stepped up to the elaborate chariot-racing mural painted across the stone wall behind Aspasius's desk. She placed her index finger on the foaming mouth of the bridled stallion and traced the taut reins to the hand of an armored charioteer. Years ago, Aspasius had locked her in his office for her unwillingness to kiss his ring. She'd nearly climbed the walls trying to escape. Quite by accident, she'd discovered the secret lever cleverly hidden in the soldier's cuff. The hammered piece of metal, a key that unlocked a secret passageway, had saved more than her sanity. It had saved the one thing that had kept her here all of these years. Good from bad. A blessing she never expected.

Magdalena stuck her finger into the cold iron ring and tugged.

The wall of stone groaned. Mortared rocks slid on a rusty iron track. Dank, cool air swirled into the office. As the horse's mouth inched slowly toward the charioteer's lap, a narrow opening exposed a dark stairwell. Magdalena reached around the stone door. Her fingers found the ledge where she kept an oil lamp for nights such as this. She struck a flint, lit the wick, then cupped the flame.

The faint glow illuminated the fear-sobered faces of her friends.

"Stay strong." Magdalena blew them a kiss and squeezed into the darkness.

9

CALFSKIN LEATHER PINCHED LISBETH'S toes. "I really can't stay, and neither should you, Ruth."

"Eat something at the feast. You'll feel better." As if they'd been best friends forever, the bishop's wife looped her arm through Lisbeth's and dragged her toward the open door at the end of the hall. "Wait until you meet the church. They're going to love you, and you'll love them."

"Church?" Lisbeth yanked free of Ruth's hold. "I thought you dressed me up like a pageant contestant to impress the bishop."

"He's with the believers."

"Believers of what?"

"The resurrection. Followers of Christ."

Snatches of Papa's history lesson sent fear rippling through Lisbeth. How had she fallen in with one of the most persecuted sects of the century? "Christians?"

Ruth nodded, her twinkling eyes offering no sign of the terror Lisbeth would have expected.

Maybe she was wrong about Rome's disdain for this religious group. She really didn't know that much about Christians. After all, she'd only attended one church service in her life. And she wouldn't have gone that time, except her roommate, Queenie, the shiny buckle on the Bible Belt, had promised a platter of her mother's homemade fried chicken afterward. Starving med students never turned down home cooking.

Lisbeth would never forget that Sunday morning in Texas. She remembered questioning the accuracy of her phone's GPS when the blinking blue ball took her to an enormous building that resembled an upscale shopping mall. She wheeled into the parking lot. Men in bright orange vests waved fluorescent wands. By the time she found an empty parking slot she was a good fifteen-minute shuttle ride from the two-story glass foyer. Once she stepped inside the door, smiling greeters stuffed slick brochures into her hands and pointed her in the direction of the coffee shop. She elbowed her way through women dressed in silk suits, fully aware that the black slacks and ballerina flats she wore were poor choices. Nearly as poor choices as agreeing to go to church in the first place. And to make matters worse, she never did find Queenie, or have that fried chicken her friend had raved about for weeks.

Lisbeth tried to extricate herself from Ruth's grasp. "I really don't have time to—"

A blur of voices, the melancholy notes of a cane lute, and the clink of silver chalices floated through the open doors.

"They've started." Ruth placed Lisbeth against the wall. "Wait here." She adjusted the pink folds of her gown. "Oh, my. You *are* striking." Obviously pleased with her handiwork, she continued, "I know Cyprian. He'll want to present you to the congregation properly. Let me go find him."

"Congregation?" Lisbeth grabbed Ruth's arm, visions of the five-thousand-seat auditorium at Queenie's church flashing before her eyes. "I'm not good in front of crowds. Can't I just sit in the back row or listen from the doorway? I had no idea you people were some kind of cult. I would have said—"

Fear flicked across Ruth's eyes. "You'll say nothing." She laid her stick-straight forefinger on Lisbeth's lips. "The proconsul does not know that Cyprian allows the believers to meet here. And he must never find out. Do you understand?"

If these people were determined to charge toward danger, who was she to stop them? But she didn't have to join them. First chance she got, she was out of here.

Lisbeth let out a frustrated sigh. "Sure. Whatever."

Besides, if this whole time-travel thing was real, who would she tell? Papa was a thousand miles and eighteen hundred years away. Even if her cell phone hadn't been smashed to bits, she doubted Queenie had enough faith to believe a text that said *Help. I'm lost in 251 AD. Captured by some kind of secret cult. Dressed to kill and headed to church.*

Right now, satisfying Ruth's good intentions was her only shot at a successful escape. She had no choice. Lisbeth sank against the wall.

"Good girl." Ruth scurried through the open doors.

The moment she disappeared, Lisbeth shot from her hiding place and peeked around the doorframe.

People of every age and, from the variety of dress, every life station were crammed into a torch-lit garden framed by two-story stone columns and balconies loaded with anxious-faced onlookers. The outdoor patio had a beautiful fountain and several stone tables laden with food and candlelight. The whole gig looked more like the casual barbecue the chief attending threw the first week of residency to welcome all the new residents. Not the state-of-the-art stadium of Queenie's church, decked out with stage lighting and headset-wearing cameramen.

In the center of this scaled-back spectacle was the one thing Queenie's church and this simple gathering had in common: a preacher . . . a stooped man with a long, weathered face and two enormous dogs flopped at his feet. The rumpled old man in a dingy white toga and a lion's mane of unruly hair resembled an unmade bed compared to Queenie's slick, three-piece-suit pastor with his militant strut. But there was no mistaking who he was.

The pontificating Santa stood atop a makeshift stage addressing the crowd and holding court with every little elf-eye glued on him. Lisbeth edged a bit closer. Surely this old man was not Caecilianus? If he was the bishop, he had to be at least thirty years older than his wife, Ruth.

"Felicissimus . . ." the eloquent speaker waved his hand in the direction of a pudgy little man who sat upon a bench with his back to do the door, a name and a hunched back Lisbeth would never forget.

Anger prickled the hairs on the back of Lisbeth's neck. What was the slave trader doing here? How dare he sell her like a used car and strip away her precious stethoscope like it was a car radio? She started toward him, when the bishop continued.

"We give you praise for the admirable work you continue to do on our Lord's behalf. Ruth tells me that together, you and Cyprian have rescued another soul from the clutches of Aspasius."

Felicissimus beamed under the praise. Lisbeth gripped the doorframe. The idea of storming the party and beating that smirking little weasel senseless pounded in her ears. If these people thought kidnapping someone and selling them to the highest bidder was admirable work, she'd been wrong in her assessment of Ruth, and she'd certainly read more kindness in Cyprian's actions than he deserved.

Cheers spilled out through the open doors, drawing her in despite the warnings sounding in her head to run. Lisbeth inched around the door. This bishop fellow had sold these people on something. She wasn't quite sure exactly what. If their enthusiasm had anything to do with her, the idea rankled every nerve in her body. Everyone was so excited, she half expected a robed choir to suddenly burst into a rousing gospel song like the two hundred voices that backed up Queenie's pastor.

"While we must do what we can to aid those held captive," someone in the balcony yelled, "what about the rumors of sickness, Bishop? Who will be left alive to help us?"

The crowd sobered. All heads turned to the man thrusting a clenched fist in the air.

"You raise a good point, Numidicus," the bishop said.

"I've got children, Caecilianus." The woman near the fountain clutched a baby. "They say the youngest are the first to die."

Concern rippled through the crowd.

The old man raised his hands, and the people immediately silenced. "Doing what we can to stop the importation of sickness into Carthage must become our next priority." The hypnotic cadence of the bishop's words cast a calming spell over his listeners . . . all but the man on the balcony who had not lowered his fist.

"But it doesn't matter what we do." The man on the balcony jumped over the railing and landed a staggered vault at the bishop's feet. Both dogs jumped to attention. Forelegs set, teeth bared, they growled. The man took a step back.

"Easy, girls." Caecilianus rubbed their ears. "Let's hear what Numidicus has to say."

With one eye on the dogs, the man continued, "Already believers are blamed for any misfortune that befalls Carthage. Persecution of the worst kind will come upon us if this sickness spreads. Aspasius will not rest until he sees us all fed to the lions. My daughter is but a child. I say we flee to the hills."

Murmurs brought some of the crowd to their feet.

"True, my dear boy." The bishop stayed his pets, then placed a gnarled hand on the man's shoulder. "But we cannot allow the fear of what might happen to enter our ranks, now can we, Numidicus?"

"We are dung on the bottom of Roman boots." The man who'd tried to rally support with his acrobatics glanced around the crowd. Sober faces registered his angst, but no one took his side. "It's not right."

Caecilianus smiled. "Like you, brave Numidicus, I chafe at the injustice. But I am not afraid to meet my maker." The bishop lifted his arms to the array of stars that crowned the open courtyard. All chins lifted upward. "Because Christ suffered for me, I will do what I can for him." The old bishop's dramatic pause held his audience captive. Slowly he lowered his arms. His eyes scanned his followers. Gathering a deep breath, he plunged toward a resounding finish. "Brothers and sisters, stay the course. Do unto others as you would have them do unto you, even to the point of death."

Flickering torchlight illuminated tears on every upturned cheek of this old preacher's congregation. He had them. They'd bought every word and guzzled the bishop's fatal Kool-Aid.

Not her. And neither had history, if Lisbeth recalled Papa's carefully planned lectures. Third-century Carthage suffered a major catastrophe. Rousing pep talks from a deranged rebel and peer pressure from his rabid followers would not stop the freight train barreling their way. If these people didn't wise up and get off the tracks, they were going to die. Trancelike stares offered little hope that they were going anywhere.

Lisbeth wanted no part of the slow, torturous suffering they'd chosen. Suffering they could've avoided by simply banding together and leaving, quarantining themselves safely out of harm's way until the unnamed virus flamed out.

Plague or no plague, the problems of these people were not her problems. Even if she could solve the mystery illness that would eventually kill thousands, the possibility that her destiny had anything to do with changing history was preposterous. Nearly as crazy as the bishop's claims that a few ill-equipped peasants could make a difference. She was getting out of here while she still could. She'd wait outside, and when the pious slave trader left church she'd confront him and demand the return of her mother's stethoscope.

Lisbeth eased into the empty hall. For the first time since this whole time-warp thing had happened, she was unattended. Free to search for the portal that had spewed her into this foreign world. No muscled hunk or his frilly little sidekick to stop her from going home.

Keeping her eyes fixed on the peculiar pep rally happening in the garden, Lisbeth backed away on tiptoes. One step. Two. Three. A startling collision with something hard. Before she regained her balance, someone gripped her elbow.

"Going somewhere?" Cyprian's arm circled her waist and drew her close. Her back went rigid against his beating chest. A clean, soapy scent replaced the equine odor she remembered from being tossed across his shoulder. "And just when we were getting to know each other." His breath brushed the top of her ear. Warmth flushed her cheeks.

"For your information, I'm"—she wrenched free and whirled to face him—"waiting."

Apparently, Cyprian had spent some time in the bath as well. Cleaned up and dressed in a more formal toga, he was gorgeous. Wet, golden waves swept back from his handsome face emphasized his aristocratic forehead, intense royal blue eyes, and cleanly shaven jaw. The blinding white folds of his garment exposed one muscular shoulder.

"Waiting for an opportunity to escape?" he goaded.

Lisbeth tucked a stray hair into the prom updo Ruth had insisted accentuated her long neck. "I'm waiting to be formally introduced to the bishop."

"Then you shall wait no more." He gently took Lisbeth's elbow and led her into the garden.

Everyone turned. Chatter ceased. Mouths hung agape. Any moment, she expected trumpets to announce the arrival of the prom king and queen. Despite the craziness, she didn't want him to let go.

"My dear friend!" The bishop opened his arms wide and beckoned them to him.

Lisbeth spoke between clenched teeth. "You didn't say you were a *Christian*."

Cyprian's dazzling smile transformed his chiseled features. On the surface, he appeared to be a kinder man, one far different than the ruthless slave buyer who'd slung her over his shoulder. Yet, beneath his facade, Lisbeth detected a hint of unbending steel. A strength that both comforted and frightened her.

"You never asked." He pressed his hand against the small of her back.

The forward thrust propelled Lisbeth through the crowd and doubled her heart rate. Why hadn't she put two and two together? Of course he had to be one of them if he was willing to risk the wrath of Rome to allow their secret meeting in his home. Yet, he was obviously a wealthy Roman. A curious mix.

They passed the gaunt-faced mother who'd voiced her concerns about the children to the bishop. Up close, Lisbeth could see that this mother and child suffered from malnutrition. If she had a stethoscope to put to the woman's sunken chest, desperation would be the scant nourishment sustaining her heart.

Lisbeth wrung her empty hands and scanned the crowd with a

professional eye. Several toddlers had the bowed legs of rickets. Numerous adults exhibited the hair and teeth loss of scurvy. Nearly every child sported the protruding belly of chronic protein deficiency. Third-world ailments easily eradicated by a proper diet and good health care. She'd been so focused on the scrappy preacher that she'd failed to notice the abject poverty of Cyprian's guests. Attired in the tattered rags of the homeless, they attacked the bread baskets as if another morsel might not come their way again.

Déjà vu memories of navigating the county hospital's over-crowded emergency room where rail-thin men in filthy army jack-ets tugged on her white coat overwhelmed her. Most of those patients suffered self-inflicted chemical addictions and poor life-style choices. Sixteen-hour days by overworked medical personnel didn't make a dent in the problem. In her exhaustion, she'd often wondered about the futility of serving the poor. She'd never have the martyr's heart of her mother.

The summer before her family went to the cave for the first time, she and Mama had accompanied Papa to Tripoli for a week. He was excavating a stunning glass and stone mosaic of an ex-hausted gladiator from the floor of an ancient Roman farmhouse. Late one night, a woman with a dead child swaddled to her breast had wandered into camp asking for bread. The emaciated woman reeked of chronic diarrhea. While Mama hurried to lace a cup of tea with honey, the young mother fell to the ground and died.

"Despite the oil riches of Libya, women and children starve." Mama shook her finger at Papa. "It's not right, Lawrence. I'll not help you rob treasures that could put food in empty bel-lies."

The suffering before Lisbeth now reminded her of the glassy eyes of that hopeless young mother. One class of society denying another to the point of starving their children, proof that greed and selfishness incited a level of suffering that transcended time. The sins of the past molding an abysmal future. Lisbeth suddenly felt very overdressed, even more out of place, and mad as Mama had been when she cradled those depleted bodies.

Cyprian ushered her toward the bishop, stopping to greet Felicissimus. "Good work, my friend."

"Thief!" Lisbeth lunged for the pudgy little man, swinging with the rage building inside her. "I want my stethoscope." She heard dogs barking and felt Cyprian reel her in. "Let me go." She hated the smug grin dimpling Felicissimus's cheeks.

"There will be plenty of time for grudges." Cyprian clamped her elbow.

"This isn't over, fat boy," Lisbeth said with a hiss as Cyprian dragged her away from the slave trader. "I'll get my stethoscope one way or another."

By the time they arrived at the bishop's small wooden dais, Ruth had joined her husband. She frowned at the displacement of Lisbeth's curls.

"My friend." Caecilianus folded Cyprian into a bear hug. His rheumy eyes appraised her over her new master's shoulder. Despite the film of cataracts, the bishop seemed to see deep into her soul, laying bare her anger, guilt, and self-doubt.

She squirmed while the crowd closed in, pushing her dangerously close to the man who thought he owned her. She felt something wet on her hand and looked down to find both dogs stationed at her feet. Running her hand over the sleek coat of the apricot-colored hound, her gaze roamed the garden for an alternate exit, one that included landing a blow squarely in the gut of that sorry slave trader on her way out of this nightmare.

"I see you have donned the white tunic of a politician, Cyprian." Disapproval clouded the face of the old priest. "Does this mean you'll run for office?"

"The time has come." Cyprian's shoulders squared. "If the power of Aspasius is to be stopped, securing a seat in the Senate is a must."

A roar of approval rattled Lisbeth to the core. These peasants would not cheer the foolish decision to take on the proconsul if they'd witnessed what she'd seen today when the woman in green silk dared to speak against the ruler of Carthage. The impertinence had most likely cost that brave woman a black eye, maybe even a broken jaw.

If Lisbeth remembered Papa's history lessons correctly, Aspasius would have obtained his appointment as ruler of this province as a reward from the Senate. He would not give up his plum position without a fight. If there was one thing she had learned growing up in camps filled with men, it was the predictability of male stubbornness.

Why did Cyprian think he could make a difference? No doubt the wealthy, well-spoken, and wildly attractive Cyprian could give the proconsul a run for his money, but Cyprian would need more than a pretty face to accomplish the nullification of the Senate's volatile political decision.

Cyprian cleared his throat. "Caecilianus, may I present the congregation with . . ." He leaned over and whispered, "You're standing on my toga."

"Oh, sorry." Lisbeth hastily lifted her foot. The heel of her sandal caught in the hem of her skirt, upsetting her balance. Arms whirling, she teetered on the podium. Cyprian's strong hand saved her from an embarrassing fall that would have surely sent her skirts sailing over her head.

". . . a woman certain to bless our efforts." His eyes did not mean a word of what his lips were saying.

"Bless what efforts?" Lisbeth shrugged free of Cyprian's clasp. "Whatever secret plans you people are scheming here does not include me!"

Suddenly a side door to the garden burst open.

A panting woman grabbed the doorframe. Blood was splattered across her green silk tunic, brown woolen cloak, and the veil across her face. "Help."

10

LISBETH SPRINTED TOWARD THE bloody woman, shouting orders. "Bring light. Bandages. Hot water."

Men leapt from their reclining couches. Mothers gathered their children close.

Two barking hounds stayed hard on Lisbeth's heels, arriving at the woman's side right after her. "Are you hurt?"

"No." The woman took Lisbeth's hand. "Come."

"Let me check your injuries."

"I can wait." She dragged Lisbeth into the hall and pointed at the two young men slumped together on one of the brocade couches. "They cannot."

The garden crowd quickly pressed in behind them, including Cyprian from the hot breath scorching Lisbeth's neck.

The dogs scrambled around her and parked themselves at the feet of the biggest boy. At first glance, Lisbeth would have guessed the late arrivals to be victims of a car wreck. They were as bloodied and battered as some of the fatalities she'd seen wheeled into the ER, but these patients seemed to have gotten themselves here by their own power, with the bigger fellow alert enough to help the unconscious smaller one.

"No! Not my son." Ruth pushed past Lisbeth and rushed to the larger boy. "Barek, Mama's here." She frantically began removing the boy's bloody cloak, searching his body for injuries.

"He's your son?" The boy looked to be about seventeen. Ruth couldn't have been much more than fifteen when she'd had him.

Caecilianus elbowed his way to the front of the crowd. "My boy. Not my boy." He crumpled next to his dogs. "What can I do?"

"Pray," Ruth mumbled. "Pray and remove these creatures from my path."

Caecilianus collared his pets and made way for his wife.

"What happened?" Lisbeth moved toward the smaller boy, the one whose head hung like a limp rag.

"Soldiers." The cloaked woman lifted the chin of the smaller boy. His eyelids fluttered. "Laurentius? Can you hear me?" An irregular-toothed smile sliced a wedge in his pie-shaped face. Then he drifted into unconsciousness. The lady in green silk removed the smaller fellow's bloody arm from Barek's shoulder. "They beat Laurentius with clubs. He may have a concussion. But I think Barek's injuries are worse. I'll tend him. You take Laurentius."

"Me?" Who was this woman ordering her around like an ER attending?

Cyprian joined the women huddled around the couch. "Did the soldiers follow you here, healer?"

Healer? Curious, Lisbeth stepped closer.

The woman in green silk shook her head. "We cut through the tenements."

"Barek's taken an arrow to the shoulder." Ruth wrapped her hand around the cock-feather fletching that adorned the shaft. "I need to pull it out."

"No!" Lisbeth and the healer shouted at the same time. Their heads snapped up. Their eyes fastened on each other. A brief, electrifying stare passed between them.

The healer was the first to recover. She quickly handed the

smaller boy over to Cyprian. "Broadheads are razor-sharp. The damage could be extensive. Ruth, help me take a look."

"I'll do it." Lisbeth eased the larger boy forward and checked his back. "It's a through and through. If the projectile punctured a lung or lacerated an artery—"

"There's only one way to find out." The healer fished something shiny out of her cloak pocket and wrapped it around her neck.

"Hey! Ruth, hold your son a minute." Lisbeth released the larger boy. He fell into Ruth's arms with a pained groan. "That's my stethoscope!"

"You can have it when I'm finished."

"You don't even know how to use it. Give it to me!" Lisbeth lunged for the woman.

They both went crashing onto the marble floor. Lisbeth tried desperately to wrestle her stethoscope from this woman's clutches.

"Stop!" Ruth screamed. "Cyprian, do something!"

Cyprian deposited the smaller boy into the arms of the bishop. His arm circled Lisbeth's waist and lifted her off the woman. "What are you doing? There's been enough bloodshed for one night."

Lisbeth's feet pedaled the air. Arms flailing, she fought to break free. "Give it back, witch!"

The healer placed a protective hand on the stethoscope and struggled to sit up. "Actually, I am not a witch, Lisbeth"—her breathy voice was no more than a whisper—"but an adequate surgeon . . . or so they used to say." The hood of her cloak had been knocked free, along with the combs that held her hair in place. Thick ebony locks streaked with gray tumbled to her waist.

"How do you know my name?" Lisbeth felt Cyprian's grip tighten around her middle. "How?"

The lady in green silk got to her feet. "This stethoscope once belonged to me." She spoke in English, her eyes locked with Lisbeth's.

A moment of stunned silence passed. When Lisbeth found her voice she answered in English. "Funny, I thought you just said this is your stethoscope."

"I did," the woman replied, and she ripped the veil from her face. "And from the efficiency of your triage, I trust you've learned to use it on more than inanimate objects."

Lisbeth went limp, the fight hemorrhaging from her extremities at a deadly rate. She tried to speak, but a million unanswered questions lodged in her throat.

The disheveled woman with sad, broken eyes could not be who she was thinking of. That woman was put together. A beautiful, self-confident doctor. And the person she'd always wanted to be.

This couldn't be happening. She must have hit her head when she fell into that stupid hole in Papa's cave. Once Nigel and Aisa hauled her out, she'd come to in a couple of days. She and Papa would sit on overturned buckets outside his tent and share warm sodas and a laugh about who was crazier . . . him or her.

Cyprian spoke into Lisbeth's ear. "Do you have healing skills?"

Lisbeth managed a numb nod.

"If you're ready to behave, I'll put you down." Cyprian lowered Lisbeth's feet to the floor.

She wanted to run toward the woman in the bloody green silk. To hug her. Or hit her. She wasn't sure. But instead she stood motionless, restrained by Cyprian and the idea that her mother was alive. "Ma—"

"Magdalena is my name." She snatched Lisbeth's hand, sending a fiery blast of joy, confusion, and anger coursing through Lisbeth's veins. She yanked her close, cutting off the questions flooding Lisbeth's mind. "Ask nothing," she whispered.

What kind of mother disappears for twenty-three years, then expects her deserted child to shelve the questions?

"But—"

"Nothing." Mama squeezed her hand until she garnered Lisbeth's pained consent. "I need your help. Now."

Emotions, raw and as bloody as the two injured boys on the couch, pumped through Lisbeth. If this woman was her mother, then her mother wasn't dead. And if she wasn't dead, why hadn't she come home? Had Mama chosen this life over the one they had together? Why didn't she want to return to her and Papa?

Fury sizzled in Lisbeth's chest, making it difficult to breathe. She'd keep quiet for now. Not because the woman who'd abandoned her when she was five deserved her obedience. She'd keep quiet because she had no words to explain the obvious. Saving ragtag rebels meant more to her mother than trying to get home to her own family.

"What do you want me to do?" Lisbeth aimed her sharp tone at her mother's jugular, knowing full well that any woman who could stand by and watch someone auction off her daughter to the highest bidder would likely bleed ice.

"Are you a surgeon?"

Technically, Lisbeth wasn't sure she was still a doctor. She shook her head.

"Then you tend Laurentius. I'll operate on Barek." Before Lisbeth could protest, her mother started again. "Quick. Let's get them laid out on a clean, flat surface." She motioned for Cyprian. "Careful with his neck." Cyprian gently guided the boy to the floor, while she turned at once to remove Barek from Ruth's arms. "Fetch the supplies I keep here."

"I can't leave my son." Panic tightened Ruth's grip on the

arrow. "This swelling will make the arrow impossible to remove. I must yank it out before he's fully awake."

Lisbeth's mother cradled Barek with one arm while she gently pried Ruth's fingers from the shaft. "You trust me, don't you, friend?" She removed the stethoscope from her neck. After listening to his heart, she held it out to Ruth. "Give this to Lisbeth, and then heat the fire poker to cauterize this wound."

Ruth kissed her son on the forehead and turned to Lisbeth. "My Barek must not die because of your bad temper." She dropped the stethoscope into Lisbeth's hand like it was a snake. "Save your fight for what matters." Ruth reluctantly parted the crowd and scurried off to fetch the ordered supplies.

Ashamed that she'd once again placed her needs before the needs of her patients, Lisbeth clutched the rubber tube. She deserved the sting of Ruth's rebuke. What kind of a doctor fights for a piece of medical equipment as if it were a locket containing faded pictures or snippets of hair?

Rubbing her finger over the engraved *M* on the bell, Lisbeth felt as if she were trying to conjure a genie. This stethoscope was more than a tangible link to the mother she had loved and lost. This stethoscope had been her lifeline to the future, to unfulfilled dreams. She'd told herself that becoming a doctor was her dream. But in truth, that dream belonged to her parents. Both of them. All Lisbeth had ever wanted was a family. The family the Hastings had been once upon a time.

Finding her mother should be the best thing that happened to her since this whole nightmare started. After all, Mama was the piece missing from the puzzle of her life, the piece she'd sought for years. Why didn't she feel happy? Why was there still a cavern-size hole in her heart?

Lisbeth felt anxious eyes boring into her hesitation. She glanced at Mama. The woman she barely recognized was busy setting up a makeshift OR. Lisbeth couldn't help envying the complete trust and confidence the crowd—especially Cyprian—had in the seasoned surgeon. Mama made practicing medicine look easy . . . even under these less than satisfactory conditions. The resident, on the other hand, was the floundering chick recently pushed from the nest. If she was to make up for her foolish and unprofessional display, she had much to prove.

Lisbeth turned her attention to the young man on the mat and gasped. So caught up in the chaos, she'd failed to give this boy more than a once-over. Was the fatal mistake she had made in the twenty-first century simply a repeat of a similar mistake made in the past? If so, she was doomed to be a careless doctor. The cheese and wine she'd had in the bath soured in her stomach.

Lisbeth knelt to examine the young man with the flattened nose, moon-shaped face, and almond-slit eyes. Down syndrome. Her eyes slid from his face to his body. Naked from the waist up, purple bruises mottled the pale skin of the boy's hairless chest. Someone much larger than Laurentius must have used blunt force to wipe the interminable smile from this innocent soul. Stubby fingers with pinkies that curved inward. Hobbit-like bare feet with larger than normal spaces between each big toe and second toe. Unlike Barek, this boy's reduced stature and thinning hair made it difficult to determine his exact age. How could someone appear so old and so childlike at the same time? The weak suffering as the strong stood by. He was a child. Someone should have defended him. Visions of Abra lying still and blue in the middle of the gurney swept over her. Her inattention and indifference had killed that child. She was no better than the soldier who'd beaten Laurentius almost to death. Lisbeth leapt from her crouched position, ran to the garden, and vomited into the nearest planter.

Next thing she knew, Cyprian stood at her side, an irritating column of unshakable durability. "Are you ill?"

"No." Lisbeth wiped her mouth with the back of her hand. "I can't go back."

Cyprian grasped her elbow. "You will."

She followed him to the wounded and her failure to defend the weak. She'd thought Mama's disappearance had made her stronger, but she was mistaken. Taking care of Papa since she was five had made her hard. Tough and calloused were not the same thing.

She stood over Laurentius. What could she do for this boy beyond a cool cloth to the forehead? If his internal injuries matched his external bruising, she had nothing to offer.

Ruth appeared with a basket filled with rags, small pouches, and an assortment of wicked iron implements, including a long iron poker that glowed red hot. "Hold this, Caecilianus."

The healer used a crude pair of scissors to cut Barek's sleeve from cuff to shoulder. "The emperor has granted Aspasius his request for additional troops."

"More soldiers?" Ruth held Barek steady. "Already they outnumber us two to one."

Cyprian weighed in on the conversation. "Rome considers Carthage hard won. I'm sure the proconsul had no trouble convincing the emperor to commission his militia to protect the wealthy and the investments they've made in the restoration of this strategic port and its aqueducts."

"Making war where there is no fight fills many coffers." Lisbeth's mother patted Barek's good shoulder. "I'm sorry. This is going to hurt." She poured brown liquid over Barek's wound. His howl echoed in the hall. "Eradicating Christians is a cheap way to occupy bored soldiers."

"Some believers say we must leave Carthage while we can." Ruth caressed Barek's hand. "Flee to the mountains."

Murmurs of agreement swept through the pressing crowd.

The healer turned to the old bishop. "Is this true, Caecilianus? Will you give in to this fear and desert the sick?" She held the flask to Barek's lips, but her eyes castigated the crowd. "I will not go."

Caecilianus studied the poker, as if answers hid in the glow. His eyes traveled to his son, then to the crowd, and finally to Ruth. Anyone paying attention could see the love and sadness passing between them. "Believers, we will stay the course." Solemnity swept across every face. "No matter the cost."

"I have a daughter." Numidicus pushed his way through the group. "What happened to these boys is a price we'll all be expected to pay."

"And they paid it gladly." Mama's glare forced Numidicus's retreat. She returned her attention to the boy with the arrow. "Cyprian, snap this arrow shaft, but leave me enough to work with so I can get the head out."

While the healer dug through a basket, Cyprian stepped into place beside Ruth. Uncertainty rippled in his tense jaw, but he set his feet.

The healer produced a handful of rags and a small cloth bundle. "Ruth, once I free that barb, you stanch the wound."

"But, what if—" Lisbeth interjected. They all turned and glared at her. "I'm just sayin', a millimeter either way, and that boy could bleed out." From their pointed silence, she knew her medical opinion was obviously of no more value here than in Dallas, and rightfully so after her little temper tantrum. "Never mind." She wasn't a surgeon. Even if that arrow had sliced some major artery, what could she do?

"I'll tend my patient," Mama said, "and I'd appreciate it if you'd get busy tending yours."

Lisbeth dropped her eyes back to Laurentius. She felt his pulse. Still unconscious and no change.

Cyprian wrapped his hand around the arrow shaft, and the

dogs began to whine. "I'll be quick, Ruth, but hold your boy steady." The muscles in his tanned arms flexed.

Crack.

Lisbeth cringed and looked up.

Cyprian fell back, holding a long portion of the jagged arrow shaft. Behind him, blood spurted from Barek's shoulder.

"Press harder, Ruth." The healer unrolled the cloth bundle, revealing a set of primitive surgical tools. "I'll have to cut him open and try to stitch the severed vessel. I'm sorry, Barek. The pain will be great."

The boy gave a wide-eyed nod.

"You're going to operate without anesthesia?" Lisbeth shouted. "You can't do—"

Mama's sideways glance skewered her. "You have a better idea?"

She didn't.

Suddenly, Laurentius's eyes fluttered open. He grasped his chest. "Can't . . . breathe." Air leaked from his voice, draining the last of the color from his skin in the process.

Cyprian flew to the boy's side and knelt beside Lisbeth. "Laurentius."

The boy didn't answer. His ragged breathing disintegrated into quick, shallow pants that mimicked a thirsty dog on a hot day. *Shortness of breath.* If the beating had broken a rib, Laurentius could have a punctured lung. Lisbeth's senses recorded the observable symptoms. *Respiratory distress. Asymmetrical chest rise. The bluing of cyanosis.* She should do something. But what? Laurentius groaned, then lost consciousness again.

Fear flashed in Cyprian's eyes. He put an ear to the boy's dark lips. "Healer, this boy is not breathing!"

"I only have two hands"—Mama remained hunched over Barek, leaving Lisbeth to deal with Laurentius on her own—"and right now they're trying to keep the bishop's son from bleeding to death. Lisbeth, Laurentius has a tension pneumothorax. Do something. Now!"

Lisbeth shoved Cyprian out of the way. She crammed the tips of her stethoscope into her ears and slapped the bell onto Laurentius's chest.

"Breath sounds unequal," she muttered, thinking through what to do next as she slid the bell back and forth along the midline. "I hear nothing over the left."

"If his lung is punctured, every exhalation pumps air into his chest cavity." Mama coached without looking up from her operating table. "Without an immediate way of escape, trapped air will compress his lungs, shift everything to one side, and affect the return of blood flow to his heart."

A certain death scenario.

"What should you do, Lisbeth?" Mama prodded. "Think. Quickly."

Lisbeth's mind kicked into high gear, the drawings in her medical books flashing before her eyes. "Relieve the pressure inside the narrow space between the lung and the protective lining of the lung."

"The pleural space," Mama concurred. "Create a release valve."

Lisbeth had observed a needle aspiration in the ER, but she'd never performed a procedure so dangerous. If she tried something this risky in these primitive conditions, she could kill him. "I can't."

"It's the only way to help the injured lung reexpand."

"But I don't have the tools to relieve the buildup." She glanced at the deepening shade of Laurentius's lips. Doing nothing meant the kid would most certainly die.

"Improvise," Mama ordered.

Lisbeth dug through the basket Ruth had placed between her and her mother. "Where's a standard intravenous hollow needle when you need one?" Her eyes shot around the room. Blood dripped from the wooden reed in Cyprian's hand.

The shaft? Approximately five millimeters in diameter. Kind of big, but the jagged end was narrow and, most importantly, hollow. It might work. Not the perfect solution, but the boy's distended neck veins and her mother's preoccupation didn't leave her a whole lot of choice. She did not want this kid to die.

"Give me that shaft, Cyprian," Lisbeth ordered. "Now!"

"This?" He presented her with the longer portion of the straight reed. "It's filthy."

"Break off the feathers." She pointed at the healer. "Then rinse the whole thing with whatever she has in that flask."

Doubt creased Cyprian's face. "How will that help?"

The healer tossed him the flask. "Do what she says!"

Cyprian doused the serrated end of the hollow reed with a red liquid. "He's dead."

In the space of a few seconds, Lisbeth's own heart rate had doubled. "He will be if we don't do something." Surging adrenaline increased the volume of her self-chatter. "Feel for the clavicle on the affected side." She located the bony ridge running along the top of the boy's shoulder. Then she ran her finger along the clavicle until she located the middle between the sterna notch and the bone's insertion into the shoulder.

Satisfied she'd located the midclavicular line, Lisbeth proceeded, talking herself through the process. "Run your finger down the midclavicular line, pressing firmly until you locate the second and third rib." She felt the rigidity of ribs, but just to be doubly sure, she started the whole process again, dragging her fingers slowly and counting out loud like a kindergartner. "Got it."

"Good!" Mama shouted over her shoulder. "Now locate the hollow between the second and third rib."

Satisfied the indention she'd found was the second intercostal space in the midclavicular line, Lisbeth marked the spot with her left finger. "Without an X-ray, there's no way to know if he has an injury to his major airway. If it's worse than we think, this kid will need more than just needle decompression to fix the air leak."

"Do it!" Mama ordered.

Lisbeth held out her right hand. "Give me that shaft."

"It's no use." Cyprian placed the broken arrow stem in her hand. "Laurentius is with God."

"He will be if you don't get out of my way." Lisbeth clutched the shaft. Keeping her eyes on the location she'd chosen, Lisbeth placed her thumb over one end of the hollow reed. "Now what?"

Mama glanced over her shoulder. "Insert the reed at a ninety-degree angle just over the third rib. Aim for bone."

"I'm glad he's unconscious, because this is going to hurt." Lisbeth took a deep breath and jabbed the sharper end of the shaft through the tight skin on Laurentius's chest. He didn't even flinch. "I've got bone."

"Good. Now walk the shaft over the rib to avoid the artery and nerves that run inferior to each rib."

Satisfied she'd cleared the rib, Lisbeth slowly advanced the reed deeper into his flesh, listening for penetration of the pleural.

Pop.

"Got it." She released the seal her thumb had formed over the exposed tip of the shaft. Immediately, air swished out through the reed.

Laurentius took a deep breath. His eyes fluttered open, muddy green irises with the telltale white Brushfield spots of his syndrome. Lisbeth filled her own lungs in relief.

"He lives?" Cyprian directed his confusion at Lisbeth. "He lives." The crowd gasped, then pressed in close.

"That he does!" Lisbeth whispered into Laurentius's ear. "Just breathe, buddy."

With each completed breath cycle, the left side of Laurentius's chest slowly expanded, gaining symmetry with the right side.

Lisbeth rocked back on her heels. Manually manipulating the occlusion, she watched a pinkish glow drive the gray from the boy's puffy cheeks. "Feel better, buddy?"

Laurentius put his hand around hers, the one she was using to steady the shaft in his heaving chest. A guttural sound croaked from his small mouth. She made out a "thank you" from his breathy Latin.

Lisbeth wiped at unexpected tears. "Easy as poking a straw through a plastic lid." Pleased at how quickly his breathing seemed to be leveling out, she looked to her mother for further instructions. Cyprian, Ruth, and Mama towered over her, their eyes glistening.

"He lives!" Cyprian knelt beside Laurentius and took his hand. "Good to have you with us again, little man."

"Good work, Lisbeth." Mama's praise felt like a 14G needle releasing the pent-up anger in Lisbeth's chest.

Laurentius struggled to sit up.

Mama knelt beside him, her hands covered in Barek's blood. "Stay still, Laurentius." She addressed the crowd. "Step back, and let her patient get some air." She found a bone needle in her basket and quickly threaded a coarse string through the tiny hole. She was left-handed, Lisbeth noticed. Like her. "You must lie very still, Laurentius. I'm afraid this will hurt." She slid the bone needle into the raw flesh and the boy yelped. With a few quick flicks of her wrist she secured the chest tube with a perfect purse-string suture. Mama glanced at Lisbeth. "We make a good team."

Before Lisbeth could refute the assumption that they were a team, Cyprian demanded, "Who are you?"

She had no intention of telling this clod anything. "I guess I'm your whore. You paid for me, remember?"

Cyprian turned to Magdalena. "She brought someone back from the dead. How can this be?"

Fear rumbled in the mob, and voices called out, "*What* is she?"

Mama smiled. "She is the answer to our prayers."

11

THE PUNGENT ODOR OF cauterized flesh lingered in the atrium long after Barek's screams dissipated.

Questions from the crowd poked Caecilianus from the shock of Mama's claim. He rose from his prayers and, with a pronounced air of authority, repeated Mama's crazy idea that God had sent another healer. A better healer with new and better ways.

Lisbeth felt the satisfaction of delivering successful care evaporate as the people pushed in to touch her. She was not their healer. If Mama wanted people to think she was magic, that was her business. Dispensing a few medical tricks here and there had probably kept the woman alive through the years. Although a part of her was grateful to learn her mother was alive, Lisbeth had no intention of mastering two-bit sleights of hand. Mama could stay here and slap Band-Aids on wounds that would never heal, but she was leaving Carthage.

Getting back in the saddle had not removed her regret, but it had surprised her to learn how much she actually wanted to be a doctor. Not for Mama. Not for Papa. But for herself. Going home to face her mistakes and take care of Papa were the right things to do.

Cyprian mingled among the excited believers, herding them toward the door. "There's nothing more any of you can do here tonight. Return to your homes in the cover of darkness. Pray and fast until you receive further word." He asked Caecilianus to speak a blessing over the agitated group and instructed Naomi to bag the leftover bread for distribution.

Parents reluctantly gathered their children and circled around the old bishop. After the preacher's lengthy prayer, families filed through the garden. Naomi doled out bundled scraps as families ducked out the back gate.

Once the great hall was cleared, only Cyprian, Ruth, Caecilianus, Mama, and the wounded boys remained.

"Give me your hand, buddy." Lisbeth wrapped Laurentius's chubby fingers around the wooden tube. "You must hold this steady. Can you do that for me?"

Laurentius gave a pained nod, his eyes becoming more aware and following her every move with an unsettling curiosity.

"Sorry to do this to you, little buddy, but I need to get you upright somehow so that tube can drain." Lisbeth wrestled Laurentius against the bench, doing her best to achieve a forty-five-degree angle of his torso without dislodging the arrow shaft. "You're a brave guy."

His smile, despite the discomfort from moving him, gave her the impression he'd fly to the moon if she issued the order.

"Wish I had some antibiotics for you, or at least something to take the edge off your pain." The adrenaline that had powered a jagged reed into this boy's chest ebbed from Lisbeth's extremities. Exhaustion, compounded by the fact that so much had happened in such a short amount of time, would soon have its victory. She needed sleep, or a stiff shot of caffeine, to keep up with her mother.

Hands trembling, Lisbeth fumbled with the excess bandages scattered about the floor. Slipping through the time portal had fried every logical synapse in her body and made her clumsy. She should give herself a break, but if she sat still for even a moment she'd need a crane to get her back on her feet. After all, in the last twenty-four hours she'd been dropped through a time warp, sold as a slave, dressed up and paraded around like a prom Barbie, forced to perform a delicate medical procedure in primitive third-world conditions, and, toughest of all, discovered her long-lost mother was alive. Those thirty-hour ER shifts were cakewalks compared to what she'd been through in Carthage.

Despite the mental pep talk, her legs had turned to jelly. If Abra's death had taught her anything it was that exhaustion leads to mistakes. Catching her breath was the right thing to do. She sank beside Laurentius. The steady rise and fall of his chest was thin comfort. He surely had so many other medical issues that things could have just as easily gone the other way—still could at this point. Who was this boy? According to Papa's history lessons, the Romans abandoned their imperfect children on the bluffs. Yet, here she sat, tending a Down syndrome child who'd survived past infancy. How had he defied history? Who had taken such good care of him? Had her mother's medical skills kept this boy alive? These questions stirred others.

Why had Mama been dodging Roman soldiers with two teen-age boys? Did she seek help at Cyprian's mansion, or had she realized these people held her daughter hostage? If so, why did Mama help them instead of trying to save her?

Finally, and most importantly, had Mama even tried to find a way back, or had she consciously chosen to stay here?

Lisbeth pried Laurentius's fingers from the reed. "I'll spell you, buddy."

Somehow she had to maneuver Mama out of earshot of these people so they could talk. Lisbeth finished bandaging the tube in place. Pleased with the rosy bloom in her patient's cheeks, she let her eyes wander the hall, searching for an exit far from the watch-ful eyes of servants guarding the front door.

Cyprian turned to Mama. "You and Laurentius must go as well, Magdalena. We cannot risk Aspasius's discovery."

"Go where?" Indignation sharpened Lisbeth's voice. "This boy can't travel."

"She's right. Laurentius can't jostle that reed." Mama doused the raw place on Barek's operative site with a golden liquid that perfumed the damp air with evergreen. "Lisbeth is a . . . healer. I'm confident she can care for both boys."

"Wait a minute," Lisbeth protested. "Who said I wanted to be in charge of *your* patients?"

"The care you offered bears witness to your heart." Mama's assumption that a few hours in the same emergency room had made them some sort of medical team did not remove Lisbeth's angst. Or cancel the doubt taking up residence in Cyprian's eyes.

From the way this handsome lawyer so expertly colluded with Felicissimus, Cyprian was a man well trained in the different shades of truth. How long before her bright-eyed captor put two and two together and figured out the true relationship between the healer and his newly purchased slave? Anybody with half a brain could spot the resemblance. Ebony hair. Sea-green eyes. Long, agile fingers. And the same sharp, outspoken mouths.

"You're right, Magdalena." Cyprian turned to Ruth. "Fetch my cloak. I'll take the healer back to Aspasius myself."

"Hold on." Lisbeth scrambled to her feet and grabbed her mother's arm. "So, let me see if I've got this straight. You're willingly going back to that jerk?"

"I have no choice." The flicker of indecision was brief, but Lisbeth hadn't missed it. "You're more than competent to handle their recovery."

"Assuming I have the medical training to handle third-world medicine is not right. In fact, it's a pitiful excuse for leaving me on call with no attending, no antibiotics, no oxygen, no nurse, and no idea of what to do next!"

"You need to rig up some sort of suction for that chest tube."

"With what?"

"Be creative." Mama handed her the flask. "Dribble a few drops over Barek's shoulder again in four hours."

Lisbeth held the vial up to the light from the torch on the wall. "What is this foul stuff?"

"Oil of cedar."

"That's it?" Anger shredded Lisbeth's vocal cords. "A bottle of Christmas perfume is the best you've got?"

"It disinfects and promotes healing. You'll be amazed." Mama raised the hood of her cloak. "Without removing the shaft, irrigate Laurentius's sutures."

Before Lisbeth could protest, Mama directed her next instruction at Ruth. "Mix a pinch of crushed yarrow leaves into a cup of warm sow's milk." As if she intended to cover all her bases before she left, Mama turned and pointed at the stethoscope wrapped around Lisbeth's neck. "May I?"

Lisbeth ripped it free. "I want it back."

Mama fingered the instrument. "Such a luxury." She dragged the bell across Barek's chest, stopping to listen intently to his heart and then his lungs. "Good. Everything sounds good." She turned and knelt beside Laurentius. "No worries. This won't hurt, boy." She completed her exam and stood, a smile spreading across her face. "Excellent work."

Lisbeth thrust out her hand. "My stethoscope."

Mama dropped the instrument into Lisbeth's palm. "Your father must be very proud."

Lisbeth flipped the rubber tube around her neck. "Papa sacrificed a great deal for me."

Pain skittered across Mama's eyes. "I knew he would."

Ruth's return with a steaming ceramic mug interrupted Lisbeth's desire to heap a few more coals upon her mother's head.

"This is a mild coagulant." Mama directed the medicinal cocktail to Lisbeth. "See that Barek takes generous sips throughout the night." She turned to leave.

"Wait." Lisbeth ran after her, frothy milk sloshing over the sides and scalding her hand. "Then what am I supposed to do?"

"The best you can." Mama caressed her cheek. "That's all any of us can ever do." She glanced at Laurentius. "Don't delay on that suction rig."

"Go ahead. Walk out!" Lisbeth shouted. "It's what *you* do best."

12

MAGDALENA SLOSHED THROUGH THE tunnel passages under the proconsul's palace. She'd been so caught up in the joy of finding her daughter she'd forgotten about the unpredictability of mugwort. If Aspasius awoke in an empty bed, she might never see Lisbeth again.

Once she reached the secret panel at the office entry, Magdalena took a deep breath and placed her ear upon the chink in the mortar.

Quiet.

She snuffed her light and returned the clay bowl to the ledge. A quick tug on the metal lever activated the stones. Through the jagged opening, Magdalena slipped into the space she would never call home.

Someone grabbed her shoulders from behind. "Where have you been?"

"Kardide?" Magdalena said with a start. "You scared me to death. What are you doing here?"

"Coming for you. We feared you'd been killed. Moments ago, soldiers reported to Aspasius that there had been trouble last night. Curfew offenders shot."

"But not apprehended." With a pleased smile, Magdalena took a small bow, then kissed her friend's cheek. "So the bear's awake?"

"Roaring like a caged animal," Kardide snatched her hand. "And demanding your presence."

Their rush through the atrium aroused the birds and sent them fluttering against their cages. Fooling Aspasius into thinking she'd merely slipped out to use the chamber pot in her room would be tricky, since his pets had sounded the alarm.

When Magdalena reached her room, she stopped. "I need to change. Fetch a breakfast tray with all of the master's favorites."

Fear crossed her friend's face. "There's no time."

"I'll be quick. Trust me." Magdalena raced inside and shut the door. She ripped off her soiled tunic, then donned the gauziest dress she could find. A couple of brushstrokes removed the cobwebs from her hair. A splash of water rinsed the blood traces of the night's trauma from her face. She gazed in the polished brass mirror. Presentable, except for the black-and-blue ring impression below her eye. No need to cover that little souvenir. Aspasius loved admiring his handiwork.

She lifted the leather cord from around her neck and kissed the gold ring. How proud Lawrence had been of his discovery when he gave it to her. She opened the nightstand drawer and buried it beneath the scarves and trinkets Aspasius insisted she wear when accompanying him in public. Her trembling fingers encountered the tiny silver box kept well hidden.

When she lifted the lid, a mixture of earthy pine bark and tannin sumac stung her nostrils. She plucked out a generous pinch of the fine wood shavings, sprinkled the flakes into a mortar bowl, then added a tablespoon of clean olive oil. With a pestle, she pulverized the ingredients into a muddy paste. She dragged a cotton ball–size piece of wool back and forth through the mixture until every last drop of liquid had been absorbed. Sitting upon the bed, she lifted her leg. She inhaled and stuffed the saturated plug deep into the scarred crevice of her body.

Whether or not her prime had safely withered was a risk she wouldn't take. Never again would she carry his child. Ignoring the sting between her legs, she tucked one of the small bags of mugwort between her breasts, an added safety precaution should his mood prove too foul.

When Magdalena exited her bedroom, Kardide stood ready with the tray. "What if he finds out where you've been?"

"He won't . . . unless you tell."

"My lips are sealed, but that scribe of his cannot be trusted."

"Then our master must be detained from business today. Tell Pytros, and anyone else who seeks an audience with the proconsul, that our master is not well." Magdalena relieved Kardide of two bowls heaped with tiny fish, a carafe of wine, and several varieties of cheese. "Do not follow me. No matter what you hear. Understand?"

Under protest, Kardide backed off and left Magdalena to travel the master's hall alone. At Aspasius's bedroom door, Magdalena balanced the tray with one hand and rapped with a clenched fist.

Quiet. Too quiet.

She clicked the latch and stepped inside. The shutters were still drawn, but the lamp beside the bed had been lit. Her eyes quickly adjusted to the dim light, then slowly made their way to the proconsul's bed.

"There you are, my pet." Aspasius lay naked upon the pillows, his body arranged as if he knew she would come to him and he intended to make her pay.

The repulsive sight incited her flight instincts, but she stood her ground. Smiling sweetly, she employed a trick learned from a college speech teacher and aimed her gaze to a point directly over his head.

She fought to control the bloodlust coursing through her veins. "I've brought sardines." She prayed the flirtatious swaying of her hips would convince him to play along, to believe that if he co-operated she would reward his preparation.

He scowled, looking her up and down. "I'm not hungry." He motioned her forward.

Was his anger left over from yesterday's defeat at the slave auction, the result of a drug-induced hangover, or brought on by the fact that she hadn't been in his bed when the soldiers shook him awake? Either way, she must douse the embers before his temper fanned into flame.

She set the tray on the table beside his bed. "Perhaps a swig of your favorite vintage to start your day then?"

He wiped the sweat from his forehead. "You know how I start my day."

"That I do." Doing her best to hold the carafe steady, she filled a chalice with wine. "Let the entertainment begin." Magdalena tossed him a provocative smile, one laced with just enough agreement to keep him waiting patiently. She turned her back. Hands trembling, she undid the tie on her garment.

As the flimsy gown slid to the floor, so did her drug packet. She didn't dare turn to see if he'd noticed, nor did she dare bend to pick it up.

"Quit stalling, wench."

Her mind raced back to her daughter and the passion dancing in her daughter's eyes, a fire she'd inherited from her father. Yet, something unsettling flickered in that flame. Fear? Insecurity? Unhappiness? Revenge? Lisbeth was obviously trained, but something had shaken her daughter's confidence; she could tell from the quiver in her voice. Talking Lisbeth through the procedure had helped, but there was still something off. Lisbeth needed her. Whether the notion was a mother's intuition or a fool's hope, the prospect of once again being involved in her daughter's life would sustain her until her message reached

Rome. Once Aspasius was removed from office, she could safely extricate her family.

"Magdalena! Now!"

She kicked the corner of her robe over the packet of mugwort, picked up the wine goblet, and climbed onto the bed.

Aspasius grabbed her wrist. "Don't lie to me again."

Did he know? He couldn't know. Kardide assured her Pytros had not been seen outside the servant quarters this morning. Who else could have told Aspasius she'd been gone for hours?

Magdalena bridled the panic clawing her insides and dipped her pinkie into the goblet. "You're much too smart for lies." She gently dragged blood-red liquid across his spreading smile. "What makes you think I've kept something from you?"

"You left my bed." His tongue shot from his mouth, and he greedily lapped away the moisture. The vein at his temple throbbed. Keeping one hand on her wrist, his other hand encircled her waist.

"Sometimes a woman just needs a private moment in the lavatorium."

He drew her so close she could smell the pickled flamingo he'd inhaled the night before. "I've worked years to have it all. I will have everything that is coming to me." His sour breath singed her cheek. "Including that pretty little jewel Cyprian stole on the slave block." He laughed when she stiffened. "Two at a time. A matched set to keep me warm." He shoved her away. "Better yet, I'll sell you and keep her all to myself."

God help her if he'd noticed the strong resemblance between her and Lisbeth. She'd clamp his nose and drown him in mugwort.

"I'm sorry I didn't tell you I had a stomachache." Stilling the tremble in her hands, she offered him the golden chalice. "Let me make it up to you."

His jowls swayed with the slight shake of his head. "Oh, you're not getting off that easy."

Before she could duck, an earsplitting punch to the side of the head sent her reeling from the bed. She scrambled to her robe and fell upon the packet. His laughter rang in her ears as he lumbered from the bed.

He came and stood over her. His kick curled her knees to her chest. "I'll make sure you never leave me again."

13

ASPASIUS CONSIDERED HIMSELF IN the mirror, then repositioned his girth so as to block out the reflection of Magdalena's bloodied body. He was tired of her treachery, and her disapproval had wearied him to the point of exasperation. Were it not for the little witch's skills at easing his headaches, he'd have ridded himself of her judgment years ago.

Magdalena was a foreigner, a captive from the barbaric frontier. What did she know of framing a civilization? She no more appreciated his political efforts than she appreciated the ample bodies of the well-fed ruling class. Granted, his uneven legs had caused him childhood ridicule, but what he lacked in agility, he more than made up for in his impressive lineage. His long list of illustrious ancestors had secured his position as the most powerful man in Carthage. It was up to him to secure his place in history.

He tugged at the heavy girdle around his waist, noting with pride the need to add two more golden links. Expansion came at a price, one he was willing to pay. For his first order of business, he intended to extend his tenure as proconsul. He'd managed to skirt the silly one-year rule in the past. He'd manage again. All he had to do was to cozy up to the emperor. But to do this, he first had to eliminate Cyprian. The godlike solicitor had an uncanny ability to bend ears with his well-honed oratorical skills. Slanderous reports that the current proconsul was failing to restore the mighty seaport of Carthage must not reach Rome.

According to the rumors, Cyprian planned to run for office once he took a wife. Therefore, he had no choice but to start some nasty rumor, something so evil no decent woman would want the man. Blocking Cyprian's election to the Senate was a chore he would enjoy as much as stamping out the religious insubordination of a nasty little uprising called Christianity. He must act quickly, or his angered gods would never lift the cursed sickness felling his stone laborers.

Aspasius left the task of clearing Magdalena's limp body away for the servants. No one cared or would dare question what he'd done to his own property. For a few coppers, she could easily be replaced with something younger and far more pliant. Like the fine little piece of flesh Cyprian had stolen out from under him. Once he ruined Cyprian's reputation, he'd strip away his vast fortune and the slave girl.

He stopped by the cages of his nightingales, ortolans, and thrushes, riling them into a frenzy that rivaled his own. "Ah, my only trustworthy companions." Their shrill songs converged into a chaotic melody that calmed him.

Aspasius swept into his office, composed and ready to get to work. His scribe waited in the corner, a stack of parchment and a new reed clutched to his chest.

"Pytros, take a letter."

The nervous little man drew up a chair, dipped his pen into the ram's horn inkwell, and readied his hand. "To whom shall I address this correspondence, sir?"

"To the Honorable Emperor Decius Trajan. Mark it urgent."

For the next hour Aspasius sat behind his desk tracing the intricate swirls in the burled mahogany with his finger while dictating his requests. His plan was simple, really. Northern Africa had become a cesspool of Jews and Roman traitors who'd converted to Christianity, people who did not appreciate what it meant to keep the gods appeased. A cleansing was necessary. A return to the pure lineage that would carry the borders of Rome to the ends of the earth. A perfect Carthage.

History would thank him one day. But waiting on posterity had no appeal. He would eagerly appease the fickle gods. Then he would take what was due him.

14

LISBETH ROUSED AT THE sound of the villa's heavy front doors being flung open and dogs licking her face. Fresh air and sunlight streamed into the atrium. "How long did I sleep?" She rubbed her eyes against the glare.

"Not long from the looks of how well these two are doing." Cyprian ordered the dogs to their mats and placed a food tray on the floor next to where she sat cross-legged between Barek and Laurentius. "Eat." He bent to wake Ruth, who slept at Barek's feet.

"No. Let her rest." Encouraging Ruth to sleep had provided Lisbeth with a moment of solitude, an opportunity to think, and time to plan. She cupped the hot mug, eyeing Cyprian's plain woolen garment. He seemed pretty comfortable for a man who'd just delivered a woman into the hands of an abuser. She had unresolved issues with Mama, but she sure didn't want her hurt. She didn't understand how Cyprian justified his decision, especially considering his elaborate and secretive scheme with Felicissimus to stop Aspasius from getting his hands on *her*. None of this made any sense.

"I'll have Naomi bring another tray later." Cyprian dismissed the slave girl, then pointed at the crude contraption attached to the arrow shaft protruding from Laurentius's chest. "What's this?"

"My version of a Pleur-Evac unit."

His brow furrowed. "A what?"

"Never mind." Lisbeth sipped the warm wine laced with spices. Not the shot of caffeine she needed, but that was probably for the best. She was already jumpy enough. "I had to figure out a way to restore the negative pressure to his lungs." Explaining physics without coffee wasn't going to happen. He knelt beside her, studying her so intently it was unnerving. She sighed and gave in. "Couldn't think of anything to substitute for rubber tubing, so I dismantled my stethoscope."

Ripping the hollow tubing from the metal headset and round chest piece had been surprisingly cathartic. A way to permanently sever the memories of playing doctor with the woman who'd walked out on her again.

"Ruth helped me attach one end of the tubing to the arrow shaft and submerge the other end in a water pot and . . . ta da . . . suction." Lisbeth glanced at the sleeping Laurentius. His respirations were still labored, but his punctured lung was producing the closest thing to a symmetrical chest rise she'd seen all night. "Poor boy wanted to suck his thumb and curl into a ball. Hardest part was keeping him upright, so gravity would work in his favor."

"Clever." A slow smile carved parenthetical dimples in Cyprian's tanned cheeks. "Maybe the healer was right about you."

Lisbeth pushed the plump pomegranate aside and dunked a hard roll into the wine. "Or maybe you people believe what you want to believe?"

"I believe this boy owes you his life."

"Apply the good deed to my tab."

"Tab?"

"You know, my bill, or whatever it's going take to buy my freedom."

His eyes locked with hers. "How did the healer know your name?" His expression remained kind enough, so why did she feel trapped on the witness stand?

"It's common enough where we come from."

He tipped his head toward the suction rig. "And the trinket you fought over? Is it common enough where you're from?"

Lisbeth stood. "I really need some more sleep." She nudged Ruth awake. "Think you can handle things while I nap for a couple of hours?"

Ruth pushed upright and immediately began asking questions. "Any change? Do they need anything? I see Cyprian is back. Did Magdalena get home?"

Lisbeth held up her hands to fend off the incessant barrage. "They finally slept, so I let them."

"What do I need to do?" Ruth brushed the back of her hand across Barek's forehead, a gesture Lisbeth remembered her mother using to check her for fever.

"Change Barek's bandages when he wakes." Lisbeth handed Ruth the mug. "Your boy will need this to keep up with all of your questions. Call me if that drain tube clogs again." She fired a laser stare at Cyprian. "And keep his foot off of my back."

Lisbeth retired to her quarters, the same room Cyprian had locked her in when she first arrived. Somehow the bed looked more inviting than she remembered. She thought she was tired after falling through the portal. Now, she was so beat she could sleep anywhere.

Bright light sliced through a large window that overlooked the garden. Plush, yet spartanly furnished by American standards, the room was larger than the entire two-bedroom apartment she shared with Queenie. Not exactly a cell, but she felt confined all the same.

Lisbeth lifted an exquisite ceramic urn and poured water into a bowl. She splashed her face, the coolness a sharp contrast to the fiery questions burning in her belly.

How was Papa? Had he slipped through the portal, too? Perhaps he was wandering around in some distant century, lost and looking for her. Maybe he'd escaped her fate only to worry himself into a complete mental meltdown at that blasted cave. She needed to locate the return portal, but she had no idea where to begin the search. Did Mama know?

Mama.

For twenty-three years she'd dreamed of finding her mother, imagined tears and hugs at their reunion. The reunion scene in her head was not the brawl they'd had in Cyprian's atrium. Who would have thought getting the one thing she wanted more than anything could leave her feeling so disappointed. So empty. So hopelessly lost.

Lisbeth gazed at her distorted reflection in the brass mirror. Dark circles under her eyes. Sunken cheeks. Bare neck. She was as broken as her stethoscope.

One by one she removed pins from the drooping curls Ruth had arranged for her debut. Ebony waves tumbled around her shoulders, reminding her of how undone Mama appeared after their fight. Had Mama envisioned a different reunion as well . . . assuming her mother wanted a reunion? So far, everything pointed to a repeat abandonment. A scenario she intended to reverse.

Lisbeth removed the heavy belt from her waist. Yards of pink fabric dropped around her ankles. She stepped over the pile, padded barefoot across the room, and closed the shutters. In the muted light, she found the bed and slipped between the luxurious sheets.

Exhaustion and life-and-death decisions did not mix. She'd sleep a couple of hours. Then she'd climb through the window, snatch Mama from this crazy world, and never look back.

15

CYPRIAN POKED HIS HEAD into the library. Light from the open balcony doors formed a halo above the white-haired man scratching upon a parchment. Sea breezes carried the scent of fish, thick oak paneling, and Caecilianus's favorite inky resin. The room had a lived-in look, a feeling of being useful for the first time in his memory. The bishop's family had forever erased quiet order from Cyprian's life. While he found the change miraculously reinvigorating, a breath of fresh air, his colleagues, who still had no idea of his conversion, abhorred his more casual manner of conducting business in the garden. Not once had he regretted the decision to bring the bishop into his home.

Cyprian stepped into the room. "I've come for my ledgers." The dogs sprawled at Caecilianus's feet raised their heads.

"A good day for settling accounts." His dear friend pawed through stacks of scrolls. Unbound rolls spilled over the desk and unfurled across the thick carpets. Both dogs leapt to their daily game of pounce. "I, too, have a score to settle."

"You?" Cyprian picked through the scattered pieces of parchment, collaring both dogs along the way to the desk. "Whom do you owe? Tell me, friend. I'll have the debt canceled immediately."

"Your generosity has blessed me and my family many times

over." The old priest waved off Cyprian's offer with a flick of the stylus. "But this debt surpasses even your impressive stores."

"I don't understand."

"It's a debt I owe the Lord . . . for sparing my son." Caecilianus's brow crinkled. "Balancing the scales is not the reason you've interrupted my study, now is it, my boy?"

Boy? Cyprian did not take offense at the term or the flinty stare daring him to offer some vague disagreement. Unlike his father, who had carried his disdain for Cyprian's imperfections with him to his grave, Caecilianus saw him as a man. A competent man. One who'd mastered the practice of the law, established a lucrative shipping company, and tripled his family's fortune. True, he was far from Caecilianus's level of spiritual maturity, but he felt the bishop's continual prodding and prayers challenged him in the area of daily growth. Given time, he'd show the old bishop that his labors were not in vain, that he had chosen well when he took on the remaking of Carthage's chief solicitor.

Settling debts was exactly the reason he'd sought his friend's counsel. He owed this man and the church more than he could ever repay. The grace he'd been given was free. He understood the concept. Embraced it even. Yet he was not a man to stand idle while interest accrued on his weighty sense of obligation. He had to do something.

"I need a wife," Cyprian blurted out, completely abandoning the script he'd worked out in his head.

"Oh?" Caecilianus punched a hole in Cyprian's solid declaration with the simple lift of his brow. "Since when?"

"According to my political advisers, if I'm to be taken seriously in this election, then a wife is a necessity."

"Don't look so distressed, my boy." Caecilianus dipped his pen into the ram's horn inkwell. "There are worse things than taking a wife."

Cyprian patted the dogs that'd stationed themselves on either side of him. "Like taking in more strays?"

"Taking the *wrong* wife." Caecilianus lowered his quill and stroked his beard with ink-stained fingers. "But then you know that, don't you?"

Cyprian paced the well-worn path in front of his desk, the rut he'd watched many of his father's debtors tread when they sought mercy, the rut his father had never allowed them to escape. "I'm quite satisfied with the current state of my household."

Caecilianus chuckled. "Is it me you try to convince or yourself?"

"Inviting you, Ruth, and Barek to share my roof was my choice." Lonely suppers in that huge *triclinium*—he at one end of the reclining couch, his father stationed as far away as possible on the other—were memories he preferred to keep distant. "Chaos suits me. I would change nothing."

"Not even to rid yourself of these ferocious eaters?" Caecilianus whistled, and the dogs flew to his outstretched palm. "Or the steady stream of problems that accompany those who choose to follow the teachings of the Galilean?"

"I risk nothing for my faith. Only those who sneak into my home to worship our God know of my conversion."

"As long as Aspasius is determined to rid Carthage of Christians, it is best to keep secret the names of all who have dared forsake the Roman gods."

"I understand the wisdom of your thinking, but . . ." Cyprian dismissed Caecilianus's protestations. "Barek was the one who put his life on the line to accompany the healer and Laurentius. Your son owes the Lord no more than me."

"Thus, you don the white toga . . . and take a wife you don't need or want."

"If I can't battle Aspasius in the court of public opinion, then winning a Senate seat is the only way we can truly help those suffering in the slums. Utilizing the power of the law is the logical course of action."

Caecilianus laid his pen aside and thoughtfully steepled his blackened fingertips. "So, in your educated opinion, relying upon the power of our Lord is futile?"

"I'm not discounting God, but surely the Lord does not expect us to sit upon our hands? Do nothing? Allow evil to run its ugly course?" Cyprian cleared a chair opposite the desk but could not make himself sit. "I think not, Bishop." His voice had slipped into the oratorical cadence capable of melting juries into whatever mold he needed. "That is why this wife of mine must have the proper connections. Money. Influence. Power enough to help me rid Carthage of Aspasius Paternus."

"And love? Is there room for love in these grand plans to take matters into your own hands?"

"Love will not bring running water to the tenements or goad Aspasius into doing what is right," Cyprian pointed out, his volume perking the dogs' ears. "God has withheld the rains for nearly two years. Drought and famine nip at the empire's heels." Cyprian took a breath and drove his closing argument home. "Improving sanitary conditions in the projects is the best way to stay this fever before sickness spreads to the wealthier districts."

"So you're running for office to secure the mortality of the rich?" Disappointment fringed his friend's voice.

"What more must I do to prove my loyalty to the cause of Christ? I've put bread in empty bellies, canceled debts, and bought every slave Felicissimus funnels my way. Doing nothing could bring death to us all. What if God awaits the relinquishment of my resources?"

Caecilianus drummed his fingers on the desk, weighing his response. "If you are determined to assume the role of God, then know this"—he pulled a ledger tablet from beneath the scrolls and slid it across the desk—"the cost will be great. Is it a price you are willing to pay?"

16

"COME QUICK." RUTH SHOOK Lisbeth awake and hurried out of the room, calling behind her, "Laurentius does not breathe."

Lisbeth bolted upright. So far, her third-century experience had been a frightening blur of disorientation and anger. She added frustration to the list as she hurriedly leapt from the bed where she'd been sacked out for more than a day, willed her body to disregard the need for a hot shower or even a sudsy soak in that huge tiled tub, and threw on the simple woolen tunic someone had left at the foot of her bed. Responding to Ruth's version of a Code Blue, she burst into the hall.

Empty.

No blood on the glistening floors. Benches completely cleared of wounded boys and crude medical equipment. No sign of the petite blonde who'd acted more like a first-rate ICU nurse than the pampered wife of a bishop. Not a trace of the man who kept her prisoner in his home.

"Ruth?" Lisbeth's voice echoed off the frescoed walls. Her bare feet slapped the marble as she trotted down the corridor, checking every door. Even the dogs were nowhere to be found. "Ruth!" She pushed open the last door.

Her gaze landed on the handsome owner of this mansion. Cyprian sat on a stool between two beds, holding out his clenched fists and encouraging her bright-eyed, chest-tubed patient to pick a hand. "Where's the grape? Right or left?" His face serious, he watched Laurentius vacillate between choices. "Careful, my little man."

Laurentius's tongue swept the circumference of his o-shaped mouth. "That one." He slapped Cyprian's right hand. Cyprian chuckled and flipped his fist. His fingers sprang open and revealed an empty palm. "You cheated." Laurentius smacked Cyprian's left hand, and the grape dropped upon the rumpled sheets. The boy snapped up the plump fruit and popped it in his mouth, chewing and smiling at the same time.

Lisbeth rushed in. "What's going on?" Purple juice dripped from Laurentius's chin, and a healthy color stained his cheeks. She immediately checked the reed's entry site. "I thought Ruth said he couldn't breathe?"

"I cleared the tube, and now he's fine." A pleased grin lit Cyprian's face. "Right, Laurentius?"

The boy nodded, then nudged her arm with his stubby index finger. "You're preddy." He ducked his chin and folded his hands, suddenly shy.

"What did you say?" Lisbeth asked Laurentius.

Cyprian lifted the boy's chin. "Tell her again. Like a man." Kindness threaded his rebuff, the same gentle prodding Papa employed with the workers he hired, especially the ones capable of little more than toting camping gear.

Laurentius's eyes flitted between her and his clenched fists. "You're preddy, Lithbutt."

"Lith-butt?" Biting back a laugh, she reached for Laurentius's wrist to check his pulse. "Who told you my name?" She gazed at Cyprian, who shrugged off any involvement in the massacre of her name.

Laurentius pointed at Cyprian. "Girlth are preddy. Boyth are hanthome."

"And did Cyprian tell you that as well?"

"No." Laurentius's tongue lapped his crooked smile. "The healer." He scanned the room, worry clouding his countenance. "Where ith thee?"

"The healer had work to do at the palace." Cyprian plucked another grape from the tray on the bedside table. "Don't worry, friend. We'll have you back at your post as soon as you're well." He held out his fists, so comfortable and at ease in his own skin. "Want to try again?"

Laurentius slapped both of Cyprian's fists with his palms, popping the fruit free. "I won."

"Cheater." Cyprian scrubbed Laurentius's head with his brawny hand. "I think he's going to make a full recovery, don't you?"

"It appears so." Lisbeth noticed the empty bed. "Where's Barek?"

"His mother insisted he bathe. And I believe we'll all be the better for it." Cyprian poured a bit of watered wine into a cup. "After I figured out how to clear Laurentius's tube, I told Ruth I'd keep an eye on this rascal while she scraped the damage of Rome from her son." He handed Laurentius the wine. "Here, my friend. Wash down that grape."

Cyprian steadied Laurentius's hand as the boy brought the cup to his lips. The gentle, caring gesture reminded her of Papa. Love buried beneath a layer of steel. Cyprian would make an excellent father someday. Would history give him that opportunity, or would this man suffer the horrible fate marching toward his city? She couldn't remember. Had she known Papa's lecture questions would become a real test, a matter of life and death, she would've paid attention, taken notes, maybe even tattooed the facts on her arms.

Why would a Roman of Cyprian's standing stoop to befriending the mentally challenged? The sight of him entertaining Laurentius with such joy reduced her disdain, but not her focus. A fleeting good impression, no matter how intoxicating, did not change the fact that this man held her prisoner. She couldn't let adolescent warm and fuzzy feelings detour her mission to free her mother and go home.

She steered her attention back to Laurentius. "I can't leave this reed in him forever. Too much risk of infection." Running her fingers along the tube, she wished Mama had reviewed the extraction steps with her before she walked out. "The only way to tell if his lung leak has sealed and regained proper adhesion is to clamp off the suction for a few hours."

With Cyprian eyeballing her every move, she took Laurentius's vitals. "Good improvement." She kinked the tube, then secured the seal with a leather cord borrowed from Cyprian's sandal. Holding her breath, she watched the rise and fall of Laurentius's chest. The bruises had changed from deep purple to mustard green. A surprisingly fast healer. Either there was something to the miraculous powers of the old bishop's prayers, or Mama's version of third-world medicine had some merit.

Laurentius grinned at her dreamily, obviously breathing comfortably as he drifted off to sleep. From the corner of her eye, Lisbeth noticed Cyprian leaning in, watching her patient intently, and matching the boy's breathing with his whole body.

He caught her smiling and immediately straightened. "Well, I'll leave you to it." He rose and strode toward the door, one used to having the final word.

"Wait." She tamped the desperate edge in her voice. "Can you explain to me how this happened?" She waved her hand over the sleeping boy.

Confusion or annoyance, she wasn't sure which, drew Cyprian's brows. "You saved his life."

"I don't mean that." Deciphering the emotions of this man was difficult, and an eighteen-hundred-year difference in their ways of thinking didn't have a thing to do with their communication barrier. His feelings were tucked so deep beneath the folds of his toga, she'd need a scalpel to dissect them. "How did a kid like this get beat up in the first place?"

"The healer said soldiers—"

"No. I understand about the soldiers—well, not really—but why were the three of them together? Barek lives here, right? And Ma . . . Magdalena and Laurentius live in Aspasius's palace, right? So how did they all end up in the same hot mess?" The twitch of his jaw muscle said she'd pushed too far, but she didn't care. Lisbeth crossed her arms, determined to wait him out. "Well?"

"Hot mess?" He repeated vernacular she'd learned from Queenie like she'd spoken Martian or something. "You are a strange woman."

"Me?"

He crossed to her, close enough that she became self-conscious of how long it had been since that luxurious scrubbing Ruth had given her in the Neptune-tiled tub. "I can't decide if you are a curse or a blessing."

"Look, the better the patient history, the better the patient care." Her failure to follow this simple standard of practice had cost a child her life. No way was she repeating that fiasco. "I need information."

Cyprian's eyes searched hers. "Since the proconsul has invoked a sundown curfew, no one should travel the streets alone. When believers at our Sabbath feast need medical attention"—he paused, as if weighing whether to say more—"I send Barek for the healer. She always brings a helper. Sometimes, the dark-skinned slave Tabari. Sometimes, this boy."

"Oh."

For a moment his eyes locked with hers. "What possessed me to acquire such an odd curiosity?" He wheeled and strode toward the exit. "You'll settle in. Give yourself time." He closed the door with a decisive click.

"I don't want to settle in!" Lisbeth spent several seconds staring at the smooth oak plank. "And for the record, I'm not the one who's odd."

Once again she'd been summarily dismissed and left to war with the infuriating odor of Cyprian's musky cologne and the fact that she wasn't making any progress toward going home and wouldn't if she didn't earn his trust. What was it about that man that pushed her blood pressure through the stratosphere? She'd encountered tough men her whole life. Papa's digs attracted all sorts of scientific bullies intent on having their own way. Med school had been worse. And residency had thrust her into a sea of testosterone teeming with pompous attendings who believed having more experience made them gods.

Yet, somehow, this third-century aristocrat, with his broad shoulders and X-ray vision, caused her to question what she thought she knew about people. She'd worked at the county hospital for six months, and not once had she seen the wealthy involve themselves in the suffering of the poor. Why did underprivileged, third-century plebs traipse into and out of Cyprian's home? What was the gain? A big part of this equation was missing. Uncertainty infuriated her. She didn't appreciate having her world turned upside down, no matter how charming or handsome the upheaver.

Lisbeth stomped to the bed of the sleeping boy with low-set ears, angelic countenance, and healing bruises. Who could have been so cruel? Apparently, not every Roman had adopted Cyprian's benevolence. She shoved her anger aside and counted her patient's respirations. Less than twenty per minute. Continued symmetrical chest rise on the inspiration. No longer short of breath. Laurentius was doing well, actually breathing easier than she was at the moment.

What was she doing here? Trying to balance the scales of justice? Seeing this child's recovery through wouldn't alleviate her failing or bring Abra back from the dead. Some scores could never be settled. She should have climbed out the window and made a run for it when she had the chance.

The door opened, and two dogs barreled toward her, followed by a freshly scoured and clothed Barek.

"I'm fine, Mother." Barek shirked the grip Ruth and Naomi had on each elbow. "Really."

"You're well when I say you're well," Ruth shot back.

The teen paused at the foot of Laurentius's bed, his eyes taking in the bruises and chest tube protruding from the boy's chest. "At least I gave it back tenfold to the ones who gave it to him."

"Barek!" Ruth said, gasping.

"I've watched my father turn the other cheek, only to see Rome slap him down again and again. I'll not do it, Mother." Barek refused to be cowed or coerced into bed. Instead, he stood as tall as his arm sling would allow, spotted Lisbeth, and redirected his venom. "Who are you?"

"She's Lisbeth. Of Dallas." Ruth smoothed the sheets. "A healer."

"We don't need her."

"You're feeling better." Lisbeth picked up the flask on the bedside table. "Let me redress your wound."

"Don't touch me, slave."

"Barek!" Obviously this wasn't the first time Ruth had struggled to control the boy who towered over her by a head. "I'm sorry, Lisbeth. My son is not easily caged, and once he regains full strength it will be difficult to keep him down."

"Then let him up." Lisbeth kept her eyes fixed on the smooth-faced teenager sure to be as handsome as his mother one day. "It's actually better for his lungs if he moves around. His body will tell him when to rest."

Barek muttered under his breath that this strange woman wasn't a real healer and she wasn't about to touch him. Loud enough to hear. Harder to ignore. Why he'd taken such an immediate dislike to her she didn't know, or care.

"You're in luck, big boy." Lisbeth shook the bottle Mama had left. "We're out of this stuff anyway."

"He'll need more," Ruth said, gratefully seizing the distraction Lisbeth offered. "Naomi has to take the laundry to the fullers. I'll have her stop by the market while she's out." She pressed Barek back upon the bed. "Where do you think you're going?"

"With Naomi," he said, huffing. "I've got scores to settle."

Lisbeth watched the ensuing disagreement with interest. Worried mother pitted against a teenager afraid to admit he was frightened. Ruth's face mirrored the frustration she'd seen on Papa's weathered brow when she resisted going to the States for medical training. Papa had thought her anger stemmed from possible separation anxiety. Anger was subterfuge, a smoke screen hiding the real truth. Truth she knew would crush him. How could she tell him that she was afraid? Frightened that at any moment she might lose him, too? Losing a parent was an experience she did not want to go through twice.

Poor Papa. Single parent. Motherless girl with raging hormones. Had she made Papa's life miserable? She'd tried to be good, to do everything she could to fill that gigantic hollow Mama's disappearance had carved in his heart.

Lisbeth stuffed the empty bottle into the pocket of her tunic. Who was she kidding? She was still that scared five-year-old scanning the desert horizon for signs of Mama.

Lisbeth interrupted. "Laurentius's chest tube must come out

in a few hours, but he's going to need something for pain. I'll go with Naomi."

Ruth wasn't so distracted by her son that she didn't catch Lisbeth's meaning. "Cyprian can fetch the healer."

"Laurentius is *my* patient," Lisbeth insisted. "I'll choose the herbs that will help him tolerate a surgical procedure. Cyprian can take a chill pill." She pointed at Barek. "And you have no idea how lucky you are to have a mother."

17

CYPRIAN PACED THE LENGTH of his library while Pontius and Felicissimus pored over the tax records the slave trader had secretly acquired from a friend in the assessor's office.

"What about Acquilina?" Pontius placed his finger on the scroll and looked up. "Her father is Blasius, the well-respected wine merchant."

"Good gods, man," Felicissimus hissed. "Have you seen her?"

"Only from a distance," Pontius confessed.

"Last year Blasius brought Acquilina to my shop when she was in need of a new handmaiden."

"And?" Cyprian hated sounding anxious, but marriage discussions reminded him of how far apart he and his father had been in their views of life and family.

"Beady eyes of a hawk. Eagle's beak for a nose." Felicissimus shook his head. "She could peck away at a man's soul with the mere flick of her head."

"Perhaps we should keep looking?" Pontius and Felicissimus returned to the list.

"What about Camilla Flaccus?" Felicissimus said proudly. "Her second husband left her extremely well placed."

"*Second* husband?" Cyprian wasn't keen on taking on the

problems inherent with another man's castoff. "What happened to her first husband?"

Felicissimus shrugged, "I assume the same thing that happened to her second?"

"And what was that?" Pontius demanded.

"Died in her bed." A twinkle lit Felicissimus's eye. "Apparently, Camilla needs a man of sturdy constitution. Which you most assuredly are, my patronus."

"Keep looking," Cyprian ordered. "You'd think in a city of this size there would be one marriageable female."

"What of the lovely Diona Cicero?" Pontius said.

"Now there's an idea," Felicissimus eagerly concurred. "A real goddess if ever there was one."

"She's only fourteen," Cyprian protested.

"But her father's quite the forward thinker. According to bathhouse rumors, Titus has granted Diona full charge of her marriage choice." Felicissimus rubbed his hands together. "And that's not the best part. Titus owns most of the fields between here and Curubis, as well as every single granary. Think of the power your combined fortunes could wield. An alliance this powerful would hold Rome by the throat."

"And if you hold Rome by the throat," Pontius added, "you will have Aspasius by the—"

"But is she a religious woman?" Cyprian had just turned thirty-four. Not only was he imagining himself as an old man tottering after a woman half his age, he was also wondering how they could possibly ever find anything in common. Especially if Diona's heart belonged to Roman gods. Perhaps Caecilianus was right. No wife was better than acquiring the wrong wife. "Why would she want to marry an old goat like me? Especially once she learns of my conversion."

"Power grows more attractive with the years. Besides, when you clean up, you're not painful to look at." Felicissimus closed the tax record. "Let's go."

Cyprian stopped Felicissimus. "You aren't going anywhere. Too risky. Return the tax records before we're found out."

"Yes, my patronus," Felicissimus said, sulking.

Two hours later, Cyprian stood on the marbled stoop of Titus Cicero. Fresh from the baths and wearing his whitest toga, he tugged at his belt. "You're certain Diona will be home?"

Pontius stood beside him with a small wooden chest tucked beneath his arm. "Her father assured me."

The door swung open. A slave girl showed them into a lush garden, a testament to Titus's green thumb.

"Solicitor." Titus swept into the room, a tall man with sprigs of gray at his temples. "May I present my daughter, Diona."

A girl with white-blond curls, pink lips, and only a year into the bloom of womanhood slipped out from behind Titus. Felicissimus was right: her perfect features rivaled the chiseled gods gracing Titus's beautiful home.

She lowered her chin. "How kind of you to come," whispered from her lips.

"Diona is . . . shy." Titus waved them toward the couches. "Please sit." He clapped, and a servant appeared with a tray of refreshments. "Let's get to the point, shall we? Diona has final say in her betrothal, but, so that there are no misunderstandings, let me lay out the terms."

"Of course." Cyprian could not help but think about how Diona had not made eye contact with him once while that snit of a slave girl he'd rescued could readily bore holes through him with her sea-green stare.

"Diona comes with a substantial dowry of jewelry, slaves, and eventually my vast land and grain holdings."

Suddenly a woman who appeared to be an older version of Diona rushed in, all aflutter in her peacock blue silk. "A word, husband."

"In a moment, my dear."

"Now, Titus."

As Titus scurried after his wife, Cyprian wondered if beneath Diona's quiet exterior her mother's temperament simmered.

Diona peered over her fan. Her eyes were two black doors closed to deeper investigation. He couldn't tell what she was thinking, and that made him even more nervous.

Titus appeared in the doorway and took a deep breath. "Cyprian, I must thank you for your offer, but I'm not quite ready to part with my little girl."

"Pontius, show him the chest." Cyprian's friend came forward and placed a large wooden box upon a stone table. "Open it."

Diona's breath caught at the sparkle of gold and rare jewels. "I choose him, Father."

"I know I gave you free rein on the selection of your husband, but you'll have to trust me on this when I say no."

"No?" Cyprian knew a fleecing when he saw one, but his list of marriage prospects was growing short. He plowed his hand into the treasure. "There's more where this came from." Coins slipped through his outstretched fingers.

"And the biggest villa on the sea. Right, solicitor?" Diona asked with a smile.

"Yes. I, too, have many holdings."

"I want him, Father."

"Diona, he has the creeping pox. We are lucky that your mother heard the news in time."

"I what?!" Cyprian shouted.

"I know I've spoiled my daughter and given her too much freedom in this matter, but she cannot marry anyone without my permission and I will not grant it in this case. And that is final."

"This is outrageous! I could very well argue the fallacy of this ridiculous rumor, but I suppose in the end only time will support my claims of perfect health." Cyprian closed the wooden box. "I thank you for your time, Titus."

"Good luck on the elections, solicitor."

18

TWO MASSIVE DOGS TRAMPLED Lisbeth's feet as she helped Ruth drag the heavy laundry cart through the villa gate. "Doesn't Cyprian have slaves to do his wash?"

"What Cyprian does with his slaves is not your concern." Ruth wrestled the worn cart handle out of Lisbeth's hand. "Besides, political togas require professional care to retain their elegant draping." She flipped the hood of her cloak over the blond coils wrapping her head and was immediately transformed from aristocrat to peasant. She lifted her chin in a quick little motion that indicated Lisbeth should do the same.

"You're sure Naomi can handle that son of yours?" Lisbeth steadied the mound of clothes the bishop's pouncing dogs seemed determined to upset. "What if his bandages need changing before we get back?" She hoped appealing to the frazzled mother's sense of guilt for leaving her injured son would entice Ruth to reinstate Naomi as her guide on the errand run. The young slave girl would be much easier to ditch.

"Say no more," Ruth said with a hiss, hammering home the fact that making friends and influencing people weren't part of Lisbeth's skill set. "Your accent will draw unwanted attention." She shooed the dogs inside the gate and set off down the street, the cart rumbling behind her.

Lisbeth knew Ruth couldn't go two minutes without talking; all Lisbeth had to do was wait the woman out. When Ruth finally cracked, she'd gather the data she needed and be on her way. Leaving the eventual removal of Laurentius's tube for Ruth's untrained hands caused a few ripples of guilt, but not enough to change her plans. An opportunity to search for the passageway connecting the centuries might not come again. Surely the tunnel between yesterday and today went both ways. Exactly how she'd find the time portal wasn't settled in her mind. The faint memory of nearly drowning was her only clue.

She'd caught a glimpse of the harbor from Cyprian's balcony. How strange to see the stone donut fully restored and two hundred ported Roman warships. Finding her entry point into this century could be a challenge.

Stepping up her pace, Lisbeth rounded the corner and scurried after Ruth, her hood sliding off her hair. "So if you had to fetch water, where would you go?" Women toting baskets on their heads and a child on each hip cast disapproving glances at Lisbeth's tumbled mass of curls.

"Raise your hood," Ruth warned.

"So where's the closest well?" Lisbeth tugged the hemp-colored hood over her hair. "Look, I know you're probably worried about leaving Barek, but he'll be fine."

"I don't know that," Ruth snapped, "and neither do you."

"We're out now and can't do anything about our patients at the moment. So why don't you tell me a little about Carthage? If I'm going to be living here and helping to run errands, it would be wise for me to get to know the city."

Ruth marched on, silent, unimpressed with Lisbeth's reasoning. They merged with the increasing foot traffic heading toward the smell of seawater and decaying fish, the same market odor she'd dreaded whenever she and Papa had traveled to Tunis for supplies.

Lisbeth hurried to keep up, determined not to lose Ruth in the crowd until she had some answers. "Is there a cistern near Felicissimus's auction block?" A woman with a large basket on her head jostled Lisbeth into an elderly peddler hawking wooden utensils. Carved spoons hit the busy street. "Sorry, sir." She bent to retrieve his wares from the filthy gutter.

"Thief!" The peddler, a lean, haggard creature with a surprisingly vigorous yell, whipped bony hands through the salty air. "I'm being robbed!"

"No." Lisbeth gathered a fistful of spoons. "I just didn't see you."

"Drop it, slave." A heavy boot came down hard, pinning her hand to the street.

Lisbeth's eyes traveled the hairy leg of a linebacker-size man. Decked out in shin greaves, a red cloak, and a crested helmet, he looked like one of those Roman soldiers immortalized on the pages of Papa's history books.

He lifted his foot and yanked her upright. Three other troopers backed him, standing ready with their boots planted on the pavement and their hands poised over gleaming swords peeking from leather scabbards. "Who is your master?" His breastplate glistened in the morning sun. "Speak or die, pleb." He squeezed her wrist, making the painful imprint of his boot on her hand inconsequential.

Fighting tears, Lisbeth searched the sea of harried shoppers, their rubbernecking slowing the flow of traffic headed toward the market booths. "Ruth!" She twisted but couldn't break free, even with the extra adrenaline pumping through her body.

"What's your hurry, girl? You have more pockets to pick?" The soldier pulled the hood from Lisbeth's head and pushed her into his uniformed pals. "Let's have some fun with this beauty."

Suddenly a blue cloak barreled into the jeering circle of testosterone. "Unhand the property of Cyprianus Thascius"—Ruth stepped between Lisbeth and the soldier—"the chief solicitor of Carthage." Ruth grabbed Lisbeth's hand, sending the wooden spoon she clutched clattering to the cobblestones. "Unless you wish to explain why you've kept the solicitor's favorite from her chores, you'll let us pass."

Lisbeth watched over her shoulder as Ruth dragged her away from the openmouthed soldiers and deeper into the maze of market stalls.

They darted into and out of the vendor booths, hurrying past the putrid scents of the carcass hanging in the butcher's stall and the toothless woman hawking bowls of soured milk curds. At the nearest alley, Ruth pulled Lisbeth into the shadows where she'd left the cart.

"Favorite?" Lisbeth asked with a huff, hands on her knees, heart pumping faster than it had when she and Queenie had tackled a marathon race in the grueling Dallas heat. "When did I become that man's favorite?"

"Shush." Ruth's normal rosy blush was missing from her face. She gathered Lisbeth's hood and returned it to her head. "Not another word from you."

"Not even thanks?"

Ruth slapped three stiff fingers to Lisbeth's lips. "Nothing." She snatched the cart handle.

Still winded, Lisbeth followed her bossy little keeper through the alley, admiring Ruth's willingness to jump in to right a wrong. Mulling over her encounter with the third century's version of real, live killing machines, she wondered if she would have had the guts to do the same. The damage Roman soldiers had inflicted upon Barek and Laurentius had surely frightened Ruth as much as they'd terrified her, yet this slip of a woman had charged in without regard to her own life. First Cyprian and now Ruth. These people succeeded where she failed. If it hadn't been for Ruth, she would have more than likely suffered far worse than a few inappropriate touches. Running out now seemed as cheap as ducking out on a restaurant tab, but what choice did she have?

They emerged in a different section of the forum, an upscale shopping mall for the rich. Booths displayed exquisite works of glass, alabaster, and ivory. Gorgeous lengths of linen and brightly colored silks swayed from long wooden poles. Tavern workers served pickled ostrich eggs and warm drinks that smelled of cinnamon to men dressed in white. Perfectly coiffed women dragged silent slaves from stall to stall, loading stacks of parcels upon their brawny arms.

Lisbeth kept her eyes peeled for the time portal. She wasn't expecting a neon sign, but maybe something familiar would jog her memory. Papa had taken her to Carthage dozens of times as a child. Together, they'd visited the local bazaars and poked through every inch of the Roman ruins. She scanned the buzzing market. Strange to see the city she knew as ruins somehow magically restored. More magnificent than the artist reconstructions in Papa's books, yet totally disorienting. Her father would jump at the opportunity to experience this post–Punic Wars rebuilding phase. She, on the other hand, just wanted out.

"You'll find what you need here." Ruth pointed out the wooden sign swinging over the door of a tiny shop. Someone had carved a snake wrapped around a staff into the weathered plank. "Don't be long."

Continuing the ruse seemed the best option, considering she hadn't seen the first thing that looked like a time portal. She left Ruth guarding the laundry and ventured into the dark, scented coolness of the third century's version of a pharmacy. Clusters of dried flowers hung from low ceiling beams. "Wish Aisa was here," Lisbeth muttered as she drew a bundle to her nose.

Papa's cook had acted as the camp doctor after Mama left. His box of brittle weeds and smelly salves comprised the sole extent of Lisbeth's knowledge of homeopathic medicine, a fact she didn't dare disclose to Ruth while making the case for doing her own herb shopping.

Lisbeth moved quickly, untying the plants she identified as a few of the remedies Aisa kept in his box. Mint for calming upset stomachs. Garlic for disinfecting wounds. And borage, a fuzzy leaf that tasted of cucumber no matter how much sugar Aisa added to the strong tea he used to treat her bouts of asthma. Upon the recommendation of the wrinkled woman trying to make a buck off a sneezing foreigner, Lisbeth purchased every dried plant that looked familiar and a few she didn't recognize. She tucked under her arm the bundle of aromatic treasures she had no intention of using and joined Ruth.

They left the main street and turned down another alley, coming face-to-face with the behind-the-scenes labor required to keep the rich looking their best. Steamy air scented with sweat, lye, and urine billowed from the open door of the fuller's shop.

Lisbeth recalled the summer she and Papa had visited the ruins of Pompeii at the base of Mount Vesuvius. Beneath excavated mounds of ash and pumice had sat a fully equipped fuller's shop. How strange now to cross the threshold here in Carthage and see real men clad only in loincloths trampling garments in the pressing bowls, their raw hands clamped on to the half walls separating each worker's water basin.

Behind the counter, a red-cheeked shopkeeper, her hair kinked by the steam of the wash pots, sorted through piles of laundry. Business was good at the cleaners. Ruth removed a numbered stone from the bowl on the counter. They assumed their place at the end of the line.

Ahead of them, a thin black girl shouldered a large bundle.

When the laundress barked out a number, the girl checked her stone, then lugged her load to the counter. The shopkeeper untied the knots and pawed through the clothes, scratching down an accounting after each piece.

"This one is covered in blood." The laundress held up a stained wad of gauzy green and eyed the girl. "The proconsul's woman have a problem the patrols need to know about?"

Lisbeth craned her neck. Icy fingers crawled up her spine. "That's Ma . . . Magdalena's dress." She started toward the counter.

Ruth grabbed her arm. "Say nothing."

What had happened after Mama left Cyprian's? Did Aspasius kill her upon her return to the palace? Or was her mother caught out after curfew again by those nasty soldiers? Lisbeth strained against Ruth's hold, intent to learn more.

"My mistress had trouble with her monthly," the slave girl mumbled.

"I don't care what the proconsul claims; that woman he drags around town is no mistress." The laundress raised a skeptical brow. "I can see you didn't soak this in cold water, Tabari. These stains are never coming out."

"No worry." Tabari lifted her chin and looked the women in the eye. "My lady has garments to spare."

"And extra blood, I pray." The laundry woman tossed the gown into a woven basket. "Next."

The dark slave girl gathered the empty cloth wrapper. "You know where to send the bill."

If this girl was the same Tabari, the one Cyprian said accompanied Mama on her missions of mercy, her retort indicated Mama was alive. Or maybe that's what Lisbeth was choosing to tell herself? The alternative sucked the air from her chest. She wanted to snatch the spindly slave girl and shake her until she spilled every detail of Mama's return to that awful man.

Lisbeth started forward, but Ruth's grip tightened on her arm. Ruth gave her another firm glare, released her, and advanced the pull cart to the counter.

"I've got to ask what she knows of Magdalena." Lisbeth wheeled. Bolting from the shop at full speed, she ran smack into a man waiting on the other side of the threshold. They tumbled onto the pavement in a tangle of arms and legs.

"Watch where you're going!" He wiggled to get free of her.

Lisbeth pushed herself off the surprised man. "Are you hurt?" Breathing hard, she offered her hand. "I'm so sorry. I didn't see—"

The man scrambled to his feet. "I must find the healer." Without taking the time to dust his filthy hands, he gripped her shoulders. "Is she here? I saw Aspasius's slave girl and took a chance that she accompanied the healer." Hope floated atop the terror spilling from his eyes. "I know you. You're the one who raised Laurentius from the dead."

Lisbeth checked the street for signs of Tabari, but she'd disappeared. "Look, I'm just—"

His dirty fingers dug into her flesh. "I need a healer." His breath reeked of a very empty stomach. "When my wife got the fever, I spent all we had on a physician. Now my daughter is very ill. Since I can't pay, the Roman dog won't come. What am I to do?"

Lisbeth suddenly remembered this man, the one the old bishop called Numidicus, the one who'd jumped from a second-story balcony to plead his concerns. She remembered the fear in his voice as he begged the bishop to reconsider staying behind. "How old is your daughter?"

"Four."

Don't get sucked in raced through Lisbeth's head as the next question spewed from her mouth. "Does she have a fever?"

He nodded. "And coughing." He released her and wiped at the

tears streaking a path over sharp crags. "I'm afraid she has the same thing that made my wife sick."

She glanced over her shoulder. Ruth had been detained by the laundress. "Take me to her now."

Relief sparked his full-on sprint down the uneven pavers. Lisbeth tightened her grip on the bag of herbs she'd purchased, her common sense flying well beyond her grasp. She hiked her tunic and trailed the man into the bowels of the city.

19

NUMIDICUS PROVED HIMSELF QUITE fleet-footed for one
so malnourished. He threaded Lisbeth through a network of
alleys, bypassing the fine houses and the red-cloaked legionnaires
that patrolled the right-angled streets.

Shallow stone steps took them deeper and deeper into a series of run-down buildings crammed little more than an arm's-
width apart. An air of neglect hung over this rough part of town
that hadn't received much in the way of Roman upgrades. Apparently the 1 percent short-changing the less desirables of society
was nothing new. The fingers of poverty reached far in every direction.

Lisbeth shooed a rail-thin dog blocking her path, silently de-
bating whether she should have at least told Ruth where she was
going. But, then again, why would she? The decision was already
made. She would not spend her life as Cyprian's slave. Accompanying this man to his daughter's sickbed wasn't a long-term commitment. She'd do what she could; then she'd disappear into the
maze of the slum district, free at last to search for Mama and the
way home.

Lost in her plans, Lisbeth ran smack into Numidicus, who
stood huffing in front of a door slightly ajar.

"I seem determined to mow you down." She surveyed rows of

warped doors running the length of the bottom floor of a six-story, multifamily apartment building. "Is this where you live?" If his home waited behind the sun-faded planks, why didn't he go in? She followed his distracted gaze to a neighboring stoop.

Three dirty children sat with their hands clasped in their laps, sad eyes begging for relief. On the balcony above these frail stick-figures, a crying woman rocked back and forth, clasping her swollen belly.

"Her husband died last night." Numidicus tore his eyes from the spectacle. "Her youngest passed the day before." He nodded toward two lumpy bundles stacked neatly on the shaded side of the alley.

Lisbeth's gaze darted between the bodies, the woman, and the hopeless children.

He grabbed her arm. "You must not leave us." Fear raised his pitch. "Please." His agitation resembled that of every parent who paced outside the ICU, praying for the best yet anticipating the worst. "You're all we have."

"If that's true, you're in trouble, mister."

He dropped to one knee and lifted clasped hands. "I beg you."

How many times had she taken a few extra minutes with a patient because she was their only shot at getting well? Not enough. Maybe never. She'd spent the first few months of her residency so tired, so stressed out, and so pressed for time that patients received only a fraction of the attention she'd sworn to give every human life.

How many people had fallen through the cracks in the medical system because Dr. Lisbeth Hastings couldn't or wouldn't stop long enough to help? Maybe Abra would still be alive if . . . "Where's your daughter?"

Numidicus jumped to his feet and opened the apartment door. Fecal-tainted air blasted Lisbeth's nostrils. She recognized the odor of bodily fluids released in death. What horror awaited her attention? Numidicus dragged her inside the sweltering little room and shut the door.

It took a moment for Lisbeth's eyes to adjust to the dim light of a single oil lamp flickering on a stone ledge. Drab, stucco-covered walls and a low ceiling formed a space no bigger than her bedroom back in Texas. She and Papa had excavated bigger burial vaults.

Numidicus seemed unwilling to step away from the door but graciously waved an offer of the only seat in the house, a crude contraption of sticks and cloth held together with strips of leather. The raspy wheeze of labored breathing drew Lisbeth's attention to the single bed at the far end of the tiny room.

"I'll need more light, Numidicus." Despite the closed door and the room's obvious lack of windows, she could still hear the cries of the distraught neighbor. "You're going to have to open that door. I can't breathe."

He shook his head. "The god of the dead must kick his way into the hovels of the poor. I'll not hold the door open for him."

Like a good Roman, Numidicus had not uttered Mor's name, but she didn't have time for foolish superstitions or nonexistent gods. "Fresh air and light. Please." As he reluctantly complied, she lifted the hem of her tunic and ripped off two strips of cloth. "Tie this over your mouth like I'm doing."

Is this what Mama would do? Magdalena Hastings wasn't around to share her expertise. She hadn't been in Lisbeth's life for the past twenty-three years, and there was a good chance she wouldn't be there for the next twenty-three. Unlike the other night, when they'd worked side by side, handling this emergency was on her.

Lisbeth picked up the lamp and headed toward the still lump in the single bed.

Not one, but two people occupied the sagging mattress. A child. And the child's obviously dead mother.

"Hold the light closer." She set her bundle of herbs on the floor and knelt beside the girl sleeping with her mouth open, each inhale creating a coarse, musical wheeze. "What's your daughter's name?"

Numidicus did not move. "Junia."

"Pretty name"—the child's olive skin sizzled beneath Lisbeth's touch—"for a pretty little girl." Junia's eyes fluttered open. The child began an uncomfortable fuss and tried to wiggle out from under the stiff arm wrapped around her. "Easy, sweetie. I'm a . . . I'm here to help you. Let's get these covers off of you." Lisbeth gently freed the child from the mother's gray limb, and that's when she noticed an angry red rash on the dead woman's arm. "What in the world?"

Junia's father stood immobile, his eyes blank screens. Was he in shock?

"When did your wife start feeling bad?" Lisbeth reached across the child and closed the mother's eyelids, taking care to avoid contact with the fiery pustules that marred her face. He didn't answer. "Numidicus, when did you notice your wife's rash?"

"Several days ago."

What kind of ancient scourge was she dealing with? Plague? Smallpox? If whatever killed this woman was contagious, Junia and Numidicus were at risk. And so was she. Why hadn't she paid better attention to Papa's lectures?

Wishing for a squirt of antibacterial soap and some gloves, Lisbeth wiped her hands on her tunic and forced herself to gather as many objective vitals as she could on Junia. Dry, deep cough. Red-rimmed, watery eyes. Runny nose. Lisbeth clasped the child's wrist and palpated a radial pulse, noting an increase in Junia's panting respirations.

"Please bring the lamp as close as possible." She snapped her fingers. "Numidicus, you have to help me. I need to take a quick peek at your daughter's throat."

He inched forward, his hands trembling. In the faint yellow glow, Lisbeth could make out the girl's swollen tonsils, but it was the red lesions with blue-white centers salting the inside mucous membranes of Junia's cheek that drew her up short.

"Koplik spots?" Lisbeth muttered under her breath, her mind racing. "Measles?"

From what she remembered from med school, measles had been eradicated, wiped from the face of the earth with the 1960s discovery of effective vaccines and massive immunization campaigns. But that medical progress had been made in her time . . . almost eighteen hundred years in the future. This third-century mother had died from a virus Lisbeth could prevent with two simple, twentieth-century inoculations . . . vaccinations she'd had as a child . . . medicine she didn't have with her now. If she didn't do something, and quickly, measles would kill this little girl.

What if she was wrong, and the wife's rash was something far worse? She checked Junia's limbs and torso for signs of the rash. *Clear.* Relieved, Lisbeth gently pried Junia's parched lips apart and peered inside again. If these lesions were Koplik spots, Junia's body would soon be consumed by the same ugly rash that covered her dead mother. She needed to check the body of the man and baby from upstairs. They may have died of measles. And if they did, who knew how many people these four people had infected? Maybe the whole housing block? If these infected carriers coughed in the communal bathrooms or sneezed while sharing a water gourd, many more neighbors could die . . . including every person who'd come in contact with Numidicus and his family at the last church gathering in Cyprian's home.

She'd never actually seen a case of measles. Without her cell phone she couldn't Google pictures, symptoms, or possible treatments to confirm. Was guessing on the exact protocol better than doing nothing? "I know what to do." She wished her voice sounded a bit more confident.

Numidicus's eyes brightened. "You can heal my daughter?"

"No. We've got to let the sickness run its course." Lisbeth hated the blow her news dealt this expectant father. "But, with your help, we can keep her alive. Understand?"

Skepticism wrinkled his brow, but he nodded.

"You must do *everything* I tell you." Lisbeth dug through her parcel, mentally cataloging supplies and tallying shortages. The minuses far outweighed the positives. "Fetch more water, lots of it. We've got to get Junia's fever down. Plus, she's very contagious."

"Contagious?"

"Don't touch Junia or anything else in this room once I scrub it clean. Understand? And you must wash your hands with soap every time you enter or leave."

"We can't afford soap."

"Hot water then. As hot as you can stand." She noticed a small bowl of untouched mush beside the bed. "Get rid of that. I'm sure she's lost her appetite, but we must keep her hydrated. I'll need honey, sea salt, and all the lemons or oranges you can find."

His head cocked to one side. "Lemons?" The unfamiliar word tangled his tongue.

"Right, not available here yet," she mumbled. She rubbed her temples. "Think, Lisbeth. What fruits were available in the third century?" The breakfast tray Cyprian had brought her that first morning, his dreamy eyes filled with compassion, popped into memory. "How about pomegranates? Think you can get your hands on a couple of those?"

"Perhaps."

"Oh, and I'm going to try and rig up some kind of vaporizer to help her breathe. But first, we must remove her mother." The man wasn't moving. "Numidicus?"

Tears trickled down his cheeks, his watery eyes fixed on the pocked face of his wife. "She was so beautiful."

"I can see that." What was one more lie? She was making things up as she went along. What did it matter if the flat, overlapping blotches had disfigured the woman's face? Truth wouldn't make this woman less dead. "If you'll help me drag that rug over here, we'll do what has to be done." She removed her cloak and draped it over the chair.

Thirty minutes later Lisbeth had finished washing the dead woman's face and tidied her dingy, threadbare tunic as best she could.

Numidicus fished a coin from a crock hidden beneath the bed. He pressed the money into his wife's clenched fist. "To pay the ferryman god, Charon." He would hear none of Lisbeth's arguments that the money might be better spent on fresh fruit and soap.

Together, they gently lifted Numidicus's wife from the bed, wrapped her in the carpet, lugged the sour bundle outside, and deposited her body next to the two corpses from upstairs. Lisbeth avoided the baby swaddled tight as an Egyptian mummy and knelt beside the man's body. She peeled back the blanket enshrouding his head. His splotchy face was frozen in horror. She quickly covered him, certain his rash matched that of the woman she'd just laid beside him.

Discarding the young mother on the curb, left to rot in the elements like trash dumped along the highway, felt criminal. But neither Numidicus nor she had the strength or time to figure out another option. Even without a proper funeral, Numidicus mourned his beloved wife, sobbing uncontrollably as he knelt by her body.

For a dangerous instant, Lisbeth allowed herself to wonder

what it would feel like to have a man miss her that much. Craig was a busy doctor; he probably hadn't even noticed she was gone. Papa may or may not have the mental capacity to miss more than his memories. And Cyprian . . . what did it matter what that man thought?

Lisbeth swiped at the tears burning her cheeks; the stink of sickness and death remained on her hands. "Numidicus," she whispered. "Junia needs us."

The distraught husband pulled himself away from his wife with admirable courage and set out in search of supplies. Lisbeth returned to Junia's sickbed.

Cracked lips framed the child's heart-shaped mouth. Without a thermometer, she could only guess at Junia's temperature, but from the heat radiating off her skin it was high. Unchecked fevers quickly sapped a child's body fluids. Plain water wouldn't replenish lost electrolytes. Junia needed an IV, or at the very least, an oral rehydration solution. She could mix one, but only if the child's father had success in finding the ingredients.

Lisbeth set to work doing what she could to disinfect the apartment without bleach. She scrubbed the walls and floor with tepid water and a generous slug from the wineskin she found hanging on the wall. Once the floor dried, she spread her cloak, lifted Junia's frail body from the soiled bed, and laid her on the pallet.

A dark red stain outlined the place where Junia's mother had lain. Numidicus's Roman physician must have used a bloodletting technique of some sort on the poor, dying woman. The only thing this barbaric treatment could have possibly accomplished was traumatizing the innocent child in bed with her. She set the bloody blanket outside the door and remade the straw tick. She gathered Junia into her arms, careful not to wake her.

After the child was settled on fresh bedding, Lisbeth watched helplessly as the girl's racking cough nearly turned her little body inside out.

Better get started on that homemade vaporizer. But with what?

Mama's word "improvise" rattled in her head. She scanned the room. Bed. Chair. Small trunk. Not much to work with. Searching the trunk, Lisbeth discovered a piece of tightly woven fabric Junia's mother was probably saving for a special occasion. Building a vaporizer so her daughter could breathe was probably not the occasion she'd had in mind. Lisbeth laid the cloth on the bed and worked to dismantle the family's only chair.

An hour later, Junia rested under a wobbly canopy of twigs and fabric. To create the needed steam for her contraption, Lisbeth filled a pot with water and went in search of the community cooking fire and possible signs of others suffering the same symptoms.

She found an open courtyard where two gaunt women eyed her suspiciously but made room for her pot on the coals. Lisbeth fanned the embers into a weak flame. A couple of tablespoons of salt dumped into the water would speed the boiling process, but without even the barest of essentials she could make nothing happen any faster in this century. Worried Junia might awaken to an empty house, she paced as she waited for the water to heat.

As soon as steam started to rise, Lisbeth hurriedly transported the pot back to Numidicus's apartment, holding the scalding slosh away from her body, and placed it beside the girl's bed. She draped a corner of the tenting fabric over the pot. Cool mist would have been better, but hopefully, captured steam would increase the moisture inside the tent and help loosen the phlegm buildup in Junia's lungs. Lisbeth stood back and surveyed her work with a surprising sense of . . . pride.

Now for the hard part. Waiting on Junia's condition to improve.

An insistent rap on the door startled her. "Numidicus?"

"No," a woman's voice whispered.

"Don't come in." Lisbeth shot to the door and cracked the plank just enough to speak. "We're under quarantine in here. Stay away."

"Lisbeth?" Mama pushed her way in, the large basket draped over her arm knocking Lisbeth aside. "What are you doing here?" Two steps in, she stopped, eyes fixed on the steam escaping a small slit in Junia's tepee. A fresh bruise darkened her right eye, and she seemed to be favoring her right side. "Pneumonia?"

"What are *you* doing here, Mama?" In truth, knowing her mother was alive was remarkably comforting, but no way was she admitting anything so infuriating.

"Whatever I can for these people." Mama fished inside the basket on her arm and produced a loaf of bread.

"No, I mean, how did you get away?"

"Aspasius is preoccupied with the Senate, trying to shore up the votes he needs to keep Cyprian from office." She smiled. "Women are not allowed in the Senate chambers." She offered the bread to Lisbeth. "The neighbor children told me Numidicus's wife was ill—"

"Dead." Lisbeth rubbed the dull ache climbing the back of her neck. "His wife is dead. She couldn't have been twenty years old."

Mama's gaze skimmed the room, sweeping Lisbeth along in her assessment. She set the bread on a small table. "And Junia's lungs?"

"If I had my stethoscope, I'd know."

"I heard what you did for Laurentius." Mama's touch on her arm sparked Lisbeth's immediate recoil. Saving her mother from an abuser was one thing. Forgiving her for never coming home was another.

Unsure of what to do with the clear message of rejection,

Mama let her hand fall to her side. "What else do you need, Dr. Hastings?"

Lisbeth snatched the basket from her. "Nothing."

"You did become a physician, right?"

"I'm *not* a doctor."

"Really?" Mama's eyes narrowed like they once did when Papa declared he'd have her returned to civilization in less than a week. "You didn't learn how to perform a needle decompression digging in your father's sand dunes."

Part of Lisbeth wanted to scream that a mother who disappeared for twenty-three years had no right to ask about what her daughter had or had not become. Another part of her, the raw, secret part she kept buried as deep as Papa's archaeological trinkets, wanted to fall into Mama's arms and pour out every failing, every fear, every ugly need. "I—"

Junia cut Lisbeth off with another agonizing round of unproductive coughing. Lisbeth could feel Mama's eyes on her as she did her best to comfort the child.

"Raising the foot of her bed will help accomplish the postural drainage she needs," Mama said after Lisbeth's efforts failed.

How dare Mama bust in and take over like she was an attending—or worse, a mother who could tell her incompetent daughter what to do? Lisbeth offered a stony, silent response.

Mama shrugged. "She's your patient. Do what *you* think is right, Lisbeth."

Her mother's use of her name, after so many years of nothing but the lonely howl of desert wind, jarred her every time.

"However," Mama continued, "the gurgling hack of Junia's cough indicates her lungs are inflamed and flooded with fluid."

Mama's eyes, calm as sea glass, assessed her refusal to speak and inability to act. "I see your father never broke you of that nasty pout."

"I do not pout."

Her brows arched. "Really?"

Lisbeth detected a riptide lurking beneath the surface of her mother's controlled reaction, a force she remembered capable of snatching the feet right out from under those lazy site excavators Papa was so fond of hiring. Mama reached inside the medical pouch slung across her shoulder.

"Here." She handed Lisbeth a bundle of dried leaves. "Crumble a handful of these, and add the powder to the boiling water. It's not an antibiotic, but the camphor in the eucalyptus will help open her airways. Oh, and take these." She pulled out a small cloth purse. "Black mustard. Don't apply these seeds directly to the child's skin, but a compress made of these little jewels is good for chest congestion."

She whirled and started for the door.

"Wait." Lisbeth's indecision hung between them, a tension so thick Mama's crude scalpel could have sliced a bloody incision. Did she want her mother's help? Or did she want Mama to walk out that door and disappear from her life once and for all? "She has measles."

"I know. No worry. You had your immunizations as a child."

"This isn't about me." Lisbeth swallowed the fear clogging her throat. "I don't know what to do with weeds and seeds."

Mama's shoulders lowered. She turned, pleasure snapping in her eyes. "Surely you saw Aisa use local remedies to treat the men in your father's camp."

"Leave Papa out of this."

Mama's cringe, albeit ever so slight, indicated Lisbeth had dealt the blow she'd wanted to deliver from the moment she realized her mother was alive and had chosen to make her life eighteen hundred years away. Despite the twinge of guilt, in Lisbeth's opinion, this woman had lost any right to claim she knew anything about the wonderful man who'd grieved her loss for two decades.

"Good luck, Lisbeth." She reached for the door.

"Wait." Lisbeth grabbed her arm, feeling every bit the frightened five-year-old who'd waited all night for Mama's return to the tent. "I don't want this child to die."

Mama's gaze probed so deeply into hers that Lisbeth feared she would discover the truth . . . that her daughter was an incompetent doctor, nothing like the doctor she'd been or had wanted her daughter to become. Lisbeth lowered her eyes and waited, the sound of her racing heart thrumming in her ears.

Mama set her basket on the floor. "Then we must do what we can . . . together."

20

Numidicus burst through the door, winded and yanking scavenged supplies from inside his ratty garment. "Soldiers are everywhere. They search for someone."

Mama snatched up the pomegranate and tossed it to Lisbeth. "Then we must be quick."

While Lisbeth carefully measured and mixed honey, salt, and pomegranate juice into a pitcher of sterilized water, Mama worked on a poultice. From the corner of her eye, Lisbeth observed this woman she no longer knew. How could someone so smart cower in the presence of an idiot like Aspasius, yet confidently concoct weedy pharmaceuticals in a mortar? What a strange and foreign person her mother had become, an emotional combination of brokenness and strength Lisbeth desperately wanted to understand.

Mama poured warm water over the powdered black mustard, then stirred until she made a goopy paste that smelled like a Fourth of July picnic with Queenie's relatives. Then, as easily as Mama used to make peanut butter and jelly sandwiches in the shade of a dig site tarp, her practiced hands spread the spicy mustard between two layers of clean cloth pilfered from her supply basket.

Holding out the steamy poultice, Mama said, "This needs to

cool a bit before we apply it to her chest. See if you can convince her to drink your tonic."

With a little coaxing, Lisbeth managed to rouse Junia. Her difficulty in swallowing even a tiny sip told Lisbeth the pocks had moved from inside her cheeks and invaded her throat. "Try to drink, sweetheart."

To Lisbeth's relief, Junia licked her lips and gulped down several ounces of the homemade Pedialyte. Lisbeth gently returned Junia's head to the pillow, dreading what was coming next for this child. Without a better option, she stepped away, and Mama moved in with the poultice.

Lisbeth couldn't stand watching Junia writhe under the discomfort, so while Numidicus propped the foot of the bed, she restocked the vaporizer pot with boiling water and a handful of crushed eucalyptus leaves.

Fifteen minutes later, Junia had finally settled into a fitful sleep. Mama produced another loaf of bread from her basket. She ripped off a hunk and dunked it in wine from the skin in her basket. "Eat, Lisbeth. You're exhausted."

"Give it to Numidicus."

Mama lifted her chin. "You know why the airline stewardess says to apply the oxygen mask to yourself before you apply it to your child?" She spoke in English. "If you don't take care of yourself, you'll do this child no good." She waved the bread under Lisbeth's nose.

Trying to get at the headache forming behind her eyes, Lisbeth ignored the bread and dragged her hands over closed eyelids. "Flight attendant, Mama," she answered. "Nobody calls them stewardesses anymore." Lisbeth opened her eyes to find Mama staring at her, silent, eyes glistening. "Is that how you justified not coming back to us, Mama?" Her voice broke. "You took care of yourself first?"

"Flight attendant?" Mama whispered, setting the bread upon an empty wooden plate, her hand quivering. "I guess I've been gone longer than I thought."

They sat in silence, Lisbeth watching a hard-shelled bug struggling to carry a bread crumb across the floor. *Beetle Bug.* That's what Papa called her. Would her father understand Mama's choice to never come home, or would it be the blow that finally killed him? She turned to tell her so and noticed Mama fingering a tiny gold ring threaded through a leather cord around her neck.

"That's the ring Papa gave you at the cave."

Mama smiled, a faraway, pleased look on her face. "Do you remember the little ceremony we had beneath the stars?"

"I remember Aisa saying it was a bad idea."

"Your father couldn't afford a diamond when we first married, so when he found this, he wanted me to have it. He said the eagle carved into the carnelian would carry my soul into the presence of the gods." A tear trickled down her swollen cheek. "Instead it carried me straight into hell. At first I was so angry at him, but as the days passed I realized it was the only thing that tied me to the future." She kissed the ring and dropped it back inside her tunic. "Time goes by so quickly, Lisbeth. Don't waste it."

Before Lisbeth could form a coherent response, Junia launched into another coughing spell. "Quick, roll her on her side," Mama ordered.

As Lisbeth rotated the child onto her left side, she pondered Mama's losses: Papa. Her. The future Mama had always wanted. Time to fix mistakes.

The possibility of time becoming confused or difficult to pin down had not even occurred to her. Had she been in the third century longer than she thought? Had Papa grown old and suffered without her there to keep his thoughts sorted? Lisbeth's knees liquefied. She sat with a thump upon the edge of the bed.

"Lisbeth?"

"I'm fine." The lie, the same one she'd told herself since she was five, rolled off her tongue and fell in line with the fortified barrier she'd erected around her heart. She wanted to tell Mama all about Papa, but the words stuck in her throat. "How long do we leave her like this?"

"A couple of minutes should do." Mama patted her hand. "You sure you're all right?"

Lisbeth began counting out loud to avoid having to lie to Mama twice. "One thousand one. One thousand two. One thousand three."

Lost seconds ticked away. Mama let the door close on the tiny crack a moment of weakness had exposed in both of them, asking no more questions.

Two minutes later they rolled Junia to her right. Racking coughs followed each repeated roll on the hay tick.

"It's not enough." Lisbeth's desperation drifted between Junia's father standing in the corner waiting for news and Mama waiting for her to make a decision. "I don't know what else to do. I wish I at least had my stethoscope."

"You have your hands."

"My hands?"

"Fremitus. The importance of a doctor's hands." Mama took Lisbeth's hand. "You felt your way through saving Laurentius, did you not?"

"I guess."

"Technology has surely increased since I've been away. Probably wouldn't know my way around an OR anymore."

"There're all kinds of fancy machines to zero in on tumors and diagnose diseases."

"But can they get to the source of a broken heart or measure the longings of the brain? I've learned that touch is the best medicine I can offer. When I place my hands on a patient and look them in the eye—there's a bond. A trust. Hope."

"They don't give us a lot of time for touching patients. I'm expected to do a full patient workup in ten minutes or less."

"A complete physical exam can be more valuable than any lab test or X-ray. When you touch a patient, it says I'm on your side. Who doesn't want someone on their side?" Mama removed the poultice from Junia's chest. "Let's sit her up."

Lisbeth helped elevate Junia to a sitting position.

"Go ahead," Mama said. "Don't be afraid to touch her."

Lisbeth remembered Abra, how if she'd taken a moment to press on that child's distended belly she would have known it was an obstructed bowel. A simple surgery fix. How could she have been so stupid? Mama showed Lisbeth how to use her hands to probe the child's body, especially the jugular vein.

"Is it distended?" Mama asked. "The vein's like a dipstick. Too much fluid backing up, you can see it in the neck. The single best tool I have is the jugular. If it's distended, it tells me what?"

"A key indicator of heart failure."

"Bravo." Magdalena moved her out of the way. "Here, let me show you." She arranged Junia into an upright sitting position. "Can you say EEEEEE?" Junia shook her head. "Try. Please. EEEEEE."

"EEeeee" rattled out of Junia.

"EEEEE." Mama encouraged Lisbeth to walk her palms down the child's small back. "Good girl. Feel right here, Lisbeth. Feel the vibration during the low frequency?"

"I do."

"Sounds clear of pneumonia, which is a good thing, since antibiotics are a luxury we don't have." Mama made a fist and began pounding the child's back. Junia started crying, but Mama didn't stop.

Together, they placed the child's right arm across her stomach and bent her knees to her chest. Three minutes later, Junia expelled phlegm, followed by a couple of successful deep breaths. The child's breathing immediately settled into a less labored rhythm.

"I can't believe this home-remedy stuff is actually working." Lisbeth offered Junia another sip of the rehydration solution. "Look at her suck it down."

Mama nodded. "Roman medicine can mend broken bones, reduce dislocations, cauterize wounds, engage in phlebotomy, and even perform various surgical operations. I have learned much from these people. And so have you."

"Like what to do with crushed eucalyptus leaves?"

"Many of the things you learned in med school were discovered centuries before you were born." Mama poured a few mustard seeds into her makeshift mortar bowl. "But when the Roman docs don't know what to do, they leave the sick to the healing power of nature."

"You mean they let them die?"

"They rely on what works. When the techniques they know fail, they do what doctors have had to do for centuries . . . they move on." She picked up the wooden spoon she used as a pestle and ground into the seeds. "Not me." Surety laced her voice.

A snort of disbelief left Lisbeth's mouth. "Does traveling through time give you supernatural powers or something? Because if it does, I'm not feeling the magic."

"No." She pulverized the tiny seeds into dust. "It gave me God."

"Don't tell me you're really one of *them*." Disgust spiked Lisbeth's voice.

Mama raised her head slowly. "Yes."

"I don't even want to know how that happened." Lisbeth snatched up an empty clay pot. "We need more hot water."

* * *

SUSPENDED BETWEEN what she knew to be an impossibility based upon her mother's nonreligious upbringing and the conviction she'd heard in her mother's own words, Lisbeth tossed chips of dried animal dung into the fire ring. Had Mama been so desperate for a sliver of kindness that she'd fallen in with a cult?

The day's meager meals had been prepared, and the plebeian women had all retreated to their cramped quarters, leaving Lisbeth to tend the fire alone.

She gathered a handful of brittle grass. Working to push away the absurd notion that Mama had fallen victim to some sort of Christian spell, Lisbeth tucked sprigs of straw beneath the scant pile of fuel. Striking the flint upon the rock, she managed a spark. She blew the tiny tendril of smoke into a little flame that set the dung ablaze. Crouched beside the fire, she waited for the water to boil.

Lisbeth made a mental list of the things she was fairly certain of. One, she was at least eighteen hundred years from everything she once knew. Two, she was a thousand miles from a father who needed her now more than ever. Three, finding her mother after all of these years had messed with her equilibrium. And four, even if she knew where the time portal was, reversing the emotional damage caused by this little foray into the third century was scientifically impossible. She would never look at her own hands and not see those of her mother. Battered and scarred from years of hard work, they possessed what she did not have . . . the touch of healing.

Steam rose from the boiling water. Lisbeth covered her hands with the frayed hem of her tunic and lifted the pot. Ready or not, she wanted to hear the truth.

21

AN OFFENSIVE SMOKE SWIRLED from the lamp's flaxen wick. Magdalena cast a futile glance around the cramped home. Quarry workers could barely afford enough olive oil to fill one small clay bowl, let alone stock reserves. She'd known Numidicus long enough to know he was no exception. Without a window, the stuffy room would be pitch black when the fuel was gone. Perhaps telling Lisbeth the truth would be easier in the dark. The lost years could not be rescued, but an honest conversation might save the future. No matter how much she dreaded reliving the horrors of the past, she prayed the Lord would give her the courage. When Lisbeth returned from the cooking fires, she would tell her everything, including the secret she'd kept from Aspasius all these years.

Magdalena poured the last of the water into the vaporizer pot. Keeping Lisbeth's clever contraption going around the clock had nearly depleted the water in the large earthenware jug. Hopefully, they could squeak by until darkness fell, and she could make the trip to the well in secrecy. No way would she send Lisbeth. Knowing how women talked, letting Lisbeth traipse back and forth between the cooking fires was already a risk. Aspasius knew the poor skirted his curfew and tended to their household chores once the sun set. Extra patrols would be stationed at every cistern, awaiting the opportunity to make an example of those who dared to defy his orders. He did not need to hear about the two women tending the ill in the tenements.

She took up the mortar bowl and ground the seeds into a paste while she still had light.

Muffled voices and heavy footfalls sounded on the other side of the door. A loud crash sent the plank splintering from the bolt. A sliver of moonlight lasered a sharp line upon the stone floor.

"It is Mor." Numidicus jumped to a defensive posture. "Death, if you must have someone, take me."

Magdalena whirled from Junia's bed, the mortar bowl clutched in her hands. "Unclean. We're unclean. Go away."

"Magdalena!" Aspasius stepped into the doorway, his white toga snug against the curve of his belly. On either side of him, two men sporting the moonlit glint of armor waited to do his bidding.

Every nerve in Magdalena's body rushed to prod her next move, but she stood silent, unable to run.

"Take her." Aspasius stepped back. Soldiers rushed in. "Kill the pleb."

Numidicus lunged for Magdalena, but the patrols snatched her from his grasp. The bowl clattered to the floor, and black mustard paste splattered the walls.

"There's fever in this house." Magdalena tried to plant her feet as the soldiers dragged her toward Aspasius. "They're dying."

"Exactly what they deserve," Aspasius said with a smug snarl. "I'll teach my slave what it means to doctor those who refuse to bow to Rome."

"Stay back, Numidicus." Despite the terror pumping through her, Magdalena kept her voice low, praying Lisbeth would not hear the ruckus and come running. When they reached the door, Aspasius's hand came down across her face. His ring tore flesh from her cheek.

"Filthy pig!" The young father's protest bounced off the stone walls.

"Hush! Numidicus!" Her warning was lost in his furor.

He lowered his head and charged like one of those crazed bulls in the arena. The biggest soldier backhanded him. Numidicus crashed into Junia's vaporizer. Sticks and heating pot splintered in every direction. The little girl startled awake and began to cry, which brought on another coughing spell and sent Numidicus scrambling to his feet.

The pointed pottery shard he brandished sliced the air. "Leave her alone!" Face grave, the desperate father stretched out his arm and rushed the soldiers again.

"No! Numidicus!" Magdalena screamed, but he kept coming.

A soldier's blade slit him belly button to sternum. Disbelief on his face, Numidicus clutched his middle and slumped to the floor.

Aspasius spun Magdalena around. "No one will want you when I'm through." He reared back his arm and slashed the whip across her face.

22

THREE DAYS HAD PASSED since Lisbeth disappeared in the marketplace, and though Cyprian had commissioned Felicissimus and Pontius to join his search of the city, no trace of her had been found.

He strode the crowded gravel paths of the bathhouse gardens, silently cursing his lack of foresight. Ruth would have been better suited to this task, especially if his missing slave hid herself among the women bathers. Men were limited to the sport courts, gymnasium, library, and massage tables. Ruth, on the other hand, would have left no pool or changing room unchecked, despite the posted warnings that prohibited bathers of the opposite sex from commingling anywhere but in the communal areas.

"Why have I invested so much effort in seeing to the return of this particularly vexing piece of property, Pontius?" Cyprian's faithful secretary offered no answer. "What need do I have for a foreign slave girl with slender hips, a sharp tongue, and a perpetual frown?" A precious waste of time better spent procuring a proper wife and putting to bed the nasty rumor that he'd contracted a disease capable of disabling his manhood, and through rather unsavory means at that. Aspasius had done everything within his power to end Cyprian's campaign before the entry deadline, and all over the fact that he'd bested him in a couple of slave-bidding wars. "What's to be gained by getting the little chit back?"

Pontius eyed him carefully, weighing his words in the manner of one accustomed to balancing Cyprian's heavy caseload against his stress level. "In spite of the woman's unorthodox healing skills, Barek and Laurentius are on the mend, sir."

"Yes, but is she going to be more trouble than she is worth?"

"Thankfully, Felicissimus returned the fortune you spent."

"In truth, I'd pay double for the opportunity to irritate the proconsul." Cyprian stopped his senseless pacing. "While we await the opening gong, I'd appreciate it if you checked the outer grounds one more time."

"But I thought you'd decided to cut your losses—"

"Humor me, Pontius."

His secretary left Cyprian to scrutinize the patrons strolling between the stone statues that populated the public places. A god on every corner rather than the one God he now carried in his heart. Had he done the right thing to realign his religious loyalties? To turn his back on the gods of his ancestors? He glanced around. Other than a few roosting matrons trading in local gossip, he was alone. He made his way to the deserted fountain in the far corner of the courtyard. "What say you, Juno? Why does this slave woman vex me so?"

The marble lady stood silent amid the patter of water in the basin, her blank-eyed stare declaring his questions foolishness. What man would dare claim to know the mind of the gods? Settling his own mind had proven to be difficult enough, a process he'd yet to complete. He was Roman. Born and bred. Adding slaves to his household staff was expected. Considering plebeians equal to the ruling patricians was one of those strange teachings of the bishop, an act of obedience his new faith required. But he found the concept difficult to embrace and harder still to put into practice.

Cyprian tossed a coin into the water. Watching it sink to the tiled mosaic of a woman's face, he asked her help in locating Lisbeth. Caecilianus would think him foolish. He could hear the lecture now. Throwing money into the ocean would be more effective than making wishes in water fountains.

Some habits die hard.

The bell sounded, signaling the opening of the baths. A burly slave clad in the uniform colors of the ruling house entered the courtyard and began clearing loiterers from the path, shoving them aside with little regard to their station.

Cyprian tightened his belt and stepped from the fountain's shadow, preparing for the puffed-up patron sure to follow in the slave's wake. *What ill luck.* Or was another chance meeting with the proconsul Juno's answer after all?

Aspasius strolled into the communal courtyard, accompanied by an entourage that included a tall, willowy man with the excess fabric of a dignitary's toga draped across his bony arm. The visitor's pointy nose sniffed the air as if the place still had the nasty reek of Phoenician plebs.

"As you can see, Sergia," Aspasius addressed his guest, oblivious to the disdainful looks the displaced crowd silently hurled behind his back. "Aqueducts from the Zaghouan Mountains are now restored, making the Bordj Djedid cisterns fully operational once again. By improving the Carthaginians' methods of water storage and distribution, I have once and for all conquered the arid region of Africa."

The thin man studied the lush grounds. "Restoring a hygienic precedent to the citizens of Carthage is key to restoring the sparkle to one of Rome's most prized jewels."

"Well said, Ambassador." Cyprian tossed another coin into the fountain. "I'm sure our esteemed proconsul would love to show off the *natatio*. He's had the entire pool space opened up. The stunning view of the sea is a bathing experience unique to Carthage, one worthy of every denarius spent."

"Cyprian?" The ambassador extended his hand and a warm smile. "Old friend." He pumped Cyprian's arm. "Still a fair-haired, bright-eyed feast for the gods."

"You've not changed a bit, dear Sergy." A lie if ever he'd told one, but it seemed a poor sport to point out his colleague's thinned hair and wasted muscles. "Once a prankster, always a prankster. You must keep the emperor on his toes."

"Sadly, it is he who keeps me busier than a one-armed gladiator." Sergia had a remarkably firm grasp for one so frail in appearance. "Maintaining order in the provinces is a never-ending task."

"Exhausting, no doubt." Cyprian cast a sly grin at Aspasius squirming in his red shoes. "A burden our esteemed proconsul can relate to well."

Aspasius cleared his throat. "Ambassador, we must keep to our rather vigorous tour schedule."

"Forgive me for going on and on, Aspasius." Sergia's half-hearted apology warmed Cyprian. The man had always valued loyalty, a trait that had endeared him to Cyprian from their first meeting. "The brilliant Cyprianus Thascius and I studied together at the feet of old Sextus in the godforsaken village of Pupput." He turned his attention back to Cyprian. "Remember those long walks on treacherous paths to reach the sweet city of Hadrumetum? And all for a decent cup of ale." They shared a laugh that excluded the fidgeting proconsul. "But I must say those harrowing excursions were worth every lash."

"Had you not dallied with the barmaid we would not have missed curfew." Cyprian and Sergia roared again, clapping each other on the back. "Did you tell your sweet Bellona of that African beauty?"

"Why crush my wife with the foolish exploits of youth?" Sergia's face sobered. He leaned in close. "Obviously, you have never married, my friend. We must find you a wife."

A wife. Could a man's character and work not stand on his own merit? Must he manage a business, his house, *and* a wife for the Senate to consider him a success? "I've got my eye on the prospect of marriage."

"How are those inquiries coming along?" Aspasius asked with a smirk.

"I'm being very selective."

"Not one positive response, I'm guessing."

"Really?" Sergia's brow wrinkled. "I remember the village maidens thinking Cyprian quite the catch." Sergia smiled. "But you were quite good at keeping your head in the books, my friend, and slipping the hook."

"School chaps?" Heat flamed Aspasius's cheeks. "How quaint." He took Sergia's elbow and led him toward the arched passageway of the men's quarters. "Our game court has been reserved to take full advantage of the shade."

"Perhaps you'd care to take in a bit of exercise with us, Cyprian?" Sergia said as he perused the mallets hanging on the wall. "I seem to recall you quite the competitor with a stick and a *paganica* ball."

Aspasius ripped a heavy pole from the rack. "I'm sure the great solicitor of Carthage has little time for whacking the leathers."

"On the contrary." Cyprian chose a sleek rod of mulberry, carved to fit his hand. "What better enjoyment than trouncing a couple of old *friends* and all the while hearing the latest from Rome?" Throwing fuel on an enemy's fire in hopes they'd burn themselves out was a business tactic he'd learned from his father. "Let me send a servant to locate my man, Pontius, and we'll make it a foursome."

Under the striped awning of the paved court, Aspasius wielded his club with a crippling force, claiming the licks he applied to Cyprian's shins during the scuffle for possession of the feather-stuffed ball were the fault of defending his goal.

"I do hate to lose." Sergia dabbed sweat from his face. "Aspasius, I believe regular bouts with my old colleague would improve your game and shrink your middle."

Struggling to wrap the towel around his waist, Aspasius dismissed the slave offering to oil him down. "When my girth hinders my ability to manage this province, then Rome can replace me." He snatched the *strigil* from the slave's hand. "Good gods, man. Leave me a bit of flesh."

Sergia allowed the slave to pass the strigil over his bare back, slinging sweat in every direction. "But have you the vigor to see to Carthage's continued rise from the ashes?"

Aspasius soured at the implied insult. "If the emperor has a problem with the way I do my job, spit it out."

"Word of sickness spreading through your tenements has reached Rome. If you cannot get things contained, then I must recommend your term as proconsul come to a premature end."

Aspasius's nostrils flared. "Why, you little—"

"I think we're all a bit overheated." Cyprian gathered his towel over his loins, anxious to divert Sergia lest Aspasius believe him responsible for this assault. "Shall we skip the *caldarium* in favor of a cold plunge in the *piscina*?"

"Excellent idea," Sergia agreed, wrapping the towel twice around his twig-like middle. He took the cup of steaming mulled cider the court attendant offered. "I'd love to hear your legal opinion on the latest edict of Decius, Cyprian."

"Edict?" Cyprian accepted a cup of the strong brew. "I wasn't aware our emperor had issued a new edict."

"The ink is barely dried on the parchment," Sergia admitted with a sigh. "I fear the ramifications will not set well, especially in the provinces."

Cyprian emptied his cup, hoping he appeared unshaken by the possibilities. "Pray tell."

"Decius fears an invasion from the Goths. He has ordered that the entire kingdom bow before the gods of Rome." Sergia sloshed the wine in his mouth, then spit into a nearby planter. "Including the captives on the various frontiers. In the past, the imperial position has been to allow conquered barbarians their worship freedoms. As long as barbarian tax dollars returned to the true throne of power, the emperor did not see the harm in humoring their little gods."

Aspasius snapped his fingers, and an attendant presented his red bath slippers with built-in wooden heels. "How are the emperor's decrees or how those decrees are carried out in *my* province of any concern to Cyprian?"

Sergia held up his skeletal fingers. "Years of political thinking may have clouded your objectivity, Consul. I think it my responsibility to judge the full impact of this decree on many levels, including those of upstanding citizens like the highly esteemed solicitor of Carthage. Our emperor deserves a full and complete report."

Aspasius threw the excess length of his towel over his shoulder. "There is an order to things. An order ordained by the gods." He stormed toward the changing-room door, the uneven click of his red shoes tapping out a warning. "Warm water after exercise is one of those indisputable orders. Seeing to the success of the dictates of my lord and emperor without questioning his imperial wisdom is another." Three servants fell in behind the proconsul, including the burly bodyguard who managed to cast a warning glare over his shoulder.

"Oh, dear," Sergia whispered to Cyprian once they were alone. "I've set him off. There'll be no reasoning with him now. If you've not considered running for the Senate, I strongly suggest that you get yourself a well-connected wife and examine the possibility. Rome could use a few good men." Sergia hustled after the proconsul, bypassing the colossal granite pillars supporting the barrel-vaulted ceiling of the *frigidarium.* "Aspasius, wait."

Cyprian looked to Pontius for support. "Can you think of a single woman willing to become the wife of an idealistic dreamer determined to set Rome on its ear?"

Pontius shrugged. "Or one who is willing to risk creeping pox?"

23

WAITING FOR THE ELEVATOR was not an option. Lisbeth flew down two flights of stairs and raced into the ER. She burst into the organized chaos of medical personnel who'd descended upon exam room 1 like worker bees summoned to the throne.

Nelda's head snapped up from the limp baby on the gurney. "I paged you . . . twice." Her laser stare stripped Lisbeth bare of excuses, while her nimble fingers removed the child's swaddling.

"Abra?" Lisbeth elbowed her way to the bed that had been rolled to the center of the room. "What happened?"

"She became lethargic and stopped breathing." Nelda slapped an endotracheal tube into Lisbeth's hand as two other nurses placed sticky cardiac pads on the small naked chest. "Dr. Redding isn't here yet. You'll have to intubate."

No attending? Lisbeth had participated in several codes but never run one. And she'd never seen a child in cardiac arrest. Her mind spun, frantic to find traction. Across the room, Abra's mother stood mute, frozen to the periphery. Terror ricocheted through Lisbeth's heart.

"Dr. Hastings, now!" Nelda's order blasted Lisbeth into action.

Someone tossed Lisbeth gloves. She positioned herself at the head of the bed. The rhythm on the cardiac monitor told her the child's heart rate was frighteningly slow and irregular. "Resume CPR!" She tilted Abra's chin toward her and pried apart her thin blue lips.

"Pedi laryngoscope." Lisbeth inserted the device over the smooth little tongue for a better view of the airway. Vomit clogged the narrow oropharynx. "Suction." She exchanged the ET tube for a mini vacuum hose. "Stay with me, little girl."

Once she had the airway cleared, Abra's tiny vocal cords came into view. Lisbeth threaded the small plastic tube down the trachea on the first try.

"Give one milligram of epi." Queenie's confident voice came as a surprise.

Lisbeth had been so preoccupied with executing a successful intubation she'd failed to notice that her best friend had slipped in and taken over chest compressions.

Confidence bolstered, Lisbeth ordered, "Go ahead and give the atropine."

Dr. Redding rushed into the room. Never had Lisbeth been so glad to see her no-nonsense attending. He surveyed the situation with seasoned skill. "We have an airway?" He assumed a position on Lisbeth's left. "How about good IV access?"

"Yes, sir." Lisbeth sounded as shaky as she felt. "She's intubated and has two good peripheral IVs."

Dr. Redding assumed command. He halted CPR and checked Abra's current cardiac rhythm, which was still dangerously slow. He palpated her femoral artery. "No pulse." Concern deepened in his eyes. "Give another milligram of epi, and check a blood gas."

Lisbeth anxiously counted the seconds. Finally, Dr. Redding gave the signal to resume CPR, and she relieved Queenie, wrapping her hands around the child's tiny chest. With each compression she prayed the heart would awaken beneath her thumbs.

"Her pH is six point five!" Nelda yelled from the back of the room. Abra's blood acidity level indicated life was not possible.

Dr. Redding kept his eyes on the monitor. "She's in vfib. Initiate shock. Clear!"

Lisbeth halted CPR, but she could not will her hands to let go.

Dr. Redding pulled on the back of her coat. "Clear, Hastings."

Abra's lifeless body jerked with the jolt of electricity. The moment the paddles were removed, Lisbeth jumped in and resumed CPR, but vfib returned. Three separate shocks failed to initiate Abra's pulse.

"Give me an intracardiac needle." Dr. Redding stuck a prefilled syringe directly into Abra's still heart. The child who'd been screaming only a few hours before didn't even flinch.

Lisbeth held her breath, alternating her attention between frantically recounting every detail of her earlier examination of this child and the bruised chest in her hands.

"Stop CPR and check rhythm." All eyes locked on the monitor. A yellow flatline raced across the screen. Dr. Redding let out an exhausted sigh. "Enough."

"No!" Lisbeth pumped harder. "I can't lose her."

Dr. Redding grabbed her hands. "Enough, Hastings." The room went silent, except for Lisbeth's labored breaths. "Call it."

She released her hold and stepped back from the blue body in the middle of the adult-size gurney. Naked and lifeless. So small. Ten fingers. Ten toes. A little upturned nose. Perfect. Except she was dead.

Lisbeth searched for anything left undone, something forgotten, something they hadn't tried. The floor and bed were littered with EKG tracings, empty medication vials, stray needles and syringes. Short of cursing, there was nothing left to do.

"Time of death . . . zero two five one" ripped from Lisbeth's throat.

Dr. Redding slung his gloves in the trash, then walked over to

Abra's mother and placed a large hand on her shoulder. He shook his head and solemnly left the room.

A razor-sharp wail jolted Lisbeth awake.

She sat upright, every nerve alerted. Sweat dripped down her back. She wasn't in the ER. She hadn't just killed a kid. And she wasn't home. Her reality came into an uneasy focus. Something was missing from the plebeian apartment she'd spent the past four days guarding. Something important. Her mind clawed through the fog of sleep deprivation for an answer.

Deathly quiet. Silence. Junia's barky cough had ceased.

"Oh, no." Lisbeth unfurled her legs from the pallet she'd made herself beside the small bed and scrambled to her feet. Tingles shot from her toes to her hips. She touched the water pot at the base of the vaporizer canopy.

Cold.

"Lord, don't let her be dead." She ripped the cloth from the frame she'd rebuilt over Junia after she came back and found the first vaporizer destroyed, Numidicus dead, and Mama gone. She grabbed Junia's wrist. "Give me a pulse, little girl."

Junia's black eyes fluttered open, alert and questioning. "Mama?"

Lisbeth released her breath. "Thank God." She stroked Junia's forehead while sucking in huge gulps of relief. "I think your fever's gone, little one." The fiery red splotches that had started on the child's face and crawled over her entire body were now a tarnished brown. "Feeling better?"

"Mama?" The rawness of the child's first attempt to speak in three days grated Lisbeth's heart. "I want my mama."

"I know, baby."

Somehow Lisbeth had managed to remove the body of Numidicus on her own, but where had her mother gone? The area was definitely not a safe one, and Lisbeth hoped, despite herself,

that Mama had walked out on her again before whatever dangerous rogue or bored, mischief-making Roman soldier had come
and killed Numidicus. At least then she would be safe. Lisbeth
couldn't face the possibility of Mama coming to the same fate as
Junia's poor father. She couldn't imagine experiencing the death of
her mother one more time. Lisbeth looked into Junia's expectant
face and saw in the girl's eyes herself all those years ago.

"I bet you're thirsty, sweetheart. I'll be right back." Lisbeth
tucked an empty terra-cotta jug under her arm. "Stay in bed. And
don't answer the door."

Lisbeth raised her cloak hood, poked her nose into the corridor, then ventured out to join the noisy line of women on their
evening pilgrimage to the well. A crowd would make it easier to
disappear if she ran into more soldiers. Until then, she must stay
alert for signs that others might be infected with measles. So far,
no nasty coughs or mothers complaining of sick kids. Perhaps Junia's family and the family upstairs were the only ones afflicted.
Lisbeth held back from the group, pretending she'd found a crack
in her jug. Feeling every bit the foreigner she was, she eaves-
dropped on the gossip. Marriage troubles. Childrearing problems. Rising prices in the market. Gossip of curses on Numidicus
for his strange beliefs. A world not so different from the one she'd
left behind.

One by one, the women filled their jugs, said their farewells,
then tramped into the deepening twilight. When the coast was
clear, Lisbeth approached the deserted well and lowered the
gourd, peering into the damp, musty cavern.

Was this the way home? With a thunk the gourd sank into
the murky darkness. Part of her wanted to hold her nose and
jump, to take her chances in the unknown rather than face another day of this constant reliving of the past and the most painful moments in her memory. Rough stone sanded Lisbeth's

palms as she lowered her head and breathed in the scent of water gurgling from somewhere deep within the earth. She couldn't back out of the promise she'd made to Numidicus. Her inattention had left one innocent child to fend for herself. She would never leave another.

The rope burned Lisbeth's hand as she raised the heavy gourd. Newly mustered bravado wouldn't do her any good once she ran out of provisions. After she mixed up this last batch of rehydration solution, everything Numidicus had scavenged and what little food she'd found in Mama's basket would be gone.

Lisbeth emptied the gourd into her jug. Water would not sustain them. Junia needed nourishment, and so did she. Either they starved, or she did the last thing she wanted to do . . . return to Cyprian.

In the predawn darkness, Lisbeth hurried to finish her preparations. If she didn't return to Cyprian's now, the odds of avoiding snarly soldiers were nil. Certain Junia was too weak to make the trip on foot, Lisbeth strapped the girl to her chest with a sling made from the last piece of clean bedding. She threw her cloak over both of them, blew out the lamp, then slipped into the ill-lighted apartment corridor.

One of the stray dogs curled on a neighboring stoop lifted his head and growled. She tossed the last of the bread crumbs in his direction, then quickly left the tenements behind, retracing Numidicus's hasty path through the maze of narrow alleys as best she could remember. She reached the darkened windows of the city's more exclusive storefronts. Feeling confident she knew the way from here, she stepped up the pace. The sun climbed over the horizon. She arrived at Cyprian's wrought-iron gates winded, arms burning from toting the four-year-old.

Recalling the noisy hinges, Lisbeth untied Junia. She stood the child upon her shaky legs, then quickly squeezed through the bars.

"Take my hand." Junia rubbed her eyes, refusing to cooperate. "Come on, kid. I know you're scared, but trust me, they have lots to eat here." She snagged a bony elbow and tugged the girl to her chest. The girl monkey-wrapped her so tight Lisbeth could barely breathe.

In the rosy glow of dawn, Cyprian's villa looked larger and strangely more welcoming than she remembered. Suddenly she felt hungry, tired, and very conflicted at the prospect of leaving an orphan on someone's doorstep. As she scurried up the walk, the dogs went bonkers, hurtling around the corner of the house like a team of spooked horses. They pounced upon the bulge under her cloak. Junia launched into a raspy, screaming fit.

So much for slipping in unnoticed.

Lisbeth wedged inside the door. The dogs clawed and barked, insisting that someone let them in.

"Lisbeth?" Ruth tied her robe as she rushed to her. "Are you all right? What happened? I looked everywhere. When I couldn't find you, I had no choice but to tell Cyprian you'd run away. He searched the city for days. Even rifled the freight aboard his fleet." She noticed Junia squirming and lifted Lisbeth's cloak. "Who is this?"

"Don't touch her." Lisbeth backed away. "I don't think she's contagious, but I'm not sure."

"Contagious?" Ruth raised a skeptical brow. "What is contagious? What's going on?"

"When I left the cleaners, I ran into Numidicus and . . ." Lisbeth shifted Junia's weight. "Look, it's a long story. I need a room where Junia can stay. One far away from everyone else."

"I should have you lashed." Ruth didn't hide the struggle with her conscience. "Come with me. I'll decide how much to tell Cyprian later." She led Lisbeth through the courtyard to a gardener's small cottage on the far corner of the property.

In a show of appreciation, Lisbeth asked questions about Barek and Laurentius. Ruth was reluctant at first, still a little miffed by Lisbeth's disappearance, but Lisbeth coaxed her until she rattled off the details of their miraculous recoveries and Laurentius's return to the proconsul's palace.

Lisbeth settled Junia on the tidy cot, surprised at the disappointment she felt at Laurentius's recovery without her and the missed opportunity to tell him good-bye.

"Ruth, I need you to listen carefully." She waited for the seriousness in her voice to stall Ruth's motor long enough for some parting orders. "The sickness sweeping the tenements is more serious than Caecilianus wants to admit. I'm pretty sure the fever killed Junia's mother and a couple of their neighbors." She'd seen cardio docs scare smokers into healthier behaviors; maybe if she scared Ruth into taking every precaution . . . "Whenever you tend Junia, you must wear something over your nose and mouth." She ripped another couple of inches from the hem of her frayed tunic and demonstrated a mask. "Wash your hands with hot water and soap. And try not to touch any oozing sores. Keep her well hydrated—I mean, make sure she drinks enough—and she should be up and around in a couple of days."

"Where are you going?" The cloth over Ruth's mouth didn't muffle her alarm.

"Home."

"But—"

A slim black girl burst into the cottage, short of breath like she'd been running for her life. "Where's the other healer?"

"Tabari?" Ruth offered a steadying hand. "What's wrong?"

Lisbeth recognized the slave girl as the one who'd delivered Mama's bloody clothes to the cleaners and then disappeared before she could get answers. "I'm the healer."

"Come quick." Tabari took Lisbeth's hand and dragged her toward the door.

Lisbeth jerked free. "I'm not going anywhere with you."

Fire leapt from Tabari's dark eyes. "Aspasius beat your mother half to death."

24

LISBETH RUMMAGED THROUGH THE pantry, her nerves on high alert. She gathered a loaf of crusty bread, two slabs of cheese, a handful of dried figs, and a large skin of wine and stuffed them into the spare medical bag her mother kept at Cyprian's. She lifted the lid on a small wooden box and looked to Ruth. "I hate to take your entire tea store, but I don't know what I'll need."

"Take it. I'll explain to Cyprian." Ruth added a wad of fresh bandages. "I should come with you."

"No." Lisbeth snapped the wooden lid and crammed it in the bag. "Everyone in this house is in quarantine now that I've brought Junia here. Besides, that child is going to need some serious mothering after all she's been through."

"Once you charge the proconsul's palace, then what?" Ruth's position had morphed from refusing to let Lisbeth go to tearful pleading that she stay.

"I'll think of something."

Ruth tossed Lisbeth a fresh tunic. "If you won't wait on Cyprian's return, at least don't disgrace his house by roaming the streets in that filthy rag." The bishop's wife had not insisted upon an explanation of how she and Mama were related, a dignified managing of her curiosity that made Lisbeth respect her all the more. Ruth fished the pieces of Lisbeth's stethoscope from her pocket. "You might need this."

Lisbeth quickly assembled the instrument, touched that Ruth had taken such good care of her treasure. "If I'm not back by sunset"—she tossed the strap of her bag over her shoulder—"promise me that you'll make sure Junia gets a good home."

"This is her home now . . . as it is yours." Ruth put a hand on Lisbeth's wrist. "Don't forget where you belong."

Soldiers in hobnailed boots strutted the main streets. Too many accusing eyes for Tabari's comfort, which, after Lisbeth's last run-in with the touchy-feely troops of Aspasius, didn't suit her well either.

"This way." The alert little slave girl darted down an alley.

The closer they got to the palace, the more patrols they encountered, even on the back streets. They rounded a corner. Tabari stopped Lisbeth with a stiff arm and pointed straight ahead. An impressive structure, the size of a small hospital, towered behind a six-foot-tall brick fence.

"Stay low." Tabari skirted the heavy ironwork of the large gate and led Lisbeth to a place along the wall safe from the view of the tower guards. The slave girl parted a thick vine and slipped through the foliage without breaking a leaf.

Lisbeth followed her through a dwarf-size opening in the brick. Once clear of the fence, they descended four stone steps that dead-ended at the palace itself. A heavy wooden plank rested flush against the massive stones. Tabari fished a rusty key from her pocket and twisted a hidden lock. She pulled the wood back. Air, as stale and damp as a sealed tomb, rushed to escape.

"Careful. There's another step." A rusty squeak accompanied Tabari's attempt to quietly shut the plank behind them. "Don't move." Tabari slid an iron bolt through a lock, then mysteriously produced a lamp and flint.

Tiny flames illuminated a low, stone ceiling.

"I hate tunnels." Lisbeth's heart hammered her chest as she felt along the wall for some sort of railing to pull herself out of the cold water covering her feet. "No, really. I'm claustrophobic."

When she was six, she had begged Papa to let her explore inside the tomb he was excavating. Walls of dirt that had not seen the sun in years hemmed her in. The confined space sent her into a full-blown panic attack. So they made a deal. While Papa dug, she explored the wide-open spaces of the desert, listening to the wind and climbing the highest peaks of any nearby landmass, pretending she could see for eternity.

In truth, she searched the barren landscape for signs of Mama. A dot in the distance. A lone tree on the horizon. An unusual rock formation. Anything could become the mother she missed more than she could confess. Then, with a visual lock on the speck of hope, she'd imagine her mother running toward her until Aisa called her to supper and the sobering and disappointing truth. There was a despair darker than any tunnel.

"Why don't I wait right outside the door, and you can bring Mama to me?" Lisbeth suggested.

"She's too ill." Tabari ducked beneath some cobwebs and set out with the light.

Lisbeth took a tentative step. Water covered her feet. "This can't be good." Her splashy footfalls on the wet cobblestones sent unidentified creatures scuttling. Twisting stairwells and narrow passageways led them deeper and deeper into the bowels of the palace.

Tabari climbed two steps, then paused at the landing outside a small door. She held the lamp close to her chest, illuminating the sheen on her forehead and her blatant disapproval of Lisbeth's slow progress.

"Please tell me this is it." Lisbeth brushed cobwebs from her cloak, but she couldn't shake the thought of being buried alive, a wide-eyed mummy discovered when Papa or some other archaeologist excavated these ruins nearly two thousand years in the future. "Well, I'm not doing my mother any good standing here. Open it."

Tabari forced the corroded hinges with a grating moan. What Lisbeth expected to see behind the door was a dusty, deserted space. Perhaps littered with discarded furniture or cast-off clutter from a palace remodel. Instead, she found a tidy, windowless room warmed by the light of a small oil lamp. Tacked to the stone walls were parchments inked with drawings of mice and crickets playing stick games with balls. Across the room, Mama lay on a tiny bed, moaning in obvious pain. To Lisbeth's left, Laurentius sat hunched over a desk covered in parchments, his clubbed fingers clutched around a stylus like a kindergartner working over a coloring book.

"Laurentius?" Her shocked voice startled him. "What are you doing here?"

The boy's lopsided smile pushed against the panic she'd been feeling, making it suddenly easier for her to breathe. "Thith ith my room." He jumped up, hugged her tight, then turned and shuffled to the bed. "I tol' you my preddy girlfrien' would come. You'll get better like me now." He nudged Magdalena's shoulder. "Wake up, Mama."

25

CHIRPING CRICKETS GAVE LAURENTIUS'S six-by-six-foot cell a calm, homey feel. Lisbeth's shattered nerves refused to transmit the deceptive sensations to her racing heart. Her world had shifted. Nothing about this shocking picture included her. Not the tiny pole bed. Not the cartoons on the wall. Not even the doting half brother eyeing her from his sentinel post at their mother's bedside. Lisbeth didn't care how many hollow explanations Mama offered; if Laurentius was her half brother, then this woman had abandoned one child to love another. A gut punch that changed everything.

She didn't know what to say in response or which language to say it in. Stalling until her breath returned, Lisbeth took the lamp from Tabari. She cupped the clay bowl in trembling hands. Not trusting her unsteady legs, she triaged Mama from a distance. "Your right shoulder looks dislocated," she said in her best Latin, unwilling to give back a single piece of their former life.

"Excellent call." Mama ignored Laurentius and his nervous fussing with her blanket, narrowing her focus directly on Lisbeth, as if they were the only two people in the world. Mother and daughter sitting once again in the shade of Papa's tent, arms wrapped around each other in a fragile, web-thin tie easily snapped. "A reduction ought to set things right, don't you think?"

Could things be set right? She doubted her world would ever be right again. "It'll hurt like hell."

Mama's grimace concurred with Lisbeth's diagnosis. "But once bone and joint are securely in place, the pain will stop immediately, right?"

She knew what Mama was saying was not what she was asking. She didn't give an answer to the possibility of mending their relationship, because there wasn't one. Lisbeth took a shaky step forward. "Manipulating broken pieces is harder than it looks." She gently nudged Laurentius aside, his doughy body tangible proof of Mama's infidelity, a truth that would crush Papa. "Fractures don't always heal like they should."

"Mama?" Laurentius's face puckered in confusion. He reached for their mother. "I don't want you to hurt."

"It's okay, son." Mama stroked his arm with her good hand, and he quickly calmed. "Tabari, can you get Laurentius started on a new drawing? Something happy. Something to celebrate that Lisbeth has finally joined us."

The servant girl settled Laurentius before a small desk fashioned from warped boards and stacked stones. She gave him a clean piece of parchment and moved the inkwell within easy reach of his stubby arms.

He dipped the stylus and held it ready, poised as if he were about to create a great work of art. "Mithe or cricketh, Mama?"

"Surprise us." Mama captured the frayed ends of her divided attention and aimed her laser stare at Lisbeth. "He's a good boy." She spoke in English, as if Laurentius deserved a special cloak of privacy, a protection from the ugly truth that she seemed more than willing to deny the daughter she hadn't seen in decades.

Secrets had been kept far too long. Lisbeth intended to get answers, details to which she and this boy Mama claimed was her half brother were entitled. She clasped her mother's wrist; pain distorted Mama's face. "Without X-rays I'll have to do this the old-fashioned way," Lisbeth said in Latin. Her mother's strong heartbeat pounded against her fingers. "Pulse is good." Lisbeth tested for sensation in her mother's lateral upper arm. Satisfied the axillary nerve had not been damaged, she ran her hand the length of Mama's dangling limb. "Does this hurt?"

Mama bit her lip and nodded.

She flexed Mama's wrist a bit harder than she needed to and immediately felt petty and immature. "What about this?"

"Yes."

"I don't think you have any broken bones." Lisbeth released her mother's hand. "Aspasius did this to you, didn't he?"

Mama reached for her with her good arm. "I couldn't let him find out about you."

Lisbeth's heart twisted. She stepped out of reach. Her mind raced back to that awful night at the tenements. Had Mama silently taken a beating to keep her from running back to the apartment? "Is Laurentius his son?"

Lisbeth could see Mama weighing her answer, searching for words to make things right. "Yes—but I named him after Lawrence." She paused, as if recounting the story would require time to regroup. "Having a little piece of your father with me made the rutting goat easier to bear."

Shards of Mama's shattered image pierced Lisbeth's soul. "Does Aspasius know about Laurentius?"

"No. He thinks he's dead. When Aspasius saw that his heir was . . . different . . . he ordered me to leave that tiny infant on the bluffs for the buzzards to peck apart, but I"—she swallowed hard—"I'd already left one child to fend for herself." Tears seeped from the corners of her eyes; regret broke her voice. "I could not bear to leave another."

The melancholic force of Mama's admission unlocked a memory buried so deep that Lisbeth felt a strange mixture of love and acid bubble forth, a deadly combination disintegrating her ability to stay focused, to stay in the presence of so much pain. Her mind slipped into darkness, tripping along until it stumbled upon the resurrected image of her and Mama sitting on overturned buckets in the shade of the camp tarp, playing doctor like they did every morning before the sun got too hot.

"Here, let me help you," Mama had said as she placed the stetho-scope ear buds in Lisbeth's tiny ear canals. "Listen carefully for the pounding of a drum." Mama slid the bell over her left breast. "Can you hear it?" Lisbeth listened intently, then sadly shook her head. "Breathe in and listen again," Mama had prodded.

Lub-dub. Lub-dub.

"I hear it!"

"Of course you do. You're going to be a great doctor someday." Mama's smile warmed her clear to her toes. "That's the sound of my love for you, a tiny seed growing into a mighty tree. A diagnosis you must never forget."

"Lisbeth?"

The desperation in Mama's pleading snatched Lisbeth from the past. She gently released her hold, unwilling to allow even a flicker of emotion for fear of releasing an uncontrollable torrent. "That slash on your face needs stitches. I'll see what I have for pain." She turned and dug in the bag she'd brought, pretending to search for some kind of analgesic while she blinked back hot tears.

"Laurentius is stronger now," Mama continued. "He had all kinds of problems at first."

"I don't have anything for pain." Lisbeth wiped the moisture from her cheeks, not wanting to hear how easily Mama could recap the details of her half brother's life. "Your injury is several days old. I think the Milch technique will be the easiest on you."

"Do whatever you think best." Mama offered a weak smile. "From the beginning, Laurentius had trouble nursing, respiratory infections, and weak ankles. He eventually managed to crawl, but I didn't know if he'd ever walk. It was all I could do to keep him alive. He could not have withstood the rigors of time travel, even if I could have found the way back. So I've kept him hidden down here."

Lisbeth wondered if her mother had ever worried over *her* health. She longed to tell her of the time she had the croup so bad that Papa had Nigel fly them to Carthage so he could rent a hotel room with a hot shower. But she decided to let it pass, afraid to interrupt the flow of information, facts she'd waited twenty-three years to hear.

"I've had to invent excuses to slip away." Mama's lip quivered.

"This is going to hurt." Lisbeth took Mama's wrist and slowly abducted the affected arm until it stretched out behind her mother's head.

"Owwww." Mama did her best to keep the volume down.

She needed to get her mother out of here. But how? She gently applied longitudinal traction while externally rotating the arm. "Ready?"

"You saved Laurentius's life." The praise, shredded and useless, slipped through her mother's gritted teeth. "Your brother thinks a lot of you."

Mama was once again asking more than she was saying. Seeking more than the formation of a bond between siblings, she sought absolution.

Seized by the sickening feeling that forgiveness was all she had to offer, Lisbeth used two fingers to locate the humeral head. She let her gaze drift to Laurentius. Hunched over a parchment, he was carefully inking a new masterpiece. Her half brother had inherited the best of Mama's qualities. A sense of selflessness, optimism, acceptance. Admirable traits. Yet something about his innocence irritated her to the core.

Laurentius lifted his eyes from his drawing and smiled. "Thith one'th for you, Lithbutt." Drool dripped from the corner of his cracked lips. The boy was a mess, one that would never be righted to perfection. But his hampered mental abilities did not obscure his message. He was happy. No matter his circumstances, he had joy. That was it. The unquenchable joy of Mama and Laurentius angered her the most. They were two united as one against their circumstances.

She wanted to believe their story. Needed to believe that had her mother not been raped and forced to hide a Down's child, she would have come home. Come back to her. But that's not what happened. So where did she fit into the story of a woman who couldn't leave a handicapped child?

A sense of shame enveloped Lisbeth. Laurentius couldn't help who his parents were any more than she could. "I'll be sure and take your art with me." Holding Mama's arm in traction, Lisbeth spoke to Tabari. "Close the door."

"He'd go with you," Mama said.

"Go where?"

"Home."

"I don't know how to go home, Mama." She pushed with all of her strength. "Do you?"

"Noooooo!" Her mother's scream echoed off the stone walls. Laurentius covered his ears and ducked his chin, turning his back so he didn't have to watch. She listened for the clunk of the humeral head sliding into the glenoid fossa, then quickly released the pressure.

When Mama finally relaxed, sweat beaded her brow. She looked lost, like her mind had traveled back to the century from which she'd been separated and the journey through so many memories had taken its toll. "Please," she said, huffing for breath. "I'm begging you. Find the portal, and take your brother away from here."

Lisbeth blinked the sting from her eyes. "What if I can't find it?"

"You must." The pleading tone of a once-proud woman begging tore through Lisbeth's heart. A single tear slid down Mama's cheek. "Laurentius is not vaccinated."

26

CYPRIAN SKIPPED THE MASSAGE tables after his plunge into the frigid political waters that surrounded the man who was supposed to have been his friend. The idea that Rome intended to impose another layer of impossible demands upon the citizens of Carthage left him in no humor for further manipulation. He and Pontius set a straight course for home, striding through the streets crowded with people who had no idea their way of life was in the crosshairs. Aspasius would use the Decian edict to beat the Christians into submission, but his evil would not stop there. The emperor had, in essence, given Aspasius the legal recourse to deal with anyone who dared defy him in any way and in whatever evil manner he saw fit.

He needed to talk over his plan with Caecilianus. The bishop would speak wisdom, but would it be enough to counteract the political double-talk that had soured his belly?

He found his mentor poring over his precious parchments in the quiet of the library, Ruth sitting nearby winding rolls of bandages while the dogs lazed at her feet. Enviable domestic tranquillity, a picture of united spirit and purpose.

"What exactly is a *libellus*?" Ruth asked.

"Written proof of sacrifice." Cyprian paced the length of the library, the dogs darting back and forth in his path.

"One more crafty way for Rome to control the thinking of its subjects." Caecilianus snagged the collar of a passing hound. "Quite similar to their secretive purpose for arena games. The masses think the bloodletting is for their entertainment when, in fact, the games are designed to entice them into a holding tank, a place to keep tabs on them, to influence their thinking, to keep the thirst for blood ever before them. How else can Rome justify its continual quest for more and more territory if their people became squeamish over the loss of human lives?" He absently patted the dog's broad head. "Lambs led to slaughter."

"Won't the issuance of such certificates increase the government's administrative responsibilities?" Ruth snapped her fingers, and the hound Caecilianus could not reach heeled at her feet. "Cost Rome more in the long run?"

"She has a point, Cyprian." Caecilianus stroked the dog's long snout. "Signed parchments can hardly guarantee the compliance of Roman subjects."

"For the right price, anything can be bought," Cyprian said.

"Not everything." Ruth sat forward. "Surely the emperor does not think he can purchase peace of mind."

"That is exactly what he hopes to secure," Cyprian exclaimed. "Decius fears Rome's inability to stop an assault on its ever-expanding borders. The emperor is desperate to summon divine protection." He plopped upon the chair opposite the desk. "And Aspasius is desperate to prolong his term. That greedy slug intends to capitalize upon the emperor's determination to maintain Rome's borders. Mark my words, our proconsul will wield this little bone of opportunity like Nero's torch. In the name of smoking out who supports the throne and who does not, he'll set fire to every freedom we hold dear." Cyprian glanced at the mallet bruises on his shins. "Our unwillingness to bow to anyone other than the one God will be declared treason."

"What are you suggesting?" Caecilianus asked.

"New aqueducts must reach the tenements. New customs must reign." Cyprian tried to assess the impact of his words upon his mentor. "New blood must infuse the Senate. Old rulers and their unreasonable edicts must be removed."

"Then we're back to where we started." Caecilianus rested his chin upon his clasped hands. "Finding you a wife."

"But who? Cyprian has already knocked on every viable door. I don't think we can outlast the women who wait to see if his sores materialize." Ruth added her bandages to the wads in the basket. "Besides, the wrong woman could do more harm than good."

"I'll do it." The voice intruding upon their private conversation was winded but sure.

Cyprian turned to see his missing slave standing in the doorway; she was disheveled and her face was as white as his toga.

"Lisbeth, your hair!" Ruth leapt from her chair and ran to Lisbeth. "You're covered in cobwebs."

Cyprian eyed his missing slave, too stunned at her voluntary return to move. "Where have you been?" A runaway's willing return was unheard of. Something wasn't right.

"To the healer."

"You went to the palace?" Cyprian sprang from his chair and grabbed her arm. "Why on earth would you risk something so foolish?"

"She was hurt." Lisbeth winced at his hold. "Only Tabari knows I was there."

"Servants talk."

Ruth charged between them, her arms spread out as if he intended to strike this young woman. "I said she could go, Cyprian."

"You? Why?" He sidestepped Ruth. "Why would you risk the welfare of everyone in my house?"

Lisbeth lifted her chin, a storm brewing in those sea-green

eyes. "After all the healer's done for you and your kind, you would let her suffer?"

"Of course not." He stiffened. "But Magdalena knew the risk of getting involved in this movement. Her misfortune does not excuse *your* disappearance. You left without *my* permission or protection."

Her stare cut him to the quick, then bounced from him to Ruth and back to him. "Would you have let me go?"

"No."

"Then you have your answer."

"I could have you flogged and shackled."

She straightened her shoulders, drawing herself up to a height that brought her full lips within easy reach of his. "Or you could marry me and put that monster out of business."

27

SILENCE PUNCTUATED THE IMPASSE of their predicament. Cyprian had no reason to trust her, and Lisbeth had no one else to trust. Her plan sounded crazier with her captor's restatement of the high points, but so far neither Cyprian nor his aged mentor had provided a better option. If she didn't stop the man torturing her family, no one would.

"Let me see if I have this straight." Cyprian rubbed his temples. "*You* are Magdalena's daughter?" Disbelief weighted every word of his question. Really, she couldn't blame him. If she hadn't pinched herself black and blue, she'd swear the whole impossible tale was nothing more than a nightmare.

Lisbeth worked to keep her voice steady. "You need a wife, and I need someone who'll help me get my mother away from Aspasius."

"And what of Laurentius?"

"He's my half brother. I won't leave him behind."

"How can that be?"

His refusal to believe a word she said left her no choice. "Aspasius raped my mother."

"What the proconsul does with his slaves is his business."

"You've got to be kidding me." She was wrong to think the man who bought her off the slave block would understand. "Help me out here, Ruth. I can't leave my mother in that situation."

Ruth floated between them in that regal way of hers that commanded control of a situation. "The marriage would put rumors of your nasty malady to rest, Cyprian."

A new round of skepticism scrunched Cyprian's handsome features. "My wife must make public appearances." He circled Lisbeth, but his agitation was aimed at Ruth. "Aspasius has seen her. He'll recognize her as the slave I stole out from under him the first time she makes an official appearance at the arena. And no matter what we think of the games, I must rub elbows in the royal arena box if I'm going to win this election."

"I was so banged up," Lisbeth countered, "I doubt he'd remember a slave girl he met only briefly."

"Aspasius forgets and forgives nothing." Cyprian spit his decision with finality: "I'll not risk such foolishness."

"We could make her over," Ruth offered. "Dye her hair. Rim her eyes with kohl. Dress her in silks. Veil part of her face. She does clean up remarkably well, remember?"

Cyprian's eyes bore into Lisbeth's, sending a fiery jolt straight through her. "No." From the discomfort on his face, he'd felt the spark that had passed between them the first time he saw her dressed as a lady, the night he'd dragged her into the church service. He took a step back, as if placing himself in that compromising position again didn't appeal to him any more than it suited her. "It's too risky."

"We don't have to have a real marriage," Lisbeth stammered. "I help you get elected, and you use the law to get my family away from Aspasius. We both get what we want, and then we go our merry ways."

"Divorce? Absolutely not." The muscle in his jaw tensed. "Fortunately, it's against Roman law for patricians and slaves to marry. And you are going nowhere."

"What if we had her liberated?" Caecilianus fiddled with a corner of parchment. "That's what you've eventually done for the other slaves you've acquired."

"I free them once they can be trusted." He glared at Lisbeth. "Look at her. She finds trouble wherever she goes."

"We'd need a magistrate to say the words over her, dear," Ruth interjected as if she'd not heard a word of Cyprian's dire predictions. "Unfortunately, all the officials in this province are tucked safely inside the belt of Aspasius. Not a one of them will help us this time."

Cyprian raked his curls. "Marrying a freedman slave offers no benefits. I need political connections if I'm to be elected. I need a life partner. The best I could hope to do without arousing suspicions about Lisbeth's origins would be to try passing her off as a lesser-known tradesman's daughter."

"Tradesmen can become quite wealthy, and wealth opens many doors." Ruth crossed her arms. She wasn't letting him off the hook easily, which made Lisbeth admire her even more. "Were you not strutting about just moments ago declaring the need for a wife? Aspasius's plot against you has already ended your chances with the Roman women of standing in Carthage. It seems to me that your only option is to marry a mysterious foreign woman." The thump of the dogs' tails upon the rug echoed in the silence. "Never have I seen the Lord answer a prayer so quickly and thoroughly. If God can provide a wife, he can see to your election."

Lisbeth didn't particularly like being considered a provision sent from God, but her opportunity to save her mother was slipping away too fast to argue religious points. "If you don't do this, Aspasius will have the liberty to do as he pleases to your little church."

"And if I do"—Cyprian eyed her coolly—"I will have the liberty to do as I please with you."

28

A S RUTH LED HIS future bride from the library, Cyprian busied himself with coaxing the knots from his belly. Most men
in his position would have jumped at the opportunity to wed such
a beauty. People marry for all sorts of reasons. Perhaps God would
count saving the church from further destruction an acceptable argument for yoking himself to an unbeliever.

Yet, here he was, shamefully hedging despite Ruth's indisputable evidence that Lisbeth of Dallas was indeed God's gift dropped
into his lap. If God had called him to save his people by engaging in
a full-on war, he would have dusted off his sparring sword and
bought a suit of armor. Buying a wedding ring was a battle he
lacked the preparation to fight.

"Take a good swig of this." Caecilianus offered him a glass of
wine. "It will knock the green from your complexion."

Cyprian let the weight of the glass anchor his roiling emotions. "Do you see another way, Bishop?"

"Sometimes God's will is not easily discerned, my boy, but
when it is . . ."

Cyprian sighed. "We must act." He took a sip, the burn sliding
into the turmoil. "Aspasius has made it clear that he has no love for
Christians. This latest edict will make his mistreatment of us legal.
And he has tarnished my name on every front."

"Sadly, my boy, the law cannot make men upright. Only grace can truly change hearts and behaviors." Caecilianus poured himself a cup of the blood-red liquid. "So tell me, do you think you can learn to love her?"

"Love her?" Cyprian choked, spraying wine everywhere. "I don't even know her. Nor do I want to. She is a pagan."

"As were you less than a year ago." Caecilianus made his way behind Cyprian's desk. "I've not detected any vulgar vices in her." He mopped wine droplets from his parchments, then lowered his lanky frame into the seat he'd made his own. "In fact, she's been remarkably helpful, considering her protestations against her situation. Virtuous enough to pass the most diligent patrician test, I'd say."

"She's caused a fight in my home, escaped at her first opportunity, and now proposes that I help her relieve the proconsul of his bed partner."

"Perhaps virtuous is stretching it a bit." The old bishop took a long, slow sip of wine that rippled over his rather large Adam's apple. He wiped wine from his lips. "There's something you should know."

Doubtful anything connected to this woman would surprise him, Cyprian pinched the bridge of his nose. "That she has bewitched us all?"

"No." Caecilianus gazed over his cup. "That your future wife has possibly brought the tenement sickness into your home."

Cyprian leaned forward. "What are you talking about?"

"Remember our dear brother Numidicus?"

The name sounded familiar, and from the fondness displayed on Caecilianus's face, Numidicus was a believer, one Cyprian was expected to know. He had tried to learn the names of the congregants that met in his home, but frankly, he'd been brought up believing that all plebeians were the same. That he'd yet to make much progress in crossing over that very well-defined line had not escaped the old bishop's watchful eye.

Cyprian took a stab at identifying the subject of Caecilianus's concern. "The quarry worker who vocalized his concerns at our last gathering?"

"Yes, impudent, outspoken Numidicus." The affection on Caecilianus's face melted into sadness. "Our dear brother and his young wife are dead."

"How?"

"Fever."

"I'm sorry." Cyprian had seen the bodies beginning to stack up when he searched the tenement streets for Lisbeth. Until now, the dead had only been nameless faces, easier to ignore. He knew he'd not completely discarded his Roman way of thinking, but how could he have maintained such a cold and callous disregard? No wonder Caecilianus would not rest until his protégé no longer went through life as an aloof patrician. "I understand the church will take this news hard, maybe even need some reassurances that we're doing everything we can to contain the spread, but—"

"Your future wife brought their orphaned child here."

"What? How did Lisbeth—"

"She was in the projects after all."

Realization punched Cyprian's gut. "She's been exposed to the sickness?"

Caecilianus's long face turned grave, the wrinkles deepening as he continued. "When Lisbeth slipped away from Ruth, she forfeited her escape plans to render aid to Numidicus. A kind thing to do, don't you agree?" His eyes brightened as if this bit of good somehow balanced the scales. "It was at the tenements that Lisbeth met up with her mother."

"The healer could have the fever, too?" Cyprian couldn't let himself imagine facing the persecution the new edict would bring without the help of the healer. Who would piece together those torn limb from limb in the arena or patch up those stoned in the square? "The church must pray for the healer and do what it can to raise the child."

"I agree, but"—Caecilianus cleared his throat—"Junia has the fever."

Cyprian's quickened heartbeat echoed the fear he heard in Caecilianus's voice. "God, please, not the child." If this sickness truly was the result of Rome's angry gods, Aspasius would see to it that Christians shouldered the brunt of the blame. Even a healthy healer could not stop the flow of blood. "My intended did the right thing to bring the child here."

"I was hoping you'd say that." Pleasure in his voice went a long way in assuring Cyprian that God had the future in his hands, even the horrible course of this plague. The old bishop rested his chin upon his steeped fingers, his hooded gaze fixed squarely upon Cyprian. "So I ask again, can you learn to love a woman who seems to have a heart of gold but lacks a dowry, a notable position, and a true grasp of our ways?"

"I don't need her money."

"You avoid the question, my friend."

"I don't need a real wife, and I won't foolishly give away my heart to win this election. I can't believe you're asking me to join myself to a pagan who plans on going her 'merry way' once she has what she wants."

Caecilianus directed Cyprian to sit. "Have I told you about Hosea?"

"The ancient prophet called to marry a harlot?"

Caecilianus nodded. "Those were dark days for God's people. An uncommon faith was required for their survival." The old bishop's face sobered. "Cyprian, dark days are upon us again." He paused, allowing the weight of his words to sink in. "Sometimes the ways of the Lord are not our ways. All we can do is walk through the doors he opens."

"And how did it end for this prophet and his pagan wife?"

"They had three children." Caecilianus smiled. "And God healed his people." The dogs whined for the bishop's attention. He stroked their heads. "Sharing your love in this life is the only way you'll win in the next, my boy."

Healing for Carthage. Was that not what he wanted?

Cyprian's mind drifted to the way Ruth and Caecilianus looked at each other, the way they worked side by side for the betterment of the kingdom, and the way they joined hands for prayer. God forgive him, but a love like his friends possessed was what he wanted. "What if she never becomes a believer?"

"Leave Lisbeth's heart up to God. He knows what he's doing."

CYPRIAN STOOD before the empty shrine cupboard in his deserted atrium. Moonlight filtered through the ceiling skylight, casting a silvery glow on the empty pedestal where the household god had presided over his family's comings and goings for years. All that remained of Lars were the sooty outlines of two tiny feet perched above the fire bowl. How many grain offerings had he and his father burned before the highly revered bronze statue? How many countless prayers were lifted before this tiny throne? His father claimed his household had prospered under the reign of that cherished little idol. They'd fought over its removal. Their last conversation had been brutal.

Should he have allowed the removal of the last ties to his upbringing? Or had his decision put those he loved at risk? Made them vulnerable as he was feeling? Was this one God of the old bishop big enough to handle the horrors Cyprian felt were sure to come?

When Caecilianus first shared the story of the Nazarene carpenter, a martyr raised from the dead, Cyprian had found the teachings impossible to believe. But something about a god who walked among men spoke to his loneliness. Day after day he had returned to Caecilianus's rug shop, hungry for the tales of the god-man called Jesus.

He would have walked away, counted the whole experience as a pleasant waste of time, had the old bishop not presented hard evidence, an original copy of the writings of Luke. A record of eyewitness testimonies supporting the resurrection of the one God. Legal proof, difficult to dispute, even in a court of law.

Cyprian traced the blackened footprints where once the eternal flames had burned. Would he have acted so rashly had he known his renunciation and removal of the gods in the cupboard would kill his father in two short days? Despite Caecilianus's teachings on forgiveness, he was glad to be out from under the constant scrutiny of a man so difficult to love. But he had only himself to blame that the grief of his father's loss had sent his dear, sweet mother to an early grave.

Now the responsibility for the health and prosperity of the vast fortune he'd inherited was his duty. He felt the burden every time he passed through the villa's heavy wooden doors. At the very least, taking a wife would give him sons, heirs who would keep his estate from becoming the property of Rome.

The slave girl seemed genuine enough in her offer to help, but so far she'd proven herself anything but trustworthy. If a barbarian with a wicked tongue and eyes that could turn a man's heart to stone was God's will for him, why did he feel like a man on the verge of making another tragic mistake? Had Hosea felt the same sense of impending doom before he took Gomer as his wife?

He closed the door to the cupboard and sought a quiet place to pray.

29

LISBETH REPLAYED CYPRIAN'S VEHEMENT reaction to her marriage offer. His expert about-face was not for her benefit. He'd conceded only to placate Ruth and Caecilianus. Cyprian may have conjured an agreeable smile, but she hadn't missed the anger those piercing blue eyes had directed her way.

Two could play his game. But only one could win. Staying one step ahead of him would require finesse and far more sleep than she'd managed to squeeze in these past few days. But freeing her mother and brother had relegated her needs to low-priority status.

Lisbeth waved off Ruth's offer of cheese and wine and rushed to the shed to check on Junia. The girl's bright eyes and renewed appetite supported Ruth's claims that the child was on the mend. Maybe if she organized proper quarantines and serious supportive care others could be saved from the fever as well. With just a little training, Ruth would be a great charge nurse, Naomi the perfect aide, and this house the perfect hospital.

The idea of making a difference, grand and unrealistic as it seemed, gave her a strange tingle of pleasure. Saving not only her mother and brother, but also a group of people she was beginning to love. An admirable mission. One that she prayed would make up for her colossal failure to save Abra.

"I want my mama." Junia's lip quivered.

"I know you do, sweetheart." Lisbeth pulled the adorable little waif into her lap. She felt heavier even though she'd only had access to an abundant supply of nutritious food for a couple of days. "I know she'd want you to get better first."

"Where is she?" Junia asked. "Where's my daddy?"

Lisbeth looked to Ruth, unable to get the words past the lump in her throat.

"They're with Jesus, Junia." Ruth offered the girl a mug of watered wine. "She wants you to live with us now."

"I want to go home."

"I know you do, baby. But you can't." All Lisbeth could do was hold her while she cried.

After Junia's racking sobs subsided, she pulled away and looked at Lisbeth. "I'll live with you." She laid her head on Lisbeth's shoulder and brought her thumb to her mouth.

Lisbeth's heart did a weird little flutter. She put her arms around the child and hugged her close. Doing what had to be done had not been easy. For the first time it occurred to Lisbeth that perhaps Mama's heart had broken when she did what she had to do.

Craig had implied on several occasions that she'd built a wall around her emotions, one that didn't allow anyone to get close. Not even him. He said she needed to do whatever it took to get over the hurt of her mother's leaving. If he thought for one moment her little indigent-care program and rescue operation was the ticket to her well-being, he'd be the first to declare this mock marriage a necessary means to an end . . . at least that's how she'd justify marrying a third-century lawyer when she returned to her twenty-first-century doctor.

Lisbeth tucked Junia into bed. As she was leaving the shed, she caught a glimpse of her dirty face in the darkened window glass. After she freshened up, she'd find Cyprian and outline the specifics of their arrangement, including reiterating one more time that this was not to be a real marriage. After she returned to Dallas, he'd be free to marry the kind of woman he deserved. One who would take up his fight for religious freedom.

She found Cyprian standing at the railing, staring out at the water and brooding silently. Moonlight silhouetted the contours of his impressive build. If she compared him to Craig, she'd lose her nerve.

Careful not to allow the click of her sandals on the tile to alert him, she tiptoed to Cyprian's side and slipped in close, so close she could feel the heat of their earlier confrontation radiating off of his bronzed flesh.

"Now what do you want?" He kept his gaze on the magnificent sight of nearly two hundred Roman warships ported inside the protection of the donut-shaped harbor. "Perhaps you'd like me to drag Aspasius into the arena for a duel, or better yet, just ask him to hand over your family. I'm sure he'd happily comply once I point out your impossible circumstances."

"If you asked nicely, I'm sure the proconsul would be happy to oblige your request, seeing as how you two are such good friends." Ignoring his obvious irritation at her sarcasm, she searched for a neutral direction to steer the conversation. "It's beautiful."

"What?"

"The harbor." Twinkling ship lights bobbed within the stone circle. "So different than I remember it, like a city I've never seen before."

"Remember?" He turned, his eyes narrowed. "You've been here before?"

Salt and sea mingled on the breeze. "Lots of times." Lisbeth clasped the railing and leaned out as far as she dared over the fifty-foot drop to the sea. "My parents brought me to Carthage when we needed supplies or when we furloughed at my grandfather's house between digs. Mama grew up not far from here." She pointed in the direction she guessed Jiddo's house might have been built nearly a thousand years later, her arm brushing against his as she did. "My grandfather is . . . was . . . will be a world-renowned heart surgeon." She cut a sideways glance to see if he'd caught her near misstep and was relieved to find him mouthing some of her strange words.

"Digs?"

"You know, assignments." She inhaled deeply, allowing the waves crashing against the stones to carry her back to happier days. Her family relaxing in Carthage. Strolling on the beach or through the ruins. Papa pointing out facts and structures from the past, Mama bringing him back to the present with her smile. "Sometimes we had to wait six months to a year for Papa's funding to come in."

"Were these *assignments* political in nature?"

"Yes . . . and no. Acquiring governmental permission to excavate in some countries often requires more effort than raising money."

"So you understand politics? When to speak and when to keep silent?"

"I'm not good at it."

"Obviously. Or you would have chosen to tell me about the feverish child stashed in my shed."

"Sorry about that. But I couldn't leave her." Lisbeth felt her cheeks heat under his scrutiny. "I don't know how much leverage this information will give you in this little election you intend to win, but if drastic measures aren't taken immediately, the sickness in the slum district will spread. Without proper vaccinations, many will die."

Cyprian's eyes bored deeply into hers. "Who are you?"

"Lisbeth . . . of Dallas."

"I know who you claim to be, but I want to know who you really are. Where did you come from? If you're from around here, how did you and your mother become separated? Why were you not sold with Magdalena?"

"What difference does it make?"

"These words you use. *Digs. Excavate. Vaccinations.*" Cyprian turned his face back to the sea, as if the answers he sought lurked beneath the glittering waves. "You speak of things that make no sense. As if you come from another world. Who are you?"

"A doctor." The word rolled off her tongue with surprising ease. "Like my mother." Lisbeth gripped the railing, wanting to tell him everything. Spill the whole crazy story. But how could she explain the time-travel thing when she didn't understand it completely herself? "So, what next?"

The muscle in his jaw tensed. "We attend the arena games, announce our engagement, and pray Aspasius will not smell the stink on our story."

"I'll tell you the rest of my story someday."

He held up his hands. "I know enough to know you cannot be trusted." Cyprian started toward the house and stopped. "The child will be safe here."

The flicker of compassion in his eyes disarmed her. "Thank you."

"Rest," he said. "The next few days will change our lives."

"I'm counting on it."

AWAKENED WITH the rise of the sun, Lisbeth stood naked before the bathroom mirror. Ruth circled, eyeing her with the same triaging gaze Cyprian had used upon her in the moonlight.

"Your first public appearance as Cyprian's future wife must be believable." She fingered the chunk of amethyst resting in the suprasternal notch of her neck. "No one can suspect that the most respected advocate in Carthage plans to marry a slave. Everything about you must change. Including the ring upon your finger." Ruth held out her hand. She'd never asked about Craig's engagement ring, and it was a good thing because Lisbeth didn't know exactly what she would say. She slipped it off and dropped the diamond into Ruth's palm.

Lisbeth eyed the pile of beauty products, grooming tools, and clothing spread around the large bath. Hospital scrubs, no makeup, and hair pulled into a ponytail usually worked for her. That last round of playing dress-up with Ruth had been a nightmare experience. "Why can't I just wear a veil over my whole face?"

"I've thought about that, but obvious beauty should silence any inquiries into your pedigree." Ruth clapped her hands, and within seconds, a team of servants closed in. "Dunk her."

Lisbeth gripped the tiled edge of the tub as Naomi dragged a strigil over the length of both arms, sanding away the top layer of her skin with each swipe. "I've seen surgical nurses who were not anywhere near this thorough in preparing patients for the OR."

"Whining does not become a lady." Ruth herded her from the hot water, insisting she plunge into the frigid cooling tub. Even though the day was already warm, Lisbeth could only tolerate the icy water for a few minutes. She scrambled out, and Ruth pointed to the massage table. Shivering, Lisbeth watched Naomi pour a puddle of golden oil into her palm.

"You must recline, my lady."

Lisbeth climbed aboard the marble slab. For the next thirty minutes, Naomi slathered floral-scented lotion neck to toe in vigorous, relaxing strokes. Slippery as a seal, it took all the concentration Lisbeth could muster to slither off the table somewhat gracefully and follow Ruth to the styling chair.

After enduring several applications of some kind of plant-based hair dye that smelled of damp clay, Lisbeth bolted for the door. Ruth cut her off, sent her back to the styling chair, and continued the torture. A towering hair arrangement was held in place by ivory combs jammed into Lisbeth's scalp. The tedious application of makeup required the use of stiff little brushes that felt more like acupuncture needles. But it was the long list of instructions Ruth shared during the pleating and repleating of the gossamer folds of her gown that nearly sent Lisbeth in search of Cyprian to renounce her foolish marriage offer.

"This fabric must have cost as much as a night's stay in a specialty hospital." Lisbeth sagged under the weight.

Ruth let the comment go and continued her lecture. "When Cyprian gives you the signal, you must put your hand in his to announce your engagement to everyone gathered in Aspasius's box."

"Me? I don't do well speaking to crowds."

She clicked the clasp on the brooch at Lisbeth's shoulder. "You will today."

By the time the team stepped back to admire their work, the morning sun had slipped through the window blinds.

"Perfect," Ruth declared. "No one will think you anything less than royalty. Should Aspasius claim that Cyprian married a servant, his supporters will take one look at you and doubt his sanity." Ruth smiled. "Go ahead. Turn around."

Lisbeth moved toward the mirror, her feet unsteady in the two-inch cork heels. "My hair is *red*."

"More of a russet really," Ruth corrected. "More becoming than blond would have been with those stunning emerald eyes of yours, don't you think?"

"I liked my old hair." Bracelets of pounded gold jangled as Lisbeth lifted her hand to touch the weighty dangles clipped to her ears. Heavy lines of kohl rimmed her eyelids, changing the shape of her eyes from round to more of an Asian almond shape. "*I* don't even recognize me." A smile slid across her deep red lips. She fastened a shimmery veil beneath her eyes. "Aspasius won't know what hit him."

30

THE LITTER TRANSPORTING LISBETH, Cyprian, and Pontius arrived at the large sports complex that claimed the western outskirts of the city. The scale and ingenuity of the newly constructed arena dwarfed Lisbeth's memories of the deserted and crumbling ruins she and Papa had explored on every supply run. According to Papa's history lessons, Rome built these colossal structures to intimidate their conquered provinces, to remind them of the obligations that accompany living in the shadow of greatness.

Cyprian lifted Lisbeth from the perfectly arranged cushions. "Ruth did a remarkable job. If you could guard that tongue of yours, even I wouldn't recognize you."

Lisbeth pondered his backhanded compliment and took it more as a warning than a rebuke as a uniformed escort whisked them and Cyprian's sidekick, Pontius, past the long line that snaked the entire stone circumference.

The escort cleared their passage through the vendors hawking everything from jugs of wine to a quick peek beneath the scanty tunics of women tethered to stakes in the ground. Lisbeth started for the hollow-eyed girls, intent to set them free, when Cyprian reeled her in. She held her tongue and followed him through a side door recessed beneath one of the many high, stone arches. They climbed the marble stairs reserved for dignitaries and walked through a system of cool hallways lit by torches stuck in metal claws. A heavy brocade curtain was parted, and blinding sunlight streamed through the giant keyhole archway.

Shielding her eyes against the brightness, Lisbeth put her other hand through the crook of Cyprian's arm, grateful for steady and firm muscle beneath her touch. "Ready?"

"God be with us," he whispered, then clasped his hand over hers, sending a jolt of electricity through Lisbeth's body. "Pontius, guard our backs."

"Count on it, my lord," the secretary confirmed with a nod.

Arm in arm, Lisbeth and Cyprian emerged onto a balcony landing. From this premium vantage point, they had a full view of the arena's multitiered interior. Lisbeth let her gaze roam over the mammoth venue. Excitement hung in the dusty air. All around the stone stadium, people haggled over seats, vying for the shade of the massive retractable roof awning sliding into place via a series of ropes and pulleys manned by sweating slaves. Unlike some of the professional sports arenas she'd visited in Dallas, there wasn't a blind spot or bad seat in the house.

The high-rent box seats rimmed the first level and were packed with men and women draped in expensive silks. Servants fanned rich patrons with large ostrich plumes or struggled under large golden trays heaped with refreshments. Even the cheap seats were fast filling up; soon it would be standing room only all around the nosebleed section.

"There must be twenty thousand people here." Heat radiated from the touch of Cyprian's hand on the small of her back.

"More like forty." He gave their engraved leather tickets to the armored man guarding the entrance. "This is our box."

Lisbeth eyed the crowded booth. On a raised platform at the back of the box, Aspasius roosted on a golden, throne-like chair, a little king of his own making. To her great relief, Mama sat beside him. Her pale face was framed by a green veil draped over her hair. Her arm hung limp in a sling of a matching fabric. Lisbeth could tell from the way Mama blinked back tears that she'd immediately recognized her. So much for Ruth's extreme makeover.

Lisbeth stepped back, running into Cyprian's unmovable form. "Maybe this whole thing was a bad idea," she said between the gritted teeth of a fake smile.

"Too late for second thoughts." Cyprian nudged her forward. "Let the games begin."

If it weren't for the possibility that contracting the measles would kill her brother and most likely Aspasius would eventually kill Mama, she wouldn't have launched this charade, let alone ever put herself within easy reach of the man who'd raped her mother. The proconsul lifted his chin in greeting.

"Let's not keep the evil brute waiting," Lisbeth said without moving her lips. She stepped into the box. Taking a moment to scan the area for three empty seats, she became fully aware of Cyprian's breath upon her neck and the need to be as inconspicuous as possible. "Are those seats taken?" she asked a plump man spitting grape seeds into a golden chalice.

The man aimed a seed at her feet and elbowed the knobby-kneed man lounging in the next seat. Ignoring her question, he said, "Who's the beauty, Cyprian?"

The thin man rose and gave a little bow in Lisbeth's direction. "I believe Cyprian took my advice."

"That I did, dear Sergy," Cyprian said, a smile making his patrician face even more handsome in the morning sun. "May I present my distant cousin, Lisbeth of Dallas."

"Dallas?" Sergy's eyes narrowed. "A province I'm not familiar with."

"The desert hinterlands," Cyprian explained with the ease of a seasoned politician.

"If only I'd had such a cousin." The bony man's red-rimmed eyes slithered over Lisbeth's body. "Perhaps I'll stay for the wedding and help you carry your prize to the bridal chamber."

"I'll not risk being thrown over for you." Cyprian had easily smoothed her entry into the upper crust with a quick comeback that did not surprise her, but his hearty laugh was an ability he'd been keeping secret. "Come, my darling. Sergia was quite the ladies' man before the lovely Bellona hung a noose about his scrawny neck. Nevertheless, I'm not certain his reformation is complete." He urged her on. "Let me seat you a safe distance from my competition."

Aspasius waved them toward him, indicating they should join him and Mama on the raised seating. Standing behind the proconsul was a man with a wax tablet in hand and stylus poised, prepared for the careful keeping of kills in the arena, no doubt. Hopefully, she would not be added to his tally by day's end.

Feeling claustrophobic and desperate for air, Lisbeth inched past Cyprian's friends. Sweat beaded on Sergia's forehead, and a feverish blush pinked his cheeks. Although the day was exceptionally warm, she couldn't help but wonder if he was ill. She gave him one last look. Probably just an overheated flush. She had to get a handle on her jumpy nerves.

Lisbeth eyeballed the arena. Armored soldiers guarded each of the eighty exits. Fear of exposing her identity before she accomplished her mission was the only thing anchoring her to this dreadful spot. Lisbeth gathered her skirts and climbed the steps, averting her eyes from Mama in case the terror ripping through her entire body somehow escaped her kohl eyeliner. The cork heels and uneven stones made her ascent clumsy. Twice she nearly landed on her face. So much for trying to pass herself off as a lady. She was a sow's ear in a silk purse, as Nigel used to say.

Aspasius shielded his eyes. "Careful, my dear." His unnerving gaze remained fixed upon her as he spoke to Cyprian. "Pray tell, wherever did you find the enchanting trinket dangling on your arm, old friend?"

"She is the match my father made for me years ago, the daughter of my wealthy cousin who controls the desert passage through the Cave of the Swimmers."

Lisbeth's legs buckled. Mama gasped.

"Are you well, my love?" Cyprian's arm quickly wrapped her waist. "Pontius, fetch a cup of wine."

What did Cyprian know about her cave? She waved off the refreshments. "It's just the heat."

"A desert flower that wilts in the heat." Aspasius resumed the same beady-eyed examination she'd suffered at the slave block. Something in his gaze seemed to border on recognition. "This one's far too fragile for such a harsh life."

"Oh, but I'm not." Lisbeth flinched at Cyprian's tightened grip about her middle. "I mean, the desert has taught me to hold my own, sir."

"Fragile, yet hearty." Aspasius held out his hand, and immediately a jeweled chalice was placed within his grasp. "You remind me of someone." He glanced keenly from her to Mama. "Does she remind you of someone, Magdalena?"

"Not anyone of recent memory, my lord." Mama raised her fan to cover her trembling lips, but her eyes telegraphed a clear message of warning. "Are you looking forward to the games, my lady?"

Screams of the big cats pacing the cages below the arena shredded the air. Papa's history lessons had included tales of aristocrats who educated their children by dragging them to the games. Someone qualified to marry a man like Cyprian would no doubt have many arena experiences to her credit, even if she came from a less civilized region. She mustn't fail in this answer. She must compose herself. Act natural . . . as any twenty-first-century woman would if she were caught in the third century.

Lisbeth anchored her gaze in her mother's and felt a surge of confidence. "I'm eager to experience all the wonders of Carthage, but even more excited to share our good news."

"News?" Mama's voice carried the fear Lisbeth had seen on her face.

Aspasius leaned forward. "What news?"

Cyprian pulled her tight against him. "It can wait until the intermission, my love."

"But I'm just so anxious to share our plans." She'd irritated him by forcing him to accept her offer of marriage, pushed him beyond what his high moral ground normally tolerated, but Cyprian wouldn't expose her. Truth be told, he and his little band of followers needed this deception to work as badly as she did. She would express her appreciation by imitating his strange customs. She searched for Cyprian's hand, then intertwined her fingers with his. "Please, my love. May I?"

His palm was damp in hers, but he did not withdraw. "What makes you happy makes me happy."

Lisbeth summoned her best smile. Now that she had the floor, she had no choice but to claim it, to appear more comfortable than she felt with forty thousand pairs of eyes staring at her. She announced over the din, "I have agreed to become the bride of the honorable Cyprianus Thascius at the next full moon."

All ears within hearing turned toward her. The slaves paused midservice. Even the caged cats ceased their roaring.

Mama lowered her fan. "That's less than a week from today."

"Show us the ring," Aspasius demanded.

"My jeweler is designing something special. Something worthy of a woman so . . . beautiful." Cyprian lifted their clasped hands to his lips. "Something that ensures Lisbeth of Dallas will always be mine."

Lisbeth pecked his cheek with a light kiss, grateful for Ruth's foresight to confiscate Craig's ring and spare their ruse another complication. "Oh, but I've been yours from the start."

IF MARRYING well equaled success in public life, Cyprian felt certain Lisbeth's disastrous introduction into the patrician world had just sealed his doom. She'd blurted out information at inappropriate times, moved about as if she wore a bedsheet, and displayed a surprisingly faint constitution at the mention of some faraway cave. Courtship was a heartless business under the best of circumstances. This knot in the pit of his stomach testified to his failure to fully weigh the pros and cons of trying to pull off a politically advantageous marriage with someone ill prepared for the task. A mistake he must quickly rectify before she ruined them both.

"Come, my love, we mustn't keep the proconsul from his official duties," Cyprian said, threading his arm around his intended's thin waist to usher her from the royal dais, but she seemed to have grown roots. Planted and stubborn, with the same determined manner she'd exhibited while attending the sick boys.

"Tell of when you first set eyes on this beauty." A dubious smirk curled Aspasius's lips. "I've time to hear of your first meeting before the start trumpets."

"Our meeting?" The stink of Felicissimus's little slave cell rose in Cyprian's memory, a stench he feared Aspasius's overheightened senses might catch wind of should he be allowed to get too close to Lisbeth. "Well, I . . ."

Lisbeth squeezed his hand. "He was on a scouting mission, a new venture to increase his vast fortune. He bravely rode into my father's camp like he owned the desert." If she felt the fear gripping his belly, her concern did not mar her confident eyes. "A bronzed god who took my breath." Her mastery of courtroom theatrics called his into question.

"Yes, and then I . . ." He looked to her, and she smiled a pleased-with-herself little grin he could see through her gauzy half veil. For the first time in his life, words had failed him. "I saw . . . uh . . ."

"He saw me directing my maid at the cooking fire," she continued, lifting a conspiratorial brow, as if to say keep up or shut up. "My hair a mess from the constant desert winds." Lisbeth's eyes twinkled. She relished jumping in to save him, humiliating him in front of the leading citizens of Carthage. "When he kindly asked me to turn over the entire stack of our freshly fried pitas, his genteel manner caused me to do so without a word of complaint."

The confident tilt of her chin made him very aware of the soft fullness of her lips. His sense of heightened danger ignited into a firestorm, along with his need to slap her and protect her at the same time. Cyprian straightened and found his voice, determined he was more than capable of playing along. "I remember the encounter a bit differently. She spit fire at my trading party, declaring us barbarians." He turned to face her. "But my heart was no longer my own. She had stolen it."

"Oh?" She pulled him close, her sweet floral scent intoxicating and alarming. "And so you bought me to get your heart back?"

"Little good it did me." He brought his lips close to hers and dropped his voice. "My heart still belongs to you and only you."

They stood, face to face, eyes locked. Around them, the arena was a beehive of random conversations. Through the clamor Cyprian could hear rakes scratching lines in the arena sand, a smoothing out of all the rough patches, an evening of the playing field. Within a breath, the anxious sounds of the arena vanished. All that remained, all that mattered, was the two of them. Slave and master bound by a fraud, quickened breaths sweeping him into chaos.

"So this is a marriage of *coemptio*?" Aspasius's verbal spear of contempt pierced the bewitching spell holding them captive. "You had to buy love to secure your election?"

"No," Cyprian and Lisbeth answered in unison, the response jerking Cyprian back to reality with a thud. They were not playing to a foolish schoolboy.

"There was no sale of this woman to be my wife." The half-truth scorched Cyprian's tongue, but he'd come too far down this treacherous path to turn back now and survive. "The relinquishment of her dowry is all very legal."

"I brag when I say he *bought* me." Lisbeth held out her arm and jangled bracelets of hammered gold. "Look at how he spoils me." She twirled, her dress floating provocatively above her ankles as she held tight to his hand. "What woman wouldn't sell her soul to be the queen of Cyprian's heart?"

Weren't they supposed to be making this stuff up? Wasn't that the game she was playing? Then why did the admiration in her voice sound as real as the crowd's chatter in his ears and make him feel so . . . he wasn't sure what being joined to this hypnotic beauty made him feel. Whatever the sensation, he'd had stomachaches from eating ill-prepared lamb kabobs that hadn't twisted his gut so tightly.

Cyprian dropped Lisbeth's hand and took a step back. He opened his mouth to fabricate an emergency that required their immediate exit when the blast of twelve silver trumpets brought the masses to their feet.

A games announcer dressed in the purple-trimmed toga of a dignitary entered the arena floor via a raised iron gate. Accompanied by a band of golden, curved horns, he led twelve gladiator combatants on a solemn march around the ring. Upon reaching the center, the announcer lifted his hands. The music and the crowd quieted. A welcoming smile split his powdered face. "Let the honorable games of Carthage begin." The perfect acoustics carried his booming voice past their box and up to the highest tiers.

Spectators went wild. Thousands of feet stamped stone. The announcer basked in the response, milking the excitement to a frenzied froth. Then he raised his hands once again, standing statue-still until silence settled upon the arena. "We give tribute to Aspasius, the proconsul of Carthage and sponsor of today's glorious entertainment." He fired a military salute toward their box, and the crowd roared, waving banners and shouting over and over the name Cyprian detested above all others.

"Aspasius! Aspasius!"

ASPASIUS ROSE from his seat. Sun glinted off the gold chains dripping from his neck. Lisbeth and Cyprian made their way back to Sergia. She seated herself between Cyprian and Sergia. *Where did that cough come from? I didn't notice that earlier.* If Cyprian's friend was ill, she wanted him as far from Cyprian as possible. She craned her neck, disgusted by the smirk curling the proconsul's lip. At the slight nod of Aspasius's bald head, the games began. They were stuck for now.

First came the mock fights. Pairs of gladiators strode onto the freshly raked sand and pummeled each other with wooden swords. No one was supposed to get hurt in the spurious bouts, but if one of the participants happened to land a blow that drew blood, the audience chanted "Finish him," leaving the more virile gladiator no choice but to beat his opponent to death with the blunt end of his wooden club.

Sergia and Cyprian chatted as if she weren't sitting between them. Neither seemed the least bit incensed by the carnage on the arena floor. As the two friends caught up on old times, her attention darted between making sure they never touched and watching the pit crew hook the dead gladiators and haul them away.

Once the sand was cleared and the blood raked into neat rows, a new team of workers scurried out and began setting up for the next display. Large wooden boxes were dragged into place. A man with a painted face ran to the center of the ring and cracked a leather whip. The crowd cheered. A gate opened, and three big cats sprang from the hold, circled the whip-cracking trainer, then obediently leapt upon the boxes. Their circus tricks held the crowd spellbound for thirty minutes. But when a wild boar was released into the mix, Lisbeth had to put her hands over her eyes to block out the bloody chaos that ensued and nearly got the trainer killed.

At high noon, vendors flooded the aisles, carrying trays of roasted game hens, burgers made of ground antelope and green peppercorns, soufflés stuffed with small fishes and raisins, eggs pickled in a mixture of vinegar and honey, and large wooden bowls of freshly cut melons. Cyprian ordered another round of wine and encouraged Lisbeth to eat.

"I think I need to stretch my legs." Lisbeth stood, determined to extricate her and Cyprian from this madness and his possible exposure to measles. "Care to join me for a little stroll, my love?"

Sergia put his hand on her arm, and she noticed he was exceptionally warm despite their shady location. "Oh, but you mustn't miss the lunch break entertainment. The hour is devoted to the execution of criminals who've committed particularly heinous crimes."

"Are you well, Sergia?" Lisbeth lowered her voice to keep the question from attracting Cyprian's attention.

"Just a bit overheated." Sergia coughed in her face. "I'm not used to this African heat. Much warmer here than in Rome."

"Ask them to add honey to your water. It will keep you

hydrated." She handed him the hanky Ruth had given her to dab away any uncomely sweat. "Cover your mouth when you cough."

"Stay." Sergia leaned in close, obediently hacking into the fine piece of linen. "Offending the proconsul would not be in Cyprian's best interests."

If Sergia had measles, she needed to get Cyprian out of harm's way without drawing the proconsul's attention. Lisbeth let her gaze slide in the direction of Aspasius, who was gnawing a large drumstick. Mama sat board-straight next to him, sipping a glass of wine with no expression on her face. Lisbeth's eyes flitted to the arena, where workers frantically removed what was left of the gutted pig, then back to Cyprian, who seemed to be holding his breath, awaiting her response.

"Perhaps we can leave after lunch then, my love?"

Cyprian tugged on her hand. "Good form demands we stay for the whole of Aspasius's entertainment."

She sat down, positioning her body as a barrier between Cyprian and his friend.

The slave assigned to Lisbeth took her plate, freed a tiny drumstick from the succulent breast of a game hen, then handed the roasted meat to her. She doubted the willingness of her stomach to welcome any nourishment, but she took the fowl and nodded her thanks to the girl.

Startling trumpets sounded again. A gate at the opposite end of the arena opened, and a guard dressed in armor that reflected the sun's glare yanked the end of a rope. A small boy stumbled from the shadows. The child was followed onto the sand by the young woman tied to him, her clothes dirty and tattered. Roped to her were two teenage boys with matted hair and pimpled complexions. They all worked together to help the elderly woman in their group shuffle as far away from the barred cages as possible. The sight of the little family clumped together in the center of the arena sent a clear message: Aspasius was Rome, and Rome could do whatever it wanted. Women and children could be sacrificed on the altar of entertainment, and there was nothing anyone could do to stop them.

"Who are they?" Lisbeth whispered to Cyprian.

"Christians."

Standing back-to-back, the ragtag group simultaneously lifted their chins and brought their folded hands to their chests, as if they wanted all of Carthage to know they faced their terror with their god's name upon their lips and their fear in check.

"Put these on," ordered the guard as he shoved white robes at them.

The young woman Lisbeth guessed to be the mother of the little boy stepped from the group. She paraded a defiant stare around the arena that silenced all forty thousand visitors. "We are here for refusing to honor your gods." Her gutsy voice floated to the highest tier. "By our death we earn the right *not* to wear your garments."

Murmurs rippled through the stands.

Aspasius stood. "Bring forth the father." An iron gate at the opposite end of the arena clanked open.

A wild-eyed man with iron shackles on his wrists scrambled into the ring. "Let them go." His desperate lunge for his family was met with the guard's quick yank on the chain. The man fell backward with a bone-breaking thud. The guard dragged him to the wall, where he promptly clipped the chain into an iron ring.

Aspasius extended his arm. Screaming cats shredded the silence. "For their treason against Rome, these plebeians are sentenced to death." He turned his thumb to the sun. Cheers exploded. Patrons began shouting their wagers to the bookies scrambling through the bleachers. As the odds takers scribbled down bets on clay-lined wooden slates, Lisbeth could not take her eyes off the child, a gaunt and fragile boy nearly the same age as Junia.

"What will happen to them?" Even as she asked, she knew. "Not the cats."

"Even the lions are subject to the yoke of Rome."

The proconsul's official scribe closed his wax tablet and put away his stylus. There would be no accounting of the traitors sacrificed in the name of entertainment. No record of the tortures performed on innocent women and children in this place. History could only guess at the horrific sight. Even Papa would find it difficult to stomach this dose of historic reality.

"This isn't right!" Lisbeth stood and leaned over the railing as far as she dared. Below their royal box, hungry cats clamored to be released. She glanced back to the center of the dusty arena. The woman with sad eyes locked with hers. Every movie Lisbeth had ever seen about the Colosseum replayed in her mind. People ripped limb from limb while the frenzied mob celebrated.

"Take my hand!" Lisbeth, leaning over the railing as far as she could, shouted to the woman.

Cyprian pulled her back. "No."

She jerked free. "Maybe you can sit here and do nothing, but I can't."

Cyprian's arm circled her waist and drew her hard against his solid body. "Say no more, woman," he warned in her ear, then silenced her completely by covering her lips with his own. Heat penetrated the fine gauze veil. Everything in the world swam from her head. Papa. Mama. Laurentius. Junia. Finding her way back.

"Ah," he said when he finished. He glanced around the box and smiled when he noticed everyone staring at them. "The craziness of new love. It can drive a man wild."

Never had a kiss induced such an onslaught of ecstasy and anger. Lisbeth swiped her hand across her lips. "How dare—"

English broke through the din of many languages and reached her ears. "Let it go," Mama was saying. "For now, you must let it go."

Lisbeth relaxed against Cyprian's hold. She swallowed the bile in the back of her throat and worked to find a smile. She lifted her veil and planted a kiss of her own squarely upon his lips. When she released him, she smiled at the tiny trickle of blood her retaliation had drawn. She blushed and cooed, blinking back tears as she dabbed at his lip with the hem of her *palla*.

Cyprian drew her close, a sheepish smirk on his face. "Such passion," he told his friends as he held her protectively.

Safety was an illusion, a fantasy that must be pushed from her mind. Never could she forget that she, like the frightened Christians on the arena floor, was a captive. And not just in another time period, but in one big, fat lie she had helped create. Any moment the jig would be up, and she could very well find herself in the jaws of a lion. For now, she had no choice but to dangle from Cyprian's arm, the prize he needed to gain his senatorial seat and the leverage she needed to free her mother. But she would not watch innocent children ripped to shreds.

Lisbeth squeezed her eyelids tight and forced her mind to find a happy place, a time when her life counted for more than just trying to stay alive. Visions of Craig and the glorious spring day when they'd skipped out on a prostate lecture in favor of a picnic at the arboretum played in her head. Walking among those incredible tulips and the stunning views of White Rock Lake with her hand in his, she'd felt hopeful. Like things would be different from what had become of her family before.

Was Craig wondering where she was? Had he grown weary of waiting on her to text him? Had he caught a plane to Africa and come in search of her? *Oh, God, please let it be so.* Craig was brilliant, first in his surgery class. If anyone could figure out where she'd gone and how to get her back, it would be her fiancé.

The crowd gasped and then fell completely silent. Curiosity immediately pried Lisbeth's eyes open. Everyone in their booth stared at the arena floor, their mouths agape. Lisbeth wiggled out of Cyprian's arms. In the middle of the arena the boy stood alone, his wide eyes darting between his father chained to the arena wall and the big cats stepping over mauled bodies while they circled him.

No one in the stands moved. Dust hung in the air. Screams of innocent women and children would echo from this place for generations, and yet not one spectator in the seats would lift a finger to stop the barbarism. Deaf ears. Blind eyes. Yet not bad men. More likely, good men and women. Good people who worked to keep their own children out of harm's way. Good people who wouldn't dream of murdering their neighbors. Yet today, they would do nothing. Good people doing nothing. The fall of every civilization playing out before her very eyes.

"What would you have me do, Lisbeth of Dallas?" Aspasius's voice rang out. "You choose the child's fate."

Had she done that very thing, chosen whether or not a child would live, when she discounted Abra's symptoms? "Not me. I'll have no part of this."

"But you must," Aspasius crooned. "It is my engagement gift to you and the solicitor of Carthage."

Lisbeth stood on shaky legs, fully aware the entire arena awaited her decision, including Cyprian. But she avoided his eyes and any judgment they may have held. She had only seconds before the cats pounced. "Amnesty is as good for those who give it as for those who receive it." How she'd conjured a Victor Hugo quote from the recesses of her literary studies she couldn't say, but if anyone understood an era of social misery and injustice, it was this avid human rights campaigner. She prayed the author's words would have the timeless impact her own ability lacked.

"Strange sentiment." Aspasius chuckled. "The boy lives." His face completely devoid of compassion, he extended his arm and gave the thumbs down. "But the father dies."

"No!" Lisbeth's scream bounced around the stone enclosure.

Aspasius turned his thumb up, and the applause of approval swallowed her disapproval whole.

Cyprian put himself between her and Aspasius. "Your gracious rule will not go unrewarded, Consul." He wrapped an arm around her shoulder and smiled at his sovereign, but Lisbeth saw tears in his eyes as he eased her back onto her seat. "Not another word," he mouthed at her.

Lisbeth sank onto the cushion. Her confidence that Cyprianus Thascius would not let this wrong go unpunished dissipated in the dust rising from the arena floor. Political justice could not restore this child's family any more than she could restore hers.

31

A SHROUD OF DARKNESS HUNG over the city when the last
dead gladiator was hooked and dragged from the arena. At
Lisbeth's insistence, Ambassador Sergia finally excused himself for
a much-needed rest. She'd doused Cyprian's hands with a flagon
of expensive wine. The added precaution may have protected him
from the measles, but no amount of scrubbing would remove the
innocent blood from their hands.

The satiated throng, rowdy from overstimulation, pushed toward the exits. Lisbeth gathered her gown's excess fabric, sadness
weighting her steps. She drew the palla hood over her head. Contemplating how much to tell Cyprian about Sergia and her suspicions of measles, she put her hand through the crook of her recently
proclaimed fiancé's arm and let him plow a wide escape path.

Outside the arena, drunken patrons jostled Lisbeth into Cyprian as they waited for their litter to be brought around. "Hold
tight to me," he said.

"My lord." Felicissimus emerged from the crush and worked
his way between her and Cyprian. "I've received word that a new
shipment of captives will reach the harbor—"

"It will have to wait, Felicissimus."

"But they will arrive within the hour," the slave trader protested.

Just as Cyprian was about to respond, the mob ripped Lisbeth from his arm. "Cyprian!"

Cyprian shoved Felicissimus aside and charged into the throng, Pontius joining him in the rescue. Cyprian reached her first. When his hand found hers, he pulled her to him, swept her into his arms, and yanked the veil from her face. "Are you hurt?"

"No." Peering over Cyprian's shoulder, she could see surprised recognition registering on the slave trader's face. "Can we go?"

"My lord, what are you doing?" Felicissimus asked. "She's a—"

"Felicissimus, I'm in no mood for you or your deplorable business tonight." Cyprian parted the litter curtains, lifted Lisbeth inside, then quickly mounted the litter and dropped the curtains in Felicissimus's shocked face. He tapped the bronze pole, and six brawny men hoisted their transport. "Pontius, pay the slave trader to bother me no more." His secretary hopped out and disappeared into the crowd.

"Can we trust him to keep our secret?" Lisbeth asked.

"Felicissimus can be a pain, but he is loyal to the core." Cyprian yanked the curtains closed.

"Maybe he was, but I don't think he appreciated you blowing him off."

"Blowing off?"

"Never mind."

Flushed and nauseated from hours of senseless killing, she didn't have the energy to worry about Felicissimus. She needed to find her bearings. To realign everything she'd seen in the arena against everything she wanted to believe true of human nature. To decide what she would do if she'd failed to protect Cyprian from contracting measles. She waited until their litter bearers had their transport free of the masses, then asked, "Could you open the curtains?"

Cyprian eyed her suspiciously, as if he wondered what had ever possessed him to agree to this folly.

"I'm not trying to escape, although I should after that little kissing exhibition you put me through."

Without speaking a word concerning their uncomfortable performance, he reluctantly complied and fell back against the pillows.

She poked her head out far enough to catch a glimpse of the night sky. Papa had taught her that if she set a course by the stars, she could always find her way home. Her way back to truth. How many nights had she and Papa sat side by side, their overturned buckets touching, the fruity tendrils of Papa's Erinmore wrapping science into a tidy package as they examined the stars . . . these very same twinkling points of light?

The thought startled her. With all that had happened since her arrival, she'd felt out of sorts. How had she missed the fact that the vast nighttime sky had remained so . . . unchanged? Proof of a consistent universe. The stability of science, her comfort even when life was overwhelmingly unstable. Yet no matter how she spun finding her mother, stumbling upon a deadly epidemic, discovering she had a half brother, witnessing the slaughter of innocent children, and agreeing to marry a guy she'd just met, none of it fit into a consistent way of thinking. Especially not the strange feelings welling up inside her for this man, this man who was a mixture of Roman and something else she couldn't put her finger on.

She inhaled the muggy breeze blowing in from the sea. "What do you know of the Cave of the Swimmers?"

Cyprian rested his head on a pillow, his eyes closed as if he nursed a headache. "Why do you ask?"

"You told Aspasius that you met me at the Cave of the Swimmers."

"I was just following your lead, making up tales to balance

yours." He rubbed his temples. "I don't know why that old legend came to my mind."

"But why the Cave of the Swimmers? Have you been there?"

"I've heard stories of caravans who sought shelter in a desert cave and then vanished, never to be seen again. I don't know. It just seemed like the impossible tale fit your strange comings and go-ings." When she said nothing, Cyprian opened his eyes. "It's only a legend but a powerful one. If Aspasius believes there is a possibil-ity you hail from such a cursed place, perhaps it will breed fear into that hardened heart of his." Cyprian turned his gaze to the stars. "Don't worry. No one knows if such a place even exists."

Lisbeth contemplated how to proceed. "So tell me about Sergia."

"Sergy? He's a friend."

"Your friend could have the fever."

Cyprian sat up. "Why didn't you say something?"

"What would you say if I told you the Cave of the Swimmers does exist?"

"I don't understand how a baseless legend has anything to do with keeping the health of my friend from me."

"What would you say if I told you that years from now a sim-ple vaccination will eradicate this fever?"

In the flickering torchlight she could see his scowl. "I would add this unfounded claim to your ever-growing list." He asked for no further explanations, and she was too upset about the day's slaughter and his nonchalant dismissal of her character to offer an-swers he didn't deserve.

She'd made the mistake of thinking a heat-filled kiss and a cou-ple of tears in his eyes meant she could trust him with the truth. Cyprian was a third-century Roman. She was a twenty-first-century woman. She would not make the mistake of forgetting the vast difference between their worlds again.

Neither said another word on the ride home. When they arrived, Lisbeth retired to her quarters and shut the door with a resolved click. She lifted an exquisite urn and poured water into a bowl, determined to wash away the stench of innocent blood. But when she looked into the hammered brass mirror, shame flushed her cheeks.

She'd sat mute while lions ripped apart human beings. One more blemish on her record. She didn't deserve to be clean. She'd seen doctors who'd worked among the ill so long they'd lost their empathy, their compassion, their ability to relate to pain or the tremendous fear that accompanied a patient's not knowing. Just a few short months in the medical system, and the same had happened to her. She'd discounted the concerns of Abra's mother, hadn't taken the time to sympathize, and totally missed the proper diagnosis. A wrong she would never be able to right.

Was she traveling the same slippery slope of apathy again? Had she become as calloused as the Roman barbarian she'd agreed to marry?

She slid between the luxurious sheets and sank into a fitful slumber. Gory images of hungry lions carrying away mothers as their children cried were intertwined with snapshots of lacy fingers that beckoned her to the cave.

"Not fair!" Lisbeth bolted upright, soaked in sweat. It took a moment for reality to register. She wrapped her arms around herself, holding tight to her damp gown.

Moonlight streamed through the shutter slats. Life wasn't fair on so many levels. She'd fought against the injustice since the day her mother disappeared, sought to make sense of a senseless world. Yet a hole too big to fill remained.

Maybe trying to fix everything was going at this problem all wrong. She'd treat one symptom at a time, and the first treatment could not wait for the dawn.

* * *

THE DISPERSING crowd jostled Felicissimus as he watched Cyprian's litter disappear into the night. How could one stand in the
middle of a throng, yet feel so very much alone? His advice on
whom Cyprian should marry had obviously been ignored, and
now Cyprian placed his loyalties to a slave woman far above him.
He'd patiently overlooked Cyprian's obvious disdain for the way
he earned a living and supported his family in the past, even as he
risked his own livelihood in their plot to foil Aspasius. But nothing was ever going to change; he saw that clearly now. He'd been a
fool to believe his simple baptismal dunking in a rich man's fount
had made them equals. Nothing bridged the gap between rich and
poor, slave and free, not even the Messiah's blood. Once Cyprian
was elected to real power, how long before he forgot his partner-
ship in their righteous crime? Or worse, somehow managed to lay
all the blame on the slave trader who trolled the back alleys?

Felicissimus checked the money pouch on his belt. Empty as
the mouths he had to feed. He hiked his tunic and set out to find
some real friends.

32

WITH THE PATIENCE OF one who'd spent his life waiting in the wings, Pytros settled into the darkened corner of the pub. The back-alley bar was crowded with quarry workers stumbling home from the games and determined to spend the last of their meager paychecks. Pytros nursed a mug of bitter ale and focused his attention on the ribald little man dressed in a urine-colored tunic. From the pout clouding the plebeian's filthy face, his conversation with the lofty Cyprian had not gone well.

Pytros had hardly been able to contain his joy when he'd spotted his master's most hated enemies visiting outside the arena. Golden opportunities to impress his owner seldom came the way of an overworked and underappreciated scribe. Keeping a sharp eye on the whereabouts of his target, Pytros had lagged behind the royal litter, ditched the proconsul's entourage in the traffic crush, and then trailed Felicissimus to this dank plebeian water hole.

Aspasius rarely sent for him anymore. If his little mission proved fruitful, his master would not only cast Magdalena from his bed but also realize that his faithful scribe was as cunning as he was beautiful.

Felicissimus tossed back one drink after another, totally unaware Pytros waited, coiled like a snake. Each round loosened the slave trader's jaw a bit more. When his legs became less and less steady, Pytros knew the opportune time had come. He ordered a jug of the best wine delivered to the man who could help him rid Carthage of Cyprian and his little wench. Aspasius would be so grateful that he'd gladly shove Magdalena aside as his favored one.

"What's this?" Felicissimus took the crock from the snaggle-toothed barmaid whose tight girdle squeezed her only assets into plain view. She whispered something in the slave trader's ear and pointed toward the corner.

Pytros raised his glass and offered the smile of one certain his risky investment was about to pay off.

33

I SHOWED THE AMBASSADOR WHO rules this province!" Aspasius bellowed as he paced his office. "Eliminating the rabble that thumb their noses at the gods of the empire is doing the emperor a great service. Left to their own devices"—he charged past Magdalena as if she didn't exist, yet refused to explain why he'd yanked her from a sound sleep—"every law would be in jeopardy. Sergia has no idea what it takes to maintain peace on the frontier. I've half a mind to write Decius myself. Tell him there's a traitor on his staff."

"There's still time to influence the ambassador's report," Magdalena said with a yawn. "I'm certain he'll extend his stay long enough to include the wedding of his old school friend Cyprianus Thascius."

"If I do not secure my tenure for another year, how will I turn things around?"

Always the consummate politician, even with her. Aspasius sounded as if he actually cared for the welfare of the poor in the tenements, the tiny businessmen trying to eke out enough to pay exorbitant tax bills and put bread on empty tables, and yet she knew his concern included only three things: Himself. His desire to impress the throne. His power.

"The bodies piled along the tenement avenues nearly did

Sergia in." Aspasius unfastened his girdle and let the weight clatter to the floor.

Why had it taken him so long to come to bed? She'd counted herself blessed when Pytros first burst in and Aspasius had dismissed her, but that was hours ago. What had Pytros said to him?

"Obviously, the boy does not have the strong stomach required to reshape a neglected barbarian province."

"Arranging burials outside the city walls would remove the stench and promote better health of—"

"Silence your prattling, woman," he ordered. "The emperor has far more pressing problems than the disposal of a few dead quarry workers in Carthage."

"I'm sure the emperor will enjoy the profit that comes from having his proconsuls declare citizens traitors in order to confiscate their property?"

"Betray the imperium and forfeit everything." Aspasius wrapped his arm around her waist and slammed her against his belly, the force wrenching her arm from its sling. "It is the law." Traces of the expensive Falerian served in his arena box still laced his breath. "The very same law that allows me to do as I please with you."

"Why waste your effort?" Pain shot the length of her arm. "I've nothing of value."

"Did you really think I wouldn't find out?" He leaned in close and nipped her earlobe with his razor-sharp teeth. "Those loyal to me were only too happy to divulge your secret."

Her breath caught. Was everything finally on the table? Did Aspasius know the truth about Lisbeth? Had he learned of Laurentius? And even more importantly, had he discovered she'd been working behind his back since she arrived?

"Who said I have secrets?" She allowed her free hand to discreetly locate her pocket and the dagger she kept there. Determined to drive the scalpel-sharp blade deep into his heart, she grabbed the knife hilt and moved in a flash.

But he caught her hand. "Where is it?" He twisted her arm until she released her weapon. "Tell me where you hide your secrets, and I may let you live."

34

A ND WHERE DO YOU think you're going?" Cyprian's voice stopped Lisbeth with the knob of the atrium door within her reach.

"I wish you wouldn't sneak up on me like that." She turned to see her soon-to-be husband standing in a puddle of silvery light, his arms folded while he waited for some type of believable explanation. *It takes a confident man to pull off wearing a dress with such masculine ease.* The liquid pool of his eyes drew her in, and for a foolish moment she wondered about the man beneath the toga. The feel of golden flesh beneath her touch. She rummaged through her sack and drew out an empty vial. "I'm headed to the market." His brows raised but he did not move, so she rambled on like some sort of blabbering schoolgirl. "For more shampoo. Something to tame these curls for the wedding."

"At this hour?" He took a step closer, the scent of him reaching her nostrils, something salty and windblown, as if he'd been on the beach. "Only the servants that empty the chamber pots upon the streets are up before the sun."

"Okay. You caught me." She wrapped both hands around the strap on her sack. "But even if you tie me to the bed, I'll figure out a way to go."

"Where?"

"To get my brother."

He pondered her admission with an appraising look that made her feel as if she'd just taken the witness stand. "Isn't getting Laurentius away from the proconsul the reason we're in this marriage mess?"

"Did you see what that monster is capable of today? I'd snatch my mother away, too, if I could, but I know we can't tip our hand to Aspasius just yet." A surprising lump rose in her throat. "The proconsul doesn't know about my brother. He can't ever find out about Laurentius."

Cyprian grabbed his cloak from the peg beside the door. "Let's go."

"I don't need your help."

"I don't need *your* permission."

Matching his pace step for step, she followed Cyprian through the dark and deserted streets, frustrated that he'd dismissed her as if she couldn't handle things on her own. "I think you should go back," she whispered. "What if we run into patrols?"

"Then my protection and my position might save your neck, since it is well past curfew."

"What if someone catches you beneath the palace? No telling what Aspasius would do."

He stopped and stared at her. "And what do you think the proconsul will do with the trespassing betrothed of his chief solicitor?" Cyprian raised her hood to cover the curls tumbling down her back. "Your hair will not stay red forever. If you get caught and are forced to stay at the palace for a prolonged period of time, Aspasius will figure out who you are soon enough, and when he does there's a good chance your head and shoulders will part company."

She raised her palms in a sign of surrender. "Okay, I get the beheading thing."

"Are we done arguing about whether or not I'm coming along?"

"As you so eloquently pointed out, *you* don't need *my* permission."

They hurried past the abandoned aqueduct construction site near the tenements. According to Cyprian, the ring of chisels had not been heard on the soaring arches of the arcade bridges in over a year. She could tell from the bite in his comment that this injustice irritated him as much as it did her.

Several blocks later, they climbed the steep street leading to the palace, the tall patrol tower pinking in the glow of the Mediterranean sunrise. At the hill's crest, she expected Cyprian to turn the lead over to her, but instead he stealthily skirted the gate and led them to the same hidden opening she and Tabari had used.

The rhythmic plink of metal studs on cobblestone marched toward them.

"Morning patrols," Cyprian whispered. He parted the tangle of leaves, pushed her inside the perimeter, then quickly fell in behind her.

Before she could start for the steps, he clapped a firm hand over her mouth and pressed her back to the wall. Sandwiched between his taut body and the hard stone, Lisbeth prayed he couldn't feel her heart beating against her chest. Heat leapt between them, igniting all sorts of feelings Lisbeth didn't want to deal with at this very moment in time.

His eyes met hers, then swept over her face. Had her eyeliner smeared? Did the curls tumbling from the holder make her look the tomboy that she was? Her questions dissolved in the dizzying intensity of danger swirling in her belly. She was anything but safe. Not so much from the patrols, but from the powerful man whose arms squeezed away the last of her defenses.

Soldiers stopped on the opposite side of the wall. They

bragged about their brothel conquests, taking their time to complete their patrol as if they had all night. Despite the danger of making even the slightest of sounds and giving them both away, she couldn't help but relax in Cyprian's hold, her body willingly melding to the contours of his. Neither of them breathed as they listened to the soldiers name the best hookers and argue over where to find the cheapest rates. She longed to probe the depths of Cyprian's alert eyes, to know how many conquests he could boast. From his quickened breathing, she wondered if he was thinking she'd soon become an additional notch on his belt.

Once the click of studs on cobblestone receded beyond the range of hearing, Cyprian's hand released her mouth, yet he continued to hold her close, with his lips lingering just inches above hers. Relieved breaths flowed between them, mingling into sweet, sensual warmth that seeped into Lisbeth's bones.

"Are you all right?" he whispered.

She could only nod.

"We must be quick. Come." His hand found hers, and he led her down the stone steps, stopping at the wooden plank. "This is as far as Magdalena would ever let me go," he confessed in hushed tones.

"Tabari had a key." Why hadn't she thought about the key or how to get in touch with Tabari? "What are we going to do?"

"Stand back." He worked his fingers beneath the board, braced his legs, and pulled with an impressive might. The board snapped under the pressure. They stood there, unmoving, listening for the return of soldiers' cleats. When they heard nothing, Cyprian peered into the musty darkness. "We should have brought a light."

"And something to slow my racing heart," Lisbeth whispered. "Those soldiers were too close for comfort." She bent to search the dark ledge inside the door. "Give me a minute." Hopefully the creatures she'd heard on her last visit didn't like fingers. "Got it." Within a few strikes of the flint, a flame sucked the oil from the clay bowl. They slipped inside the narrow passage.

Cyprian pressed against her, the bulk of him swallowing up the majority of the space. "Which way?" He pointed out the choice of two different tunnels.

Lisbeth held the tiny flame out as far as she could. "I'm guessing the one with less cobwebs." She nodded in the direction of the right tunnel.

He took the light from her. "I'll lead."

"This is *my* rescue mission."

"And *my* reputation on the line."

She gave a mock curtsy. If he wanted to be the gentleman, then let him. "Then I'm only too happy to let you clear the rodents." As they slogged through the ankle-deep water, the narrow stone walls seemed to close in on her. Papa's catacomb lessons on the persecuted Christians forced underground popped into her head. How did they stand it? How had Laurentius lived his life down here? She wished she'd thought to bring something to leave along the path that would help them retrace their steps after they found her brother.

Cyprian stepped on something that squealed and skittered off in the water. "That can't be good." His hand found hers. "Stick close."

"Do you hear that?"

"Sounds like humming."

"Laurentius hums while he draws. We must be getting closer."

Several wrong turns and dead ends later they ended up at a door that looked like her brother's room. "I think this is it." Lisbeth tapped lightly, and the humming stopped. "Laurentius?" She tried the knob, but it was locked. Ear to the thick wood, she tapped again. "It's Lisbeth, Laurentius. It's safe to open the door."

The bolt slid on the other side; then the door slowly creaked open. Laurentius's almond-shaped eyes peeked around the edge.

"Lithbutt?" Thin black hairs stood on end all over his head. Bedhead like Papa used to have every morning. How could he be anything like her father? "Mama thaid don't open the door, thon. Thranger danger."

"But I'm not a stranger, Laurentius." Seeing him there, eyeing her carefully as he weighed his options was the best sight she'd seen in days. "And you know Cyprian. Remember?"

His eyes shot to Cyprian. "He cheats."

"Me?" Cyprian's laughter rumbled in his chest. "Weren't *you* the one who slapped both of my hands at the same time?"

Levity didn't help the feeling that the tunnel seemed to be closing in on her. The sooner they got out of here, the better. "Can we come in, Laurentius?"

"No." He started to close the door. "Mama thays don't open the door when I'm not here, thon."

Lisbeth stuffed her foot in the space between the door and the jamb. "But I promised Cyprian he could see your drawings."

"Ooooh. Why didn't you thay tho?" Laurentius smiled and pulled the door open. "You like mithe or crickeths, Thiprian?"

"I had a pet cricket once." Cyprian left Lisbeth standing on the threshold trying to imagine him as a boy who had played with bugs. Was he an only child? Did he have to entertain himself like she did? Did they have more in common than wanting to see Aspasius defeated after all? She watched Cyprian waltz into the room and take it over with the same confidence he'd displayed when he mounted Aspasius's box at the arena. Add to the list that they were both really good fakers when it came to acting like they had everything under control.

"Hey, wait for me." Lisbeth rushed in after him.

Cyprian stood in the middle of the tiny cell, staring at the walls with his mouth open. "I had no idea he lived like this. I thought he was a servant in the house. An entertainment like the dwarf Aspasius bought for the games." Tear-filled eyes glistened in the light. The impact of his caring surprised her with a deep, visceral thawing of cold, dark recesses his touch hadn't even aroused. "Who does this to a person?"

Before she could answer, Laurentius grabbed Cyprian's hand. "Mithe on this thide. Cricketh on that thide."

"Did you draw all of these, my friend?"

Laurentius nodded. Lisbeth swallowed an unexpected lump of pride and admiration as her little brother marched Cyprian from parchment to parchment. Cyprian listened carefully to the story behind every intricate cartoon as if he cared. If she didn't watch herself, she might even learn to like this guy despite her hard and fast rule to avoid dangerous emotional attachments.

Extracting Laurentius from his home wasn't going to be easy, maybe even as difficult as pulling her father from that cave he couldn't seem to forget. Her original plan to fly to Africa, get Papa, and go back to Dallas seemed like a mission from so long ago. How could the tragedy that befell her and Mama be in their past, yet such a part of this boy's future? Somehow, some way, she must survive all of this. Sort out a way for the four of them—Mama, Papa, Laurentius, and her—to be together. To settle somewhere. Maybe even back in the States. Somewhere they could be a family and get to know each other again. Somewhere far away from toga-clad men who accelerated her heart rate.

"Boys, art appreciation is going to have to wait. We have to get out of here before dawn." Lisbeth gathered the tunic draped over the desk chair and stuffed it in her bag. "Let's go, Laurentius."

"Go?" Laurentius shook his head and backed away. "Where?"

"To Cyprian's house."

"No."

"You've been there. Remember? After the soldiers hurt you, and I helped you get better."

Laurentius shook his head. "No."

"You can have a room of your own with a window and everything," Cyprian added.

"I can't go. Mama thays don't go anywhere without me. Ever."

She hadn't considered the idea that a boy raised underground might feel safer burrowed away, especially after the trauma of his last foray aboveground. And since she'd spent most of her life without her mother, it never occurred to her that he wouldn't go without Mama. Moving him from this dungeon to Cyprian's villa would be as foreign to him as falling through the time portal had been to her. "But Mama wanted you to go with me. She told me to take you when I was here, but I was too afraid." She reached for his arm. "I'm not afraid now."

"No!" He shook her off. "I won't leave my mithe!"

"Let's take them with us," Cyprian offered. "In fact, I've been looking for an artist to paint a mural on the wall in my library. I think you're the man for the job, Laurentius." He went to one of the parchments stuck to the stones. "These wrestling rats would make the old bishop smile, don't you agree?" While he spoke, Cyprian carefully removed parchments from the wall and rolled them up. "These will be our patterns."

"Be careful." Laurentius rocked heel to toe, wringing his hands. "If I'm gone when Mama comes, she will cry."

"We'll leave her a note." Cyprian wrapped his arm around Laurentius and guided him to the door. "Tell her where she can find you."

"No."

"Does Mama bring your breakfast?" Lisbeth asked.

"Yeth."

"Then we'll wait." Mama used to rouse her with a kiss and a

bowl of Cocoa Krispies floating in goat's milk. She hadn't thought of those wonderful mornings in years, and strangely, thinking of them now didn't drive a dagger through her heart. "Mama should be here soon."

"And then what?" Cyprian asked.

"I guess we'll have to take her, too," Lisbeth said, plopping on the bed. "Families should stick together, right, little brother?"

MAGDALENA CLUNG to the rickety tunnel handrail, praying that by some miracle Laurentius would sleep through the commotion and not come looking for his breakfast. Her own terror she could deal with, had dealt with for years, but it was the realization that her son would soon be gazing into the eyes of evil that released her hold and sent her stumbling into Aspasius.

"I don't know why you think I'd spend any time down here," she said with a gasp, her mind scrambling for some sort of plan, a way out of this hell.

He grabbed a handful of her hair. "I should have known this is how you disappear." He waded through the water, dragging her by the hair with one hand, holding a lamp with his other. "Sewer rats nest with their own kind."

At the tunnel split, he paused. "Did you hear that?"

She listened, terror ripping through her that Laurentius was up and humming already. When she didn't answer he lifted his nose, sniffed the air, and listened. The faint sound of footsteps going the opposite direction echoed from the tunnel that led directly to her boy.

Aspasius let out a low, feral growl. "This way."

All sorts of explanations for not following his orders to murder their son pinged in Magdalena's head. None of them would satisfy Aspasius's wrath. She and Laurentius would suffer a horrible death in the arena . . . the death of traitors who dared defy the pro-consul's orders. Were it not for Lisbeth and Laurentius, death was a fate she would gladly welcome, an end to the years of suffering.

By the time they reached Laurentius's room, Magdalena could scarcely breathe.

"Open it," he ordered.

"But—"

"Now!"

THE GRATE of stone moving over stone echoed in the tunnel. Low, hostile voices rumbled along the passage, growing closer by the minute.

"Let's go." Cyprian herded Laurentius toward the exit. "Now!"

"No!" A woman's distant scream funneled along the damp walls. "There's nothing down here."

Laurentius's head snapped up. "Mama!" He dropped his parchments and bolted toward the stairs.

"Hush, little man." Cyprian collared Laurentius, clamped a hand over his mouth, and dragged him in the opposite direction. "We must leave now," he whispered to Lisbeth.

Laurentius bit Cyprian's hand, then shouted out, "My mi-theth!" He wiggled free and plunged in after the soggy rolls.

"I'll get them." Lisbeth fished what drawings she could out of the foul water, while Cyprian reeled in Laurentius. "Go!" She stuffed dripping parchments in her sack.

"You'll be right behind us?" Cyprian ordered more than asked.

"Yes. Go!" Lisbeth watched until Cyprian's cloak disappeared into the darkness.

She ran back and snuffed the lamp. She slung her sack over her shoulder and exited the room, quietly closing the door behind her. She slid a few feet into the tunnel blackness to wait. Working to keep her breath to short, inaudible gasps, she leaned against the damp stones, contemplating the execution of her next move. She heard the splash of someone coming from the opposite direction of Cyprian's escape . . . and the distinct sound of Mama's voice.

"There's nothing down here. I promise." Mama's cries grew louder and more cryptic, meant to be secret warnings Lisbeth was sure, secret warnings Laurentius would never have deciphered. "I'll do anything you want, just—" A loud, resounding crack cut off Mama's bargain, but only for a brief second. "Anything down here would RUN at the ugly sight of you!" she shouted.

Lisbeth's mind formed the picture of Mama stumbling, blood dripping from her mouth, but fighting to get in one more distress signal. Fighting to protect her child as the life was knocked out of her. In that moment, Lisbeth knew her mother had tried just as hard to get to her, to come home, but the circumstances holding her back had been too great.

She scoured the tunnel for a weapon. Why hadn't she brought a knife, a stick, a club, anything? Lisbeth whispered a prayer in case Cyprian's God was listening, braced her feet, and prepared to swing her sack with every ounce of force she could put behind it. Suddenly a hand came through the darkness and clamped her mouth. Before she could break free, someone dragged her in the opposite direction of her mother's agonizing pleas for mercy.

35

EMPTY DELIVERY CARTS CLATTERED over the cobblestones, eager to exit the city before sunup. Pale, defeated rays of light slithered through the bedroom shutters. Lisbeth stretched the kinks of restless sleep from her body, but shame remained coiled deep in her gut. Today she would rise from her soft bed as one of the soon-to-be wealthy residents of Carthage. She would be expected to join in the idle prattle of a patrician's wife and go about her day with no thought of yesterday's carnage. No thought of those suffering unimaginable horrors in dark places.

Contemplating her surroundings, Lisbeth slid her gaze along the wall murals and the room's rich furnishings. Security and riches were little comfort considering she'd left her mother to fend for herself in a dungeon cell. Hands trembling, Lisbeth reached for the stethoscope on the nightstand and cradled the tangle of rubber and metal to her chest. No comfort there either. No absolution for her growing list of monumental failings. Abra. Papa. And now Mama. No matter how Cyprian tried to spin the need to get them out of there, successfully rescuing her brother offered no justification for leaving Mama to endure another round of Aspasius's brutality.

Lisbeth crawled out from under the sheets. Her mother's screams still rang in her ears and made her unsteady on her feet.

Why had Cyprian insisted on coming back for her? He'd saved the weaker, mentally challenged boy, something his faith would have expected. But surely even his one God didn't expect him to risk his life for a stubborn, outspoken slave girl. He could have washed his hands of her. Left the daughter of foreigners to suffer whatever fate the gods dealt. Then he could have found himself a well-connected Roman to marry—one who hopefully had not heard the rumors Aspasius had been spreading about him—and called it a day, a day he was probably as anxious as she to forget.

But he didn't do either of those easy things. He'd pressed them through the tunnel, practically carrying the clumsy Laurentius every terrifying step of the way back to his villa. And once they'd settled her brother in a clean bed, he'd insisted she rest and let him have the first watch. Even if his impeccable morals wouldn't have allowed him to leave them to die, he could have put an end to the whole charade once they were safe. Instead, he'd let her sleep under his roof and protection. Why? Had he felt the chemistry between them? Was he beginning to wish their upcoming marriage wasn't a sham?

All of a sudden it hit her. Cyprian was being kind. Putting her needs before his. He was acting Christian, and she liked it. The unexpected notion pulled her up short, knocked the dizziness from her head.

Selflessness was a trait she'd never assigned to any man, not even Papa. Something within her gut warned that this type of behavior was dangerous. She didn't like the idea of being in someone's debt. When expectations were too high, disappointment followed. And that's exactly what would happen if she didn't distance herself from Cyprian. He'd done too much for her not to expect some type of repayment. She could never live up to his ideals. Or become a fine Christian woman like Ruth.

Just to be safe, she'd separate herself quickly, before these crazy romantic notions made going home an impossibility. Before she began to hope that this time things would be different, that she might actually be able to have that family she'd always wanted.

Lisbeth poured water into the basin and splashed her face, the tragedy of how close she'd come to wanting to be married to the wrong man playing in her mind. In less than a week, Cyprian could legally take her to his bed. Legally, he could have had her at any time since her purchase. His reluctance to enter into this arrangement proved he was far too principled to sleep with a woman without the benefit of marriage. But would the principles of a man who would not let her die hold up once she said "I do"?

36

R UTH INHALED DEEPLY OF the woody aroma filling Lisbeth's room. "I love this Arabian nard Cyprian ordered for you." In one elegant gesture, she returned the lid to the tiny jar and placed it among the collection of vials and smudge pots she'd gathered over the past few days. "The sheen on your skin will be exquisite."

"Sounds expensive." Lisbeth sniffed the fiery red ends of her own freshly treated hair, unable to escape the earthy scent of hemp.

"Exorbitant. But not nearly as costly as fetching snow from the mountains to chill the wine."

"I wish he wouldn't make such a big deal of this marriage thing." Lisbeth plopped upon the bed. "No one invests this much money and effort into a wedding ceremony without expecting some kind of reward." Since their successful rescue of Laurentius, she'd not had a minute alone with Cyprian to thank him, to check him for signs of measles, or, more importantly, to reinforce the platonic terms of their agreement.

"When someone of Cyprian's social standing marries, it *is*, as you say, a big deal." Ruth gathered the discarded tunics she'd rejected because they did not adequately show off Lisbeth's features. "Work to remove that scowl from your face, or I'll have to send someone to the desert for sand to scrub those lines from your fore-head."

"At least let me help." Lisbeth handed Ruth a tunic she'd missed. "What about the guest list?" Inviting Aspasius was dan-gerous, but short of finding some way to make contact with Tabari, she could think of no other way to learn her mother's fate. If he'd killed Mama, Lisbeth's reason for this wedding had died as well. Surprising sadness pricked her heart. "Will you invite the proconsul?"

"His invitation was the first designed and delivered." Ruth cocked her head, understanding and compassion lighting her eyes. "Who the surly beast will bring as his guest is anyone's guess."

"What about the menu? I used to help Papa's cook, so I could—"

Wide-eyed horror swept Ruth's face. "A patrician's wife never cooks. Cyprian's capable staff will have the scullions stoking the cooking fires day and night."

"The music?"

"Hired from Italy and setting up in the garden as we speak."

"Flowers?"

"Imported from the best growers."

"I guess that leaves just the dress." Lisbeth sighed. "But unless it's a laceration in need of sutures, I don't sew."

"Cyprian employs two of the best tailors in Carthage. They'll conduct your fitting within the hour. That leaves just enough time for Naomi to assist with your bath. Go and let her scrub until she finds your smile." Ruth patted her cheek. "A happy bride is a beau-tiful bride." She turned to leave, then stopped, hugging the gar-ments tightly. "You might learn to love him, you know."

I already have.

Where in the world had that come from? Lisbeth shuddered at the jarring thought. Quickly tucking away the insane notion, she blurted, "Business and love don't mix." Trying not to meet Ruth's eyes, she went in search of Cyprian to remind him of that very fact, even if she had to tell him the entire truth. Her bath could wait. Cyprian deserved to know who she was, and he deserved to hear the whole crazy story from her before Laurentius repeated something he shouldn't, something that would raise questions she couldn't dodge.

She stopped by her brother's room for a shot of courage, amazed at how quickly he'd wormed his way into her heart. "Hey, buddy."

"Lithbutt!" Her brother showed off his ample supply of paints. "I get the whole wall." He danced in front of the large, empty space Cyprian had given him to practice upon before tackling the library mural.

Once again, Cyprian's extraordinary kindnesses made Lisbeth keenly aware of her own tendency to be self-absorbed. Why had this stubborn Roman patrician overlooked Laurentius's disability? Treating her flawed brother as a human being of equal value was a huge deviation from his survival-of-the-fittest culture. Perhaps Cyprian had succumbed to the teachings of his mentor and become far more forward-thinking than she'd originally thought. If so, could he offer her and her incredible story the same grace? There she was worrying about herself again. Worrying about what someone would think of her, of how this situation affected her.

She pushed her selfishness aside and plodded to the library, intent on making things right. To prove to Cyprian and to herself that she, too, could act with selfless motives.

The old bishop sat hunched over the desk, struggling to read a scroll in the dim light.

She tapped on the doorframe. "Caecilianus."

He raised his gray head. "Ah, the lovely bride." He motioned her in with an affable smile, the same twinkle of delight that won over nearly anyone who encountered him. "You sound as though you could use a respite from my wife's zealous ministrations." His dogs stretched but remained stationed at his feet, regarding her more as family than an intruder these days. That was some progress, at least.

"Ruth means well." Lisbeth marveled at the ability of one with advanced cataracts to see so clearly into the heart of a matter. This preacher was more than rhetoric and platitudes. Exactly what made him different, she'd yet to pinpoint. "I'm looking for Cyprian."

"Our boy's been called to the Senate."

"No trouble, I hope."

"More of a sadness, I'm afraid. He must make funeral arrangements for one of those political horse traders." He offered her the seat across from his cluttered desk.

His disapproving tone surprised her. Weren't priests required to love everybody? "Who died?"

"Sergia."

"The ambassador from Rome?" Her heart stuttered. "How?"

Caecilianus shrugged. "He dropped dead in the middle of a torrid disagreement with Aspasius late yesterday afternoon."

"No!" She bolted for the door and set the dogs charging after her in hot pursuit.

"Wait." Caecilianus leapt from behind the desk, covered the length of the library with remarkable speed, and snagged her arm as she reached the hall. "You can't go."

"You don't understand." Dogs circled her feet. "Sergia had measles. If Cyprian touches him, he could die, too."

"Slow down." Caecilianus clasped her shoulders. "I think you have something to tell me." He led her to a cushioned couch. "Sit."

The weight of doing too little too late sagged Lisbeth's shoulders. She obeyed like one of the bishop's dogs and dropped onto the couch. What difference would a couple of minutes matter now? Cyprian's contact with Sergia at the arena had probably sealed her future husband's fate. Whether or not Cyprian believed her time-travel tale wouldn't matter anymore if the man she was supposed to marry was dead in a couple of weeks.

Caecilianus pulled up a chair and leaned in close. "What are these . . . *meezeles*?"

"Measles," she corrected.

Lisbeth hesitated as she considered what to say. Telling the truth of where she came from might affect her relationship with Cyprian, but bringing twenty-first-century medicine into a third-century plague could change the course of history. Yes, she'd already stepped in to save a few lives, but this was so much bigger. Was stopping a pandemic her place? Even if it wasn't, there was too much hanging in the balance.

Risking everything, she took a deep breath and let the story gush forth. She told of Papa's search for the mythical desert cave and Mama's unexplainable disappearance shortly after their arrival. She briefly mentioned how she'd only pursued medicine because she wanted to be like her mother. She even went so far as to enumerate some of the medical advances in the future. Her claims of a vaccine that could prevent the fever raised Caecilianus's bushy brows. Her failings in the medical profession and Papa's apparent descent into madness she kept to herself. She held her breath as she awaited his response.

"Another time?" Caecilianus ran a hand over his stubble. "The future, you say?"

She nodded.

"But I don't understand how you came to be in Carthage."

Lisbeth sighed. "Me either." Grateful he'd not dismissed her story as foolishness, she felt her lungs expand with her first deep breath since landing in Carthage.

Lisbeth stroked the dog's head resting in her lap. "The last thing I remember is touching a faded cave painting of some pot-bellied swimmers." She went on to tell about waking up in Felicis-simus's dark cell, unsure of how she'd landed in the third century.

"You did the right thing to tell me."

"You don't think it's crazy that I'm here?"

"You, my dear, are exactly where God intended."

"God didn't push me down that hole. It just happened. I can't explain time travel or how or why I ended here . . . I just did."

"Everything happens for a reason." From under his hooded eyelids, his certainty bore deep into her soul. "Magdalena is right. You are the answer to our prayers."

"What will you tell Cyprian?"

"Nothing."

Who was this guy? She'd just told him this mind-blowing story, and he'd swallowed it. No questions asked. But of course he also drank the Kool-Aid on the whole Jesus-raised-from-the-dead thing, too. "Don't you think my fiancé deserves to know the truth?"

"Your story is not mine to tell."

The dogs stirred and rushed to the door, barking a welcome as Cyprian entered. With his cloak askew and his hair tousled, he looked as if he'd run the entire distance between the Senate and his villa. Sweat dripped from his pale face. "Sergia has brought fever to the doorsteps of the wealthy. Aspasius has finally rallied full sena-torial support to pursue all who refuse to bow to the Roman gods."

37

LISBETH STOOD ALONE ON the balcony. Sea breezes whispered over the moonlit water, changing the shape of the waves.

She'd thought telling Caecilianus about her arrival from the twenty-first century would lift the weight of keeping the truth from people she was beginning to love, and for a brief moment the wonder on his craggy face had given her a reprieve. But when the old bishop proclaimed her an angel, she'd felt hemmed in and suddenly unsure, caught in a web of unrealistic expectations.

Lisbeth lifted her eyes and searched the inky sky for Orion or the Bear. These strange people who'd taken her in believed these pinpricks of light proved a shiny god existed beyond the darkness. In Dallas, the night sky came and went, and no one seemed to notice. Even she'd been too busy trying to keep up with school and residency to give the sky much thought. But here, watching the moonrise fill the universe with a glorious glow, she missed Papa and the heavenly compass he used to find his way home.

There was no going back. There was no fixing the mistakes of the past or the future. There was only her current reality. Time had played a cruel trick.

She was not an angel. She wasn't even a good doctor. How could she possibly be the answer to the Christians' prayers?

Despite the warm night, a desperate chill shuddered her body.

Lisbeth tightened the shawl across her shoulders. Caecilianus had said the story was hers alone to share. She'd wanted Ruth's advice on the best way to break such an incredible tale to Cyprian or, at the very least, to get a couple of tips on how to navigate this pickle before she jumped in. For some crazy reason, he mattered to her. But Ruth was far too distracted with the wedding preparations for a serious heart-to-heart about the best way to proceed with a pretend marriage.

She'd considered telling Cyprian the truth at the dinner the church hosted in their honor in the triclinium. But when her fiancé had finally emerged from the library, it was not to accompany her to church but rather to attend Sergia's burial. He'd brushed her off and hurried away like she was the one with the plague and had ended up missing the dinner his friends had worked on for days. His indifference stung a bit, but she'd decided to use the pain to remind her not to play with the fire that leapt in her belly every time they got within spitting distance of each other.

Her finger dragged along the limestone railing. She'd tried to remain detached, even stuffed the obvious physical attraction she felt for Cyprian. But then she'd catch him tossing Junia in the air or sprawled across the library rug helping Laurentius color one of his drawings. This powerful man was such a contradiction of hard edges and a soft heart. She'd been dreading taking Papa into her home, and here Cyprian had generously opened his villa to Caecilianus and his family and anyone else needing a roof over their head. Cyprianus Thascius was obviously made of finer stuff than she. A benevolent and selfless man was not an easy man to ignore, let alone hate.

Lisbeth's thoughts turned to Caecilianus's conclusions. They were crazy, but she couldn't quit thinking about them. Had the crusty bishop's one God sent her here for the purpose of altering the demise of the Roman Empire? What if destiny was not a finite theory? Could a human being alter the preordered boundaries of time enough to make a difference? What if fate had given her an unprecedented opportunity to right her own wrong? Shame on her if she stood by and did nothing.

Far below, along the water's edge, someone strode into view. Those broad shoulders and that determined gait could belong to only one man.

"Cyprian!" If fate had turned in her favor, clearing up his misconception of her would be one of the first wrongs she would right. Her heart did a strange little skip. "Cyprian!" Lisbeth called out again, adding a wave this time. Either he ignored her or he couldn't hear her over the roar of the sea. Raised on her tiptoes, Lisbeth leaned over the rail and yelled at the top of her lungs.

Without so much as a backward glance, Cyprian peeled out of his toga, tossed it upon the sand, and dove into the water like a muscled torpedo.

"What's he doing?" Lisbeth's muttered question floated away on the wind, but the image of his almost naked body stuck tight in her mind.

Stroke after graceful stroke, Cyprian progressed toward the ships anchored in the harbor. In breathless admiration, Lisbeth watched his powerful arms slice the sea without effort. Left. Right. Left. His confidence in the water equaled his confidence in life, in the future he believed was his. A stark contrast to the doubt in her desert. Had his newfound faith given him that purpose, or had he always been a man on a mission?

From the corner of her eye, a flash of moving light on the wharf drew her attention. In the faint glow, she could make out the sheen of soldier armor marching toward the place where Cyprian had entered the water. What would they do to him if they caught him out after curfew?

He must be warned. She gathered her skirts and hurried toward the stairwell, unwilling to play it safe anymore. Descending the stone steps from the balcony to the beach, she kept an eye on the approaching torches. Once she reached the sand, she removed her sandals, hooked the ankle straps over her finger, and quickly followed the trodden path that led to the waterfront. Gauging her proximity to the ships, she guessed herself to be very near her family's favorite shady picnic spot . . . a circle of pillar ruins.

Crouched behind a tuft of sea grass, she waited for the bank of angry clouds rising from the horizon to obscure the low-hanging moon. Taking advantage of the hazy light, Lisbeth ventured down the shoreline in search of more substantial cover. Right where she remembered the ruins to be, she found the concrete pillars, whole and in perfect condition. The newness of everything still boggled her mind. Papa had surmised the crumbling structure held Roman gods to watch the harbor, but he'd not guessed it to be an extravagant stone gazebo constructed for the sole purpose of stealing a romantic kiss or welcoming a weary sailor home.

Stepping from the sudsy foam lapping the gazebo stone, Lisbeth scurried inside and hunched deep into the shadows. She peeked around the pillar and scanned the sea for Cyprian's bobbing head. Across the harbor, she spotted him climbing up a rope ladder that dangled from over the side of one of the wooden ships.

A hand clamped upon her shoulder, giving her a start that launched a piercing scream.

"I told you I saw someone on the beach." The soldier yanked Lisbeth from her hiding place and hauled her out to a broken patch of moonlight. She remembered this guy's face from their market run-in. Hopefully he wouldn't recognize her. "You shouldn't be here."

She shrugged free of his hold, determined to rein in her fight-or-flight reflexes before she did something stupid. "Since when does a lady have to have Rome's permission to stroll her private beach?" Lisbeth tossed her loosened hair so that they could catch a glimpse of the jewels she still wore from dinner. "You are the trespassers, sirs."

He clapped a gloved hand around her wrist. "*You* are under arrest."

"What?" She failed to break his killer grip. "My husband won't appreciate having to bail me out of jail."

"Bail?" His hearty laugh rang out. "This curfew offender wants bail, boys!" His patrol buddies joined in with taunts and began shoving Lisbeth between them.

"You just wait until my husband hears about how you've treated me! This isn't right!"

"Cry to the proconsul, lady. You don't have rights."

"Since when are prominent Roman citizens denied their rights?" Cyprian emerged from the sea, slicking his hair back with his hands. Even dripping wet he was beautiful. *Darn it.*

He strode toward them. "I'd appreciate it if you'd release my bride, gentlemen."

"Bride?" The patrol leader laughed.

Cyprian trotted out a roguish grin. "As you can see, we had plans." One of his broad hands created a fig leaf over his skimpy undergarment. His other snagged her arm and towed her toward him, stretching Lisbeth between the two men like two dogs fighting over a bone. He was staring at her in a way that made her sizzle. "Come, my love. The water is perfect tonight."

The soldier squeezed her arm a bit tighter, determined to win this tug-of-war. "I have my orders."

"And do they include depriving the solicitor of Carthage his pleasure?" He gave Lisbeth a lewd wink. "My love, this is what we get for rushing the wedding night. If wagging tongues get word of us frolicking about in the surf the night before our wedding, my election hopes will be dashed."

The soldier dropped Lisbeth's arm. "Cyprianus Thascius?"

"*The* Cyprianus Thascius." Lisbeth rushed into Cyprian's open arms. He pulled her against his slick physique, and her sudden sense of panic morphed into an exhilarating tingle that traveled the length of her body. She tossed a wicked laugh over her shoulder, then threw her arms around his neck. "If the ranks are going to talk about us, let's give them something to talk about, *my love.*"

"THANKS FOR making an exception, boys." Cyprian didn't wait for the slack-jawed soldiers to go on about their patrols. "Keep up the good work." He swept Lisbeth off her feet and tumbled into the surf with her.

She came up sputtering salt water and reacting defensively to his attempt to keep her from hightailing it back to shore. "What the—"

He snagged her arm as she attempted to bolt. "Trust me," he whispered, noting the starfish eyelashes that framed the liquid pools of her eyes, the kind of eyes that reflected the one observing them a bit too clearly for his comfort. A quick perusal of the beach told him the soldiers were taking their time returning to their patrol beat. "Come on." He hooked her waist with one arm and ripped single-limbed strokes that carried them into deeper water. Several yards offshore, he turned her to face him, noting the soldiers still eyeing them from the shore. He began treading water. "This is where you act like you're having fun. Put your arms around my neck again and kiss me." The undercurrent of warning was not to be missed in his voice.

"What?"

He gave a swift scissor kick that buoyed them like a wine cork. "Do it."

She obeyed, flinging her slender arms across his shoulders.

Without hesitation, her lips found his. Fresh-bread soft and setting off a hunger in his belly he longed to quench. Instinctively, he moved toward her, devouring the salty taste of lips he'd imagined the flavor of honey since the first day she'd told him off. He clasped her waist, then scissor-kicked again while drawing her against him. Every curve of her body melded with his, as if the water had dissolved her tunic. Strong. Healthy. Sensual. Flesh against flesh, sucking him deep into a liquid vortex where he couldn't breathe.

He broke from her lips, yet kept his arms under hers.

Her eyes flew open, wide and wondering. "Are we done now?"

Working to keep her afloat was more difficult now that she had stiffened. A cautious survey of the shore proved them finally alone, but he kept his voice low in case his words carried over the water. "I know where the fever is coming from."

"What?" Now it was her turn to check for soldiers. She relaxed and drifted close again. "How?"

He put a dripping finger to her lips and lowered his voice even more. "According to my sources, the sickness originated in Ethiopia, then migrated to Egypt. But I wondered why we've seen such an increase in deaths despite the closure of the land trade routes." He nodded toward the ships. "Then Sergia died. He traveled to Carthage via Egypt on a Roman frigate."

"Is that what you were doing? Looking for measles?" Her laughter, a surprising delight that buoyed him, would also convince anyone lurking in the shadows that they were lovers. "I thought you were trying to get out of marrying me."

"There are easier ways to dissolve a betrothal contract, woman."

Her arms circled his neck, and their legs tangled. "Don't ships have to go through customs or something?"

"Only the freighters." They kicked in unison, working together to stay afloat, sharing the burden in a way he'd not expected possible of one who couldn't understand the intricate politics involved.

"The troop reinforcements ordered by Aspasius!" Exceptional brilliance shone in her eyes.

"Warships answer to no port authority."

"Well, something has to be done." Her dauntless conviction was fascinating. "The port needs to be shut down, the crews quarantined until I determine they're fever free."

"Even if Aspasius admitted that his military transports are hauling sickness and death, it would be political suicide to let a woman close his port."

Lisbeth released him, and he felt himself sink. "I'm going to check it out." She glided in the direction of the ship.

"Wait." He darted after her and caught her arm in midstroke. "We've drawn enough attention tonight."

"*We* aren't going. I am." Stubborn determination bubbled in her eyes.

"No." He hauled her toward shore.

"If they have measles, you could catch them," she sputtered.

Ignoring her pounding on his arm, he trawled to the shallows. When she found footing, she wiggled free and stood. She kicked water and sand in his face.

He wiped the salt from his eyes. "That's my thanks for saving your life?"

"It's for whoever is watching the show." Lisbeth turned and marched toward the villa, her bare feet leaving angry imprints in the sand, her glistening shoulders leaving an even deeper indentation in his heart.

Tossing his recovered tunic over his shoulder, he cursed the day he'd listened to Felicissimus and bought the beautiful slave girl from Dallas . . . or wherever it was his client had found such a maddening bundle of trouble.

38

LISBETH'S STOMACH HAD A great deal of experience surviving various levels of nervous discomfort. Butterflies before her move to the States. Small birds when she took the MCAT. Vultures while she waited on her residency match. But she hadn't anticipated flying pterodactyls the day of her wedding. The few grapes Ruth had encouraged her to eat for lunch had not stayed down. Finishing the late afternoon snack of olives and cold meat Naomi had delivered was out of the question.

She didn't need food. She needed rest. The continual replay of Cyprian's body against hers as they kissed had kept her up the entire night. Craig's kisses had never ignited such passion.

Infuriating as Cyprian could be, she had to admit he was right about not going to the ships with soldier patrols crawling all over the wharf. But she was right, too. If the ships did indeed harbor the virus, they needed to be burned. Somehow, winning the plague war had diminished in importance compared to a more pressing battle raging inside her.

Despite days of planning, too many things could go wrong at this wedding. Things like Laurentius blurting out something that would expose her or Mama. Or what if Aspasius suddenly remembered her from the slave cell? Or worse, she imagined Cyprian stomping to the altar and announcing that he'd changed his mind, that the attraction they felt as he held her afloat was just part of some crazy horror show. What if he decided she wasn't worth the risk?

Heady scents of rose, crocus, and myrtle hung in the heavy steam of the bathroom. Lisbeth sank into the tub and slowly dragged the strigil over her body, flinching as the thin blade rounded the tiny curve of her breast. Had Cyprian noted her lack of Roman bosoms and wider hips like she'd noticed every sculpted contour of him? Had he observed that his touch caused her to tremble like a willow in a windstorm?

Usually she didn't care what men thought of her, but she couldn't help wondering what was going on in that handsome head of his. Was he attracted to her at all? Or was the physical tension she felt every time he took her in his arms merely the adrenaline rush of the life-and-death situations her presence always seemed to bring down upon his head?

She clambered out of the tub and climbed aboard the massage slab without complaint. For once she didn't mind the primping and pampering. Queenie always said she'd turn heads if she fixed up a bit. This was her wedding day, after all. Call her shallow, but she wanted to be as beautiful as possible.

Naomi slathered Arabian nard over every inch of Lisbeth's freshly scraped and scrubbed skin. Ruth was right. This oily stuff was worth every penny. Submitting to the languid motions, Lisbeth allowed her mind to revisit the pleasure of Cyprian's touch, the protective pressure of his palm on the small of her back, the sure grip of his large hands around her waist, the beat of his heart matching hers with each scissor kick.

Given different circumstances, in a different time, in a different world, perhaps both of them would have willingly embraced the idea of becoming husband and wife. At least that's what she told herself. What Cyprian was telling himself, she could only guess.

Perfumed and wrapped in a thin robe, Lisbeth waltzed into the bedroom where Ruth and Junia waited for her. "Well, what do you think?"

"You smell good." Junia shot out from under Ruth's grip and bounded into her arms. "You should see your dress. Ruth says my dress matches yours." At the corner of her perfect lips, one dimple-size mark remained. A scar to forever remind this child of the parents she had lost. "Can I try on your shoes?"

Lisbeth hugged her. "Okay, but don't trip." She set Junia down and joined Ruth at the bed. "Oh, my. What's all of this?"

"I hope you're pleased." Ruth proudly pointed to the stunning array of garments, jewels, and the exquisite red sandals with ivory buckles that Junia was already happily clomping about in. "Well, what do you think?"

Lisbeth ran her hand over a piece of linen woven with the reddish-violet hues of an African sunset. "I feel like Cinderella."

"Who?" Junia asked as she tried to balance herself in the shoes.

"Never mind." Lisbeth took her hand and helped steady her. Nothing in the bridal magazines she and Queenie had flipped through could compare to the beautiful wedding trousseau laid out before her. "How did you get this together so fast, Ruth?"

"Proper connections and proper help. You'll learn." Ruth's eyes slid from Junia parading across the room in the sandals back to Lisbeth. "The right of dressing the bride belongs to the bride's mother."

A twinge of regret prickled Lisbeth's glistening skin. Mama had missed so much. The loss of Lisbeth's first tooth. The arrival of her first zit. The onset of her daughter's menstrual cycle. Poor Papa, he hadn't known what to do when Lisbeth thought she was bleeding to death. Mama was absent when Papa put her on a plane bound for the States, when she rented her first apartment, and when she graduated from med school. And now Mama would miss the joy of yet another important rite of passage . . . dressing her daughter for a wedding ceremony.

Up until a few days ago, Mama's absence would have made Lisbeth angry, salt in a raw wound. But after hearing Mama's fight to get to Laurentius, she knew her mother would have done anything to attend the wedding. Lisbeth swallowed all the things she wished she'd said but hadn't that day she went to set her mother's dislocated shoulder. "Mama would be pleased to have you take her place, Ruth. If she makes it to the wedding, it will be more than I deserve."

"We'll start with the sleeveless chemise." Ruth slid a straight, close-fitting tunic of delicate white fabric over Lisbeth's head. The slip-like garment molded to Lisbeth's slight curves, and the hem of intricate embroidery brushed the tops of her bare feet. "Since it's so warm this evening, I think we'll do your hair first, and then you can step into your *stola* later."

Ruth spent the next hour brushing a lustrous sheen into Lisbeth's curls. Next, Ruth divided the shimmering mass into six sections with an iron spearhead. She arranged the strands around a small cone she'd fastened to Lisbeth's head with hand-carved ivory combs. Two hours later, Ruth finally gave the chair a spin.

The princess in the mirror took Lisbeth's breath away.

"I wish you knew how beautiful you are." Ruth gathered the ruby-colored stola. "The sun will set soon. We must not keep the bridal party waiting." Lisbeth stepped into the crisp, linen folds. Ruth wrapped a thin cord of golden threads around Lisbeth's waist and tied the strands into the knot of Hercules—

guardian of wedded life. "Only your husband may untie this knot." Her sly smile sent the pterodactyls soaring again in Lisbeth's stomach.

Ruth lifted a transparent, flame-colored veil and secured it to Lisbeth's head with a wreath of amaracus flowers. "Junia, get out of those shoes."

39

PYTROS PRODDED THE COALS beneath the bronze feet of his master's household god. Across the atrium, different-colored birds protested their confinement in the golden cages. Magpies, starlings, finches, and a rare nightingale . . . all trapped. Pytros understood their frustration. He, too, was trapped. A slave bound by love to a heartless master. He'd risked so much to pry information from Felicissimus and bring Aspasius the secret of how Magdalena had managed to run around behind his back. And how had he been rewarded? He hadn't. Pytros jabbed the poker into the altar fire and sent coals bouncing across the marble floor.

The uneven click of Aspasius's built-up shoes echoed in the hall. "There you are, Pytros." He swept into the atrium, running his hand along the row of gilded bars. A flurry of feathers and empty seed shells spilled through the bars.

"I'm in trouble." Aspasius stepped up to the cupboard.

Pytros ceased his manipulation of the fire. Had Aspasius just confided something personal, something more deep and meaningful? "I am here to serve, my lord. How can I help?"

"Offerings must be made to Mercury until the gods are appeased."

"I'm honored to assist such a powerful man. A noble man. A

man admired by the gods." Pytros stirred the coals. "I'm sure the gods will eagerly answer your prayers."

"Then why is there such trouble in Carthage?" Aspasius stared at the rise of a single yellow flame. "There are still some in the Senate who disagree with my tactics to bring the Christians into submission. The fever among my stone workers has brought several renovation projects to a halt. And if Cyprian's wedding is not stopped, his election will be secured. He's very favored, especially with those who adored his father."

A blue flame joined the attack upon the slivers of wood Pytros fed the fire. He'd considered the merit of laying another option upon the altar. But why? His last attempt had resulted in dashed hopes. So far, his disgusting groveling and fawning over Aspasius had gotten him nowhere.

"What should I do?" Had Aspasius spoken to Mercury or to him?

Pytros cocked his head. "Must you stop the wedding, my lord?"

"I must, if I don't want to be banished from Carthage." Aspasius snorted and pulled a small packet of grain from his pocket. "Wishing Cyprian dead would defile all of my sacrifices. I cannot afford to anger the gods worse than they already are." Hand over the brazier, Aspasius funneled the finest oats money could buy onto the smoldering wood.

Greedy flames leapt from the center of the bowl. Within seconds every kernel had been devoured. A grain-fueled glow reflected red on Aspasius's distraught face. Oh, how this man needed him, Pytros thought. It was all he could do not to wrap his arms around his master's expansive girth and hold him close.

Pytros checked the hall for signs of that wretched woman Aspasius had kept chained to his bed since he discovered her secret life. Perhaps the time had come to share the rest of what

Felicissimus had told him. "I believe there is another way, my lord."

Aspasius turned slowly and smiled; a flicker of appreciation registered in the simmering coals of his eyes. Pytros was delightfully encouraged. Aspasius took the fire poker from Pytros's hand and hung it on the iron hook beside the cupboard. "Tell me more." He clasped Pytros's shoulder.

Hope, as greedy and warm as the altar flames, sparked in Pytros's loins. He gazed into the black eyes of his master, hungry for a kernel of fuel.

Pytros followed Aspasius from the atrium. As he passed the bird cages, he dragged his free hand along the bars and joyfully sent the aviary into another round of enviable protest.

40

O UR NUMBERS ARE GROWING, Bishop." Felicissimus paced the library with the chip on his shoulder that he'd worn since Cyprian dismissed him at the arena. "Why not stage a rebellion? Have Cyprian publicly proclaim his allegiance to Christ, and storm the proconsul's palace? War seems a better plan than this marriage."

"For whom? Do you plan to take up the sword, little man?" Caecilianus closed the door, shutting off the view of the nosy wedding guests mingling in the hall. "The church must never become the spear pointed at Rome."

"Better we remain the dung beneath Rome's boot?" Felicissimus asked with a growl, casting his disapproval before Cyprian, who stood staring out the windows that overlooked the garden. "What say you, solicitor?"

Caecilianus jumped in with an answer. "I'm certain Cyprian is grateful for your concern, but he's graciously agreed to this wedding as a means to a peaceful, legal resolution."

"Is it true, then, my patronus?" Felicissimus's outrage bore into Cyprian's back, but he continued watching the slaves flutter about, lighting lamps and candles for the biggest night of his life. In the eyes of the one God he and Felicissimus may be equals, but in his house he did not have to explain his decisions to one of his clients. "You intend to marry the slave girl I found floating in a cistern?"

Cyprian could take no more of this badgering. "In less than ten minutes I'm placing a ring on the finger of a woman I hardly know. A woman whose crazy ways scramble every logical thought in my head. The very woman the Lord provided . . . through you, I might add." He turned and faced Felicissimus. "Who are you to question from whence our blessing came?" Cyprian hooked his finger to loosen the neck of his wedding tunic, and still he found it difficult to breathe. "We all must work with what God has given us . . . even if that means working with—" Cyprian cut himself off, but he could see he was too late. His irritation had wounded Felicissimus. He put a hand to the little man's shoulder. "Forgive me, friend. I know you have the best interests of the church at heart . . . as do I."

"So the church must play charades while Aspasius gathers soldiers?" Felicissimus asked, his disapproval obvious. "It's not how I'd run things."

"If the one God were to ever appoint you bishop," Caecilianus said, patting the slave trader's shoulder, "then *you* can do as the one God commands you."

41

DRESSED IN FULL WEDDING finery and feeling every bit the fairy-tale princess, Lisbeth sipped honeyed wine near the atrium fountain.

Ruth pulled her aside. "Before I fetch Junia, let me pray for you."

After all this woman had done for her, Lisbeth could hardly say no. She bowed her head and thought of Queenie and the pleased grin that would split her churchgoing friend's face if she could see her dressed for the red carpet and praying. She could almost hear Queenie's hearty belly laugh. Lisbeth cracked open one eye. No Queenie. No hospital break room. Nothing familiar. Funny how her mind insisted on believing her old life waited for her to come home. Everyone had probably moved on without so much as one backward thought.

When Ruth's prayer ended, Lisbeth did feel a bit better, as if the blessings Ruth had pronounced over her might actually compensate for her losses and somehow make this day bearable.

"I wish I could believe in your God."

"Only fools say there is no God. And I have never believed you a fool, Lisbeth of Dallas."

A warm calm crept through Lisbeth's veins despite the fact that she was about to marry a man under false pretenses. A man she hardly knew, a strong, powerful man who judged her to be beneath his station. A man who believed her to be a third-century slave on the one hand and a royal pain on the other. While normal men tended to shy away from her intelligence and drive, Cyprian was not the least bit intimidated. Figuring out the best way to keep him on board with her mission once he knew the truth would not be easy.

"My lady?" Naomi appeared.

Lisbeth handed her the silver chalice. "Is she here?"

The nod of Naomi's head indicated that Lisbeth should turn around.

Lisbeth whirled. "Mama?" Her mother's dual black eyes drew Lisbeth up short, but relief that she was alive won out. She threw her arms around the neck she hadn't hugged since she was five. "I knew you'd come."

"I've missed so much of your life. I couldn't miss your wedding." Mama held her tightly, as if she'd never let her go again. Lisbeth drank in the smell of her, a combination of the dusty herbs she kept in her medical bag.

Laughter spilling over from the garden broke the spell.

"Let me look at you." Mama reluctantly released her and gave her a one-eyed appraisal. Lisbeth could only guess what this day had cost her mother. Shame didn't begin to describe what she felt—thinking about herself and what Mama's absence from her life had meant to *her* while her mother thought only of protecting her children. "You're absolutely beautiful . . . even with red hair."

The praise washed across Lisbeth's parched soul. It was pathetic to think that she'd wasted so many years believing her mother had left her on purpose. Even if she spent the rest of her life making it up to this woman, it wouldn't be enough. "Like mother, like daughter."

"Far better. Some of your father, too." Mama's trembling hand went to her eye, deflecting a flash of deep regret. "Thanks for getting Laurentius."

"So Tabari got word to you that he was safe?"

"She did." Mama led her away from the garden door. "God help me, but I had prepared myself to kill that brute if I had to."

"It would have been self-defense, but I'm glad God did help you." Taking a life when her mother had worked for years to save lives would destroy her, a truth Lisbeth knew all too well. "Hopefully, Laurentius won't say anything when he sees you. He's been so excited all week that we thought about not letting him come to the wedding. But Cyprian didn't have the heart to lock him away." She'd meant the comment to be a compliment to Cyprian rather than a judgment on the choices her mother had been forced to make, but she could tell from Mama's flinch that keeping Laurentius hidden all these years had not been easy. "I know you only did what you had to do."

"We've practiced acting like he doesn't know me, but sometimes he forgets." She patted the Herculean knot at Lisbeth's waist and changed the subject. "Cyprian is a good man."

"This isn't a real wedding. I'm—"

"Here." Mama fished the leather cord out from under the veil around her bruised neck. "I want you to have this."

"I can't take Papa's ring."

"Your father and I had our differences, but I know he loved me. I pray you'll know the kind of love that lasts a lifetime." She tied the cord around Lisbeth's neck and hid the ring in the folds of her gown.

Aspasius's shrill laughter drifted from the garden. Mama shuddered, then quickly kissed Lisbeth's cheek. "Don't acknowledge me in any way. No matter what happens. Promise?"

"Magdalena?" Ruth appeared in the atrium with a scrubbed and polished Junia in tow. "Aspasius mustn't see you together. The resemblance between you is uncanny. Even with the changes we've made."

"I can't thank you enough for what you've done for my daughter, Ruth."

Ruth waved her on. "Return to Aspasius's side before he sends someone to search for you."

Mama blew a kiss over her shoulder and hurried back to the garden.

Ruth adjusted the wedding veil and ran a horsehair brush of crimson lip dye over Lisbeth's lips one last time. "I got some on your teeth."

Lisbeth finger-scrubbed her teeth. "Ready or not, here I go."

Ruth handed Junia a basket filled with flowers. "Remember what I told you? Toss a few of these petals around as you walk straight to me. Understand?"

Junia nodded. "I'm a princess."

"That you are, my sweets." Ruth gave the little girl a squeeze. This child had found a new home, and the thought pleased Lisbeth. "Now, smile, everyone." Ruth threw open the double doors to the garden and darted out of the way.

All eyes turned toward Lisbeth. Before her, a sea of dignitary white and purple perched upon cushioned couches. Although the Senate council had been invited out of propriety, the curious pride of hungry lions attended mostly out of fear. Fear that this woman from the desert might possess a power capable of destroying them all. She must be careful and remember every instruction Ruth had given her. One mistake and Aspasius would end their ruse with a vicious swipe of his claw.

She tried to move forward, but her body was as frozen as the fountain statute. Only her eyes responded to the frantic transmissions her brain issued, two organic cameras that scanned the crowd. Aspasius had his arm draped over her mother. She couldn't afford to dwell on how badly she wanted to hurt that monster. She pried her gaze from him and visually searched for her groom.

Cyprian stood next to Caecilianus atop the dais. Both were dressed in the heavy white woolen robes this formal occasion required, but they might as well have been worlds apart. The wrinkled bishop with caterpillars for eyebrows looked like he'd grabbed his sheet and jumped out of bed without combing his hair. Cyprian, on the other hand, stood tall in an expertly arranged toga, the pressed creases of the one-shouldered drape tailored to his sculpted body. His hair had been brushed back from his aristocratic forehead, and for a brief moment, she thought she saw his smooth lips toy with a smile. But when she checked again, his face had become expressionless and totally unreadable.

Flute music floated into the hall.

"Do I go now, Ruth?" Junia shouted.

Everyone snickered. "Yes." Ruth crouched before the dais and waved the child forward. "Take Lisbeth's hand."

"Don't be scared." Junia placed her hand in Lisbeth's. "I'm right here."

Lisbeth's feet, heavy as iron, broke free and slid toward Cyprian as if his inscrutable eyes were magnets.

Junia marched her under the swag of lush greenery strung across the transom and into a pillared paradise. The casual beach wedding she and Craig had once discussed had nothing in common with the formality of candlelit tables covered in fine linens and strewn with silver and delicate white flowers.

Laurentius stood in the shadows with Naomi, his lopsided grin bigger than ever. He put his finger up across his lips in the be-quiet symbol they'd practiced. It was all Lisbeth could do not to snatch Mama from her seat beside Aspasius, then grab her half brother and beat it out of there.

Whispers spread through the sober-faced guests as Lisbeth

followed Junia to the dais, where Cyprian waited. From her vantage point of staring up at him, he looked like a Greek god. Bronze, polished, and undeniably handsome. Ruth's instructions, as well as Lisbeth's flimsy escape plan, flew from her head. So Lisbeth just stood there, staring at this man she'd known only a few weeks and contemplating what it would be like to know him a lifetime. Did these heat-inducing thoughts mean she loved him? No, she couldn't. Love would make everything too complicated.

Cyprian stepped forward and offered his hand. Lisbeth laid her palm in his broad, smooth grasp. This was the hand of a man used to pushing paper rather than patients. Would his hands once again circle her waist or draw her to him? Surety pulsed in his clasp. Strength lifted her to his side.

"Follow my lead." Fresh mint tinged his whispered instructions, but Cyprian's steady composure offered no trace of what he was thinking. No hint of the pressure he must be under. Admirable quality. Worthy of imitating. Which she would . . . if she could breathe. Her goal for the moment was trying to keep her knees from locking and passing out in front of fifty people looking for any reason to end Cyprian's bid for office.

She stared at her future husband's mouth. Lips that spoke hard truths as easily as soft kindnesses. Lips that were certain. Lips that could talk their way out of any trouble. And for a brief instant, she wanted to kiss him like she had on the beach, to be sucked into his world with no thought of what she'd left behind.

"Cyprianus Thascius, do you grant your consent?" The old bishop looked up from his scroll. "Cyprian?"

Apparently she wasn't the only one who had been rendered speechless by the words of the marriage contract Caecilianus read before the witnesses. From the faraway look in Cyprian's eyes, his thoughts had stalled as well, or was he bailing? Lisbeth's heart dropped to her stomach. He hadn't wanted this in the first place.

What if their kiss had changed his mind? Maybe he'd decided he didn't want to give this woman he barely knew a legally binding commitment? Most men didn't. Truth be known, Craig was probably secretly relieved she'd disappeared. That way they didn't have to fight over the prenup he'd insisted she sign.

Cyprian turned and faced her. "I do." His confidence launched a shudder that shook Lisbeth's courage. His commitment sounded genuine, like a marriage was a better idea than a wedding.

"And Lisbeth of Dallas, what say you?" Caecilianus asked.

She'd never put herself out there romantically. Not really. Not even with Craig. She'd always reserved that secret part of herself, held it back, kept it safe from the pain that comes with loving someone too much. What if the tiny seed of love, or like, or whatever it was that had been growing in her heart, took root and tangled her emotions and her plans? Then what? Mama, Laurentius, and her decision to do what she could to stop the growing epidemic had already made cutting free of the third century very complicated. She managed a weak nod.

Cyprian lifted her left hand. His eyes bore into hers as if he were casting an anchor into a troubled sea. He slid a gold band with a pearl setting on her third finger, kissed her hand, and set the anchor's metal flukes deep in her heart. If his ship was to sink, she was going down with him. Lisbeth closed her eyes and braced for his lips on hers. Instead, Cyprian lifted their clenched hands high. Her eyes fluttered open just as the sedate wedding guests clapped their approval.

Hiding her unexplainable disappointment, she accompanied Cyprian to the empty cushions at the head table's reclining couch. Along the way, Cyprian stopped to accept congratulations from important senators and to make formal and uncomfortable introductions of his new wife.

The U-shaped head table glittered with the details of Ruth's attention. Aspasius and Mama waited for them on long couches that graced one side. Caecilianus and Ruth lounged on the other. She and Cyprian took their place between them, settling into the plush cushions. Bare shoulders touching, Lisbeth reached for a glass of wine to douse the flame physical contact ignited. Cyprian was far too smart to shift away or force a space between them. Was his action false bravado, or the need to offset the volatility of the proconsul to her right? Either way, she couldn't resist leaning as close to her new husband as possible. Slaves arranged the folds of their wedding garments and quietly removed their matching red sandals.

Cyprian glanced at her and smiled as if he, too, was genuinely relieved they'd made it this far. "Shall we eat, then?" He clapped once, and servants shuttled from the shadows, toting silver goblets filled with honeyed wine. Next, they served appetizers of pickled guinea eggs, salt-water eel imported from Tartessus, and Spanish snails braised to a golden crisp and floating in melted goat butter.

Aspasius devoured an entire skewer of grilled peacock, then tossed the stick. "I see you've spared no expense, solicitor."

"My father always said to buy the best wine you can afford or notice the difference in the morning." Cyprian jabbed a stiff piece of bread into the goose liver pâté.

"Your father understood that impressions are everything." Aspasius licked his fingers, then reached for another snail. His black irises had become beady little stones swimming in jaundiced sclera. "Weddings are not so different from public office. Once the honeymoon is over, the term of service can seem interminable."

"The best is yet to come." Cyprian kissed Lisbeth's cheek with a flirtatious ease that aroused giggles from the servants and sent a rush of heat to Lisbeth's face. "Isn't that so, my love?"

"Absolutely." Lisbeth ducked as a huge steamed lobster was placed on Cyprian's plate.

Cyprian examined the succulent crustacean, then gave a pleased nod. A piping hot boar covered in wild truffles and roasted in a pit of coals was carried in on a platter that required two men to haul. Everyone clapped . . . everyone but Aspasius.

By the time the guests had polished off the pork, several rounds of media beer had also been consumed. Spirits were high. Even Lisbeth felt her defenses melting.

"And for dessert?" Cyprian asked Ruth.

"A fine Falernian wine chilled in snow transported from the Atlas Mountains." She lifted her chin and waited as the admiration of Cyprian's generosity spread through greedy guests reaching for frosty glasses. "And a confectionary delight of dried fruit preserves sealed inside a flaky maize crust."

Aspasius's head snapped up, then wavered like he had no business trying to walk a straight line. Eyes bloodshot, he placed his palms on the table and worked to push himself upright. "What? No cake offering for Jupiter?" His slurred voice had the sharp edge of a man armed with a dagger of damaging information he intended to use. "Won't the gods be angry?"

Silence ripped through the garden. Cyprian shifted away from Lisbeth, and she felt the anchor that had tethered them together plow a trench in her brief sense of security. The storm they'd feared had come ashore.

Aspasius shook his finger at Cyprian. "Why would a good Roman risk angering the gods?" His hand came down heavily, rattling the silver and giving Lisbeth and Magdalena a start. "There's only one reason a man seeking office would do something so foolish." The proconsul shoved back from the table, placed his hand on Mama's shoulder, then struggled to his feet. He waivered for a moment, swaying like a drunken sailor, then fell face-first into the dried remains of goose pâté.

42

Most of the wedding candles had melted into glossy puddles by the time the bodyguards of Aspasius had his limp body scraped off the head table. A muddy brown splotch of avian pâté dripped from his broken nose.

"I drugged him." Mama spoke English as she tucked a small glass vial between her breasts. "Come morning, he'll have a black eye as noteworthy as the ones he gives me." She gave Lisbeth a coy smile, as the entourage of eight burly servants hauled Aspasius from the garden to the waiting litter. "Hopefully he won't remember a thing."

Lisbeth wished she could remove her own spinning head from her shoulders. "How did he find out?"

"I have my suspicions," Mama whispered. "You must be careful."

Lisbeth knew Mama must leave, so why did she feel like she was five years old again and begging her mother not to leave her tent? "Are you safe?"

"You have bigger worries than me. Look at their faces." The uncomfortable silence that had pervaded the garden after Aspasius's partial accusation had not dissipated with Mama's pronouncement of her master's inability to stomach cheap snails. Doubt and wary suspicion clouded every focused eye. "If you don't go through with the rest of the wedding festivities, I'm afraid raising the charge that Cyprian violated his obligations to the gods will be enough to end Cyprian's bid for office." She gave Lisbeth's arm a squeeze. "Don't worry. God brought you here, and he has a way of bringing a person exactly where they need to be."

God . . . or fate? The question lingered in Lisbeth's mind as she watched her mother disappear in a swirl of green silk. How could everyone be so sure the third century was her destiny?

Murmured voices summoned Lisbeth from her thoughts. She turned to find Cyprian standing by her side. A look of understanding passed between them. He, too, was conscious of the guests staring at them, rubberneckers waiting on their precarious house of cards to implode. One false move, and their deception would be over.

She took his hand. "Surely we're not going to let a drunken guest ruin our wedding night."

"Nor our future." Cyprian clapped, and servants scurried into place. Naomi handed Cyprian a bundle of sticks dipped in resin. With a steady hand, he held the torch to a flickering candle. Bursting flame broke the dour spell hanging over the garden and spawned a tittering of nervous laughter. Cyprian passed the light to one of the young torchbearers, who turned and lit the torches of two other escorts.

Ruth stepped up behind Lisbeth and put her hands on her shoulders, whispering, "May I stand in for your mother?"

Lisbeth looked around for Laurentius, hoping he'd not felt as deserted as she. He watched from the shadows, his thumb in his mouth. She could do this for her brother. She could do this for her mother. "She'd be pleased."

Ruth wrapped her arms around Lisbeth's waist and began shouting feigned words of trying to save her. The crowd pressed

Cyprian toward her, urging him to take what was now lawfully his with a phony show of outrage.

In a pretend show of force that suited this situation perfectly, Cyprian ripped Lisbeth free of Ruth's embrace. Roars of approval drowned Ruth's fake protest. Three young torchbearers led them from the garden, shouting off-color jokes.

Cyprian's hand swallowed hers. "This could hurt."

"I don't like the sound of that." This wasn't a real marriage. This was a business arrangement, and the jury was still out on whether their plan was going to work. Suddenly a walnut struck Lisbeth's shoulder. "Ouch. What the—?"

"Symbols of fertility." Cyprian did his best to shield her with his body while nuts pounded the cocoon created by the excess folds of his toga. "I told you this marriage would be painful."

"Let's get out of here."

Hurled walnuts and curious stares accompanied their race through the villa's marbled halls. Growing anticipation thrummed in Lisbeth's veins.

By the time they arrived at Cyprian's master quarters, most of the breathless guests were thankfully empty-handed. They paused outside the bedroom door. Cyprian attempted to thank everyone for coming and send them on their way.

"Kiss her!" Laurentius shouted. And the crowd quickly joined his chant. "Kiss her. Kiss her."

Cyprian held up a hand to silence them. "But what if she bites?" He turned to her, his eyes twinkling mischief in the torchlight.

"Kiss her anyway," Laurentius said. And everyone started the chants again.

"They won't go until I do." Before she could grant permission, Cyprian's lips landed lightly upon hers. A delicious taste of honeyed wine and salty eel registered in her rapidly clearing brain.

He pulled free, leaving Lisbeth gasping for air. Loving Cyprian Thascius was a lost cause. But she couldn't make herself stop.

A tinge of pink in his cheeks, he bowed to the whistles and shouts. "Now, my friends, you must leave me to fulfill my duties." His muscled arms scooped her up, and he kicked the door open. Howling cheers erupted. Holding her tightly against his chest, he stepped inside and slammed the door shut with his foot.

Arms snaked around his neck, Lisbeth was aware of the fruity remains of well-aged wine on his breath and the six o'clock shadow on his square jaw. Breathing hard, he stood there, holding her in his arms. Neither of them daring to look into the other's eyes. Neither of them speaking. Neither of them willing to make the first move. Frozen in time as they listened to the receding laughter of the crowd.

Warning sirens, blaring like ambulances in the distance, sounded in her head. Lisbeth released her hold on his neck and braced for whatever was to come next. Not sure what to do with her arms, she glanced around the candlelit room, searching for an escape. The massive bed brought her quest to a screeching halt. Someone had turned the master's room into a honeymoon suite. A decanter of wine chilled in a crock of snow was placed on the nightstand. Roman symbols of fertility—flowers, greenery, and fruit—were strewn everywhere. She felt her skin grow hot as the coals glowing in the brass brazier. Ruth had taken this wedding thing way too far.

"Well, I think we survived the wedding feast fiasco." Cyprian set her feet upon the thick carpet warmed by the charcoal fire, but he kept a hand on her arm.

"Now, if we can only survive the marriage until after the election." Lisbeth's knees were not cooperating.

He moved to steady her. "Depends on how much Aspasius knows."

Lisbeth held her breath, her eyes fastened upon his. "Either way," she stammered. "I guess it will be the survival of the fittest."

He considered her comment for a moment, exploring her face as if seeing it clearly for the first time but revealing nothing of what he thought. His eyes slowly lowered, and she could feel his gaze scanning the entirety of her body with the intensity of an MRI machine. "You're a strange one, Lisbeth of Dallas." He reached for the knot at her waist, his bold, possessive touch causing an involuntary shudder. Dropping to his knees, he began meticulously unraveling the twisted cord. As he concentrated on his task, Lisbeth turned over several options. She could run. Kick him where it hurt. Or believe that he wanted her as badly as she wanted him.

She focused on the golden waves of his hair. They'd both had too much to drink. He should be stopped before boundaries were crossed, before this wedding night farce went too far. Remind him again that theirs was a marriage of convenience. A ruse to get him elected and her family freed from the clutches of the Roman proconsul. A historical necessity.

Lisbeth raised her hand to push him off, but instead her fingers plunged into the soft, thick strands of his golden hair, a force that took him by surprise and tilted his head toward her. She held him in her grasp, the sharp lines of his face softened by the muted light. Heart beating against her heaving breasts, she was sure of what she wanted to do next. Sure, but not sure.

A PLEASED smiled curled Cyprian's lips, and he felt the knot give way. Lisbeth's arms fell limp at her sides. He held up the freed belt. "Feel better?"

Folds of fabric slid from her shoulders and fell at her feet, exposing the tight-fitting chemise tunic. She nodded. Her breath short, restricted spurts despite her expanding rib cage.

He rose slowly and tossed the cord upon the bed. The back of his hand skimmed her cheek and tucked a stray hair behind her ear. His index finger followed the curve of her lips and drifted down her neck, tracing the fine bones of her neck where he felt the lump of excited anticipation rising in her throat.

His finger hooked the leather string hanging from her neck. "What's this?"

"The ring my father gave my mother."

"And did your father love your mother?"

"Yes."

He said nothing, but his breathing rate slowed. His fist opened with the natural insistence of a blooming rose and slid across her shoulder.

Her breath caught, but she did not take her eyes off his. He could feel alarm pulsing beneath her thin gown. He didn't want to frighten her, but he could not stop touching her. With both hands, he encircled her waist, a power that rendered her defenseless against his six-foot-two frame.

Holding her at arm's length, he assessed her. "I don't like your hair."

Lisbeth released an embarrassed snort. "Me either."

"May I?" He raised his hands and removed the wreath of flowers. His body loomed close. The heady scent of Arabian nard propelled his senses into high alert. The veil fell to the floor, and they both chuckled with nervous relief. "Hold still." One by one he removed the pins that had secured the hideous styling cone.

"Ah." Lisbeth shook her mane free. "Ruth's hairdo gave me such a headache."

His fingers toyed with the curly ends spilling over her bare shoulders. He reached up with both hands and wove his fingers into the tangled auburn mess. His thumbs massaged her temples, and he watched her tension ease away. His eyes sought hers and locked. He longed to see deep inside her soul.

His hands cupped her face, and her eyes flew open. He smiled and gently lifted her chin. His mouth hovered over hers. "You're beautiful," he whispered.

"Uh, I appreciate that, but this isn't a real marriage, remember? We had an agreement."

He closed the space between them, slipped his arms around her waist, and covered her mouth with the tender brush of his.

A DEFIBRILLATING jolt shot through Lisbeth. He gathered her body against his, while his lips explored hers with a thirsty passion. Deep. Long. Fully. She'd been kissed before by men who claimed they loved her, but even Craig had never caused such an intense warmth to spread through her limbs or press the traces of doubt from her thoughts. Her arms slowly twined around his neck. Everything else fell away: Papa. Tumbling through the portal. Mama. Laurentius. Measles. Gone. Nothing but the sound of the sea, a thrashing against the rocks. She kissed him back hungrily, filling her own emptiness.

Suddenly he broke free and pushed away. Cold distance, similar to the chilling shock of being ripped out of a warm bed on a winter morning, hung between them.

"I can't do this." Breathing like he'd just finished a marathon, he turned and snatched the exquisite coverlet from the bed. Fruit and flowers bounced across the floor.

"What's wrong?" Lisbeth tried to move toward him, to climb back into those arms of safety, but the yards of loosened fabric held her prisoner. "What did I do?"

A flick of Cyprian's wrist billowed the coverlet and sent it floating to the carpet. "Sleep." He dropped to the crude pallet, crossed his arms over his head to create a pillow, and made himself comfortable.

"Sleep? You get me all hot, and now you want me to sleep?"

"You agreed to be mine, to allow me to do as I please with you, remember?" He nodded toward the bed, indicating she should retire alone. "Tomorrow the real games begin."

The kiss had shattered the facade. She'd seen desire in his eyes. "Don't pretend you don't want me."

"Well rested and at your best is what I want."

"Okay, we can do that after . . . I thought you—"

"Enough!" He raised himself up on one elbow, a look on his face that she could only interpret as sadness. "God may ask many things of me, Lisbeth of Dallas. But taking advantage of you is something I could never do." And he blew out the candle.

43

Lisbeth tossed and turned in the gilded bed, the emptiness of another rejection rattling inside. Cyprian's gentle snore wafted from his pallet. How could he sleep?

She eased from the bed and slipped out to the balcony, hoping the enormity of the night would swallow up this hollow, tingling sensation. Who was this God who owned Cyprian's heart? This God who compelled people to think of others before thinking of themselves?

After pacing for a couple of hours and feeling no change, she padded back into the room. Moonlight framed Cyprian's face and bare chest. She bent and touched his hair, but he just mumbled and turned his back to her. She left him on the floor and fell upon the downy tick. Pillow plopped over her head, she eventually drifted into a fitful sleep.

"My lady." Ruth poked Lisbeth's shoulder. "I hate to bother you before your wedding breakfast, but—"

Lisbeth lifted the pillow. Light flooded the room. Someone had tucked the coverlet around her, wrapping her in a cocoon as if they expected her to awaken transformed. "What time is it?"

"Nearly noon." Without a single question as to why she alone occupied the marriage bed, Ruth freed Lisbeth from the blanket and helped her rise to a sitting position. "I need your assistance."

Head pounding, Lisbeth rubbed her eyes and tried to concentrate on something other than the humiliating fiasco of her wedding night. "What?" The doors leading to the balcony were open. Cyprian's pallet was empty.

"A father and two children arrived this morning."

Now that she was the wife of a wealthy politician, did Ruth expect her to care about the comings and goings of her husband's clientele? "What are you talking about?"

"They're sick." Ruth offered her a mug of something steamy. "And while they were preparing to come, the mother went into labor."

"Labor?" She'd awoken a different woman, in different circumstances, and yet something familiar suddenly kicked in. "Are they coughing?"

"Yes."

"Don't touch them or anything they brought with them, Ruth." Lisbeth threw back the covers. "Keep Laurentius in his room." She jumped from the bed and downed a quick sip of hot tea.

"The man hated to leave his laboring wife, but she couldn't walk . . . so." Ruth held out the tunic of a slave. "Cyprian said you could go with him to get her, but no one must know."

"Really? My husband's going to move a laboring woman? Obviously he's never had a baby." Neither had she, and she felt even less prepared to deliver one on her own; even the thought of it made her palms sweat. "I'm going alone."

"No. It's too dangerous."

"Everything is risky business around here."

"You husband waits for you in the library."

"He can't go." Lisbeth wiggled into the scratchy, brown sack dress. "If he thinks he can get away from me by catching measles and dying, he's got another thing coming."

"Do you want me to go?"

"No. Neither one of you should risk exposure."

"What about the father and his children? I can't turn them away."

Lisbeth gathered her hair into a ponytail. "Let's put them in my old room. Once I deliver the baby, I'll decide what to do with the whole family." She secured her red mane with the pins Cyprian had scattered across the floor. That his touch still seared her cheek scared her more than the thought of delivering a baby alone. "In the meantime, gather supplies and stack them outside my bedroom door." She rattled off the things needed for making vaporizers, mustard poultices, and hydrating solutions. "Is there any snow left from last night?"

Ruth shook her head.

"Then send for more. It will help bring down their fevers, but don't touch them. I'll give them sponge baths when I get back." Lisbeth noticed a sheepish look on Ruth's face. "Have you touched them?"

Ruth nodded. "They needed help."

"Your big heart will be the death of you." Lisbeth pointed to the basin. "Wash your hands with soap; then wash them again with the hottest water you can stand." A search for shoes yielded those horrible red sandals, another reminder of last night's catastrophe. "These will give me away." She threw them on the bed. "I'll stop by my room for another pair, and while I'm there, I'll get my patients settled." She poured water in the basin and splashed her face. "No matter how sick they seem, promise me you'll stay away from them until I get back."

Ruth's lack of commitment left Lisbeth more than a little worried, but all she could do was allow her friend to join her at the basin for a good hand scrubbing.

"So how was it?" Ruth asked, her eyes cutting Lisbeth's way.

Lisbeth backed away from the question she'd been dreading. "How was what?"

"Your first time together." Ruth's smile refused to be contained. "I pray he was gentle."

Something akin to shame accompanied Lisbeth's reflection in the polished brass mirror. Everyone expected her to emerge from her husband's chambers as a *matrona*, a satisfied and happy wife in every sense of the word. "More merciful than I deserved." Another lie to add to the stack she was accumulating, but this was no time to seek aid for a rebuffed schoolgirl crush.

"Details will have to wait." Lisbeth dried her hands on her tunic and hurried to the atrium. The little family huddled together on one of the couches, their faces splotchy with measles. Without taking time for a thorough examination, she scooped both boys into her arms. She turned to find Cyprian standing in the doorway. "Get back."

"Let me help," he insisted.

"No way. They're very contagious." She awaited his reluctant retreat, then spoke to the father. "Sir, can you walk?" The man didn't waste effort on an answer. Instead, he raised himself from the bench. "Good. I need you to follow me." Lisbeth moved the little family to her room as quickly as she could.

All three of her new cases fell into the bed. The two brothers were asleep before she could remove their filthy shoes. Between the father's coughing spells, she managed to get directions to his apartment and his wife's name: Eunike, a Greek by the sound of it.

Weighed down by the dual burden of trying to save them and a sick woman in labor, Lisbeth retrieved her mother's stethoscope from the nightstand. If only Mama were here. As much as she hated to admit it, she would need Cyprian's help in locating Eunike.

Stethoscope lassoed around her neck, Lisbeth went in search of her new husband.

Ruth met her outside the library door with her mother's medical bag and Junia in tow. "I added suture supplies, a couple of clean tunics, wine, and a blanket for the baby."

"You're a terrific nurse." She took the bag, grateful to have another piece of her mother to take with her. "But remember what I told you: stay far away from my patients."

"Should I give them something to eat?"

"No!" Yelling was not going to deter Ruth's passion for strays. "Junia's immune now. Let her serve them tea and honey." Lisbeth squatted next to the quiet, wide-eyed girl, no doubt reliving the death of her own parents. "You can be my big-girl helper and give them a drink, right?"

Junia swallowed, then threw her arms around Lisbeth's neck. "Don't let their mama die."

How could she make that kind of a promise? Even if she had access to the best medical supplies, which a few rags and some wine were not, she couldn't guarantee her ability to save a life. Abra had taught her that hard lesson, and she would never forget it. "Ruth, help me out here."

"Come on, Junia. Let's fix some eucalyptus tea." Ruth untangled Junia's arms and led her toward the kitchen. "You're such a brave girl. I'm glad you're here."

Lisbeth rose to her feet. When she turned, Cyprian and Caecilianus stood in the library doorway, compassion on their faces.

With a sigh of resignation, she held out the directions she'd scribbled on a piece of papyrus. "I don't know how to find this man's wife."

44

A S THEY SEARCHED THE polluted tenement alleys for the laboring mother, Lisbeth prayed the scanty knowledge she'd accumulated on her brief labor-and-delivery rotation would outweigh the fear pulsing through her veins. The last time she'd dealt with a baby, things hadn't ended well.

Lisbeth stepped over sour-smelling refuse that littered the uneven streets and hurried to catch up with Cyprian. Home births had been the de facto method of delivery for centuries. This woman could probably drop a baby in the field, strap it to her breast, and go right back to work. Needless worry about possible complications would not help her get the job done.

Cyprian waited outside a door where a woman's labored screams pierced the wood. "I think we've found Eunike." He knocked, and the door creaked open. "Want me to go first?"

"No." Lisbeth didn't move.

"I'm right behind you, then."

"Right." Heart pounding out *get a grip, get a grip, get a grip,* Lisbeth eased inside. "Eunike?"

The little apartment was a mirror image of the one where she'd found Junia, except even more crowded because of the paraphernalia of everyday life and empty pallets taking up the floor space. On the narrow bed, a young woman wearing a soiled nightdress lay spread-eagled, one leg slung over the dirty sheets, the other foot resting on the floor.

"Oh." Cyprian diverted his eyes, but he didn't back out of the room like she'd seen Craig do at his first delivery. "What do you need?"

"Water. Lots of it." Lisbeth snatched an empty crock from the corner. "And get it hot." Although embarrassed, he seemed reluctant to leave her. "Go." Once she had him out of her way, Lisbeth went to the woman, whose eyes were clamped shut in an effort to concentrate on her pain. "Eunike? Your husband sent me."

The woman's eyes flew open. "Help. Me."

"That's what I intend to do." Lisbeth did a quick preliminary exam, noting the woman seemed pretty worn out and possibly dehydrated, but she'd progressed to complete dilation, with the fetal head properly aligned in the birthing canal.

"Hurry," Eunike said, huffing. "I need to push."

"Hang on. Breathe through your nose." Lisbeth dropped to the floor and positioned her mother's medical bag for easy access. "Cyprian!" She dug out some clean rags to glove her hands for the baby catch. "Can you sit up, Eunike?"

"No," the woman replied, panting.

Cyprian burst into the room, water sloshing everywhere, alarm on his face. "What?"

"Help me get her upright."

He hastily placed the pot on the floor and raced into position behind Eunike. His strong arms easily and gently raised the exhausted woman. "This good?"

"Ease her to the edge of the bed." Lisbeth wiped her hands on her tunic. "Eunike, I'm going to put your feet on my shoulders. Wait to push until I say."

The woman expelled a shattering howl. "Hurry!"

"We've got crowning." Lisbeth eyed the dark bulge in the cervix. "Is this your third baby?"

"Fifth," Eunike answered between labored breaths. "Two girls died before they walked."

Lisbeth glanced at Cyprian. The color had left his face. But his steady focus was aimed directly at her, communicating that he believed she could do this. "Let's get this kiddo out and into her mama's hands as quick as we can." Another contraction tightened the swollen belly. "Chin to chest, Eunike." Lisbeth readied for the head. "Okay, girl. Push where it counts."

The baby's head, topped with an abundance of dark, curly hair, appeared. Lisbeth couldn't contain her smile or her relief. "Halfway there, Eunike. Another good push should do it." She patted Eunike's leg. "This one better be a girl, because it's a beauty. Can you give me another good push?"

Gasping for air, the laboring woman spat out, "I *am* pushing."

The fetal head suddenly retracted against the mother's perineum, causing the baby's cheeks to bulge like a turtle pulling its head back into its shell.

Eunike went limp in Cyprian's arms.

"Oh, no." Should she apply a bit of force or allow nature to take its course?

"What's wrong?" he asked.

"I don't know. Something's holding up the delivery." Possibilities tumbled in Lisbeth's mind. The cord? Baby too big? Suddenly a med school test question came to mind . . . shoulder dystocia?

Lisbeth cursed. "The baby's stuck."

"Why?" Cyprian's eyes were wide.

"The shoulder has impacted the maternal symphysis."

Shifting Eunike's weight, Cyprian asked, "What are you talking about?"

"It's rare. This is where I call in an attending. Get some help. But I—"

Cyprian cast a narrow look her way, his disapproval of her fear evident. "Fix it," he ordered, a man used to clapping his hands and having the world scurry to do his bidding.

"Fix it?" She laughed to keep from crying. "She could hemorrhage. The baby could suffer permanent injury. You only have to look at Laurentius to know how well that works out in this society."

He didn't deserve her verbal slap, but right now she felt completely helpless. This rare complication wasn't any more Cyprian's fault than the fact that she was trapped in a serious medical situation with no anesthesiologist, attending, or surgical options.

"If you do nothing . . . they'll die." Cyprian eyed her calmly, a reminder that the best way through this was to stay in control of her terror. To keep her composure so as to not panic the mother. When had she become so risk-averse that she wouldn't try everything she knew rather than let a mother and baby die? *God, help me.*

"Quick, grab her legs." Lisbeth clasped Eunike's ankles and hyperflexed the woman's knees against her abdomen. "You're going to hold her legs against her belly. Hopefully shifting positions will open the pelvis and free the shoulder—" The baby shot out in a gush of reddish water. "Whoa. I almost didn't catch—" Lisbeth looked up. "It's a girl." Cyprian's smile unlocked a deep longing, a heat that warmed her intimate, empty spaces.

"Why isn't she crying?" Eunike's concern snapped Lisbeth out of her trance.

Lisbeth's blurry gaze leapt from Cyprian's to the waxy form in her hands. "Let's find out." She turned the baby facedown and worked mucus from both nostrils. A gentle pat on a miniature foot roused a lusty cry. "Thank God." She and Cyprian shared a relieved laugh and a look that said he was in awe of what she'd accomplished.

"I've helped horses foal"—he steadied Eunike, who was leaning forward with outstretched arms—"but I had no idea."

Lisbeth swallowed the lump his praise had raised in her throat. "Help Eunike lie back." She placed the baby on the woman's naked belly and asked, "What's her name?"

Eunike stroked the tiny head. "What's your name?"

"Lisbeth," Cyprian answered before Lisbeth could speak, a different tone in his voice, a pride that melted Lisbeth on the spot. "Of Dallas."

"*Thascius*," Lisbeth corrected, her eyes locked with Cyprian's. "As of last night."

"Then she shall be called Lisbeth," Eunike declared, "as a wedding gift to you both."

A child named after her was a gift she didn't deserve, but one she would cherish nearly as much as the picture of Cyprian's beaming face.

While Eunike and Cyprian counted fingers and toes, Lisbeth cut the cord and delivered the placenta with no problems. "Let me clean her up, and then you can nurse her."

Eunike relinquished her baby long enough for a brisk rubdown. Lisbeth wrapped the pinking girl in one of the blankets Ruth had sent. The child fit in her arms as if she were her own. She couldn't resist kissing the puckered forehead gearing up for a hungry cry. With an unexpected tug of regret, she handed the baby back to her mother. What was happening to her? She wasn't an emotional person, and here she was on the verge of completely losing control.

"I think she's hungry." Lisbeth watched the infant greedily attach to her mother's breast. Security. That positive touch of humanity. Unconditional love. A primordial glimpse into humans treating others well. Humanity at its best.

Within seconds both mother and child were sound asleep.

Lisbeth glanced at Cyprian standing stone still over the bed and barely breathing. "Baby Lisbeth is beautiful, don't you think?" he whispered, his admiration directed not at the satisfied bundle in Eunike's arms but at her.

Here she was, eighteen hundred years removed from the past she'd rather forget, and all she wanted to do was tell this man the truth, to tell him she didn't deserve his respect. To beg his absolution and forgiveness. "The most beautiful thing I've ever seen."

He moved toward her and lifted her trembling hands to his lips and kissed her ring. "Who are you, Lisbeth of Dallas?"

"Thascius." The word rolled off her tongue, leaving a sweet taste in her mouth. She pointed to the hand he held. "Proof that I am the wife of the solicitor of Carthage."

"A hollow title without the truth." He kissed her.

"You deserve the truth."

The old bishop had been right to insist that the story come from her. Now would be the perfect time to tell her new husband everything, before she fell so far in love with him that she'd never recover from the dissolution of his respect and admiration.

He pulled her to him. "It won't change how I feel about you."

"It might."

The chatter of women returning from the well drifted through the open door.

"Let me clean up; then we'll talk." She snatched the empty crock. "I need some more water."

"I'll fetch it." Cyprian tried to take the jug from her hand.

"No. Fresh air will clear my head, allow my adrenaline to dissipate." Lisbeth gathered the bloody cloths to toss upon the trash heap on her way to the well. "Don't look so terrified. I'll only be gone a few minutes. They'll be fine."

By the time she reached the worn path to the cistern, evening shadows had lowered the temperature several degrees. It had taken all day to find their way to the correct apartment and deliver Eunike's baby. A good day, one of the best days of practicing medicine she'd ever had. She would relive the moment of the baby's arrival the rest of her life. Was it Cyprian's presence that made all the difference? Or was it getting back in the saddle again and having some success after her dismal failure with Abra? Or maybe she felt ten pounds lighter, because Craig was right. She was cut out for obstetrics.

Craig. Obstetrics? The thought stopped her in the middle of the path. The truth, a big, ugly roadblock she hadn't noticed before, now stared her in the face, and she couldn't navigate around it.

He was the one who had convinced her to trade places with him that night in the emergency room. She'd let him blind her with that dreamy smile. Craig Sutton hadn't cared about her hopes and dreams, what she wanted. He'd been more focused on his own career, on the triple gunshot surgery that would add another notch to his belt, than on even considering what would be best for his assigned patient and for the woman he supposedly loved. Even when he had offered to stand up for her at the morbidity and mortality conference, deep down she must have known his promise was nothing but another puff of smoke. Because if he'd really wanted to go to bat for her, he wouldn't have hidden out in the OR during the exact time she was scheduled to report.

And then there was Cyprian. She was kidding herself to even hope . . .

Lisbeth stomped to the well and tossed the roped gourd down the dark cavern. *Thunk.* The last of her hopes and dreams disappeared in the gurgling sounds. Hand over hand, she reeled the heavy gourd to the surface. Wrestling the water to the ledge, she bumped the empty jug with her elbow. Crockery shattered around her feet. Kicking at the pieces of clay in frustration, she turned and slid down the limestone, defeated.

She lifted her chin to search the sky, to find a star, any star, in the deepening darkness. Instead, her line of sight landed underneath the cistern's rocky lip. Swimmers? Yellow and red hand-painted cave swimmers tucked out of sight.

Lisbeth flipped to her knees, her hands shaking as she visually examined the replica of the same three potbellied swimmers from Papa's cave. The Hastings family, he'd called them. Eroded memories suddenly became whole, vivid, and compelling. The last thing she remembered was reaching for the painting of a crimson child with outstretched arms.

She'd found the way home. "Thank God." Lisbeth scrambled to her feet and lifted her hand to touch the scarlet child.

CYPRIAN PACED the length of the birthing bed, his eyes shamefully captivated by the sight of a mother nursing her child. How much more protective would he feel if that were his wife and daughter? Desire so strong rose up within him that he thought his heart would burst. Lisbeth may not completely embrace his faith, but only a good woman would risk everything to deliver a child under such risky circumstances.

He glanced out the open door, noting that the stream of women returning from the well had trickled down to only an occasional passerby. Where was Lisbeth? She'd assured him she would not be gone long and that mother and child would sleep while she cleaned up, but he lacked her abundant confidence when it came to women and babies.

"I'm thirsty." Eunike's damp hair clung to her forehead.

"My wife has gone for water." He jumped when the baby released her hold with a popping smack. "Can you wait, or should I fetch her?"

Milk dribbled from the baby's tiny chin. If she'd had her fill, why did her mouth suck the air like a hungry carp? He had lots to learn before his child suckled at Lisbeth's swollen breast. Desire pumped through his limbs, flooding him with a want he was wrong to even consider.

Lisbeth was his wife in name only, a bargaining chip he was playing in a deadly game. Tell himself what he may, he could no more wipe Lisbeth's quick-to-miss-nothing eyes from his memory than he could yank out his conflicted heart. Her long, slender fingers had freed the trapped child before he could blink. Lisbeth of Dallas would just as easily free herself from him once she had her family safe and secure.

"Burp her." Eunike thrust the fussy baby at him.

"What?"

"Put her against your chest," Eunike said, panting. "And pat her back."

As an only child, he'd never held a baby. Tossing Junia around made him nervous, and she was not as easily broken and very capable of communicating exactly what she did and did not like. "Maybe we should wait for Lisbeth."

"You." Insisting had sapped the last of Eunike's strength.

He didn't have the heart to make an exhausted woman listen to an unhappy baby. Scooping the newborn from Eunike's arms, his hand brushed against the intense heat of her skin.

"Oh, no." Weightless bundle clutched in his trembling hands, Cyprian flew from the room. "Measles."

"LISBETH!" CYPRIAN'S voice carried through the mazelike corridors of the plebeian slums. "Lisbeth!" Breathless and toting a baby, he burst into the courtyard. "Eunike has fever."

Lisbeth's arm hung suspended between where she'd been and where she was going . . . immobilized in an excruciating vise of decision. Stay or go?

"Lisbeth?" Cyprian jostled the screaming infant. "Did you hear me? We can't leave them here."

Her eyes darted between the handsome man holding a baby and the bodies of the faded family clinging to the limestone. Father. Child. Mother. Tangible reminders of everything she knew. If she went home to Papa, she could save him and her old life. If she stayed in the third century, she could save Mama, Laurentius, and Cyprian's city.

"Lisbeth!" Cyprian stuck his little finger in the baby's mouth. "I don't know what to do. I need you."

If she stayed here . . . maybe the man she loved could save *her*.

45

MAGDALENA WHISTLED AS SHE filled the feeders in the bird cages. God had heard her prayers. Brought her daughter and son to safety. Her redemption was near. She'd felt the Lord's hand upon her when the litter bearers had hauled Aspasius from her daughter's wedding. Exactly how all of this was going to work out, she wasn't sure. Would she and Laurentius go back to the twenty-first century with Lisbeth? Or would Lisbeth fall so deeply in love with Cyprian that she would stay in the third century with them? She'd seen the way those two looked at each other. They didn't know it yet, but theirs was a love like she and Lawrence had once shared. As much as she longed to return to her husband, she wasn't sure what she would do if the Lord asked her to leave her daughter behind . . . again.

Magdalena closed the container on the birdseed. What was she thinking? Planning ahead as if God had revealed the passageway home and given her options, which he had not. More than two decades she'd waited, and not once had she come across anything resembling a portal to her old life. And Lisbeth had no better recollection of her fateful entry than she.

Regret tangled the memories of the night she'd allowed a fight with Lawrence to send her stomping off in the dark. In her dreams she imagined him searching the desert, calling her name. And every waking minute she wondered if he missed her as much as she missed him.

She would never know. Some decisions yield consequences that can never be undone. And some decisions change a person in such a profound way that she would be a different person without the consequences. Laurentius and his lopsided smile was a treasured consequence. That Lisbeth had granted her forgiveness for her inability to leave Laurentius was a huge consolation she would forever cherish.

Voices jarred Magdalena from her thoughts and drew her toward the open door to the garden. Tiptoeing across the atrium, she worked to place the men talking with Aspasius.

One was definitely that sneaky little scribe Pytros.

The other . . . Felicissimus.

46

MOONLIGHT SPILLED ACROSS THE bed, wrapping their bodies in a beautiful silvery blanket. Lisbeth pressed Cyprian's arm across her chest and snuggled deeper into the perfect fit of their spoon. She'd wasted so much time and energy looking in all the wrong places for safety and happiness. Content in Cyprian's embrace, the ancient swimmers on the cistern wall seemed a million miles away.

She was home.

"Are you still awake?" Her husband's breath warmed the back of her neck.

Her husband. "Yes."

He lifted her hair from her neck and kissed the soft spot behind her ear. "Aren't you exhausted?"

The last twenty-four hours had been packed with a flurry of physically and emotionally draining activity. A wedding. More plague patients. A complicated labor and delivery. Transporting and reuniting a sick mother with her ill family. And finally, after all this time and hesitation, locking eyes with Cyprian and knowing with surety that what had been growing between them was more than a ruse.

"The best kind of tired ever." She turned to face him. "Why?"

"Because we never had that talk, remember?" He took her face in his hands and kissed her, tenderly at first, and then with the passion that made her insides quiver. "I don't want there to be any secrets between us," he whispered. "Tell me who you are, even if you belong to another."

His desperate need to know sent a painful jab to Lisbeth's chest. She drew a deep breath. "Come with me." She slid from his arms. "Don't just lie there staring; come on." While she wiggled into a shimmering robe, she watched him rise from the bed. A breathtaking male specimen. Rock-solid, yet gentle as a new kitten. And hers, if she could keep the truth as simple and painless as possible. She tossed him a loincloth. "Not interested in sharing you with the world."

He twined the fabric around his middle. "We're going far?"

"Farther than you could imagine." She slipped her hand in his and led him through the open doors and out onto the balcony.

A sea-scented breeze swept her hair from her shoulders and ruffled the dark waves against the harbor rock. They moved across the cool pavers to the railing. Moonlight silhouetted Cyprian's solid build. Call it selfish or simply self-preservation, either way, she took a moment to soak in the calm of his demeanor before shattering the peace they had found together.

The list of people she must take with her whenever she finally made her break for the twenty-first century was growing. His name was now permanently lumped in with Mama and Laurentius. However, she knew executing her plan and even evading capture would not be nearly as difficult as convincing Cyprian of his need to come with her. Not his need. Hers. She was the one who couldn't imagine a lifetime without him.

He drew her into his arms and kissed her. He tasted of sea salt, their lovemaking, and hope. For a few seconds she allowed herself to feel safe, to rest in the security of her husband's strong arms. But time and experience had exposed the futility of such an illusion.

Taming the danger of tomorrow was as futile as trying to erase the mistakes of yesterday. She pulled away reluctantly but determined to say what she should have said from the start.

"You better sit down."

He reeled her back into his arms. "I'd rather hold you." A long, slow press of his lips to hers and Lisbeth felt her resolve melt.

She wiggled free. "I'd rather look you in the eye." She held him at arm's length. "So you can see that everything I'm going to tell you is true."

"Have you not always told me the truth?"

"Technically . . . yes . . . what I've *told* you is true." Lying by omission was still lying in her book, a realization that didn't make her feel any better. This wasn't going to be easy. Maybe it was best if she took it slowly. "Please, sit."

He bowed assent. "Your wish is my command." He took a seat on a bench near the balustrade. "Speak, my love."

Lisbeth hesitated; her courage suddenly vanished. What if he didn't believe time travel possible? She really couldn't blame him. After all, she would have admitted Cyprian to a psych ward if he'd fallen into her century spouting a story this preposterous.

His head cocked in an expectant manner. "Well?" He gestured for her to get on with it.

"You're right. Let's get this over with." She perched on the opposite bench, her knees touching his for the added support. Whatever happened, for a few brief moments in time, everything had been perfect, and she would carry those memories with her forever.

She took a deep breath and dredged the truth into the open. Every incredible, unbelievable detail of the story, starting with Abra.

He pulled back. It was slight, but the distance was enough to make her reconsider this whole honesty thing. She reached for his hand as if her touch would keep him from leaving her or declaring her insane. He didn't withdraw, but something had changed between them. His face had hardened into an unreadable mask. Anxious to get this behind her, she continued on with the telling of the strange letter from Papa.

Nigel was right, she thought as she explained flying to the camp. A person either loved endless horizons or hated them. Cyprian listened to her tale of cars, cell phones, and fast food with a baffled expression that made discerning his take on modern horizons difficult.

But she was in this far and he hadn't bolted, so she risked a bit more. She told him about her parents and their quest to explore the Cave of the Swimmers. She recounted the night her mother disappeared, growing up in Papa's excavation camps, her travels to a place called the United States so she could attend med school, and she even threw in her friend Queenie and her crazy ten-thousand-member church, a number so staggering she finally garnered a reaction from Cyprian—granted it was a head shake of doubtful amazement, but at least he was still listening.

When she reached the chapter about Craig, she hesitated again. Cyprian was just now coming around, seeming a little less skeptical. Bringing up an old boyfriend seemed an unnecessary risk, especially since their love was so new. How could she explain that although she would always be somewhat divided between two worlds, somewhere in the midst of the adventures she'd shared with Cyprian, things had forever changed? She now belonged wholly to him. Every inch of her heart, soul, and very satisfied body.

For now she would skip Craig altogether, as well as her discovery of the way home, and move on to the impossibility of two women falling down the very same hole in the ancient cave, the exact same one he'd mentioned at the arena. But when the full impact of time travel registered in his thinking, his lips stretched into a tight line. He'd heard enough for one sitting.

Lisbeth took a relieved breath and let the information sink in. When she could stand his contemplative gaze no longer, she said, "Well? Say something."

His eyes drifted from her to the stars overhead. "So you want me to believe that people can fly?"

Lisbeth burst out laughing—releasing the tension that had been building since the day she arrived. "After all I said, that's what you heard? That Nigel flew me out to the desert to get my father?"

"What kind of wings does this Nigel have?"

"Pilots don't have wings. They fly planes." Lisbeth pointed to the harbor. "Ships with sails designed for the sky."

"Sometimes my clients tell me incredible stories." He stroked his stubbly chin. "Tales to hide the truth." He didn't believe her.

Had she chosen him over going back to the life she knew for nothing? "So what do you do?"

"I defend them anyway." Cyprian scooped her into his arms and headed for their bed.

She wrapped her arms around Cyprian's neck and kissed him. If she could stop time, she would stop it at this very moment.

They fell into bed. But even as they pulled the sheets over their heads, Lisbeth knew they couldn't hide from the future. It was a greedy and relentless master that wanted her back. The only way to alter her destiny was to change the past.

47

A COUPLE OF DAYS AFTER Lisbeth told him everything, Cyprian confessed to Caecilianus that he had a list of questions concerning his wife's dire predictions. Parts of her story were harder to believe than Caecilianus's claims of the Messiah. How could the past intersect the future to create a tenable present?

However crazy her claims, he had no interest in crushing the trust developing between them, a trust he treasured more than he could have ever anticipated. He did, however, take comfort in knowing he wasn't losing his mind. His wife really was different. He suspected her an exception to the rule the minute he'd laid eyes on her and knew her peculiarities to be fact once she opened her mouth. Yet he loved her, and he did not regret giving in to those feelings.

What to do about his beautiful wife's fledgling faith was something Caecilianus assured him the Lord would work out in time. Already he could see her heart softening. For now, he would keep his priority focused on securing the quarantine Lisbeth believed necessary to stop this plague. Since they had transported Eunike and her new baby to his villa, others afflicted with the sickness had flocked to his doorstep.

He sat upon the bed and stared at the sleeping woman who'd stolen his affections. Both of her new patients had endured a restless night. Therefore, Lisbeth hadn't slept either. He hated to wake her.

Lifting an auburn curl, he let the curly tendril wrap his finger. He couldn't wait for the hideous color to fade. Thank God her face had been scrubbed clean of all that ridiculous paint Ruth insisted she wear in public. He loved the natural shape of Lisbeth's eyes, blazing emeralds that did not need the harsh outline of kohl to captivate.

"My love." He ran his finger down her naked shoulder and along the curve of her exposed hip.

She rolled over and smiled. "Waking up to you is so much better than the alarm on my phone."

Alarms? Phones? Her strange ways would keep him occupied for a lifetime. "I hate to cut your slumber short, but we've got four new arrivals waiting in the atrium."

Her eyes snapped open, immediately alert. "Thank God you must have some kind of natural immunity."

THANKS TO a couple hours of sleep in Cyprian's arms and a good breakfast, Lisbeth had gained an entirely new perspective on the plague situation. Why had she not thought of it before? The people of Carthage did not have to sit idly by and wait on Aspasius to do something about the continual infiltration of the virus. They could band together. Turn Cyprian's home into a makeshift hospital. Organize a place where she could control the quarantine. It wasn't much, but doing something was better than doing nothing. Armed with a plan, a tangible way to slow the spread of the disease, Cyprian would have an easier time rallying governmental support.

In the remaining hours of daylight, Lisbeth shooed Laurentius, Junia, and Barek out to the shed to prepare it for those who'd not had measles. Next, she and Ruth gathered the supplies needed to pull this hospital thing off. Organizing the logistics was a slow process, one Lisbeth wished her mother were here to direct. But she hadn't seen Mama since the wedding. Fearing the worst, she'd scarcely allowed her mind to visit the question of what had happened to her mother once Aspasius sobered up. Now that she'd finally found Mama, she wanted her safe and close. Sharing the things mothers and daughters shared. Like how much she loved Cyprian, and that she'd discovered the secret of the cistern. She wasn't sure she wanted to go back anymore, but Mama had the right to decide whether she wanted to take Laurentius and go home . . . to go back to Papa.

Lisbeth tucked away the guilty niggling of having left Papa to fend for himself. Tomorrow, albeit eighteen hundred years away, had enough trouble of its own. She would do what she could to make today a better day.

Several hours later, Lisbeth and Ruth surveyed their work. Every mattress had been stripped from the beds and carried to the hall. Eunike's family had been placed on some of the woven hemp mats outfitted with vaporizers cobbled together out of sticks pruned from the trees in the garden and shredded stolas from Ruth's wardrobe. The villa looked more like the Thascius family was hosting a carnival rather than expecting an onslaught of deadly disease. Who knew an assortment of gaily colored silks and the addition of a new baby in the house could add such a festive touch to the starkness of their situation?

Exhausted and dirty, Lisbeth and Ruth stopped long enough to make a meal out of a small round of hard cheese and warm wine.

"Here are the things we're certain of." Lisbeth broke off a chunk of cheese. "Word will spread quickly. We'll be overrun with cases of every kind. We must prioritize those in the earliest stages. They are the most contagious. Separating them from the others is imperative." Lisbeth took a large gulp of watered wine. "Even though I'm pretty sure Cyprian must be immune, I want him to stay with you, Caecilianus, Barek, and my brother in the shed." Lisbeth held up her hand. "Don't argue with me, Ruth. We must keep anyone who has not had measles away from the sickness as much as possible."

"And Junia?"

"She can stay with me, since she's had measles. She'll make a great little helper."

"God will protect." Ruth stuffed a hunk of bread in her mouth, determined to once again get in the last word.

"Let's hope so." Lisbeth gazed at their crude setup. Papa's dig sites were better equipped for medical emergencies than this third-world stopgap. What had she been thinking? "A few home remedies and a little help from above are about all we've got going for us."

They finished their lunch in silence; then Lisbeth encouraged Ruth to take a rest on one of the mats in the library. Lisbeth thought about doing the same, but she stayed in the atrium and within easy access of Eunike and her little family. Fear that she might have overlooked some detail kept her eyes from closing. What if she couldn't pull this off? She didn't have a single vial of vaccine, antibiotic, or even a bag of intravenous fluid. Basically, she was waving a stick at a hungry lion.

48

MAGDALENA HID IN THE shadows as storm clouds gathered in the chambers of the Supreme Council. The Carthaginian Senate was a group of venerable men clad in purple and gold chains who'd been elected from the nobility of Carthage. Aspasius was seated in the leader chair. While she knew Aspasius said he was only too happy to entertain Cyprian's proposal, the men in the ornately furnished room had no idea the proconsul meant something totally different.

Cyprian had come armed with a pile of sketches, statistics, and cost estimates for the completion of the aqueducts, as well as an unheard-of plan to slow the spread of the disease plaguing the tenements, something that must have come from Lisbeth's twenty-first-century mind.

He stood head and shoulders above any man who'd taken the floor. Aspasius's elevator shoes failed to compensate for the difference, and his irritation showed on his face as he stepped aside in order for Cyprian to make yet another flawless argument.

"With the fever taking such a large toll on the general population"—Cyprian spoke confidently despite the obvious hostility of the audience—"further reducing the workforce by singling out those who do not bow to Roman gods is foolishness." This fine young man was her son-in-law, not that she could tell anyone, but knowing something good had come from this life-changing experience was a blessing Magdalena intended to count. "Can religious freedom not be extended or, at the very least, our differences tabled until after this crisis has passed?"

"Why such a fondness for these Christians, Cyprian?" Aspasius gnawed the solicitor's name and let it hang in the air like a shredded sheet.

"I see no advantage to destroying any segment of your workforce."

"I agree, but if these Christians continue to multiply faster than rats, the gods will withhold their blessings. Already these heretics fill far too many places among us. The shops, the harbor, the forum." He turned and addressed his colleagues. "Next thing you know, our honorable solicitor will have vermin filling not only our Senate seats but also the palace of our emperor and the temples to our gods."

Murmurs swelled in the giant hall. Magdalena peeked around a pillar.

Cyprian's smile faded into controlled calculation. "We'll see whose generosity the emperor rewards."

Aspasius chuckled. "Generosity?"

"I intend to raise the finances myself."

Aspasius let the silence grow thick in the room, the same type of dramatic pause that always preceded the impact of his fist into Magdalena's face. If she shouted out a warning, Cyprian's pride would not be the only casualty. All she could do was watch and pray.

"More than one reputation has found its grave at the walls of Carthage." Aspasius patted his belly. "If you choose to bury yours for those who dare to anger the gods, I shall miss you, Cyprian. You are a worthy opponent. But don't think others will join you in this. Now that Rome has turned a hungry eye upon Africa, I have the support I need. A vote in opposition to your plan is merely my concession to the council's vanity."

"Politicians, hear this!" Cyprian's voice rang out as he gathered his sketches. "A pound of words for an ounce of action will not pacify the dying masses for long."

"Best of luck in the election." Aspasius's shrill laughter needled Cyprian's back on his way out the door and punctured Magdalena's last hope of her son-in-law securing her family's freedom.

IT HAD been weeks since Cyprian exercised his oratorical privileges on the council. He expected to be a bit rusty. That he'd become totally ineffective was a shock. He'd not intended to storm from the assembly of senators, but he'd been so incensed by their total disregard for human life that he'd grabbed Pontius and fled.

"Poor sanitary conditions will kill Carthage." Cyprian and Pontius jumped aboard the waiting litter. "As long as the patricians can escape to their summer homes, why should they care what happens to the plebs left behind?"

"We were outmaneuvered," Pontius stated flatly, "but we are not defeated."

"Short of mounting a rebellion, I have no backup plan."

"Did you not just say there is more than one way to finance a worthy project?"

"So right, my friend." Cyprian halted the litter. "Pontius, stop at the market and order large quantities of fruits and herbs for the sickly multitude that has taken over my house. While you're at it, pay the fuller's bill, and have the clean bedding delivered later today."

Pontius climbed out of the rig. "And where are you going?"

"To sell off part of my shipping fleet."

49

MIDDAY SIESTA HAD BROUGHT a welcome quiet to the house. Lisbeth circulated among the hospital mats, filling vaporizer pots, adding herbs, and taking vitals. When those jobs were finished, she realized that despite the lack of modern medicine, all of her patients were fairly comfortable.

Taking advantage of the moment of peace, she decided to scrounge up something to eat. She tiptoed to the kitchen door, which served as the invisible boundary between those who'd survived measles and those who had not been exposed. Servants came and went with the supplies she ordered, but they never stepped over the line. Not even Cyprian, though it was all she could do not to cheat and fling herself into his embrace. More than she wanted a sandwich, she needed a moment with her husband. To feel his arms around her and taste his lips upon hers. How quickly she'd come to rely upon his strength, his reassurance, and his belief that she could do this. The brief notes he wrote and tucked into her dinner tray had been her salvation.

Lisbeth washed her hands with the last of the hot water and peered into the quiet kitchen. No Cyprian. No Ruth. Even the cook had deserted her. She hopped across the invisible line, put another pot of water on to boil, and snagged a round of bread.

Cawing seagulls drew Lisbeth's attention to the open doors

leading to the balcony. She padded across the atrium and stepped into the bright sunlight. Inhaling deep breaths of fresh air for the first time in several days, she lifted a few crumbs for the wily scavengers swooping overhead.

Anchored ships swayed in the harbor's pristine waters, and a soft breeze indicated a slight cooling trend might be coming this way. Idyllic, really. No wonder Mama loved growing up on the Mediterranean. Except for the seriousness of this plague, Carthage would make a great place for a real honeymoon with Cyprian.

"BISHOP!" FELICISSIMUS hammered at the door.

Lisbeth came running.

The slave trader burst into the atrium. "Bishop!"

"Stay back, Felicissimus!" She dodged occupied mats and whizzed past Caecilianus and Barek, who were sticking their heads in from the kitchen. "What's happened?"

"A Roman warship has drifted into port." Red-faced and gasping for breath, the tubby slave trader had obviously run some distance. "All aboard have perished."

Panic tore through the ill, roused from their naps.

"Brother and sisters," Caecilianus shouted over the coughing and shuffling about in the beds, "I urge you to remain calm!"

"Did I not warn you, Bishop?" Felicissimus heaved his girth atop a stone bench, then held up his hands as if he intended to preach a sermon. "This plague is sweeping the empire faster than Christian persecution."

"We don't know why those sailors died," pointed out Ruth as she and Barek joined Caecilianus at the door. "Or if they are dead for certain."

"Does this woman you bed think for you, too, Bishop?" The

chubby little man seemed pleased that his insult had recaptured the attention of the crowd.

"Hey, don't talk about my mother." Barek started over the line, but Ruth pulled him back.

Felicissimus shook a finger at Lisbeth. "Cyprian has sent me to warn you."

"Cyprian?" Not caring that she might be contaminated, Lisbeth jerked the squatty slave trader down from the bench. Her face in his, she shouted, "Where is my husband?!"

"If we stand idle, we'll no longer have to fear the arena. There'll be no one left alive for the wild cats to shred." Buoyed by cheers of support, Felicissimus raised a clenched fist above his head. "Christians must leave while we still have breath. We owe the empire nothing."

"Where is my husband?" Lisbeth demanded, tightening her grip on his collar. "Tell me now."

"He's on the ship."

"No!" screeched out of Lisbeth. "Ruth, get my cloak!"

"I'm coming with you." Ruth gave orders to her son before Lisbeth could argue. "Barek, fetch Magdalena."

Minutes later, Lisbeth and Ruth were flying down the balcony steps. "Maybe those sailors simply died of scurvy or some kind of environmental contamination."

Ruth dared to say the words out loud that might seal a fate Lisbeth wasn't ready to accept. "If they had the plague and Cyprian was on that boat . . ."

"They don't."

She and Ruth arrived at the harbor, agitated as the circling seabirds.

"If those are the troops Aspasius ordered," Ruth cautioned, "he will not be happy with anything less than a boatload of able-bodied men."

Lisbeth and Ruth stood shoulder-to-shoulder on the wharf, sucking in the scents of seaweed, sewage, and spice while contemplating the next move. "Do you see that, Ruth?" Lisbeth pointed to the water and the flame moving toward the wooden vessel listing to one side, its square mainsail the only one hoisted in the entire port. "What is it?"

"A torch." Ruth shielded her eyes against the sun. "And Cyprian."

"What's he doing?"

Ruth's face went pale. "He's going to burn the ship."

"If he burns that ship, the proconsul can claim his soldiers were murdered by Christians." Lisbeth shed her cloak. "I've got to stop him."

Ruth laid a hand on her arm. "But if we let a plague-ridden ship dock, we risk far more."

"Agreed."

Saving a dying world, a world that according to history eventually recovered and swept the heroism of Christians into obscurity, would have to take second place to saving her husband. Scanning the port, Lisbeth noticed the manmade island in the center of the harbor. Narrow launching ramps, perfect for the flotilla of military triremes docked in the slipways.

For her, leapfrogging from vessel dock to vessel dock was the fastest way to her husband. "I'm going after him." Lisbeth pulled off her sandals.

"I'm coming with you."

"I've had every vaccination known to man. You haven't."

"Are you determined to get yourself killed?"

"Quite the contrary, my friend. I have every reason to live." She raced down the dock, weaving through stacks of wine crocks and clay jars filled with fish sauce awaiting export. Once she was even with the ship Cyprian was nearing, she drew the hem of her garment between her legs, looped the excess fabric through the front of her belt, and dove into the water.

Stroke for stroke, she swam toward the life-size version of Papa's museum model ships. Her father would have given his right arm for this incredible opportunity to actually board one. She, on the other hand, prayed she didn't have to, but she would to save her husband.

As she neared the warship's keel, she called out, "Cyprian!"

"Lisbeth?" He popped around the bulk of the ship, bobbing in the water like a floating candle. "What are you doing here?"

"I could ask you the same question."

"Careful. There's a razor-sharp ramming beak lurking just below the waterline." He swam toward her, the torch in his hand.

She dodged the primitive missile and met him. Throwing her arms around his neck, she didn't know whether to kiss him or strangle him for stupidity. She opted for the kiss. "Let's go home."

"This ship can't reach shore."

"Then I'll go aboard and—"

"No, you won't."

They argued over who should go aboard the warship. He pointed out that while her sharp tongue could hold its own against the blade of any soldier, a man was better suited to handle the unknown dangers. He lunged for the rope ladder, leaving Lisbeth to tread water and fume.

Cyprian's toga clung to his body and sinewy legs as he scrambled toward the outspread sail of purple, the torch in one hand. They were from such different worlds, and though they were in love, every time those worlds collided, sparks flew.

Treading water in the shadow of creaking hull timbers, Lisbeth nervously picked at one of the barnacles stuck to the tarred planks. The crustacean fell into her hand. Gazing at the spot where it had resided, Lisbeth noticed the heads of several copper nails aged to a green patina. Romans were known for keeping their fleet freshly painted and scoured immaculately clean. This boat had to have been at sea for a long while. Why?

She kicked against the chill. "Cyprian! Come back!"

When he didn't answer, she grabbed hold of the ladder's first slippery rung. "I'm coming up." Doubling her effort to compensate for the weight of her gown, she strained to hoist herself out of the water.

As she neared the top rung, she heard a frantic clip-clop pounding on the deck. Toes curled around the rope, she slowly pushed up. When her eyes cleared the railing, she saw an emaciated stallion pawing the air.

The horse's hooves struck the deck with a wood-splintering crack. Cyprian dropped his torch in a copper fire pit and approached the wild-eyed beast. He talked in low, soothing tones as he reached for the loose tether. The horse, wanting no part of this stranger, reared again, then lunged. Right before impact, Cyprian stepped aside. The horse sailed over the railing, his front hooves nearly brushing the top of Lisbeth's head.

"Whoa!" Clinging to the swaying ladder, she watched the animal land a belly flop, lift his nose in the air, and begin a desperate paddle for the shore.

When she glanced up, Cyprian was staring down at her. "You could have been killed."

"Me? What about you?" She struggled for a firm grip on the railing. "What in the world was that?"

Cyprian offered his hand. "Commander's mount." He hauled her over the rail, and she tumbled into his arms. "Poor animal was near starved to death. Hasn't been tended for days. You hurt?"

"No." Except for the horse's droppings, the deck was devoid of any recent signs of life. Cookpots, some caked with dried stew, were scattered about. Several wine amphorae lay uncorked, their spilled contents allowed to stain the salty boards. Lisbeth couldn't imagine healthy soldiers wasting the emperor's premium alcohol. Something wasn't right with this picture. "Where is everyone?"

"Let's check the holds." He took her elbow. "Careful, these boards are slick."

They padded around the large stash of untouched wine stacked beside a huge pile of basketball-size stones covered in something similar to dried moss.

"What are these?" she asked.

"Fireballs."

She nudged one with her toe. It didn't budge. "What are they for?"

"Soldiers light them, then launch the flaming balls from this catapult." He placed his hand on a wooden A-frame contraption that resembled the construction project required by her college physics professor, only this one looked like it might actually work. Disapproval on his face, Cyprian added, "Very destructive for those at the wrong end of the spear."

"I'm just thinking out loud here." She pointed at the fireballs. "Why would Rome send a trireme armed for a fight, unless—"

"Aspasius doesn't plan to police the Christians." Cyprian cut her off, fire rimming his eyes. "That dog plans to have us destroyed."

"What are you doing?"

"Altering the proconsul's orders."

"How?"

"Burning not only this ship, but his entire fleet."

"How will that help? Aspasius will just order more troops, and Rome will send more ships and more soldiers. And then they'll come after you." Lisbeth stayed his hand. "If this crew died of the plague, which we have no way of knowing, since I haven't seen the first dead body, then the plague has already spread throughout the entire empire. Burning a few warships is about as useless as a screen door on a submarine."

"What?"

"Never mind." Lisbeth pointed at the iron ring attached to a trapdoor that she surmised led to the trilevel holds. "Someone could still be alive down there."

"Not for long."

"Really?" She stayed the hand that brandished the torch. "You're going to burn them alive?"

He didn't answer.

"You're no better than those who throw your people to the lions in the arena." Flickering flames reflected in Cyprian's eyes. "Do you or do you not believe all that *do unto others* stuff the bishop was saying?"

He released an exasperated sigh, but she didn't miss the desire to slap some sense into her that was still registered on his face. "We must be quick." He returned the lit torch in the copper cauldron.

A man willing to listen to reason was surprisingly attractive. Hopefully, he could forgive a woman willing to say what she had to in order to accomplish her goal.

Lisbeth bent and ripped a strip of fabric from her hem. "Tie this over your nose and mouth like this." She demonstrated how to make a surgical mask. "And don't touch a thing."

Wishing for a pair of latex gloves and a decent backup plan if they did find someone alive down in the hold, she watched Cyprian brace his muscular legs and heave the door aside.

Putrid gases, ripe with the smell of rancid meat and rotten eggs, gushed forth along with an agonizing scream that came from the belly of the ship.

As they took a step back, a bare-chested man charged up the stairs and body-slammed Cyprian. Both of them went skidding across the deck.

Blades flashed, and the clank of metal upon metal punctuated their groans as they tumbled end over end.

Lisbeth followed the dueling duo around the deck, yelling for them to stop and tried to get a closer look at the filthy man who was acting as erratic as a deprived drug seeker.

Although the man appeared malnourished and coughed like a chain smoker, he managed to point both of his feet at Cyprian's chest and give a good, strong kick. Cyprian slammed into the fire pit, which launched the blazing torch into the fireballs. Flames exploded and greedily licked their way toward the wine jugs.

"Cyprian!" Lisbeth ran toward him. "Fire!"

He leapt to his feet. "Run, Lisbeth!"

The man from the hold swayed. "Those Roman cowards locked us in the filth and jumped ship." He waved a knife with one hand and dug at the dark red boils blanketing his entire torso with the other. "The fever killed everyone but me."

Lisbeth would have preferred a brief peek inside his mouth to check for Koplik spots, but from the maniacal glaze of his red eyes that wasn't happening. So she did her clinical assessment from three feet away. Runny nose, cheeks flush with fever, and that awful hacking cough. Measles. "Calm down." She inched forward, hand extended. "I'm a doctor. Let me help you."

The man lowered his head and charged. Before she could get out of the way, he head-butted her stomach. Doubled in pain, she flew backward. Her right wrist struck the glowing edge of the fire pit. She could hear skin sizzling but was too winded to move.

Cyprian snatched her up and snuffed her burning flesh with the hem of his wet tunic. "Swim to shore." Crackling flames greedily devoured the tar-sealed planks.

She struggled to get loose. "I need to examine him."

"No time. This ship is going down."

Fire climbed the oiled ropes of the mast and gobbled the square topsail in an instant. Black smoke billowed in the breeze. If Aspasius didn't know things were amiss down at the port, these smoke signals would alert him soon enough.

Lisbeth spotted the delirious man, laughing and running circles around the deck. "It will only take me a second." Before she could move, the crazy man raised his knife and charged again. "Look out!" Lisbeth screamed.

Cyprian wheeled, dove, and tackled the man with the force of a seasoned linebacker. Knife spinning across the deck, both men scrambled to gain possession of the blade.

The sick man beat Cyprian to the prize. He leapt to his feet with knife raised and came at Lisbeth.

Cyprian intercepted the man and wrestled him into the obscurity of the roiling dark cloud of smoke taking over the deck. Struggling to breathe, Lisbeth searched for a weapon of her own.

Suddenly the man with the wild hair shot out of the sooty haze and lunged at her with a black scowl and his knife poised over his head. She dodged the impact, but he pivoted with remarkable agility and stamina, then barreled in her direction again. Lisbeth stuck out her foot as he flew past. Down he went with a sickening thud. His body quivered, then stilled. She cautiously stepped forward and checked for a pulse. Nothing. She rolled him over and discovered the knife handle protruding from his diaphragm.

"Cyprian!" She ran into the smoke. "Answer me!"

Two strong hands grabbed her shoulders, hands she knew instantly, hands she trusted. Before she could tell him what she'd done, he scooped her up and emerged from the smoke in an explosive gasp.

"Must get you out of here." Cradling her in his arms, he

raced across the deck. At the railing, he peeled her arms from his neck. "Go."

Lisbeth sailed over the railing and cannonballed into the sea. Kicking against the pull of the water, she fought to reach the surface.

KABOOM!

50

ARM HOOKED UNDER CYPRIAN'S chin, Lisbeth kicked toward the shore. Her thoughts ping-ponged between the past and the future, devising plans to reweave the tapestry, to rewrite the outcomes she knew awaited her. Mama would not leave her to grow up without a mother. Craig would be nothing more than an ambitious colleague. The child she'd misdiagnosed would live. Somehow Cyprian would survive. And together they would rewrite history.

Ruth and Barek rushed into the surf to help Lisbeth drag Cyprian's limp body to the shore. She pressed her lips to his. *Breath, thank goodness.* "Stay with me."

"I went for the healer," Barek said, huffing, "but she must wait until Aspasius leaves for the harbor."

Lisbeth bent to check Cyprian's pulse. "Aspasius is coming here?"

"Him and every available soldier." Barek nodded toward the patrols gathering on the dock and pointing at the plume of black smoke. "We've got to get him out of here."

"He's alive." Lisbeth's quick examination didn't reveal any visible wounds. "I don't know about internal injuries."

Soldiers thundered down the wharf.

"We've been spotted." Barek slid his arms under Cyprian's shoulders. "Grab his feet."

When they arrived back at the villa, Felicissimus stood waiting, wringing his hands. "Oh, dear. Not my patronus. What can I do?"

"Stay out of my way."

51

LAURENTIUS PACED THE LIBRARY Lisbeth had converted into a private ICU ward for Cyprian. Her brother had became so uncontrollable when they hauled Cyprian's unconscious body into the villa she'd had to grant him limited access to his hero just so he could breathe. But without knowing the root cause of Cyprian's refusal to wake up, Laurentius's presence in the same room as her husband made Lisbeth very nervous.

Was Cyprian's fever the result of some kind of infection from his near drowning, or had he not been immune to measles after all? Until the incubation period had passed, she preferred sending her little brother back to the palace. Not the best option, but she didn't have the heart to lock him in the shed. At least in the dank, little underground cell the boy's life would go back to his normal.

Laurentius plunked down beside her. "Don't worry, Lithbutt. I'm praying." He patted her hand, as if these simple words solved everything. "Thyprian will be okay."

Her brother may be a bit out of sorts, but he was the only one in the household who'd not adopted Lisbeth's pensive mood. Even the frequent appearances of Ruth and Barek at the library door were clouded with worry. If only she saw life as simply as her brother. For a brief instant she was envious of the comfort his unsinkable hope must have given Mama over the years.

Remembering how Mama used distraction to redirect Laurentius, Lisbeth kissed his chubby cheek and said, "Why don't you draw Cyprian a picture?"

Smiling, he shot from the room and left her to fulfill her craving for a moment alone with Cyprian. She gently lifted one of her husband's slack eyelids. The blank stare remained. "Please wake up, my love."

Three days of stubbly growth darkened Cyprian's slack jaw. She missed the way his smile pushed parenthetical lines on either side of his full lips. What would she do if he never regained consciousness? *The twenty-first century has lost its appeal.* The idea struck her hard, as if someone had shouted and slapped her at the same time. She sat up straight and glanced around the room.

Nothing had changed. The dogs still slept at her feet. A sea breeze was still drifting through the open balcony doors and ruffling abandoned parchments spread across the desk. She was still treating a critically ill patient with a wooden bowl of broth and a clay mug of strong tea. And yet, everything about this picture felt right. She was home. She belonged here in the ancient impracticality of the third century. She'd fallen in love with this man, his people, and his problems.

A firm hand came to rest upon Lisbeth's shoulder. "Caecilianus? You shouldn't be in here. Cyprian may have the virus." She rose from the chair and tried to push him toward the door. "And measles are no respecter of social standing."

"Nor am I." The old bishop gently moved her aside. "I've come to pray."

Determination twinkled beneath Caecilianus's hooded eyelids. Lisbeth stood transfixed and unable to further protest. If she'd admired the bishop's speaking skills from afar, up close she found the ready-to-take-action confidence of this grandfatherly man overwhelming. No wonder followers like Cyprian were so de-voted.

Caecilianus withdrew a small vial from his tunic, poured a drop of golden liquid on his finger, then smeared it on Cyprian's forehead. The bishop placed a large, gnarled hand over the shiny spot. "In the name of Jesus Christ, the Messiah, who rose from the grave on the third day, I command this spirit of sickness to leave this young man. Bring him peace, Father. Bring him rest. Bring him healing."

The earthy fragrance of blessed olive oil reached Lisbeth's nostrils and stirred impossible expectations. Foolish hopes similar to those who paced the hospital rooms of the dying. Holding her breath, she leaned forward, waiting and watching.

Another round of unintelligible delirium tumbled from Cyprian's lips, and he began to convulse like a man with fever.

She placed her palm on his clammy forehead. No change. "Now what?" she asked, her disapproval far more obvious than she'd intended.

"We wait upon the Lord."

Lisbeth crawled in next to Cyprian, twining her arms and legs around his in an attempt to calm him. But his excessive heat did little to warm the dread that chilled her to the core. Would he ever ask her to explain flying once again? Or insist that he go first when they approached danger? Or sleep contentedly after they made love? She waited for the click of the library door latch before she flooded her husband's chest with tears of disappointment. She was going to lose him along with everything she'd come to love. His body slowly stilled, and Lisbeth couldn't bring herself to move.

"I dreamed I'd lost you," Cyprian's parched voice rumbled beneath her ear.

She popped up on her elbow. "You're alive!" Without taking

the time to examine him, she threw her arms around his neck, laughing and crying at the same time. "It worked. The bishop's prayers worked."

"I didn't lose you?"

"No." Thinking he may not be as recovered as she thought, she sat up. She knew his lips, had watched the various changes in coloring during these frightening days, but she never dreamed how grateful a smile could make her feel. "I'm right where God wants me."

"I love you." He pulled her to him, and she was hopelessly lost.

52

AFTER THE INCUBATION PERIOD passed and Cyprian remained measles-free, Lisbeth declared him one lucky man. Cyprian claimed luck had nothing to do with his protection. God had spared him. Since Lisbeth had no better explanation for his escape from contracting the virus after his wrestling match with the man on the ship, she had to agree. God had given her her husband back, and she was going to cherish every moment.

Today was one of those moments. Caecilianus felt the church needed to gather. Many had lost loved ones to the fever. The old bishop thought the survivors needed encouragement and a strategy to cope with their losses going forward. Lisbeth had agreed, with a few stipulations. Only those who had survived the fever or had remained in her controlled quarantine were allowed to attend.

Without grousing, Lisbeth joined Cyprian and the cleared believers in the garden for worship. Miraculous recovery buzzed on everyone's lips as they swarmed Cyprian like it was Old Home Week. The survivors had been so grateful for Lisbeth's care that they willingly volunteered to help her nurse the new measles cases that arrived every day. In the process, these people had lost their suspicions of her, and she'd come to admire her brave new friends.

In the middle of Caecilianus's prayer of thanksgiving,

Felicissimus burst into the garden. "Rumor has it that Aspasius blames the Christians for the fire that destroyed his ship."

Lisbeth and Cyprian exchanged nervous glances. Besides the paunchy slave trader, only Barek, Ruth, and Caecilianus knew about the ship. And they would never tell. Had the soldiers gotten a better look as they fled the scene that day than they had thought? Had Aspasius discovered their connection to the church?

Looking as sour-faced as ever, Felicissimus continued, "He promises to kill a priest every full moon until he has the one responsible."

53

MAGDALENA RELIEVED TABARI OF the watering can and dismissed her from the daily task of cleaning bird cages. She wanted the atrium to herself while she confirmed her suspicions, because she hadn't decided exactly what she'd do with the information once she had it.

The sound of someone tapping on a door down the hall caused Magdalena to glance in the direction of Aspasius's office. Pytros, tablets in hand, stood ready to enter. He caught sight of Magdalena staring at him and cast a smug smile her way. Then, without further ado, he waltzed into the room and shut the door. What was that little weasel up to? Who else was in there?

She busied herself with the care of the birds for nearly an hour, but when she could no longer stand the suspense, she set aside the soiled parchment liners. Ears and eyes on high alert, she padded down the hall and carefully placed her ear to the carved door.

"I've only found two." The voice belonged to Felicissimus, the mystery man she'd seen scampering down the hall like the rat that he was.

"And where do you find these slaves?" Aspasius demanded.

"In the tenement cistern."

A gut-punched gasp escaped Magdalena's lips.

The cistern. Of course.

Lost details buried deep in her memory awakened with an electrifying intensity. Faded paintings on the sandstone cave wall flickered like a slideshow in her mind. She paused on the grainy picture of the family of potbellied swimmers with the scarlet child. Those tiny outstretched arms had reminded her of Lisbeth, the rag doll caught between her and Lawrence in a desperate tug-of-war on how they were going to live.

She remembered feeling responsible for her daughter's happiness, and failing. She wanted to provide Lisbeth with the same wonderful life she'd had growing up. Proper schools, friends, museums, concerts, a house by the sea. Not a canvas tent in the middle of nowhere.

That night in the desert, when she'd stomped off, she wasn't running away from their nomadic life as much as desperately running toward the hope of a normal, stable life. Seeing the family of swimmers on the wall that reminded her so much of what she hoped to have, she'd touched the scarlet child. A choice she would regret as long as she lived. A choice that could never be undone.

Falling through the hole must have somehow funneled her into one of those subterranean aquifers Lawrence believed crisscrossed the Sahara and emptied in Carthage.

Felicissimus said he'd found her at the tenement cisterns. The painting on the cave wall was the exact same painting she'd noticed on the cistern stones years ago. She'd seen the family of potbellied swimmers every time she fetched water to tend the sick. Why had she never connected the two? Unless subconsciously she knew that the guilt over how she was raising her daughter had propelled her into this world, and guilt for what would happen to her son had kept her from returning.

Adrenaline pumped through Magdalena's limbs. She knew exactly where to find the portal Felicissimus had mentioned. She knew exactly what she must do to go home.

Magdalena bolted down the hall.

54

I'M NOT ABOUT TO let Aspasius keep me from doing my job."
Lisbeth had been arguing with Cyprian and Barek since breakfast, and she was making no headway. "I need those supplies." She
turned to Felicissimus, who sat quietly sipping a cup of tea. "Help
me out here, Felicissimus. Tell him the streets are safe."

The slave trader, whose daily visits had not only cheered Cyprian in his recovery but also kept him apprised of Aspasius's plans,
held up a grubby hand. "I'm just here to give a report on the latest
slave shipments, not to referee a domestic dispute. Barek, you'd do
well to follow my lead and keep your opinions to yourself." He set
the cup upon the library desk. "I'll let myself out. Good to see you
feeling better, my patronus."

Cyprian clasped his hand. "Thank you, friend."

Lisbeth wasn't sad to see Felicissimus go. Unlike Cyprian, she
didn't trust the man. To her, his presence was like fingernails on a
chalkboard, especially after that shameful stunt of trying to get the
believers to leave town. Someday she'd tell Cyprian what a little rat
his slave trader friend really was, but not until he regained his
strength.

"Let me or Barek run your errand," Cyprian offered once Felicissimus was out of earshot.

"You're still convalescing." Lisbeth crossed her arms. She'd underestimated the power of coupling prayer with the will to live, but he could still use a few more days of rest. Especially if the reports were true and Aspasius had put a price on her husband's head. "And Barek wouldn't know a eucalyptus leaf from a mustard seed. Would you, boy?" Barek gave her the fish eye. "I didn't think so." A kiss to Cyprian's cheek let him know that she hadn't totally dismissed his concerns. She didn't want to worry him, but drastic times called for drastic measures. "Ruth and I will be quick and discreet."

"At least take Barek with you."

Lisbeth gave a resigned sigh. "If it will help you sleep better." Barek puffed like a peacock, then smugly marched from the library to fetch his mother. "Maybe taking him along will ease the animosity he has toward me." Lisbeth kissed Cyprian properly, allowing her lips to linger on his with a whispered promise of more when she returned home.

"No heroics." Cyprian held her a minute more. "Promise."

"Straight to the herbalist and back. I promise."

Ruth and Lisbeth donned their cloaks. Barek leading the way, they set off to restock their empty herb baskets. The streets were eerily quiet. For some unknown reason patrons and shopkeepers had taken their midday siesta several hours early.

They trudged on toward the marketplace in silence. None of them admitted the uneasiness drawing their muscles taut as a bowstring, but each of them took turns glancing over their shoulders. Every ounce of wit and cunning would be needed if they encountered patrols. As they neared an intersection obscured by a tall building, yelling and sounds of a scuffle met their ears.

"Trouble." Barek halted Lisbeth and Ruth with his outstretched arms, acting far more grown-up and brave than his wide-eyed stare suggested. "Stay behind me."

Barek peeked around the corner. Before he could draw Cyprian's borrowed dagger, soldiers ambushed them from behind. The impulse to save herself thrummed through Lisbeth's veins. She turned and saw that the soldier corral had circled around them. Lisbeth's nose stung with the sharp smell of sweat, spilled beer, and desperation.

Guards snarled at them. "Bow to the gods of Rome."

"We will not," Ruth said with lifted chin.

"Bow or suffer the consequences." Swords drawn, they shouted accusations of treason and promises of death in the arena.

Barek finally freed the dagger. "Stand down."

Laughing, the soldiers continued to close in with a uniform precision.

Ruth screeched, "Run, Barek!" In a flash, a brawny soldier clamped on to her and hurled her to the pavement. Ruth's head hit with a thump. Her body jerked for a second, then did not move again.

"Mother!" Barek broke free of the two patrols binding him. He lowered his head and rammed his curls into the armored belly of the soldier who'd discarded Ruth. "I'll kill you." Their bodies fell in a writhing heap upon the cobblestones. Barek swung his fists, pounding the soldier's face with the fury of a boy set on vindication for the beating he'd taken at their hands. Blood spurted everywhere.

"Ruth!" Lisbeth called, but her friend did not respond. Lisbeth followed Barek's leading and sank her teeth into the hand of the soldier cuffing her wrist. The big lout released her with a howl. She lunged across the pavement, pulled Barek free, and screamed, "Run!" The shocked boy could only stare, blood dripping from his hands. "Now!" she commanded.

As the soldiers pounced on her, Lisbeth saw Barek sprint from the chaos and disappear into a darkened alley.

55

I T'S NOT FAIR." BAREK retched into the crock Caecilianus held
before him for the second time. Both dogs stood guard next to
the lad as if they understood his pain. "They set us up. A trap for
believers. Lambs led to slaughter."

"No, it is not fair." The old bishop comforted his son who so
wanted to be a man. Why he wasn't pressing the boy for more details had Cyprian on the verge of exploding. "But it's not your fault.
This is a fallen world."

Cyprian could stand the platitudes no longer. "Where have
they taken them?"

"I don't know." Barek trickled out the rest of the story in painful, mortified gasps. "When I circled back, Mother and Lisbeth
were being carted off in chains. Mother is alive. Injured badly, but
alive."

Cyprian loaded his belt and cloak with every weapon he could
find. "I'm going after them."

Someone hammered the front door, and both dogs sprang at
the wood in a snarling frenzy.

"Soldiers." Barek spat the word in a hiccupped sob, fear flashing in his wide eyes. "They've come for us, too."

Cyprian gestured for silence, and the dogs receded with a
low, ready-to-attack growl. Caecilianus folded Barek to his chest.

Dagger drawn, Cyprian proceeded to the door and yanked it open.

Magdalena rushed past. "I know the way back. I've found the por—" She slid to a stop and spun around in the atrium. The smile, along with any good news she might have carried, melted from her face. "What's happened?" The distraught state of the men registered in an instant. "Where's my daughter?"

Barek was the first to speak, his cheeks hot with shame. "Arrested."

"Nooooo!" Magdalena's scream set the dogs to howling.

"Mama?" Laurentius shouted from the library. "Tholdiers have our Lithbutt."

Magdalena threw her arms open. "Come."

Laurentius hesitated, considering whether to break the quarantine rules Lisbeth had so carefully taught him, but in the end he couldn't stand everyone being on the other side of the line and ran to his mother. "Where are we going?"

"To bring your sister home," Magdalena declared.

"I'm coming with you." Cyprian linked his arm with hers.

Barek swiped his chin. "Me, too."

"No." Caecilianus put himself between them and the door, the dogs flanking him on either side. "It is the priests they want. Kill us, and they kill the rebellion."

"What are you saying?" Cyprian asked.

"A priest is all we have to offer in exchange for the women's freedom."

"Father, no!" Barek flung himself at his father's feet. "I can't lose you, too."

"Caecilianus, you can't . . . the believers need you," Cyprian pleaded. "Your son needs you. Let me offer money. Aspasius won't turn down an opportunity to gorge his coffers."

The old bishop shook his head. "I've had my time, my friend. The future is up to you."

"Me? I can't—"

"You can." Caecilianus's eyes filled with tears. "I've taught you everything I know, but you, my dear Cyprian, have skills I cannot teach. An abiding strength and deep sense of purpose I do not possess. People will follow your leading. You are the future of the church, not I. Care for the believers with the same love you've given me."

"This is ridiculous. I'm not letting you do this."

Caecilianus silenced his protest, then lifted Barek to his feet. He clamped a shaky hand on his son's shoulder and presented him to Cyprian. "You are the only man I trust with my family."

"If I'm the best you've got, then I've no choice but to keep you alive."

56

LISBETH AWOKE IN TOTAL darkness, cold, naked, and certain she'd been beaten. A shroud of dank, musty air was all that covered the different aches of her ravished body. The putrid smells reminded her of the tunnels beneath the proconsul's palace. Head throbbing, she raised her hand to her scalp and discovered a large goose egg. Who knew how long she'd been out?

Moaning drew her attention to her right, but she couldn't see her hand in front of her face, let alone tell who else was in pain. "Ruth?"

"Over here." Ruth's voice sounded weak and parched.

Lisbeth managed to roll to her hands and knees. Ignoring her fear of confined spaces, she blindly crawled across cool, damp stones, searching for her friend. "Are you all right?"

"I'm not dead yet."

"Could have fooled me." She found Ruth's hand, and though it was cold, she'd never held anything that warmed her more. "I'm afraid I got us into a real mess this time, friend." She clamped Ruth's birdlike wrist for a quick pulse check. "What hurts?"

"Everything." Emotion cracked Ruth's voice. "Where's my son?"

"Bringing the cavalry, I hope."

"Who?"

"Never mind." The scuffling of boots sounded outside the door. "Shhh. We've got company."

"Lisbeth, are you naked, too?"

"Yes."

"God help us," Ruth whispered.

The door flew open with a shudder, and a soldier bearing a torch entered their cell. "Up."

The women were dragged through the tunnels. Water and filth squished between Lisbeth's toes. When they arrived at some stairs, they were ordered to climb. Lisbeth went first, doing her best to keep from slipping, considering the slime on her feet. When she reached the top step, someone shoved her through an opening in the stone wall. Lisbeth stumbled over a thick carpet and landed face-first in an expansive room lined with soldiers' boots, red patrician sandals, and floor-to-ceiling bookshelves. Soldiers jerked her to her feet. Several men in purple togas turned to appraise the scuffle with scorn, but without a word of comment on her surprising entrance or her obvious state of undress. Lisbeth did her best to cover her naked body with her arms.

Seconds later, Ruth made the exact same entry. Lisbeth helped her up before the soldiers had an opportunity to manhandle her friend. The light streaming through the large windows gave Lisbeth her first good look at Ruth. Other than the hematoma where her head hit the cobblestones, Ruth had no other visible signs of injury. At least being unconscious had protected this fragile woman from the beating she'd taken.

Side by side, Lisbeth and Ruth did their best to cover each other as they digested the silent scene. Where were they? And what in the world was going to happen next? The raspy sound of an unseen throat clearing parted the sea of toga-clad men ogling them and exposed the one man Lisbeth had never wanted to see again.

"Aspasius."

The proconsul sat behind a giant desk, drumming his fingers on the burled mahogany. A pleased sneer crossed his lips. "Well, I never expected the bodies of treason to be so . . . feminine." He rose slowly, commanding the attention of every high-ranking politician in the room. One hand resting on the ledge of his belly, Aspasius swept around the desk and came to stand before Lisbeth and Ruth. "What a waste of such perfectly divine flesh." He pulled a dagger from his belt. Sliding the blunt side across Lisbeth's neck, he circled her slowly, reminiscent of the day he'd inspected her in the slave cell.

From behind, he leaned in and whispered in Lisbeth's ear. "I may keep you to torture myself." He slipped an arm about her neck and pressed the blade point to the fear pulsing through her throat. She could smell his last meal—a sickening combination of garlic and fermented grapes. "We have unfinished business, you and I. Remember?" He knew who she was. How? Who had told him?

"Let her go," Ruth demanded.

Without releasing Lisbeth, the proconsul backhanded Ruth. "The wench of a Christian I can do without."

Ruth stumbled but quickly regained her footing. She came at him with everything she had. "Let her go!" Two soldiers clamped on to Ruth's arms and pulled her back kicking and screaming.

Raised voices outside the library's closed door snapped Aspasius's head in that direction. The door flew open, and the old bishop, dressed in a fine white cloak and toga, both edged in purple, stormed into the room.

"Caecilianus!" Ruth seemed relieved and terrified at the same time. She covered herself as best she could. "Go back."

Fury shot from the old bishop's eyes. He removed his cloak and tossed it to Ruth. "Release my wife and take me."

"And me!" Cyprian marched into the room and took his place

beside the bishop. Standing taller than anyone in the room, he commanded immediate attention in his election toga. He, too, sent his cloak hurtling in Lisbeth's direction. She snatched it up and wrapped herself in its warmth and protection. The senators glanced at each other nervously, murmuring that this whole thing had gotten out of hand.

Lisbeth could understand why Caecilianus would give himself for his wife. They'd been married for years. They had a son. And most importantly, Caecilianus was a priest. History was full of men of God who sacrificed themselves for others. He was simply living up to those same expectations.

What she couldn't comprehend was why Cyprian would offer himself for her. She knew he loved her, but they'd only been married a couple of weeks. As near as she could tell, she often drove him mad with her outspoken, hardheaded ways. Other than to patch him up after the boat explosion, she'd done nothing to earn this level of sacrifice.

Aspasius holstered his dagger. "Silence."

"By what authority do you hold upstanding Roman citizens without trial?" Cyprian demanded, his eyes ringed in fire.

"Not that I have to explain myself to one not yet elected to our council, but so that there is no question as to my authority"—he paused and surveyed the room with a dare-to-challenge-me glare—"the emperor himself."

"I want proof that Rome no longer grants its citizens a fair trial." Cyprian's voice rang above the murmurs.

"The illegal act of inciting citizens against the throne is punishable by death." Controlled accusation laced Aspasius's tone. "Christians will bring destruction upon us if they are not stopped."

"Who said they were Christians?" Cyprian demanded.

Aspasius turned to Caecilianus. "Do you deny your treasonous faith? That you are, in fact, the leader of these troublemakers?"

"No," the old bishop answered without hesitation.

"Soldiers started this, not us." Lisbeth struggled to break loose of the two brutes cuffing her arms. "But you know that, don't you?"

Aspasius eyed her carefully, as if he could see every naked inch of her beneath Cyprian's cloak. "Since we have no witnesses, I will take your offer, Bishop. Your wife's freedom in exchange for your life." Something new rang in his voice. Something cold. Something even more evil. "Seize the old man and remove his head."

The astonishing declaration scorched Lisbeth's brain. What had sweet Caecilianus done to deserve death?

"No!" Ruth broke free of her guard and flung herself at the feet of Aspasius. "Take me."

"Hush, my love." Caecilianus stooped and drew her to his chest. He held her face in his hands and kissed her gently. "Go to our boy."

In the confusion of Ruth and Caecilianus being escorted from the room, Lisbeth stood spellbound, sucked into the vortex of an impossibly hard-to-believe moment.

The man who'd just given the execution order for the peace-loving patron of Rome returned to his desk. He smiled calmly, as if he'd ordered a tuna sandwich for lunch. "Now what to do with you, solicitor."

"Am I under arrest?"

"You housed the Christians; therefore you, too, are condemned for treason . . . unless"—Aspasius gave a nod, and soldiers seized Cyprian—"you can offer something in trade."

"He has me." Mama swept into the room, dressed in a stunning sea-green silk. "Take me."

"No. Me!" Lisbeth screamed. "Take me."

With a chuckle, Aspasius lifted the glass wine decanter on his desk and poured liquid the color of dark blood into a silver chalice. "My friend, it appears you have two women grousing for you. Such an unexpected and delightful entertainment. Perhaps it would profit me more to move this interchange to the arena."

"By what right do you hold me?" Cyprian demanded in that commanding way of his.

"Letters given to me by the sacred emperor, letters that order every Roman to comply with our ceremonial worship practices." Aspasius sloshed wine around in his mouth, then swallowed slowly. "Answer me this: did you know Christians lived in your home?"

"Yes."

"Well then, do you bow to the god of the bishop or the gods of Rome?"

Dead silence weighted the air for an eternity. Cyprian and Aspasius locked in a death stare, neither of them willing to blink first. Lisbeth was too paralyzed to even take a breath. Little by little, the senators shook off their shock at the sentencing of Caecilianus, along with the challenge of what Aspasius had just put before their favorite solicitor. Quarreling among themselves started with a low rumble, then quickly escalated into a full-on debate of the merits of such unprecedented proceedings for the most highly respected barrister of Carthage.

"Quiet!" Aspasius ordered. "What is your answer, solicitor?"

Cyprian turned to Lisbeth, his eyes frantically searching hers. What did he want from her? Absolution for what she was certain he was about to do. She hated herself, but she couldn't give it.

He squared his shoulders. "I am a Christian, sir. And the newly appointed bishop of the Lord's church. A good that God knows cannot be altered."

The senators gasped.

A pleased smile slid across Aspasius's face. "Shall the record show that you persisted in your treason?"

Cyprian looked at her. "Lisbeth."

With that one word, she knew. He had made the only choice he could. The love of her life would sacrifice his life for the lives of those scrappy little believers huddled in his house and scattered about the city. It was stupid, yet noble at the same time. And she couldn't help but love him more.

A crippling ache cut her in half, and she screamed, "No!"

Cyprian turned a steely gaze back to Aspasius. "I know no other gods but the one and true God who made heaven and earth, the sea, and all that is in them. This God we Christians serve: to him we pray day and night, for ourselves and for all men, and for the safety of the emperors themselves."

"You are then sentenced to the same fate as your old friend."

"Let him go, and you can have me." Lisbeth's heart thundered against her chest. "You wanted me once." She threw off the cloak. "Take what he robbed from you, and finish our business together."

"Lisbeth, no!" Cyprian thrashed against his captors, ordering her to flee. But his efforts were useless.

She could not let the family she'd always wanted and was finally piecing together be destroyed. Keenly aware of the stench of her fear, she threw herself at the feet of Aspasius, offering herself in Cyprian's place.

Recognition brought a roaring laugh from Aspasius. "The confessions of a slave girl. Oh, this is sweet." Aspasius lifted her chin. "Yes, my beauty, we do have unfinished business." Aspasius slapped her hard, and Lisbeth crumpled. "Still want the deal?"

Hot, metallic blood stung her tongue. "Yes." She'd never wanted anything more.

Cyprian struggled to come to her. "No, Lisbeth. I can't let you do this."

"You have no choice." Aspasius polished his ring on his tunic. "I keep her, and you go into exile."

"Exile?" Lisbeth scrambled to her feet. "You sorry son of a—"

"Send him to Curubis." Aspasius waved his hand, and soldiers started dragging Cyprian from the room. "One more thing, solicitor. Before I defile your wife"—he laughed as Cyprian lunged against the chains being slapped upon his wrists—"give me the names of the other Christians scuttling about my province."

"By your own laws you have wisely forbidden informers, so I'm not able to reveal their names and betray them." Cyprian lifted his chin in a final show of defiance.

"May your obstinate determination keep you alive on those lonely nights when all you have for comfort is knowing that I bed your wife." Aspasius's eyes narrowed. His jaw clenched. He'd had enough. "Banish him."

57

Felicissimus glanced around the room to make sure no one was listening. "But I held up my end of the deal."

"Not completely." Aspasius twirled the end of his belt like a whip. "I want the names of every presbyter in my province."

The slave trader wrung his hands. "Is littering the throne with martyrs a wise idea?"

Aspasius moved forward. "Who are you to question me?" He blew a cloud of sour breath over the weasel. At the first opportunity, he would part company with this one and see to it that he never caused him trouble again. "What I do with these traitors is my business."

"And once you have them, then we'll be even?"

Aspasius laughed. "We're even when I say we're even."

58

EXCEPT FOR THE FEW times she'd prowled the secret tunnels, Lisbeth had never been inside an occupied palace, let alone lived in one. She and Papa had traipsed through plenty of ruins, allowing their imaginations to complete walls, add furniture, and fantasize about the lives of those who possessed such wealth. Childhood imaginings paled compared to the actual horrors she'd witnessed these past few days inside these ancient chamber halls.

Lisbeth's sandals clicked against the cold granite tiles. Ironic that a brisk fall day so full of promise was also the day Cyprian would leave her hopeless. She pulled her wrap tightly against the chilly sense of abandonment that had once again found her after so many years. Curubis was forty miles away by ship. Mama had only been a water slide ride away. In truth, without a plan, both destinations were light-years out of her reach.

By the slant of the sun streaming through the shutters, she had little time. She intended to watch Cyprian's ship sail from the harbor even if Aspasius followed through on his threat to kill her should she be caught anywhere near the balcony.

How had Aspasius known that she and Ruth would be in the marketplace? That their capture would bring Caecilianus and Cyprian running? And even more puzzling, how had he learned of their Christianity?

The sound of someone coming yanked Lisbeth from the questions that had plagued her since the day of Cyprian's sentencing in the kangaroo court. She slipped behind a large pillar and waited for the man coming her way to pass. She held her breath, waited until he clattered down the hall, then peered around the column. She'd recognized that pompous strut anywhere. "Felicissimus?"

The startled slave trader halted and turned. "Lisbeth." Sheepish embarrassment soon gave way to righteous indignation. "I see the red is fading from your hair. Just as well, I suppose, since keeping your identity secret is no longer an issue."

"You're the traitor?"

"Not a traitor." He patted his belly. "The rightful bishop of Carthage." He whistled as he left the palace.

Waves of sadness battered Lisbeth's stomach as she stepped onto the proconsul's balcony. Felicissimus had betrayed Cyprian, and for what? Did he really believe Aspasius would allow the church to continue? Felicissimus would be the king of nothing, or he, too, would be dead. Even so, the truth of such deep deception would kill her husband. She wanted to strangle Felicissimus. But her desire to see her husband once more far outweighed her immediate need for vengeance. For now, she would do what she came for and trust God to deal with the traitor.

Trust God. Where was this God she'd grown to love? The thought played in Lisbeth's mind as she scanned the multitudes gathered along the shoreline. Word of an official exile had brought the masses out in droves. If any of the onlookers had the measles, the close contact would speed the spread of the disease.

For once, she didn't care.

An arm slipped around Lisbeth's waist, and she jumped with a start. "Mama? What are you doing here?"

"I couldn't let you go through this alone." She gave Lisbeth a little squeeze.

Lisbeth rested her head on her mother's shoulder. "I love you, Mama." The words rolled out from a place deep within her. They felt good in her mouth and tasted sweet on her tongue. Healing. Her mother had not left her on purpose, and neither had her husband. Both had given everything to spare her a painful future.

Suddenly someone in the crowd spotted the man they'd waited to see. The mob shifted. Cyprian, accompanied by his faithful deacon Pontius, strode through the people jostling to touch his snowy-white toga. One last in-your-face proclamation to the citizens of Carthage of just whom Aspasius was banishing that made Lisbeth smile.

With a dignified bearing, Cyprian marched up the gangplank of the ship. Right before he stepped aboard the Roman freighter, Cyprian removed his toga and tossed it into the water. Wearing only his under tunic, he shouted to the crowd, "Romans, lords of this world, know that I renounce the race that wears the toga. From this day forward, I serve the one God."

Soldiers pulled him and Pontius onto the deck and raised the gangplank.

"Cyprian!" Lisbeth didn't recognize her shredded voice. "Cyprian!"

Her husband cuffed his eyes and scanned the homes stacked along the shore. When he spotted her on Aspasius's balcony, he blew a kiss.

As the boat carrying her love drifted out of earshot, Lisbeth continued to scream Cyprian's name even though she knew he wouldn't hear it. Eyes straining and arms outstretched, she watched the sails of Cyprian's ship recede.

"Come, daughter." Mama tried to move her from the railing.

"How have you stood this world?" Lisbeth turned her face into the blustery wind and allowed the salt to scrub her cheeks raw.

59

During the long, dark days that followed, Lisbeth felt completely unhinged, like she was lost in a bad dream. But an eerie sense of hopelessness had swallowed her ability to sleep, so the despair was real. This pressure crushing her bones was beyond the reach of reason. She'd known Cyprian only a month. Falling so head over heels in thirty days was about as logical as time travel. This couldn't be real love. Yet she could not stop crying.

In Lisbeth's zombielike state, Mama handled her tenderly, supplying bowls of broth or wine laced with herbal cocktails that numbed the pain. Which was just as well. Letting her mind consider what Mama was doing behind the scenes to keep Aspasius at bay would be the nail in her coffin.

So when Mama appeared at her chamber door with a beautiful silk gown draped over her arm, the reality of what was about to happen hit her like the aftershock that topples the remaining shaky structures after an earthquake.

"He's ordered you to dine with him." Mama cleared her throat. "You are to be scrubbed and decked out in my finest." Mama's lips quivered. "I'm to take you to the Baths of Antoninus and parade you among the senators' wives as a reminder to never cross the proconsul. You remember those ruins, correct?"

Lisbeth nodded. "Papa loved them."

"Yes." Mama offered her hand. "Your father." She led Lisbeth from her room. Immediately outside her door stood the scribe Lisbeth had seen attending Aspasius at the arena. "I've got it from here, Pytros," Mama tossed over her shoulder as they hurried down the hall.

Once they cleared the palace gates, Mama spoke in hushed English, a gleam of emotion in her eye Lisbeth could not interpret. "We've not but a minute." She glanced around as if she thought them followed. "I've secured your passage."

"To Curubis?"

"To safety."

"And you're coming with me, right?"

Mama hesitated, then offered a reluctant smile. "Yes. Of course."

"And Laurentius?"

"Him, too. Ruth will bring him to the port—"

"Let's go."

"We must wait until dark." Mama checked once again to see if they were followed. "I know a place where we can hide. Where Aspasius will never think to look."

They turned toward the mountains, quickly putting an uncomfortable distance between them and the harbor. "But what about Ruth and Laurentius?" Lisbeth asked as the tenements came into view.

"Trust me." Mama dragged her faster and faster through the darkened alleys and narrow slum dwellings. They zigged and zagged until Lisbeth was hopelessly lost.

Suddenly they passed through the outdoor kitchen where Lisbeth had boiled the water for Junia's vaporizer and Eunike's baby. "I know this place." She froze. "It's near the cisterns."

"Come." Mama tugged on her hand, hauling her into a familiar courtyard that surrounded the stone structure of the wells, the structure with the cave swimmers symbol, the way back.

Ruth and Laurentius huddled near the cistern wall.

"No. I won't go. Not without Cyprian." Lisbeth planted her feet near the stone lip of the well. The smell of cold, dark water sent her heart pounding in her ears.

Mama pulled her stethoscope from her tunic pocket and tied it around Lisbeth's wrist. "Laurentius and I will be right behind you."

Laurentius peered into the well and shook his head, backing up. "I don't want to go, Mama."

"Soldiers!" As the word left Ruth's mouth, the courtyard filled with armed guards. Two soldiers seized Laurentius by the tunic.

"Let him go!" Lisbeth lunged for her brother, but Mama grabbed her.

"He'll never touch you." Mama snatched Lisbeth's hand, the one with the stethoscope tied around the wrist, and plastered it against the painting of the swimmers.

Heat seared Lisbeth's palm. "No!"

"I love you." Mama's fists pounded Lisbeth's chest with an incredible force. "Forever."

Lisbeth tumbled backward, flipped over the well's edge, and spiraled into the deepest darkness she had ever known.

60

"Beetle bug?"

Lisbeth felt her father desperately pat her hand for the thousandth time as they jetted back to the States. She tore her gaze away from the vast emptiness outside the plane window and inside her spirit. "I'm good, Papa." Adding reassurance to the response she'd given over and over didn't seem to help. Her father still looked at her like she was the one who'd lost her mind.

She fingered the stethoscope Papa said had been tied to her wrist.

Two weeks ago, she'd awakened in a Carthage hospital, bruised, battered, and unsure of her name. When Papa asked her about the ring on the cord around her neck, she remembered that she'd found her mother alive in the third century. While he wept, she'd told him about her mentally challenged half brother whose refusal to jump had probably cost both him and Mama their lives. Her preposterous claims were met with one phrase: "I knew your mother would have come to me if she could."

Instead of facing the possibility that what she thought happened was the result of a traumatic head injury, she allowed Nigel and Aisa to fuss over her and argue about who had actually saved her from that hellish water shaft.

She squeezed her father's hand as the plane's landing gear

intersected the Dallas tarmac. "I'm glad you came back with me, Papa."

"You're my Beetle Bug."

He seemed lucid enough now, but she intended to use this opportunity to run him through a battery of medical tests. Even if her extended absence had broken her probation and ruined her chances of ever being a doctor again, she knew where to find some of the best physicians in the world.

Lisbeth paid the taxi driver while Papa gathered their luggage. Together they took the stairs to her apartment. Fumbling with the key, she accidentally pushed the doorbell.

The door flew open. "There you are." Queenie parked her hands on her hips. "I've been calling you for hours."

"Sorry, I lost my phone and—"

"I thought you said your daddy wasn't coming for Christmas." Queenie latched on to Papa's hand. "You come right on in, Dr. H. If my momma knew you were coming she'd have baked you some corn bread."

"Queenie, we've got to—"

Lisbeth's roommate glanced at her watch and gasped. "Go!"

"Go?" Lisbeth asked. "Go where?"

Queenie tapped her watch. "Call. Christmas Eve. First years. Bottom of the food chain. Short straw."

"It's Christmas Eve . . . when?"

Her roommate's brow wrinkled in confusion. "Girl, you should have taken a nap and let me go to the airport to get your daddy." Queenie tossed Lisbeth her white coat, which was draped over a chair. "If Nurse Ratched gets wind that you're tired, she'll run your legs off." Queenie hooked Lisbeth's arm. "Dr. H., you just help yourself to anything in the fridge. I'll have her back in thirty grueling hours."

Mama's stethoscope in hand, Lisbeth mutely followed Queenie to the parking garage, too confused to argue.

Queenie sped down the freeway, jabbering about an OB resident who'd asked her out. "He'll want to have kids, and then what? I'm not a barefoot-and-pregnant kind of girl." She squealed into the parking garage. "Earth to Lisbeth."

Lisbeth dug through her quickly eroding memories. Were the past moments of love, laughter, family, and hope real or wishful thinking? "Can we sit here a minute?" She glanced at the scar on her wrist, a pale pink line. Where had that come from? From the ship where she and Cyprian had found the crazed sailor? Or had she gotten the scar as a child playing too close to the campfire? Her mind couldn't seem to sort it out.

Queenie's big black eyes regarded her thoughtfully. "Girlfriend, who are you, and what have you done with the girl who had places to go and people to meet?" She yanked the keys out of the ignition. "No, we can't sit here. We're late. Ratched will serve our heads on a platter for Christmas supper."

Following Queenie through the well-lit parking garage, Lisbeth shrugged into her white coat. Had she made the whole time-travel thing up? Had some kind of crazy brain short to compensate for the fact that her papa could be losing his marbles? Searching for a piece of gum, Lisbeth crammed her hand into her pocket.

The letter?

Exactly where she'd put it before everything went south. Still perfectly intact. Not soggy and ruined by the waterslide ride she had taken to the third century. Shaking off the confused feeling, she sprinted through the hospital door.

Around midnight Queenie announced that she'd eat the arm off the next patient if she and Lisbeth didn't bail and hit the Taco Hut. Afraid Nelda would catch them, they headed to the break room instead. Lisbeth bought a tuna sandwich. She'd barely sat down when the page came. *Incoming gunshot wounds.*

Sandwich in hand, Lisbeth flew down two flights of stairs and barged into the emergency room. Arms circled her from behind. "Hey, beautiful. I need an examination."

"Knock it off, Craig." Lisbeth wiggled free. "Nurse Ratched has spies everywhere."

"You speak Arabic, right?"

A déjà vu feeling swept over Lisbeth. "Yeah. So?"

"This is a triple gunshot."

"Yeah, and it's mine."

He cranked up the charm. "You know I want this surgery, love. Nelda dumped a baby on me. Projectile vomiting." Nose wrinkled, Craig thrust a triage chart into Lisbeth's hands. "Women are better at this kid stuff than men."

"What?"

He held up his hands to block the possibility of her slapping him. "You know what I mean, more nurturing."

Lisbeth stopped and stared at him. "Craig?" From the way he was running his finger along her hip he obviously thought they were still engaged. "What do you want?"

He leaned in close, and she could smell his expensive cologne. "How about a little trade?"

"What kind of trade?"

He waved the chart. "Baby for gunshot." He raised his eyebrows seductively. "You know you want to."

"Why would I *want* to do that?"

"Because you love me, right?" Then he kissed her cheek. "And you know deep down women are better suited for pediatrics."

She ripped the chart from Craig's hand. "We're done."

"What?"

"You heard me."

He held up his palms in surrender. "Hey, no offense."

"Why would you assume a woman is better suited to peds? Do you even care about my hopes and dreams? Or does it always have to be about you and your career?" She looked at his blank face and realized she was wasting her breath. "Never mind. I'll do it. Give me her chart."

"You're just tired." He reached for her, and she stepped back. "We'll get some breakfast at the end of call and then, you know, celebrate Christmas."

"What part of *never in this life* don't you understand?" She reached to yank the engagement ring from her left hand, but it was gone. "I'll get your ring back to you . . . later."

Craig gave her a puzzled look, then stalked off, commenting under his breath that she'd be sorry. For the first time since her return, Lisbeth's senses did not burn with shame. She felt remarkably free.

Lisbeth took a deep breath, then walked into the examination room. She was rewarded with the sight of a mother dressed in head-to-toe black and holding a baby. "What's her name?" she asked in Arabic.

The mother released a relieved breath. "Abra."

Lisbeth paused to gather her composure.

She smiled and offered her hand. "I'm Dr. Hastings."

Epilogue

THE BLUE PLUS SIGN on the pregnancy test wand confirmed the reason for her upset stomach. Lisbeth checked the device again just to be sure.

Yes, positive.

A piece of the past tucked so far inside of her that no one could take from her what she'd believed to be true all along.

She carried Cyprian's child. The brave young noble from the third century. The missing part of her that made her whole.

Lisbeth gazed into the mirror above the bathroom sink. Her cheeks were pink, and her eyes were bright despite the nausea. The woman smiling back at her was exactly who Lisbeth wanted to be . . . a woman brave enough to do whatever it took to save her husband and his people.

She ran the palms of her hands across her tender breasts and let them caress the flatness of her belly.

"Papa!" she called to her father, who was smoking his pipe on the tiny apartment balcony. "We're going back!"

Author's Note

I FIRST LEARNED ABOUT THE Cave of the Swimmers from the movie *The English Patient*. Although the movie was filmed on a set, the real cave is in the southern quadrant of the Sahara. Prehistoric paintings of little swimmers cover the sandstone walls. Except for a labyrinth of underground aquifers that exists beneath the desert floor, the nearest water source is nearly a thousand miles away. What happened to the water? And, even more fascinating, what happened to the Neolithic artists?

In 2008, a group of Egyptian tourists was kidnapped while exploring the cave. My imagination conjured all sorts of scenarios. What if they weren't actually kidnapped? What if they just mysteriously vanished?

It wasn't until 2010 that I discovered a specific time and place to drop a brave heroine who might have disappeared into an unexpected rip in time. I was eavesdropping on a conversation about the origin of organized health care when someone mentioned the Plague of Cyprian, a third-century pandemic that nearly destroyed Carthage.

By AD 253, the epidemic was killing an estimated five thousand people a day. Only wealthy citizens had access to the empire's few physicians. Organized health care for the masses was nonexistent. Interestingly enough, even while the Roman civilization struggled to survive the fever, Christian persecution increased to an all-time high. The fledgling church faced an impossible choice: stay and care for their persecutors, or flee and protect themselves.

Enter a real hero: Cyprianus Thascius, the wealthy son of a Roman senator. According to extensive historical accounts written by this accomplished orator and respected lawyer, an old bishop named Caecilianus converted Cyprian to Christianity.

Cyprian opened his home, used his massive wealth to care for the sick, and organized a scruffy little band of believers into an army who stared down adversity. This risky decision cost Cyprian a shameful exile.

On the plus side, Cyprian's radical concept of medical charity revolutionized health care and became the founding basis of the world's earliest hospitals. But more importantly, as Christians rendered aid to the pagans, their actions breached social barriers, touched hearts, and spurred the eventual legalization of Christianity.

The plague virus has not been conclusively identified by historians, though Gary B. Ferngren's *Medicine & Health Care in Early Christianity* was an invaluable resource during my research. Some scholars believe the plague could have been smallpox, some measles. Since I wanted my heroine immune, I chose measles, because we no longer vaccinate against smallpox.

The ancient Carthage I re-created is populated with historical characters, as well as fictional characters running around in my head. The real-life records of Cyprian mention his faithful friend Pontius, a political enemy named Aspasius Paternus, and Felicissimus, a betrayer who broke Cyprian's heart and nearly destroyed the church. Lisbeth Hastings represents the brave woman I'd like to think I would be in the face of such insurmountable odds. But I wonder. The cost of true courage is great, and few are willing to pay the price.

Acknowledgments

MANY HAVE ENCOURAGED ME on this writing journey, and I am filled with gratitude.

Thanks to my husband, Lonnie, who believed me an accomplished storyteller from the first time I said he was perfect. A truth that needs no embellishment. He is perfect for me.

I want to thank the medical intern who let me peek into the grueling process of becoming a doctor. Any malpractice found in these pages is purely my own. Thanks to the theological graduate student who helped me research early church history. Any historical liberties taken are mine.

Thanks to cheerleaders Diane, Grant, Michael, Lindsey, Kellie, Julie, Lisa, Janice, and my precious Bunco pals. Jackie Castle deserves the credit for creating the beautiful map.

A special thanks to my agent, Sandra Bishop, for knocking on doors; to my editor, Jessica Wong, for polishing this crazy story nugget into a diamond; and to the great team at Howard Books for getting this story into the hands of readers.

And finally, all praise is due the Great Physician, the true healer of body and soul.

A Howard Reading Group Guide

HEALER

of

CARTHAGE

Lynne Gentry

Introduction

THE FIRST IN THE series, *Healer of Carthage* takes readers through a journey in time when Dr. Lisbeth Hastings falls through a hidden hole in her father's archaeological dig site and awakens in third-century Carthage. Propelled into the unknown, she grapples to rescue those she loves, risking much, while simultaneously experiencing her own rescuing. Slavery, religious persecution, and disease serve as a dark backdrop for romance, justice, and courage, and the stage for a dramatic, suspenseful story of freedom.

Topics and Questions for Discussion

1. Lisbeth meets Cyprian for the first time when she is sold to him as a slave. To win Lisbeth, Cyprian intentionally bids higher than the proconsul because "rescuing those the proconsul keeps in bondage is worth the risk" (page 48). Explain the risks Cyprian takes in outbidding the proconsul. How does the theme of both rescue and risk characterize Lisbeth and Cyprian at this point?

2. In Chapter 7, Lisbeth realizes that her fall has taken her back in time to mid-third-century Roman Carthage. Lisbeth recalls that Roman rule and the city change drastically during this time period with a "bloody, volatile mess in the African provinces" (page 60). If you could choose a previous time period to live in, which one would it be and why? What historic challenges are associated with that time period?

3. When Lisbeth first discovers her mother is alive, she is filled with a myriad of emotions as to why her mother had not returned to them. "Had Mama chosen this life over the one they'd had together? Why didn't she want to return to her and Papa?" (page 82). Have you ever assumed you'd been rejected or abandoned by a loved one? If so, how has time and further communication changed your perspective on the decisions this loved one made?

4. One of the believers, Numidicus, expresses concern over Christian persecution in Carthage: "Already believers are blamed

for any misfortune that befalls Carthage. Persecution of the worst kind will come upon us if this sickness spreads. Aspasius will not rest until he sees us all fed to the lions" (page 70). He wishes to take his daughter and leave Carthage to flee from the spreading sickness and persecution, encouraging other believers to do so. If you were in third-century Carthage at this time, would you have stayed or left? Why?

5. Aspasius's evil plan of destruction through a cleansing was designed to enable a "return to the pure lineage that would carry the borders of Rome to the ends of the earth" and create a "perfect Carthage" (page 107). Describe other real-life cleansings that have occurred or are occurring in the world. How do you see social, economic, or religious injustices play out in present-day American culture?

6. In order to stop Aspasius's inflicting rule, Cyprian seeks a seat in the senate. Bishop Caecilianus asks Cyprian a question that contrasts with his desire to take proactive steps to secure a better Carthage: "So, in your educated opinion, relying upon the power of our Lord is futile?" (page 115). Cyprian responds that he is "not discounting God, but surely the Lord does not expect us to sit upon our hands? Do nothing? Allow evil to run its ugly course?" (page 115). Do you think the bishop's, or Cyprian's, perspective is the better path to take? Why? How do you personally navigate relying on the power of the Lord or others, versus proactively engaging in righting the wrong or striving for good?

7. Shortly after saving Junia from the measles, Lisbeth helps heal her mother from one of Aspasius's beatings and discovers that the Down-syndrome boy, Laurentius, is her half brother. How

do these encounters alter Lisbeth? How does Lisbeth begin to see her mother? How have you been changed by helping another?

8. How does Lisbeth's offer to marry Cyprian compare and contrast with the decision of her mother to stay in Carthage for so long?

9. Lisbeth asks herself, "Could a human being alter the preordered boundaries of time enough to make a difference? What if fate had given her an unprecedented opportunity to right her own wrong?" (page 262). How do your actions today alter the preordered boundaries of time, specifically the future? Choose one area in your life that will impact your future *and* that you would like to change. Develop a plan to change it. Conversely, if given an opportunity to redo a wrong, which one would it be? And what would you do differently?

10. How does the status and progression of Lisbeth's relationship with her mother parallel Lisbeth's relationship with and actions toward Abra, Junia, and Laurentius?

11. When Lisbeth finds the way to return home she is faced with a decision. If she returns home, she could save her Papa and her old life. If she stays in the third century, she could save Mama, Laurentius, and Carthage. She also wonders if Cyprian can save *her*. What do you think she means by the latter thought? Discuss how Cyprian, Lisbeth, and Magdalena are *both* rescuers and the ones being rescued. How is this true of your life?

12. A horrifying and unjust scene unfolds in Chapter 56 when Aspasius accuses Ruth, Lisbeth, Cyprian, and Caecilianus. Was there a particular hero that emerged? Explain. Could you

imagine yourself facing death for refusal to bow to a god different than your own? Could you imagine giving yourself up for a loved one in order to prevent their death? Which of these would be easier for you to do? Why?

13. Consider the relationship between Magdalena and Lisbeth. How do you think Magdalena must have felt as a mother with a son to protect in one world and a beloved daughter in another world? After all the heartache, why do you think Magdalena sacrifices the nearness of her precious daughter once again when she pushes Lisbeth down the cistern?

14. The story opens and closes with Lisbeth's evaluation of an Arabic baby named Abra. How does Lisbeth's medical failure as a doctor in the opening scene compel and affect her throughout the book? In what ways has a failure in your life compelled and affected your journey?

Enhance Your Book Club

1. Research the Cave of the Swimmers. Who discovered it and when? Where is its actual location? Who are the Neolithic artists proposed to be?

2. As Christians rendered aid to both believers and nonbelievers during the third-century health crisis of Carthage, social barriers were breached and Christianity spread. Select a time for the group to volunteer with an existing organization that will allow you to breach the social, economic, or religious barriers outside of your everyday norm.

3. Identify someone in your life that has sacrificed to allow you to be where you are today, rescuing you in some way. Share that story with the group, or write the individual a letter to express your gratitude.

4. Lisbeth carried her Mama's stethoscope with her for years, a tangible reminder of her nearness and love. Identify an object, or craft one that represents who you are. If fitting, perhaps this item can be given to a loved one.

5. Lisbeth is forced to learn natural remedies in order to care for the sick in third-century Carthage. Research the various ways you can use lemon, honey, and sea salt as natural remedies for things such as skin care, sore throats, electrolyte imbalance, and more!

A Conversation with Lynne Gentry

Who or what inspired you to write *Healer of Carthage*?
The call of adventure. Those who know me best know that I long to travel. To live unfettered by the restraints of time and money, to see the world, and experience many different cultures. Reading takes me to those places. So when I read about a group of tourists kidnapped from the Cave of the Swimmers, my mind immediately joined their exotic desert excursion. It was as if I touched the faded swimmers painted upon the sandstone walls and disappeared into third-century Carthage. My expedition into this ancient world of danger and intrigue has been the most exciting and satisfying mind trip yet.

You are not only a writer but also a dramatist with an educational background in speech and theater. How does this background influence your writing and storytelling process?
When actors are afraid to let their minds venture into the world of make-believe, their characters remain flat and unconvincing. That's why I use lots of imagination games that teach my student actors how to take mental risks. When my fictional characters are reluctant to step outside their comfort zone, I have been known to pull out an acting exercise that will nudge them in the right direction.

Who is your favorite character? Why?
Lisbeth's Down-syndrome half brother Laurentius. The original purpose of adding this young man to the cast was to demonstrate the easy-to-overlook compassionate side of the Romans. I didn't know he was Lisbeth's secret sibling until after she performed her rescue procedure. The moment Laurentius opened those almond-shaped eyes and

offered Lisbeth unconditional love, I knew this boy had been loved. But by whom? I looked across the room and there was Magdalena glancing anxiously over her shoulder, and suddenly I had the reason Lisbeth's mother could not return home. I couldn't have left Laurentius either.

Describe your favorite writing location or room.
My creativity is stimulated by interactions with real people. Most of my writing is done in the thick of our family life—at the kitchen table. I have a lovely office, but it is tucked away on the second floor. Too far from the action for this extrovert. If I really need to concentrate on writing details, I will trudge the stairs. But after three or four hours of isolation, I'm breaking free.

Your research process was thorough and tapped into the knowledge of a medical intern, a theological graduate student, and historical resources. How long did the research process take you? How long did the writing process take you?
My fascination with history originated with the books I read as a kid. I loved the daring spirit of the pioneers of Little House on the Prairie *and the against-all-odds survivor story of* The Swiss Family Robinson. *I spent hours contemplating how those people lived without electricity, indoor toilets, modern medical care, or a good hair dryer. Over the years I've collected boxes of research and stacks of historical books. Creating an imaginary world from the gathered bits and pieces has been a lifelong journey. Actually putting the story on the page took about twelve months.*

What would you describe as the main theme(s) in *Healer of Carthage*?
On the surface, the story's theme is mercy. The mercy God freely gives us and our willingness to offer mercy to others. But, to me, this story is really about the mercy we extend to ourselves. Like so many of us, Lisbeth

was stuck. Hanging on to the past was sabotaging her future. It wasn't until she accidentally fell into the biggest adventure of her life that she learned how to forgive herself and move forward.

What do you want readers to experience or take away from this novel?

I hope readers close the last page and say, "Whew! That was one wild and courageous ride." I marvel at how a scruffy little band of misfits changed history. Their bravery bolsters my courage to love with reckless abandon.

In the Author's Notes section you say, "The cost of true courage is great, and few are willing to pay the price." How has your own journey of courage shaped the path Lisbeth takes?

Courage is not the absence of fear. Real courage is being scared to death but doing it anyway. When this story idea came to me, I was afraid to write something so different. But a still small voice inside kept saying, "Trust me." So while the laundry and dishes piled up, I wrote. Day after day. Even when I didn't see the point. Even when I wanted to stop. So many times in this story, Lisbeth is faced with the same questions that plagued my unexpected undertaking. Why me? Why this place? Will I be sorry if I don't give it my all? If you've been called to do something that scares you to death, let me encourage you to take the risk. Living with regret is not living.

You are a co-founder of The Echo Project, a humanitarian organization that brings aid to those in Africa. *Healer of Carthage* also touches on the theme of bringing aid and relief to those who are without. Discuss this passion for justice and mercy in your life.

In the 1940s a polio epidemic swept the world. Everyone was terrified. My mother was one of the half-million children who contracted the crippling disease. If Berni's country doctor hadn't risked breaking the quarantine, she would have died. It makes me mad when children suffer, whether from disease, poverty, or lack of opportunity. I want to pack my bags and rescue little ones around the world. But until that is financially feasible, co-founder Lisa Harris and I are doing what we can to give voice to those who cannot speak for themselves. If you'd like to learn more about what we do for kids, visit www.theechoproject.org.

An excerpt from the sequel *Return to Exile* begins with the following line: "Time is not the healer of all things." Is this an idea that you would like your readers to grasp? Why?

Who hasn't wanted to turn the clock back and change things? Yet, as we all know, some choices leave wounds so deep they never heal. The whole idea of fixing mistakes implies that we can eliminate the consequences. But can we? This intriguing conundrum drives Dr. Lisbeth Hastings's quest to right her wrongs. But if she eliminates the consequences of her first visit to Carthage, she also stands to eliminate the thing she loves the most. Now that's an adventure I don't want to miss.

Keep reading for an excerpt from
Return to Exile,
the second book in
The Carthage Chronicles!

1

*T*IME IS NOT THE *healer of all things.*

Dr. Lisbeth Hastings grabbed her stethoscope and sprinted through a gurney gauntlet. The exceptionally high onslaught of feverish patients had increased her workload tenfold and kept her at the hospital long past her call shift. So much for spending Christmas Eve with her family. So much for believing that this time she had everything under control.

Lisbeth skidded around the corner, out of breath and in a cold sweat. Her patient's worried husband paced outside the room where the code had been called. He jostled a crying toddler and pleaded for answers she didn't have.

"I'll get back to you soon as I can." Lisbeth shot past him and burst into the crowded room. "What happened?"

Nelda, the charge nurse, shrugged. "Fine one minute. Convulsing the next." She quietly started closing drawers on the red crash cart.

"Not another one!" Lisbeth plowed through the litter left by the team of airway specialists, nurses, and ICU attendings. She'd attended and assisted at hundreds of Code Blues. Heroic measures inflicted unavoidable trauma on crashing patients. Yet, when she reached the body lying on the bed, she gasped at the total loss of dignity.

Damp, blond strands stuck to the dead woman's face. Red-rimmed eyes. Blue lips. Fiery pustules that made her look like some kind of distorted monster. Her hands were curled as if she'd tried to hang on to the last breath. Lines of all sorts tethered her rigid frame to silent machines.

Two days ago this woman and her beautiful two-year-old were enjoying Disney World. If this woman died of what Lisbeth feared, she was probably contagious the day her family flew home from Orlando, plus the three days they were in the theme park before her rash appeared, and probably even on the initial trip to their vacation destination. If Lisbeth let herself think about how many lives this woman had touched between Dallas and Florida in the past six days, she'd lose what was left of the sandwich she'd choked down ten hours ago.

Lisbeth pulled a penlight from her pocket and lifted the woman's eyelid. Foolish, she knew, but she wanted a reaction. Needed this young wife to wake up and prove her theory wrong. She flicked a beam of light across each eye. Pupils blown beyond repair were nothing but large, black holes that pushed away any trace of the former color. Lisbeth clicked the pen off.

"Dr. Hastings?" Nelda sidled around the equipment and handed her the chart. "You want to tell the husband?"

"Tell him what? Merry Christmas, and oh, by the way, you're a single father now." Powerlessness shook her insides. "Hard enough to tell someone their spouse died, but when it could have been prevented, what do you say?" Two decades without a single case reported in Texas. Now there'd been three senseless deaths presenting similar symptoms in the past twenty-four hours. "I'm sorry, Nelda. It's not your fault that more and more people insist on skipping their vaccinations." She took a step back from the bed. "Drop your gown and gloves on the floor. Cordon off this room."

"Do we need to quarantine the father and daughter?"

Lisbeth nodded. "And contact the CDC." The tiled walls seemed to be closing in, squeezing the breath from her chest. This couldn't be happening again. "We may have a pandemic on our hands."

LISBETH WHIPPED her old Toyota into the parking garage of her downtown loft apartment. She killed the engine and dropped her head onto the steering wheel. If she'd stomped out this disease when she had the chance, that mother would be home hugging her baby, not lying on a morgue slab.

In the tomblike darkness, fingers of cold snaked through the vehicle's broken window seals. A guilty shudder ripped through Lisbeth's exhausted body. The past had caught up with the future, and it was all her fault.

Lisbeth grabbed the sanitizer out of the console and scrubbed her hands. Even though she'd showered and disposed of her scrubs before she left the hospital, she reeked of failure. Thankfully, Papa and Maggie were current on their shots, but would their vaccinations be enough, especially if the virus was gaining the advantage over herd immunity?

She glanced at her cell phone: 3:00 a.m. If she was lucky, she'd have time to see Maggie before the CDC's chartered jet arrived. The governmental investigators would expect every local infectious disease specialist to be front and center until they'd contained the danger. She yanked the phone from the charger and dragged herself from the car.

The elevator dinged. Lisbeth trudged the apartment corridor. A glass of milk and a plate of homemade cookies waited on the welcome mat outside her home. She bent to read a note written in red crayon.

Dear Santa,

I want my daddy.

Maggie

Santa could easier give her five-year-old daughter the moon. Lisbeth scooped up the cookies, drank the milk, then slid the key into the front-door lock. She slipped inside the quiet apartment.

Oatmeal and cinnamon lingered in the air. Papa snored on the couch, an afghan snugged up tightly beneath his chin. White lights twinkled on the spindly spruce leaning against the TV. Under the tree was Maggie's new Ashton Drake doll. Her father had remembered her instructions to get the doll out of the closet. This bit of progress was a surprisingly bright spot in a very dark day.

"Papa?" Lisbeth pressed her fingers into his sinewy shoulders.

He roused with a start and opened one eye. "Home already?"

Life with her father had been like growing up with Indiana Jones. She'd been just five years old when Mama disappeared at the Cave of the Swimmers. For the next thirteen years, she and Papa took on the world, leapfrogging from one archaeological dig after another. They'd probably still be digging together if Papa hadn't sent her to the States to become a doctor . . . to be more like Mama. Their years apart had made Lisbeth hard and determined, but the separation almost killed Papa.

"Got to go back when the CDC calls."

"So it's measles?"

"Yes. Maybe worse."

Papa pushed himself upright, his white hair as wild and restless as a desert wind. He eyed her carefully. "What do you mean?"

"A virus must mutate to survive. Epidemic is its ultimate goal."

Papa wrestled his lanky frame from the afghan. "How about I fix you something hot and solid?"

"Not hungry." It took everything she had not to throw herself into his arms. "Thanks for making Santa cookies with Maggie."

"A real corker, that one. Got your beauty and my brains." Papa swung his legs off the couch. "We had to put Santa's setup by the front door. In Miss Magdalena's opinion, the man in the red suit's way too fat and way too smart to try comin' in through this fake gas fireplace." Papa's refusal to call Maggie by anything other than her proper name was a battle Lisbeth would have continued if she hadn't been so tired. "That girl won't be put off much longer. You're going to have to tell her about her daddy."

"I saw her note."

"Anyone smart enough to write notes to Santa is smart enough to ask why he didn't deliver."

"She's not ready."

"Neither were you, but we managed."

"This is different. You didn't know what happened to Mama."

"And you know where her father is."

"Going there's too risky. What good would it do to tell her about a father she can never meet?"

Papa raked his hands through his hair. He'd lost this round, but she felt certain they'd have this fight again. "Should we wake her now? Let her have her Christmas before you get called out."

Lisbeth shook her head. "They're sending a team from Atlanta. That gives me a few hours before I have to disappoint my daughter again."

"You could use a little shut-eye."

"I can't let measles win this time."

Papa drew her into his arms. Six years since he'd last poked through the ruins of some ancient civilization and he still smelled of the desert right before the rain. He could read ancient signs in the sand better than anyone in the world, but unlocking this virus wasn't the same as piecing together shards of pottery. "I ordered some old articles from the National Library of Medicine." He kissed the top of her head, his scraggly beard sanding a few of the splinters from her ragged thoughts. "Maybe there's something in the archives we've missed."

"I've turned over every rock." Lisbeth pulled back, checking his eyes for clarity, a habit she couldn't seem to break since she'd brought him back to the States. "Go on to bed, Papa."

"It's already Christmas in the Middle East. Think I'll catch CNN. See if Santa left *me* a little present." Unlike her, he hadn't given up on the hope that one day he would be allowed access to the cave that had changed everything.

Lisbeth patted his shoulder. "You think Santa has any pull in Egypt?"

"No." He grinned. "But God does."

Lisbeth headed toward Maggie's room, contemplating the changes in Papa since he'd hauled her from the secret shaft at the Cave of the Swimmers. Not only had his mind cleared, his sole reliance upon science had shifted to a strong conviction in a higher power. According to Papa's new way of thinking, the same God who'd created the unknown dimensions of time had also created scientific minds determined to unravel the mysteries. Maggie's birth had given him hope that he would see Mama again. Bile burned Lisbeth's throat. Papa still believed there was a chance she was still alive. He refused to accept the probability that her sacrificial decision to protect Lisbeth from the Roman proconsul had probably ended Mama's life.

Light from the Little Mermaid lamp plugged in next to Maggie's twin-size bed cast a blue glow over the Mediterranean wall mural she'd commissioned. A splurge on a hospitalist's salary, especially since they were living in an apartment, but it wasn't Maggie's fault Lisbeth was not ready to put down roots. Maggie deserved a normal life . . . if anything about birthing a child conceived from a time-travel marriage could ever be considered normal.

Maggie's pale legs sprawled atop the covers were cool to the touch. Maggie had inherited her silky blond tresses from her aristocratic father, but her fear of tight spaces came directly from her mother. No matter what they tried, Maggie refused anything that could pin her arms and legs. Lisbeth found it easier to wait until her daughter was sound asleep before attempting a proper tucking in.

Lisbeth kicked off her shoes and lifted the covers. She slid in next to the perfect little body.

Maggie roused and snuggled into the crook of her arm. "Mommy?" Her hand found Lisbeth's face. "Did he come?" she asked without opening her eyes.

"Who?"

"My daddy."

Lisbeth brought Maggie's hand to her lips. She kissed every chubby finger. Her daughter's vaccinations might be enough to fend off a large-scale virus transmission, but she knew for certain the shot had not been invented that would protect her daughter from a broken heart. "Not yet, baby."

"Santa will bring him, right?" Maggie nuzzled her nose deeper into Lisbeth's neck.

Inhaling the scent of tear-free shampoo, Lisbeth wished she could seal her baby inside a sterile bubble. A place where nothing bad ever happened to mothers or their children. A place where little girls didn't wish for parents who couldn't return. A place where families were never separated. No such place existed.

She pulled Maggie close. Her fist-size heartbeat steady beneath her thin Little Mermaid gown.

Maggie's question reminded her of another Christmas Eve, one she'd never allow herself to forget, even if it had been six years ago, when she was an intern. Exhausted and distracted, she'd nearly made a tragic mistake with a child—no, she had made the mistake. Remembered every guilty second that ensued. But by some strange twist of fate, she had been granted an opportunity to right the wrong. To redo those tragic minutes. She might not get a second chance with her own child.

Lisbeth swallowed the lump in her throat. "If you believe, my love, your father will come to you. Somehow. Some way. I promise."

Maggie wriggled free. "Too tight, Mommy."

"Sorry." Lisbeth eased her grip, and Maggie's tiny body relaxed. "Night, baby." Maybe her worry was out of proportion. Papa was right. Maggie was a smart kid. They had time to work through Maggie's need for a father, and when she was old enough to understand the whole crazy story, they would.

Maggie drifted back to sleep. Lisbeth tucked little arms and legs inside the blanket, relishing the feeling that, for this minute, her baby was safe. She'd never understood how much her mother loved her until she became a mother herself. The moment the nurse placed Maggie in her arms, she knew why small animals fought predators twice their size. She could do it. Fight to save her young. Much as she hated violence, she would kill anyone who tried to hurt her daughter. Even a virus. But how could she permanently take out something she couldn't see? Something that didn't fight fair? Something that had the potential to come at her again and again?

Lisbeth snuggled in beside Maggie, breathing in the scent of her like someone who'd just surfaced from being underwater too long. In through the nose. Out through the mouth. In through the nose. Out through the mouth.

For now, she'd focus on getting this measles outbreak under control. There had to be a simple explanation for the patients she'd lost in the past few days. Compromised immune systems. Weakened hearts. Something. Until she had full autopsies, speculating that the virus had morphed into a superbug was borrowing trouble and wasting valuable time and energy.

Lisbeth gave in to the exhaustion, allowing her heavy eyelids to close and shut off the nagging feeling that she'd missed something important. Gradually her own respirations synced with the peaceful in and out of Maggie's slumber.

The vibration of her phone jerked Lisbeth alert. One arm around Maggie, she struggled to fish the cell from her pocket.

A text from Nelda glowed on the screen.

Five new cases. Help.